Praise for *Bend Toward the Sun*

"A steamy romance about humans' ability to grow and heal, and about the power of love."
—Ali Hazelwood, *New York Times* bestselling author of *Love, Theoretically*

"One of the best books of the year." —*Paste*

"A lushly drawn portrait of two people with a magnetic, soul-deep connection, wrapped up in a gorgeous story of hope and healing."
—Rachel Lynn Solomon, *New York Times* bestselling author

"Devon breaks hearts and puts them back together again. . . . [A] tear-jerking debut." —*Publishers Weekly*

"A gorgeous love story full of lyrical writing and raw emotion." —Jennifer Probst, *New York Times* bestselling author

"*Bend Toward the Sun* hits all the perfect notes."
—Trish Doller, author of *Float Plan*

"An achingly beautiful romance . . . soul satisfying, sensual, and unforgettable." —Libby Hubscher, author of *Meet Me in Paradise*

"Intoxicatingly sensual and undeniably sexy, *Bend Toward the Sun* stole my heart from page one and never let go."
—Mazey Eddings,
author of *A Brush with Love*

"Sweeping and lush, *Bend Toward the Sun* is one of my favorite kinds of books."
—Anita Kelly, author
of *Love & Other Disasters*

"Smart and riveting . . . Jen Devon knows her way around the human heart."
—Camille Pagán, bestselling
author of *Everything Must Go*

"A breathtaking, beautiful debut!"
—Priscilla Oliveras, *USA Today* bestselling
author of *Anchored Hearts*

"An inspiring tale of love that sweeps you into a world you'll never want to leave."
—Brooke Burroughs,
author of *The Marriage Code*

"A masterpiece."
—Sonia Hartl, author
of *Heartbreak for Hire*

"One of the best contemporary romances I've read in years."
—Elizabeth Everett, author of *A Lady's Formula for Love* and *A Perfect Equation*

BY JEN DEVON

Bend Toward the Sun

Bend Toward the Sun

JEN DEVON

St. Martin's Paperbacks

This is a work of fiction. All of the characters, organizations, and events portrayed in this novel are either products of the author's imagination or are used fictitiously.

Published in the United States by St. Martin's Paperbacks, an imprint of St. Martin's Publishing Group.

BEND TOWARD THE SUN

Copyright © 2022 by Jen Devon.

All rights reserved.

For information, address St. Martin's Publishing Group, 120 Broadway, New York, NY 10271.

www.stmartins.com

Library of Congress Catalog Card Number: 2022006001

ISBN: 978-1-250-91032-5

Our books may be purchased in bulk for promotional, educational, or business use. Please contact your local bookseller or the Macmillan Corporate and Premium Sales Department at 1-800-221-7945, ext. 5442, or by email at MacmillanSpecialMarkets@macmillan.com.

Printed in the United States of America

St. Martin's Griffin edition published 2022
St. Martin's Paperbacks edition / May 2024

10 9 8 7 6 5 4 3 2 1

For Keith. You're my favorite.

PART ONE

CHAPTER ONE

Rowan

Rowan McKinnon crouched in an abandoned greenhouse in the rural Pennsylvania darkness, trying not to pee her pants. She'd have taken it a bit easier on the Cabernet tonight if she'd known the party at the old vineyard would include a game of hide-and-seek.

The greenhouse was a good hiding place for a botanist. Rowan was wildly curious to see what grew there in the light of day. The clouded glass ceiling was tall and cathedral-shaped, allowing only enough silvery moonlight through to see the place was a mess. Wooden floorboards were warped by moisture and fuzzy with moss. Beneath vented roof panels, little islands of plants overflowed pots to ramble across a maze of tables and benches. Life had flourished and thrived there, despite years of apparent neglect.

Rowan felt a pang of kinship.

In the darkness outside, someone's scream dissolved into laughter, the sound followed by whoops of triumphant men's voices. The hairs on the back of Rowan's neck involuntarily rose.

"Just a game," she murmured, shifting her weight from foot to foot.

Four weeks ago, she'd packed up her two suitcases

of belongings and left Cornell to head back to Philadelphia. Philly wasn't home—nowhere was, really—but Temperance and Frankie were still there. The three of them had been best friends since undergrad, and Rowan needed a quiet place to revise her research manuscript. Only days after she'd defended her dissertation, her department chair had called to report "significant complications" about her data sets. Suddenly, her world of stable, deliberate plans became a world of roadblocks and uncertainties. She couldn't publish until she did major recalculations and rewrites, and she couldn't apply for worthwhile postdoctoral fellowships until she published.

Couldn't recognize herself without that academic lens.

Couldn't manage to peel herself off Temperance's couch.

Frankie had visited early in the week, unable to entice Rowan out of her funk even with the promise of Robustelli's cheesesteaks and famous truffle Parmesan fries. Rowan had instead subsisted exclusively on caramel popcorn and cherry soda for days, watching and rewatching David Attenborough's *The Private Life of Plants* and repotting her small collection of succulents in Temperance's little kitchen.

Rowan wondered if Temperance would have still dragged her along tonight if she'd have pantomimed self-care by conspicuously eating a banana or an apple a time or two. Maybe Temperance would have left her alone if she'd managed to change out of her pajamas. At least once.

Tonight's revelry was a housewarming party to celebrate the Brady family's new ownership of the property. Temperance was a de facto member of the Brady family—her older sister, Maren, was married to one of the Brady sons. Rowan grudgingly found the Bradys charming, but they had big-family camaraderie, the kind of overt, playful loudness that came from a lifetime of knowing exactly who your people were. It was a stark, slap-in-the-face contrast to her own lonely childhood, and being there in the midst of it, she felt as conspicuous as a toad on a birthday cake. *"Like recognizes like,"* her mother always used to say. Even as a child Rowan had been able to infer that "like" also recognized *other.*

So, she'd sipped wine—a lot of it—around the bonfire, introverting like a card-carrying professional, until she was unceremoniously opted in to the hide-and-seek game by a determined Temperance and Frankie. "Team Tag" the Bradys called it, a decades-old tradition at their family gatherings. A handsome older man in a barbecue apron emblazoned with WELL SEASONED—presumably the Brady patriarch, William—had stood on a picnic table to belt out the game's rules for the newcomers. Teams were the Brady family versus non-Bradys. Timed rounds, whoever captures the most members of the other team in thirty minutes wins. Everyone got a little pocket flashlight, for safety. They were all branded with BRADY BROTHERS CONTRACTING in typeface straight from the 1980s. Cute.

The only family traditions Rowan had were trips to Kmart with Grandma Edie for new shoes before each new school year, and hot cocoa from cheap powdered packets on Christmas Eve. Imagine having an entire *game* as a tradition. With branded swag.

When Rowan had arrived, her eyes had been drawn to the Victorian-style greenhouse on the rise at the top of the property. The glass panes had shone like amethysts in the sunset. But now that she was inside it, the big building had lost its whimsy. The white metal frame instead seemed to hunch over her like a massive skeletal rib cage.

Even before academic calamity had her spiraling into existential self-doubt, Rowan had always been an anxious, awkward sort. For kids and well-adjusted adults, this game was probably pure, primal adrenaline-tripping. A thrill of imminent danger, with no real-world consequences. But Rowan had no childhood frame of reference to compare to, no baseline to determine whether her sprinting pulse and sweaty neck were typical, or over-reactions.

She was hurtling toward thirty and had never played hide-and-seek.

As she'd raced across a wide lawn and up the hill after the starting whistle blew, a latecomer's car headlights briefly illuminated her as it pulled up the gravel drive. Aside from that, there'd been no sign she'd been seen or followed.

Until now.

A shadow passed across the glass at the front of the greenhouse.

"Just a game," she reminded herself again. Sweat was slippery behind her knees. Her rapid breathing was strangely muffled by the dense greenery and heavy air. Late summer humidity made copper curls pull free from her braid, coiling outward in serpentine mayhem around her face. She blew the strands back and peeked over the edge of the potting cabinet she'd chosen for cover. Silence.

Shoes skidded on the gravel outside the greenhouse door. Rowan gasped, clumsily brandishing the little flashlight like a weapon.

A wide-shouldered, undeniably male form filled the

doorway, backlit by the weak porch lamp outside. He made a little "gah" sound as her light hit him in the eyes. In the narrow beam, Rowan took rapid inventory of him: body lanky, very tall. Golden hair, winging from the sides of a frayed ball cap. Thin, angular face, new beard—and not the well-managed, trendy kind. It was the scruff of a man who couldn't be bothered to shave, let alone give any shits about beard combs and balms.

Being discovered so quickly wouldn't have been a problem, really. She'd simply go drink more wine around the fire while everyone else played out the game.

The *problem* was—this rangy, disheveled man wasn't someone she recognized from the party. By his height alone, Rowan certainly would have remembered him.

She snapped the flashlight off and tucked it into the pocket of her cutoffs. She pivoted, leaping over a knee-high bench.

"Hey!" the man said. Footfalls thudded on creaky floorboards as he gave chase.

Rowan heard a smack and answering groan as he slammed into one of the heavy tables. Then, a burst of filthy, breathless words. The baritone rasp of his voice drew goose bumps across her skin like a needle pulling thread.

Jumping a few more short benches, Rowan shoved several stacks of plastic nursery pots off a table, sending them tumbling in the direction opposite from the one she headed in. While the pots clattered to the ground, she froze, using the commotion for cover. She opened her mouth wide to catch her breath. Her tongue felt as dry as old newspaper.

Again, she heard the unmistakable crack of a shin or ankle bone meeting wood. A groan, and "Mother-*fucker.*" Then he went as quiet as her.

A solitary cricket whirred once, twice, testing the silence. Outside, another bubbly scream split the night, followed by peals of familiar, obnoxious laughter. Frankie must have gotten caught. It annoyed Rowan that she couldn't force her brain to find that same uncomplicated joy in the experience.

Could she get around the guy and out the front door? Possibly, if she could pinpoint where he was and get him moving in the wrong direction before she made her break. But the tables and benches weren't arranged in any pattern. It had been sheer luck she hadn't yet tripped ass over ankles and busted out a tooth.

From where she squatted, the wide windows along the back wall of the greenhouse were far closer than the front door. One of them was cracked open.

She could get there.

A rumbly sigh came from an indeterminate place in the shadows. "I think you're out of bounds, this far away from base." His voice was smoother now that it wasn't grinding out obscenities. It had a cultured cadence to it that opposed his rumpled appearance.

Was he *teasing* her?

Rowan caught her lips between her teeth and fought the impulse to retort. He'd homed in on the only thing that might make her give away her position—and her advantage: an accusation that she wasn't following the rules.

At least she knew now he was part of the game, and not some vagrant from Linden, the closest town over on the way back to Philly. Still, it seemed strange she hadn't seen him until now. Maybe he'd been the latecomer in the car. That would explain why he didn't have a flashlight.

Rowan's knees and ankles burned from crouching, and *god,* her bladder.

Outside, two male voices shouted to each other from different directions, coordinating with militaristic urgency. Moments later, another high-pitched scream floated up the hill before dissolving into giggles. Her teammates were dropping like flies.

A plastic pot rolled across the floor in the darkness. Her pursuer was on the move, but heading toward the wrong side of the greenhouse, by the sound of it. Rowan seized the opportunity, shooting to her feet to make for the back wall.

The guy went down again as he tried to swivel and pursue. This time, his growling groan sounded muffled, like his mouth was pressed against the ground. She almost felt sorry for him, but her haywire sense of self-preservation wouldn't let her stop to check on him.

Rowan wanted to shout with relief as her hand closed on the lever-like handle of the partially open window at the back of the greenhouse. She grasped the latch in both hands and shoved, hard.

Nothing.

No movement. It was frozen into a foot-wide opening by rust and time.

Shit.

As circulation returned, her legs felt like they were full of buzzing bees. The eruption of sensation nearly buckled her knees. She blurted an agonized, frantic laugh.

"No way you're getting through that," the guy called. He grunted, pushing to his feet.

Rusty joints screamed like a banshee and the pane gave. She pushed it up and outward, as wide as it would go, then dipped her head through. Way too far down to go headfirst.

Rowan hooked each of her legs through the bottom lip of the window, squeezing her backside through with a shimmy of her hips. For a mortifying moment, she imagined becoming stuck, wedged there between the glass, squished out like a specimen on a microscope slide.

"Told you."

His smug tone pissed her off. Squeezing her butt tight, she wiggled centimeters farther out the window. She'd make it. There were still too many tables between them for him to reach her before she was fully through. A petty surge of triumph buoyed her.

But then, everything changed. When Rowan looked back again, he was retreating, fading quickly away in the darkness.

He headed for the door.

Oh, god. He was going to intercept her outside.

"Shit, shit, *shit,*" Rowan wheezed. She'd wedged too far into the window to pull herself back inside, and her feet hadn't hit the ground yet, so she had no leverage. She dangled there, inert, limp as a flag on a windless day.

It was a miracle her shorts hadn't ripped yet. With a desperate final squeeze of her ass, she made it the rest of the way through the window, hitting the ground below with a molar-clacking impact.

"Just a game," she panted.

The guy was already around the side of the greenhouse, and the moon seemed to shine a spotlight on her. Adrenaline pumped wildfire into her bloodstream. But it didn't matter. His legs were longer, and he had a head start.

In a few long strides, his arms snapped around her torso like a living straitjacket. "You're caught. You're done," he said, his breath igniting a hot trail from her earlobe to her collarbone.

Cinnamon gum.

The primitive part of her brain did a strange double-duty analysis, acknowledging the alarm of being caught, while simultaneously detecting that her captor smelled *delicious.* Somehow like marshmallows, undercut with sharp, peppery juniper and clean sweat. That weird juxtaposition of sensory delight with the compounded anxiety from the entire evening made her light-headed.

More screams in the distance, more laughter, more hoots of victory from male voices. Really, had the rest of her team hidden behind bushes and tree trunks?

Rowan jerked against his grip.

"Easy," the guy said, letting his arms fall away. At the same time, she twisted to face him to push free, and the momentum made her bounce her nose sharply against his breastbone like a choreographed slapstick gag.

Phantom stars instantly bloomed behind her eyes, a firework of pain. Tears welled, her scalp prickled. The stranger reached out and slid his hands down the backs of her arms, clutching lightly to keep her steady.

Rowan moaned into her cupped hands.

"Damn it, sorry. Let me see." He removed his ball cap, and a boyish swoop of hair fell over his forehead. He tossed the locks back with an upward jerk of his chin, then reseated the cap bill-backward on his head. Gently, he cuffed her wrists and pulled her hands away from her nose.

"Bleeding?" she mumbled.

"Ah, you *can* speak." He tucked a knuckle under her

chin to tilt her face to the moonlight, bringing his face close to hers.

Rowan glared. It was her first real look at him in the glow of the moon. His height disoriented her—she wasn't used to having to look up to meet someone's eyes. His clothes were too big for his lean frame. Hollows bracketed his mouth beneath too-sharp cheekbones. The edges of gleaming white teeth showed beneath a vaguely snarly top lip as he struggled to catch his breath.

There was an intangible vulnerability about him that tempered her combativeness. Something about his posture, or the way his concerned frown made his eyebrows dip down at the outer edges. The backward ball cap, or the spicy scent of his gum.

One of his hands maintained a warm, proprietary grip on her arm, his thumb absently passing up and down her bicep. His other hand cupped her opposite elbow. Awareness stirred inside her—an explicit human-to-human recognition of warm, healthy skin against her own. Somehow, this entire bizarre situation was beginning to turn her on, muddling her instinct to run.

Of *course* her libido would make this even weirder.

"I look like a goblin shark now, don't I?" she said. Her voice sounded nasally to her own ears, but the tingling pain had already faded, urged on its way by the long-fingered hands steadying her. Soothing her.

"Ah—I'm not sure if I should take you straight to an emergency room or a reconstructive surgeon."

His expression was placid on the surface, but something in his eyes churned like a rip current. As he studied her face, Rowan caught a glimpse of his tongue, nudging against the tip of a perfect incisor.

"Ha, ha," she deadpanned.

While evading him in the dark greenhouse, her

rampaging imagination had painted him as a faceless wraith. A thing devoid of personhood. But now that she was close enough to him that she *smelled* his body heat and felt the gusts of his breath against her mouth, it was impossible to ignore his very appealing humanity.

With a lover's familiarity, he tucked a loose curl behind her ear. The pads of his fingertips brushed along the sensitive curve of the lobe. "You good now?" he said. His eyes dipped to her lips. It sent a sucker punch of desire straight to her belly.

She didn't know his name.

The narrow space between them changed and charged, like the air pressure plunge before a major storm. They breathed each other, inhaling what the other exhaled. The greedy ache in her belly unwound and spread lower until it found a home between her hip bones. Rowan tipped her head back and narrowed her eyes in silent challenge, daring him to make a move.

Did people hook up at housewarming parties?

She didn't *need* to know his name for that.

A few flyaway filaments of her hair floated upward, caressing his face. He dipped his head subtly to the side, questioning, calculating. A modest forward nudge, a deeper downward exhale, and his mouth would be on hers. Curiosity and panic and recklessness expanded in her chest like an intoxicant-filled balloon.

God, she'd never felt anything like it before, and she didn't even know his name.

The loud bleat of an air horn shattered the silence. The guy flinched like he'd been slapped, throat convulsing in a hard swallow as he glanced down the hill and back to her. They stared at each other, chests rising and falling in unison.

"What's that mean?" Rowan asked. "The horn."

He blinked, squeezed his eyes shut, and blinked again. "Ah—only one person left on your team. One person who hasn't been caught yet."

The hand on her elbow tightened, and it boomeranged her back to reality. *She* was the one person left. Rowan tried to pull away.

"I caught you, fair and square." The guy laughed, tugging her toward the hill leading down to the campfire. "I'm not letting you go."

Like hell.

She could win this for her team. Her, the rookie. It was childish, it was petty, but she wanted—needed—to feel in control of *something* tonight.

Rowan thrust her knee upward. It glanced across his thigh, just missing his balls. Surprised breath whooshed out of him, and his free arm noodled like a faulty parachute cord. She overcorrected as she pulled away, tripping backward and bouncing hard on her ass. The impact sent a bolt of pain up her spine and into her skull.

For a few silent seconds, they faced off, each with the wind knocked out of them. The guy was fixed in place, body bent at the waist, hands planted on spread knees. His eyes ignited in the gauzy moonlight.

"Christ, woman. It's just a game," he croaked.

Rowan felt like a clown. What could she say now?

"Nice to meet you, sorry I have the manners of a feral cat."

"Sorry, I've had a really bad week and really need to win this children's game to salvage what's left of my self-esteem."

"Sorry about my knee, do you still want to kiss?"

Instead, she opted for awkward silence and scuttled backward like a crab, then pushed to her feet.

"Who the hell are you?" His voice was sandpaper on sandstone.

Rowan flexed her toes, priming her body to flee.

"I'm the one winning this game," she said, and ran.

CHAPTER TWO

Rowan

Rowan managed to hide in the western vineyard until the clock ran out. In the next round, her team secured the win by finding all the Bradys within the first fifteen minutes.

Everyone gave her credit for the victory. She was high enough on adrenaline and a fresh glass of wine that she managed to weather her newfound popularity gracefully, surprising herself by small-talking with strangers and only hating it a little bit. People from both teams congratulated her, toasting her as they walked by, patting her on the back, giving her shoulders a good-natured jostle. She hadn't been touched so much in years.

Maybe never.

Once the game ended, Greenhouse Guy was conspicuously absent from the rekindled revelry around the bonfire. Rowan scanned the crowd for his tall, sharp-shouldered form. At one point, she found herself alone with someone's elderly aunt, who hoarded an entire platter of bacon-wrapped dates and lamented seasonal allergies. When Rowan had offhandedly mentioned that pollen was plant sperm, the old lady looked at her aghast, as if Rowan had licked each of the hors d'oeuvres and placed them back on the tray. Then the woman scurried away with her contraband appetizers, leaving Rowan alone at the edge of the crowd with a renewed loathing for small talk.

Later, she found Temperance standing under a halo of paper lanterns suspended from the lower branches of a huge sugar maple. Her friend's pale hair was in a twist so smooth it shone like a mirror under the lights. A single dimple notched her cheek as she summoned Rowan over.

"I barely know what to do with myself in the presence of a newly minted Team Tag legend." Temperance pushed tortoiseshell cat-eye glasses up her nose. "Everyone is talking about you."

A pediatric resident in Philadelphia, Temperance Jean Madigan—T.J. to friends and family—had a heart as big as a mountain, but she was outwardly stoic and elegant. Some people assumed she was cold, but really, T.J. was an adrenaline junkie with a corny sense of humor, and any perceived aloofness was simply her steadfast refusal to deal with anyone else's bullshit.

Rowan groaned. "I'm going to need to sleep for two days after this. Being social is exhausting."

"You're doing fine." Temperance clinked a tumbler of gin and tonic against Rowan's wineglass. "Thank you for not wearing one of those plant pun T-shirts tonight, by the way."

Rowan sniffed. "I think my PARTY THYME shirt would have been perfectly appropriate."

Temperance hummed a noncommittal sound and crunched a piece of ice in her teeth. "Harry's here tonight. I can't wait for you to finally meet him. He got here late."

Late.

The headlights.

There it was—Greenhouse Guy was one of the Brady brothers. A ribbon of unease unwound in Rowan's belly. "Oh, boy. I may have already met him," she mumbled into her wine.

Temperance cocked a hip. "What, now?"

Dots of sweat sprung up at Rowan's temples. "Your friend, Harry. I think he was the one trying to catch me up at the greenhouse."

"What did he look like?"

"Tall."

"Sixth graders are taller than me," Temperance said. "Do better."

"Well, he *was* tall, damn it. Taller than me. By a few inches. Lanky. Newish beard, light brown hair. Maybe blond. Wavy."

Temperance's nostrils flared and she held her breath. It was one of her tells—she was trying not to laugh. "Was this guy wearing a UCLA ball cap?"

"Are you serious? It was really dark."

Temperance twisted her bottom lip between her thumb and forefinger. "I bet it was Harry."

"He scared the crap out of me, T.J. He was intense."

Laughter bubbled up, but Temperance locked it down between pressed lips. "I'm sorry. This would be funnier for you if you knew them. The Bradys are really good people, honey. Only one of them is an asshole."

Rowan had a hard time keeping up. "Wait, what?"

Temperance muttered more to herself than in reply to Rowan. "Actually, *two* of the brothers are assholes, but you'll probably never meet Malcolm. He lives in New York and is even more socially avoidant than you are."

"I have no idea what you're talking about."

Temperance blinked. "They take that game really seriously."

"No shit."

"Couldn't have been that bad."

"I tried to knee him in the balls, T.J."

Temperance's eyes widened. "Ooh. In that case, it's too bad it wasn't Duncan."

"The big guy, right? The only Brady you haven't introduced me to tonight."

Temperance frowned and evaded by sipping her drink. Slim arms wrapped around Rowan's waist, and a chin propped on her shoulder from behind. Already on edge, Rowan startled and sloshed wine over the rim of her glass. The embrace ended as quickly as it began, and a luminous tawny-skinned brunette slid in front of her.

"Frankie. You spilled my wine. This is an act of aggression," Rowan said.

"You're being uncharacteristically social tonight. Who are you, and what have you done with Rowan?" Frankie Moreau's voice was a husky alto, rich as the bourbon in the glass she held.

"I've been reveling in the adulation of the masses for my Team Tag tactics," Rowan said. "And offending old ladies by talking about plant sperm."

"As one does." Temperance crunched more ice.

"That's my girl." Frankie smiled, then pointed at Rowan's glass. "You spilled your own wine."

With no sense of fashion and a lack of social graces, Rowan always felt like a hulking mess around Frankie. She was a photographer and former model, always effortlessly immaculate. Her sleek dark hair slanted in a bob that framed her exquisite face, and she never had flyaways or broke out in situationally inappropriate sweats. Frankie's physical perfection was paired with a sweet personality and playful intelligence that made her impossible not to love.

Temperance and Frankie had been friends since they'd matched as undergraduates in random roommate assignments. Rowan was a year older than them, and she'd been a senior when her living situation had drastically and desperately changed. She'd answered the first "roommate wanted" ad she came across in the university paper, and moved in with them the next day, carrying a single suitcase of clothes, a rolling tote full of books, and a shitload of emotional baggage.

"T.J., stop eating ice. You're going to mess up your teeth," Frankie said.

"Thanks, Mom."

Frankie rolled her eyes and redirected to Rowan. "What finally lured you off that couch, Rosebud?"

Temperance cut in. "Rowan's been splitting her time getting potting soil all over my apartment and emasculating perfectly nice men."

Rowan snorted. "Everyone knows I'm trashing your apartment ninety percent of the time. Emasculation is only a side hustle."

"Ah, permission to approach?" A familiar baritone cut in from behind her, and Rowan smelled him before she saw him.

Juniper. Cinnamon gum.

Oh, boy. Here we go. She felt tangible warmth at her back as a large body drew close. Her insides pitched downward like she was on a poorly balanced ride at the county fair.

Temperance lit up and extended her arms. "There he is."

Heat flooded up Rowan's neck to splotch her cheeks and ears with red. Frankie clicked her tongue, unapologetically curious.

Greenhouse Guy entered their little ring of light like

a lanky, earthbound archangel, and greeted Temperance with a hug. The scruffy beard and ball cap from earlier had hidden a face a decade younger than she'd originally assumed. Now, he looked like he'd stepped from the pages of a J.Crew catalogue.

His hair was brown sugar generously brushed with honey, slightly damp at the tips from a recent shower. It curled in wide waves away from his face, like Michelangelo's freaking *David*. He'd shaved, revealing a deeply dimpled chin below a luscious mouth. A hint of overbite made his top lip slightly fuller than the bottom one. Rowan was typically unmoved by conventionally attractive men, but this guy was more than classically handsome. Something about the arrangement of his features and the way he moved his body made it difficult for her to look away.

He was mesmerizing.

God, if she'd known he looked like this under the scruff, she'd have let him capture her.

Temperance leaned into him, and he bent low to drop a casual kiss on the top of her head. The two were conspicuously, comfortably beautiful together as they shared the brief hug and murmured greeting.

"Did you need to shower off the shame of being on the losing team of Brady Team Tag?" Temperance teased.

The corners of his mouth tipped into a slight smile. "I'll need to have a good cry later."

"I didn't even know you'd arrived until an hour ago," Temperance said.

He kept one arm around Temperance's shoulders, tucked the opposite hand in the pocket of pants so wrinkled they'd obviously been hastily removed from luggage. "Cab dropped me off, and I jumped right into the game." He looked straight at Rowan. "Couldn't resist."

Rowan swallowed so hard it hurt. In the distance, she saw moonlight shimmer on a small body of water. She wanted to dive in headfirst and never surface again.

Instead, she did the next best thing: she hid in plain sight behind Frankie's overt charisma and innate knack for small talk. Really, it was a superpower.

"Who do we have here? T.J., have you been hiding a boyfriend from us?" Frankie said.

"Are we too old to say 'boyfriend'?" Temperance smirked. "Also, not my boyfriend." She and Greenhouse Guy shared a look that suggested it was the most absurd thing they'd ever heard.

"Cousin?"

"Not that I'm aware of."

"Masseur."

"Nope."

"Gardener," Rowan murmured into her wine. Her friends didn't hear, but one of Greenhouse Guy's brows quirked, and a vague smile hovered on his lips.

He stepped away from Temperance and extended a hand to Frankie. "Harrison Brady, and I'm, ah"—he glanced over his shoulder at Temperance—"I guess we're siblings-in-law? Is that a thing?"

Temperance nodded. "My sister, Maren, is married to his brother Nathan. But more important than that, Harry and I are *friends*."

"I'm Frances Moreau." Frankie captured his hand and made warm, genuine social interaction look effortless. "My friends call me Frankie."

"My friends call me Harry," he said.

"Why haven't we ever met?" Frankie asked.

"He's been in California for the last five years," Temperance answered, before he could.

Harrison smiled at Frankie, then diverted to shake Rowan's hand. That damned hunk of honey hair fell across his forehead as he leaned toward her. "I feel like I already know you," he said, ostensibly to both her and Frankie, but his attention fixed like an electromagnet on Rowan.

His long fingers slipped across her knuckles to fasten her palm to his, and he gave her an unmistakable squeeze. Adversarial and vaguely teasing, while his expression remained judiciously neutral. Rowan squeezed back, feeling the elegant array of bones in his hand shift against hers. Even though this man had already put his hands all over her tonight, the innocent contact made her cheeks bloom with heat.

If other people wore their hearts on their sleeves, she wore her entire circulatory system on her face.

He held on for a bit longer than he should've, then straightened again to Temperance's side, tucking his fists away into the pockets of his pants. Though he'd relinquished her hand, his eyes remained locked on hers. He wasn't simply watching her.

He was *concentrating*.

Rowan barely contained a nervous, explosive laugh. She awkwardly wiped her hand on the thigh of her shorts. Her organs were in complete disarray—heart in her neck, stomach on the ground.

Thank goodness for Frankie. "Tell us more about you, Mr. Brady. Actually, it's Dr. Brady, isn't it?"

He hesitated, and his congenial mask slipped a bit. Little muscles ticked at his temples as he flexed his jaw. "I'm a doctor, yeah. Harry is fine, though. Just Harry."

Temperance slipped her arm through his. It was subtle, but to Rowan, it was transparent—her friend was *protective* of this man.

Frankie continued, "What kind of doctor are you? Pediatrician, like our T.J.?"

Again, a brief pause before he responded. "I'm an obstetrician." The mild strain in his tone contrasted with the casual nature of the conversation.

Silence.

The moment was so loaded with awkwardness, Rowan's mouth outpaced her brain. "So you—know your way around a vagina. Professionally speaking."

"Oh my god, Rowan." Temperance slid her arm free of Harrison's to remove her glasses and pinch the bridge of her nose.

Harrison's mouth drifted open, but he snapped it shut. Then he chuckled and shook his head, and some of the tension evaporated from his posture. "There's a lot more anatomy within my professional purview than vaginas, Ms.—?"

She hadn't introduced herself during the handshake. What an ass.

"I'm Rowan. My friends call me—Rowan."

Jesus *Christ*.

Frankie shot her a look oozing with empathetic embarrassment, and Harrison stared at her with fascinated bewilderment. Rowan didn't avert her eyes from his, but she had to bite the tip of her tongue to keep from losing it.

Temperance narrowed her eyes at the optical combustion between them. Again, she twined her arm around Harrison's. "Want a beer?" Her voice was high.

He diverted his gaze from Rowan to look down at Temperance. "I've been eating airport junk all day. I do need to track down some food, but I keep getting lost."

"Stick with me, big guy. I gotcha." Temperance nudged him into the crowd. Over her shoulder, she mouthed, *"Don't even think about it"* to Rowan and Frankie.

"Good meeting you," Harrison called as Temperance led him away. Frankie gave a little wave with her fingers, and Rowan nodded, afraid to open her mouth.

It felt like she'd been kicked in the chest by a horse. She took a big drink of wine, focusing on Harrison Brady's broad back, and the golden ducktail curls brushing the collar of his shirt.

Right before the crowd claimed him, he looked back a final time, straight into her eyes.

Busted.

Alcohol burned her vocal cords as she choked on the wine. She coughed until she was hoarse, and tears squeezed from the corners of her eyes.

Frankie patted her blithely on the back. "Well. That was impressive, Rosebud. I'm not sure if it was flirtation or sexual harassment."

"I get nervous meeting new people."

"Obviously. Your level of inappropriateness increases exponentially the more awkward you feel."

"Why am I like this?"

Frankie made a thoughtful sound as she sipped her bourbon. "I'm calling dibs on your behalf."

"No. Oh, no. Not interested."

Frankie touched the back of her hand to Rowan's forehead. "You literally choked on your drink as you watched him walk away."

"I wasn't watching him."

"You're a damn liar."

"Not my type," Rowan said.

"What, because he seemed *nice*?"

"Exactly. Too nice for me."

"That man is a sad, gorgeous cinnamon roll in need

of your weird Earth-goddess energy to snap him out of whatever funk he's in."

Rowan sniffed. "I don't understand anything you just said."

Frankie made a circle with her thumb and forefinger, and plunged two fingers from her other hand through. "You two need to get horizontal. Together."

Rowan laughed. "You're a ridiculous flirt, Frances Moreau."

"Exactly. I was flirting my ass off, giving him full-force Frankie doe eyes and sex voice. He *literally* couldn't take his eyes off *you*."

"That was fear. Like when a mouse keeps a house cat in its line of sight. It's survival instinct, not attraction."

Frankie did a slow blink. "Now it's my turn to not understand anything you just said."

"He looked at me like that because I tried to knee him in the nuts during Team Tag, Frances. He probably hates me."

At the greenhouse, Rowan's body had been primed for confrontation, completely marinated in adrenaline. This sudden fascination with Harrison Brady had to be misattribution of arousal—a psychological phenomenon where a person mistakenly thinks they're attracted to *anyone* they encounter during a stress-elevated situation. Honestly, it was the only reasonable explanation of why a woman like *the* Joan Wilder would have fallen for a dick like Jack T. Colton in *Romancing the Stone*.

Rowan wasn't *actually* into Harrison Brady.

In any other circumstance, the taste of his exhaled breath and the scent of his heated skin wouldn't have done anything for her. The primitive parts of her brain had simply tangled reality with biochemistry.

It was science. That's all.

"Anyway." Rowan gestured toward where Temperance had disappeared with him. "There's obviously something between those two."

"Bullshit. That vibe was strictly sibling, sweetheart."

"I disagree. They're both single. They're both gorgeous. Hell, they're both single, gorgeous *doctors*. Didn't you feel like an extra in an episode of *Grey's Anatomy* just now? And did you not see Temperance giving me her scary 'do not engage' eyes?"

"My intuition is very rarely wrong," Frankie said.

Rowan raised a brow. "Mason Dingle."

Frankie snorted. "Okay, one flub in a history of near-flawless romantic intuition. Oh, god, I can still see my brother's face when he told me about their first date."

"Your brother just didn't want to date someone with the last name 'Dingle,' " Rowan said.

"No, he didn't want to date a guy with a TikTok dedicated to his dog in a Dolly Parton wig," Frankie sniffed.

"How could anyone dislike Dolly Barkin'?"

Frankie nodded solemnly. "Look. If the morose but sexy Dr. Brady and T.J. are anything more than close friends, I'll shave off my eyebrows. Your people skills are not your strong suit. Stick with the plants, leave the love stuff to me."

Rowan rolled her eyes. "Are you confident enough to make this a Cheesesteak Friday wager?"

Frankie dipped her chin and dropped her voice in a faux conspiratorial tone. "I'm listening."

"I say they're sleeping together, or will be shortly. You say they're not. Loser pays for Cheesesteak Friday."

"Meh." Frankie looked at her nails.

"For a whole *month*," Rowan added.

"Better." Frankie lifted a brow. "What kind of time frame are we thinking?"

"We could ask Temperance later tonight. Easy."

Frankie tapped a manicured nail on the rim of her glass tumbler. "You lost me again. Let's raise the stakes."

Rowan snorted. "Was that—a cheesesteak pun?"

"Obviously. And I'm serious, let's make this more interesting. I propose that not only are Dr. Brady and T.J. not romantically inclined, that man is hot for *you*."

"Sounds like a plan—"

"Addendum," Frankie interrupted, holding up a finger. "*And* you're going to be in love with each other by spring."

Rowan blurted a laugh.

Please.

That word. Love. Unquantifiable, misused, meaningless. For Rowan, *love* was two hands pushed deep into fragrant black earth. In nurturing seedlings, in ankle-deep mud, in scorching sunshine and lip-numbing autumn chill. Seeing the first bees in springtime. The open air of fieldwork. In books, in research, in the acquisition of knowledge. In solitude.

Music began playing from the direction of a big gazebo in the center lawn. Rowan pulled her braid over her shoulder to remove the elastic. She combed fingers through the curly strands to let her hair hang loose. "Frankie, I'm not even going to see him after this weekend."

Frankie ignored her. "When I win, you know I prefer Robustelli's. Something about their cheese is—" She made a chef's kiss gesture with her fingers, then gave Rowan a sideways squeeze. "I think there's dancing happening. See you in a bit."

Rowan watched her friend disappear in the direction of the music. "I didn't take the bet," she called after her.

"Coward," Frankie volleyed back in a singsong voice.

For the first time since she'd squatted in that green-house, Rowan was alone. From her vantage, she saw a couple on the steps of the gazebo, illuminated by fairy lights and leading a toast. She'd met them earlier in the night—Patrick Brady and Mercedes Hudson. They were a movie-star sort of couple, impossibly attractive and plainly wild about each other. Newly engaged. Rowan viewed that kind of romance the same way she'd observe a compelling painting—appreciative of the beauty, while acknowledging it as only an approximation of reality.

The problem with marriage was that its ongoing in-tegrity depended on the inherent goodness of the two people entering the union—and not all humans were in-herently good.

Rowan had always felt half-good. Built only for tran-sience, never attachment. She'd felt that way even as a child.

Get out, before they discover what's missing from you. Before they see your not-good half.

She suddenly felt embarrassed to be there. A cynical fraud. Rowan ducked out of the halo of light cast by the paper lanterns, lifted a mostly full bottle of uncorked wine from the minibar at the edge of the party, and headed toward the pond where it was dark.

She didn't bother to grab a glass.

CHAPTER THREE

Harry

On the pond along the eastern edge of the Brady family's new property, Harry and his brother Duncan sat on a bench at the end of an old dock. The wood felt smooth with age and warm to the touch, like it had banked some of the day's late summer sun. Harry breathed in the mineral tang of mud and the fresh smell of the water. The air felt lighter and cleaner in his lungs than the air in Los Angeles ever had.

Five years he'd been gone. He'd missed the East Coast. Missed his family.

"Glad you could get here in time for this," Duncan said. "Means a lot to Ma and Dad."

Harry's answering smile was humorless. "My schedule was pretty open."

"You know they used to call housewarming parties 'Food Pounders' back in the day?"

Harry raised a brow.

"Sometimes they just called them 'Poundings,'" Duncan said.

"Who the hell is 'they'?" Harry asked.

Duncan shrugged. "I dunno. Horny old ladies."

Harry smirked. "Sounds like your kind of party."

They laughed, then went quiet for a while.

Duncan broke the silence. "Ma and Dad have lost their fucking minds, you know that?"

"Can't be that bad," Harry said.

Duncan grunted. "Wait until you see those vineyards in the daylight."

The elder Bradys had closed on the property just last week. Decades ago, a young Gia Brady had grown up at Vega Vineyards—her grandparents' vineyard in northwest Spain. Now Vega was a million-dollar operation run by Harry's aunt Renata. Ma fancied she knew winecraft via some kind of mystical genetic osmosis, the same way her sister did. Said it was in her blood. And now that she and Dad were retired, Ma decided she wanted to make wine, and run a bed-and-breakfast. They were gambling a huge chunk of their retirement savings on the prospect.

"Dad can handle it," Harry said. Will Brady was an architectural wizard, competent from blueprint to construction. He'd never seen Dad attempt to undertake anything he didn't finish with grace and style.

Duncan leaned out to look at Harry in the darkness. "You haven't heard?" he laughed. "Dad has decided his role in this new Brady enterprise is head *chef.* Head chef—at the bed-and-breakfast that doesn't exist yet."

"No shit?"

"No shit. He's been watching too much *Great British Bake Off.*"

"Still working out what he wants to be when he grows up," Harry said.

Again, they laughed.

"I'm doing all the general contracting." Duncan popped knuckles on his big hands, and hesitated. "They asked me to fully take over Brady Brothers, I couldn't say no. Nate and Maren are handling the business stuff."

Harry knew this thing would succeed because Ma and Dad had each other and the family behind them. The only thing he'd ever wanted more than a career in medicine was a family like the one Gia and Will Brady had created—an indelible, rock-solid partnership. They loved each other with a luminous, tangible kind of affection, the kind where they'd simply share space, and the weight and warmth of their love would overflow to everyone around them.

This place was where his parents would grow old. Where Harry would see his brothers and his sister, Arden, on holidays. It was where, someday, he would bring his wife and children to visit their grandparents and cousins, to build new family traditions. To play that ridiculous game of Team Tag on nights like this.

Wife. Children.

Well, hell.

Christ, his life felt so unrecognizable now. His big family felt like a brand-new puzzle, and he was the final unplaced piece. He belonged in the Harry-shaped space, but the fit was snug now, like a bit of extra effort was necessary to notch him properly into his spot.

Party sounds drifted down the hill, muted and merry.

Silence lingered between Harry and Duncan. They hadn't seen each other in over a year, but it didn't matter—the quiet was comfortable. The only thing strange about it was that his younger brother hadn't yet made some kind of wiseass comment or a dick joke. That Duncan was being so sedate made Harry realize how deeply messed up his family must think he was.

"Nicola know you left California?" Duncan asked.

Harry slid his hands together and looked down at the water, like he could somehow conjure a decent answer from it. He'd managed to hide from Dr. Bridger—

his own therapist—that it had been a year since he and Nicola had lived under the same roof. That put him on some kind of next-level plane of fucked-up denial, he was sure of it. What was the point of having a therapist if he didn't tell her the truth?

His relationship with Nicola had been in a state of mostly benign but irreversible decline over the past two years, but they were both too busy with residency to bother with the formalities of ending it. Her cardiology career had skyrocketed, and she slept at the hospital most nights, by choice. It wasn't until Harry's world crumbled after he lost a patient and she'd been incapable of being there for him—physically, mentally, and emotionally—that he realized he needed more.

He needed . . . *real.*

Nicola agreed, and did the thing he'd been too much of a coward to do.

Dr. Bridger had suggested a change in scenery. Get out of the city, she'd said. Maybe a trip into the foothills, or tent camping on Catalina Island.

Instead, Harry dumped most of his belongings into a suburban Los Angeles storage unit, took a leave of absence from the job he'd barely been at a year, and got on a plane east. Home.

Was this really *home,* though? The only thing that made this place home was the fact that his folks were here. He didn't even know where he was sleeping tonight.

"I'm not Nicola's problem anymore," Harry eventually replied.

Duncan made a low sound in his throat. "You're not a problem, man. For anyone."

Losing a patient in his first post-residency year hadn't been a thing Harry had prepared for. All doctors acknowledged the inevitability of this loss, and they learned tools to cope. Counseling. Meditation. Morbid humor, emotional numbing. Harry hadn't been able to do any of it. Hell, he'd barely been able to even *try*. Maybe he was too naive. Maybe it was hubris. Maybe he was a shitty doctor.

All of the goddamn above.

Whatever it was, he hated himself for it.

Duncan clapped a big hand on Harry's knee and squeezed before he stood. "All right, enough emotional shit. I need to get back. This entire soiree will collapse without my rakish charm to hold it together."

Harry gave Duncan a tight-lipped smile as he left. The dock swayed in the wake of his heavy steps.

For a while, he stargazed, looking for constellations—another thing rural Pennsylvania had on L.A. There, light pollution made it difficult to see many stars at all, unless he drove into the foothills. But he'd barely left his condo for most of the summer, let alone gone out of his way to stargaze in L.A. County.

He found Cassiopeia in the near-midnight sky, then let his eyes drift shut.

What in the *fuck* was he doing here?

The reset button on his life had been pounded with an unflinching hand, with a third of it already behind him. Four years with Nicola, over. Six figures of school loan debt, and no career in medicine to show for it. All because he was unable to get a fucking grip on his mental health.

Harry pulled and squeezed locks of hair in closed fists, hard enough to make his eyes water.

After a moment, he looked up. The greenhouse sat there, on the hill.

Cloudy moonlight turned it into a dully gleaming diamond. The skin of his forearm was ravaged with a dozen razor-thin cuts from the thorns of some renegade plant, and by tomorrow, souvenir bruises would bloom all over his aching body.

But he *felt* something other than despair. And it wasn't only the physical discomfort of his injuries.

He felt *her*.

Her name was Rowan.

Earlier in the car on the way from the airport, two of his brothers had sent texts to taunt him about missing the inaugural Team Tag at the new homestead. When the cab had pulled up the drive to drop him off, the game had just gotten under way, and she'd been the first person he'd seen, running up the hill. Nobody else around. Flying completely under anyone's radar.

Her long braid had slapped rhythmically down her back as she'd loped away, as if to beckon him. He'd paid the cab, dropped his bags in the grass, and took off toward her before greeting anyone else. Ma had given him hell later for not saying hello before diving in to the game.

Rowan.

She'd moved through the forsaken glass building like a nocturnal animal. For every time she'd woven through the maze of tables, or sailed effortlessly over a bench, Harry had bounced his shins against them like a Ping-Pong ball. He was convinced a skeletal hand had snagged his ankle and yanked him to the floor, like the greenhouse itself had come alive to prevent him from reaching her. He'd been so desperately outclassed and outmaneuvered by her, he should've given up in the first five minutes.

But then he'd seen her face in the glow of the moon, and suddenly, it wasn't about winning the game anymore.

An extraordinary face. Her features were too ineffable

and unique to merely be called *beautiful*. A galaxy of freckles spread across her nose and cheeks, dense enough to be visible even in the relative darkness. The most sensual mouth he'd ever seen had panted with exertion after the chase.

Harry swiped a hand across his own mouth, wishing he'd brought a drink with him.

If he'd been in remotely better shape, he'd have chased her again when she'd run into the vineyard. But after losing nearly twenty pounds of weight and muscle tone over the last six months—along with his laughably poor nutrition—he'd been breathless even *before* she'd grazed his junk with her knee.

The stars had shifted noticeably westward in the night sky when he felt the dock dip hard behind him. Harry turned. A raspy voice softly muttered, *"Shit,"* and a silhouette with a nebula of wind-stirred curls came onto the dock, arms spread like a tightrope walker.

Rowan.

For a moment, he considered lurking in silence. Maybe she'd leave after a few minutes. But when the dock swayed harder, and she crouched low and squeaked out an "Ooop," he stood. The only thing that would make this more awkward was if she took a drunken header into the water and he had to jump in after her.

Harry sighed inwardly and stood. "Pool's closed."

CHAPTER FOUR

Harry

A wordless rush of surprised sound escaped her and she sat back hard, making the dock sway side to side. Wine sloshed out of an open bottle top.

Harry bent at the waist as he approached to keep his center of gravity low, and managed to make it to her without dumping them both into the murky water.

Her legs were splayed out in front of her like a rag doll's. She held up a hand, palm out. "Damn it," she said. "Once my head stops spinning, I'll go."

"Not necessary. Plenty of room for both of us."

She made a soft, grumbly sound.

They sat in silence, and the rocking eased.

She held up a mostly full bottle of wine and criss-crossed her legs under her. "I'm working on drowning something, see? Might be sorrows, might be boredom." Her words were syrupy, as fluid and dark as the water around them. "I guess I can share."

"Ah, I'm afraid what ails me is far beyond what that bottle of wine can cure," Harry said.

"Won't know unless you try."

Backlit by the glittering lights of the party, her gaze was compelling and direct. Her feet were bare. Harry noticed her toenails were unpainted and charmingly, perfectly rounded.

"Where are your shoes?"

She flexed her toes. "Took 'em off. I hate shoes."

"Why are you out here alone?"

"Why are you?" she deflected.

Harry responded with a quiet smile. Rowan picked at the edge of the bottle's label. They both turned their attention to the water. A reflected beam of moonlight bisected the surface, pointing like an arrow straight toward them.

She answered first. "Alone is my favorite place to be."

"Ah, maybe I'm the one who should go?" Harry moved to stand, and the dock tilted sideways again. His thighs tightened.

"No, no. You were here first. I hate small talk, though. Don't small-talk at me." She sighed, and her posture shrank a bit, like she'd shed some invisible outer armor. Securing the bottle between her legs, she leaned back on her palms, shaking out her hair behind her. When she turned her face up to the sky, moonlight slid along her jaw and cheekbones.

"Not a fan of small talk either," he said. "This is actually one of the longest conversations I've had with another person in about three months."

Her head tipped down. "After the first hour of a party, I usually start hiding out in bathrooms."

"I mostly let others talk."

"Another solid strategy." She swept him with an unreadable look.

"Maybe we can share tips," Harry said.

"How does a doctor avoid small talk, though?"

The word *doctor* made his guts clench. He frowned. "That's different."

"Hmm," she murmured. "Temperance mentioned you live in L.A.? You're a long way from sunny California, Dr. Brady."

"That's the idea."

"You came all the way across the country for your family's bonfire?"

"Ah, not exactly."

"Why are you here, then?" she pressed.

Escape, Harry thought.

"I have a thing for ponds," he said instead.

Pause, then a small sideways smile. "I didn't mean here on the dock, Doc."

Harry chuckled. "My folks retired this year and bought this place. They don't know how to be idle, I guess. Big plans. I took a leave of absence. To help."

Liar.

"You planning to trade the stethoscope for some by-pass pruners, then?"

Harry shrugged. "I'm not sure what bypass pruners are, but that vineyard is a mess, from what I hear."

Rowan took a long drink of the wine. She blinked slowly, watching him.

"Shit, was that small talk?" Harry said.

"No. But it wasn't an answer, either."

"Maybe I'm afraid you'll *think* my answer is small talk? I don't want you to hide in bathrooms every time you see me."

"Wow, you're really overthinking this," she laughed.

"Overthinking used to be all I did. Now, I, ah—do everything *without* thinking." Harry tucked a hand back through his hair.

"You still haven't answered my question. Why are you *here*? If I ever take a leave of absence, I'd go somewhere that's—not Pennsylvania."

"My family wanted me closer," he said. "So, here I am."

"No strings to tie you down, then?"

"Are you asking if I'm married, or if I'm Pinocchio?"

Confusion briefly crumpled her features, then a loud, bubbling laugh. "Funny. *Are* you?"

He didn't answer and looked out over the pond. Night wind pleated the surface of the water like black silk.

She sat forward, pushing the bottle of wine to him. Her fingernails were short, and a narrow sliver of soil darkened her thumb's cuticle. "You brought more baggage with you than would fit in the overhead bin, didn't you, Dr. Brady?"

A self-destructive kernel lurked in his mind, urging him to rip open that baggage and spill it into the dark air between them. A masochistic off-loading, to see how she'd handle it. Instead, he kept his reply as sterile as a surgical field.

"Sounds about right."

A bullshit reply. But the answering depth of understanding in her eyes felt weighty, palpable. Not the vacant, template sympathy he'd gotten from so many others back in L.A. Not the impatience and "tough love" he'd always gotten from Nicola. Everyone there wanted to fix him. Not because they cared. Because his despair was inconvenient and uncomfortable for *them*. No, he didn't want to do yoga, or pray, or try fucking CrossFit or essential oils or burn a goddamned Himalayan salt lamp.

Rowan didn't cluck her tongue and offer nonspecific apologies or spiritual solutions or trite greeting-card pleasantries. This woman seemed to know what it meant to be damaged. She was simply allowing him to be . . . not okay.

Until now, Harry hadn't realized what a gift that was.

He felt seen for the first time in six months. Like more than only a vessel for his virulent self-loathing.

He felt *human*.

Harry took the bottle and held it up in a solitary toast. His hand shook.

As he drank, Rowan looked down at her own hands and rubbed them together. "There have been times in my life where the only thing getting me out of bed in the morning was stubborn curiosity about what might happen that day."

Harry drank and gave a little grunt of acknowledgment. Simple curiosity. Such a pragmatic reason to survive. Curiosity was at the heart of science, and one of the reasons he'd fallen in love with medicine.

He certainly felt curious about the woman sitting across from him now.

Some of the party lights winked out behind her. Night coalesced around them, silent and substantial.

"I don't know why I told you that," she said.

"I have one of those faces, I guess. Maybe I should have gone into psychiatry instead of obstetrics."

"Delivering babies is pretty important."

He took a deep breath in through his nose, blew it out through tight lips. "So is mental health."

"I might have been a doctor," she said. "But I like and understand plants a lot more than people."

Hell. He might've been a doctor, too.

He took another pull on the wine, and she watched. Her gaze felt heavy on his mouth, and he imagined he could taste her on the smooth glass rim of the bottle. It sent an unexpected bolt of heat straight to his groin.

"Well. My family is glad to have me back." Harry swallowed hard and swiped the pad of his thumb across his lips. "Med school took me to Baltimore, then California for four years of residency. Arden—ah, that's my little sister—she was still in middle school when I left. Now she's in college. I don't even know what she's majoring in."

For a while, they bobbed in silence. Harry passed the wine back to Rowan, and she tucked the neck of the bottle in her fist. She took a long drink, then licked her bottom lip with a generous swirl of her tongue. His jeans felt uncomfortably snug in the front.

At least that part of him wasn't broken. Maybe he simply needed generic human contact. Another person's heat. A willing mouth and body to use as a tool to slow the spread of darkness inside him.

"It's not polite to stare," she said, snatching him out of his trance.

Harry cleared his throat, shook his head, averted his eyes. "You're a botanist, right?"

"I will be once I'm employed, I suppose."

"Tell me about what you do."

That loud, sudden laugh again. "Okay, now you're just being polite."

He couldn't help smiling. "I never ask questions I don't want to know the answer to."

"Are you just trying to keep me here?"

"What if I am?"

"Not sure if that's creepy or charming." An unmistakable flush darkened her neck, but her tone was playful. "I'm leaning toward creepy."

"That's fair," he laughed.

"My research looks at the effect of using native cover

crops on fruit yields in cider apple orchards and vine-yards."

"Interesting. Lots of money in the alcohol business."

More lights winked out behind her, and the music stopped. In the sudden quiet, Harry heard the wind slither through cattail reeds at the pond's edge. Rowan's eyes glittered, her face underlit by the moon's reflection on the water. "Exactly why I chose that direction for my research. I wanted to do science without the hassle of having to beg for money to do it with. I was better funded than anyone else in the department."

"Smart. What's next?"

A beat of hesitation as she looked down at her hands. "There were some—complications with my current project. Some of my data sets turned out to be unusable, so I'm writing a lot from scratch with the numbers that are still sound. Publish, hopefully, by next summer. Postdoc afterward." Abruptly, she shifted to a hip and pushed to her feet. "I should get back."

Standing, she stumbled sideways and tilted per-ilously toward the water. Harry vaulted to his feet to steady her, planting his feet wide for stability. Her fingers latched hard onto his forearms, and the fresh cuts from the greenhouse thorns stung under the fabric of his shirt. With his hands socketed snug against her hips, they clung to each other, still as statues.

Christ, she smelled good. Lush and green.

Her hair brushed under his chin as she stared at the collar of his shirt, unmoving. Warmth from her breasts and belly infused him. The edges of reality came into bold focus, like an oversharpened photograph. It wasn't generic human contact he needed. Everything inside him called out for *this* woman. This stranger.

"Is your family going to demolish that greenhouse?" Rowan said to his neck.

"No idea, but I'm definitely making sure it is off-limits for Team Tag in the future."

"Funny."

"Do you not want them to? Tear it down?" he asked.

"What I want is irrelevant."

"Is it?"

The dock no longer swayed, and they could've safely let go of each other.

They didn't.

"Why did you come after me? In the game?" she asked.

"I'm the only one who saw you. It's—ah, a point of pride. Brady team hasn't lost in a while."

"So I broke the streak."

"You're not supposed to run after you've been caught," he said. "Technically, you cheated."

Rowan stiffened in his arms. He'd meant the accusation to be playful, but her quick intake of breath made it plain that he'd said the wrong thing. She pulled abruptly away and made a vague gesture to his crotch. "How's your—um?"

Harry stuffed fists into the front pockets of his pants. "All good. Glancing blow."

"Good thing for terrible aim, then." She frowned and shifted from foot to foot. For a moment, the silence felt loaded. Then she kissed the tip of her pointer finger and touched just below his bottom lip. "It's a crime to hide this chin dimple behind a beard, Dr. Brady."

She stepped off the dock into the grass. As she walked away, her hair floated with the cadence of her steps, like the tendrils of a sea anemone in a quiet ocean. Harry bent down to pick up the empty wine bottle, rubbing a thumb over the smooth glass opening where they'd both pressed their mouths to drink.

A part of him that had been dormant for months sparked to life, like kindling catching flame after too long in the cold.

CHAPTER FIVE

Harry

"Rise and shine, Doctor Strange," Duncan yelled through the door, pounding a fist to punctuate.

Harry cracked open a grainy eye. Last night, it had been just before 4:00 A.M. when he'd glanced at the clock on his phone. When he finally fell asleep, his subconscious was unsettled, and he dreamed of bourbon-hued eyes.

Rowan.

Groaning, he lay back on the pillow with an arm over his face.

Somehow, she'd been aloof and earnest at the same time. Effortlessly engaging, unpolished, funny. Vulnerable in ways she probably tried not to acknowledge, but shrewdly self-contained. A woman well-armored.

And Christ, she was gorgeous.

Duncan pummeled the door again. "Dude."

"Fuck *off*," Harry growled, yanking down the zipper of his sleeping bag. When he rolled onto his side, his back and right hip screamed in protest. He had no extra weight on his already lean runner's body. The air mattress in the otherwise empty room had lost volume in the night, leaving his ass and shoulder to hit the hardwood beneath.

Harry made a wrong turn upstairs and got lost on the way to the kitchen. After living in an L.A. condo for nearly ten years, the house felt mammoth inside, like a museum. The walnut floors had been refinished to their former glory, but they were creaky, giving little discordant squeaks here and there. Each room was awash in sunlight, and most were bare, with no drapes or blinds on the windows. To make the move easier, Ma and Dad had sold most of the furnishings from the house where Harry'd grown up. The result was a mostly vacant space where the loud voices and laughter of his noisy family bounced freely off the freshly primer-painted walls.

When he made it to the kitchen, Duncan was cracking a wiseass comment to their brother Nathan. They were the bookend brothers—Nate was the oldest Brady kid by seven minutes, a fact he never let his twin, Patrick, forget. Duncan was the youngest son, and originally the only one who'd stuck around to help with the family contracting business. Patrick was a pharmacist in Philly, their brother Malcolm was a big shot author living in New York, and Arden, the youngest child and only daughter, was off at college in Ohio.

"He lives!" Duncan's voice reverberated between the kitchen's cream tile and high post-and-beam ceiling. "Listen, something's wrong with the plumbing in the second-floor bathrooms, so we're sharing the one down here, between the three of us. Be quick about your business."

"You're one to talk, Ducky. I heard about your forty-five-minute showers in high school," Nate said.

"We barely had time to brush our teeth some mornings because you always took so long to jerk off," Harry added.

Duncan speared a middle finger at them both.

Harry hopped up to sit on the edge of the kitchen countertop, and Duncan handed him a mug of coffee. Nate tossed him a roll of powdered doughnuts and a Tastykake. "Bon appétit, lad," he said. Harry caught the doughnuts, but the Tastykake hit the floor.

"You two are trying to kill me," Harry mumbled. He sipped the coffee and grimaced. "Duncan, did you brew this coffee with piss?"

"Kiss my ass," Duncan growled. "This isn't the Holiday fucking Inn."

Duncan picked up the Tastykake, ripped open the crinkly plastic package, and ate most of it in one bite without getting a single crumb in his tidily trimmed black beard. He squinted at Harry. "What kind of breakfast do you require, Dr. House? Figs and granola and endive, or some shit like that?"

"Hey man, you pronounced 'endive' correctly. I'm impressed," Harry said.

Duncan grunted. "Last woman I dated was a vegetarian," he muttered around a mouthful of Tastykake.

They all nodded sagely, and Nate handed Harry a banana. "Family meeting is in twenty minutes, bud. At least go put a shirt on."

* * *

THE BRADY FAMILY sat in a semicircle on the floor of the sunken den, one of the few carpeted rooms in the house. The morning was cool, so the two-story fireplace along the back wall housed a crackling fire made from wood they must have scavenged from around the property. Above the den, an open-railed mezzanine led to the hallway where the upstairs bedrooms were.

"Let's talk about getting that vineyard into shape." Gia Brady's hair was cropped into a lively bob, the silky black strands threaded liberally with silver. Harry had never seen Ma's hair cut so short, but it suited her. She wore a bright melon-colored sweater paired with a green-and-burnt-orange plaid scarf that complemented her dark skin. Her only jewelry was a simple gold wedding band.

"Maybe we should have furniture and working bathrooms before we start worrying about the grapevines?" said Dad. A hot mug of coffee sat poised in his big paw-like fist. Harry wondered if he'd discovered yet how awful it tasted.

Gia blinked at her husband over a pair of square-framed reading glasses, tapping a pen against a notebook. "I want as much work as possible done by hand out there, William."

Duncan breezed in, sighing loudly as he lowered himself to the carpet. "It's not even nine in the morning and you're already talking business? Jesus, woman."

Ma jabbed a pointed fingernail at him. "Do not blaspheme under my roof, Duncan Callum."

"Harry," Nate said, "tell us about the botanist."

Harry sat up straighter. "Ah, what about her?"

"You're the only one of us who has really met her. We got her résumé for the consultant job we posted in the Linden newspaper."

"Really? Already?" That didn't match up with what she'd told him last night at the party. Harry distractedly rubbed the pad of his thumb across his chin where she'd pressed a kiss with the tip of her finger. "Is Duncan going to give me shit if I talk about business?"

Duncan smirked.

"He will not," Ma said. "But I will, if you don't watch your mouth in my home."

"Is it really a home if there's no furniture in it?" Nate said.

Ma swung her attention to Nate, pointing at him with her pen. "Don't you start too."

"Boys," Dad interjected. "Stop giving your mother shit."

Ma bent her neck and pinched the bridge of her nose.

When Harry spoke, he was careful to keep his tone mild. "Her name is Rowan, and she's—ah, a botanist. Which you already know. I'm not sure what else to say."

"What's she like?" Nate asked.

She's gorgeous and funny, and she smells like lush green things growing in dark, fragrant earth, Harry thought. "Ah, she's smart. Tenacious. A little distant. She's Temperance's best friend. What more do you want to know?"

Nate raised an eyebrow. "I can think of a few things."

"Do we know if she really wants a vineyard job?" Dad added. "Being a botanist doesn't mean she knows about grapes."

"Neither does having family who runs a vineyard on the other side of the Atlantic." Duncan grinned at Ma, earning himself a *shoosh* and an onyx-eyed glare.

"She worked in orchards and vineyards for her Ph.D. research." Harry held up his hands. "Look, I don't know why I'm the go-to guy here. She told me she was working on publishing a paper. Wants to do a postdoc. I don't know how working here fits in with that. But generally, when someone submits a résumé, it means they want a job, Dad."

"Point of order," Duncan interjected. Everyone turned their attention to him, and he paused dramatically before continuing. "Is she as cute as Temperance?"

Harry sighed. "You're an asshole."

Nate barked a laugh and lobbed a crumpled piece of

paper at Duncan's head. "T.J. Madigan is way overpunting your coverage, Ducky."

"Kiss my ass," Duncan said.

"Boys," Ma said.

Nate's wife, Maren, came into the den with a mug of tea. "Point of order," she echoed Duncan, sliding her eyes to him. "First of all, that's my little sister you're objectifying." She sat next to Ma. "Temperance told me she's the one who sent the résumé, Gia. Not Rowan."

"Oh." Ma looked down at her notepad. Her pen moved like she was writing something, but Harry could tell she was just scribbling tiny circles. The corners of her mouth turned downward, and she nodded. Her disappointment was plain.

"I can talk to her if you want me to," Harry said, quickly.

Duncan leaned back on his hands and crossed heavily booted feet at the ankles. "She *must* be as cute as Temperance."

"Fuck off, Duncan," Harry said.

"Harrison Bryant."

"Sorry, Ma. Look. You said you wanted me to get involved here. This is a way I can contribute."

Something shifted in her eyes, a spark of shrewdness. She cut her eyes over to Dad, who ducked his chin and raised his eyebrows.

"Pretty sure she meant with project stuff, not woman stuff, big brother," Duncan said.

"Jesus *Christ,* Duncan, will you knock it off?" Harry growled.

"I'm still not convinced we needed to put out that job listing." Dad raised his voice. Even though they were all grown men, it still worked to quell their bullshit bickering. "I don't even know where all the bathrooms in the house are yet. The vineyard is a low priority."

Ma clamped and unclamped her teeth on the pen. "Renata says if we don't get the grapes pruned down this winter, we'll lose a whole season in the vineyard. We can't cut things back once they bud out in the spring."

Dad replied with a *huh* and a nod. "Well, there we go. Why do we need to pay someone to advise us when we can call your sister? Get her on a video chat, and—"

"Renata doesn't have time for our little project, my love."

"'Little project'?" Duncan laughed. "Understatement of the decade."

Harry interjected, "If we hired Rowan, you all could focus on getting other things around the property into shape."

Nate flipped his own pen in his fingers. "Your timeline for getting the bed-and-breakfast up and running *is* pretty ambitious, Dad, if you want to have guests here by the end of next year."

Dad scratched his cheek. "Fine. Say, hypothetically, we wanted to hire her. How do we pay someone without a cash flow?"

Duncan shrugged. "We were planning to hire through Brady Brothers Contracting. I've got some wiggle room in my payroll."

Ma turned to Nathan. "Is that going to work?"

"Well, technically yes, but aren't we putting the plow before the horse, here?" Nate said. "We still don't know if she would accept what we can offer."

Dad opened his mouth to respond, but Ma laid her hand on his forearm. They shared a look, doing the thing Harry had seen thousands of times, where they conducted an entire conversation without a single spoken syllable. By Dad's sigh and Ma's self-satisfied smile, he could see she'd prevailed.

Dad began slowly. "I *do* like the idea of asking her to consult on what she thinks needs to be done in the vineyard. Short term. And your mother needs help identifying all the plants around the property. Maybe we can get a few hours of her time to help us figure out a business model and hiring forecast."

"Now you're talkin' my language." Nate rubbed his hands together. "I'll call her later today."

* * *

LATER THAT MORNING, Harry stood with Duncan and Nate in front of the main house. Duncan twisted a bit of his beard between his fingers with one hand and gestured southward with his travel mug. "Carriage house is the building right as you pull onto the property. Renovation there is finishing up by the middle of next week, if all goes well. Ma and Dad haven't had time to look in any of the other outbuildings yet. Might be some kind of animal living in that pool house, based on the smell down there. Key to that one is nonexistent, so I'm going to have to break a window." He took an eager swig of coffee, cringing as he swallowed. "Fuck me, that's bad."

"Told you," Harry said.

Duncan dumped the coffee onto the gravel driveway and gestured up the hill. "There's also a gardener's cottage next to that disaster of a greenhouse, but I haven't been able to figure out which key works for it yet. And who the hell knows what we're going to find in that bank barn." He pointed east.

The bank barn—named for how it nestled partially into the hillside embankment—was gray stone, and enormous. It was bordered behind by dense conifer forest, the spaces between the trees still black in the morning gloom. According to Nate, the front of the barn would become a boutique tasting room, and the deeper parts would house the tanks and casks for the winery operations. Since the structure's lower levels were half-buried under the hillside, the temperatures there would stay naturally cool year-round, ideal for crafting wine.

The bank barn dominated the lowest point on the property, while the greenhouse overlooked from the highest. Two huge structures, neglected to time, to nature. The true magnitude of work facing his family hadn't hit Harry until that moment.

The entirety of the modest suburban Philadelphia ranch home he'd grown up in—including its postage-stamp lawn—would fit into a single one of the vineyard blocks here, with room to spare. That house had always had the loveliest landscaping in the neighborhood, despite six kids' best attempts to destroy it with bikes and skateboards and runaway basketballs. There had been an apple tree in the backyard that always bloomed prettily, but never actually produced apples. Ma always had a little vegetable garden where she grew tomatoes for her Spanish tomato toast and homemade gazpacho.

Harry had always hated the fucking gazpacho. Soup shouldn't ever intentionally be eaten cold.

Dad had built a little pergola over the back porch, which Ma had eventually covered in Concord grapevines. Late every summer, ripe clusters would hang down from the top and sides of it, and they'd taste like grape jelly straight from the jar. Harry and his brothers would spit the seeds at each other with as much velocity as they could muster.

As far as Harry could see, there were grapevines. After months of turtling in his little L.A. condo, this new world seemed impossibly vast. According to Dad, there were only nine acres of vineyard, but it seemed an enormous undertaking. Ma's hobby garden in the suburbs had nothing on this.

Hell, if fresh air and hard labor really were what he needed to help him heal, he'd certainly get plenty of both here.

The brothers separated. Nate and Duncan headed off to start projects, leaving Harry to get to know the property. He walked alone down the gravel drive leading away from the main house. At the end of the lane loomed a huge double gate, its hinges rusted permanently open.

A massive weeping willow stood next to the brick building Duncan had called the carriage house. As Harry approached, the wind lifted the droopy, golden-leaved branches in welcome. The motion had a slow sensuality to it that reminded him of Rowan's butterscotch curls.

Ornamental gardens encircled the little house, but they'd been reclaimed by nature long ago. Weeds weaved throughout the spent blooms, but Harry still recognized the innate beauty of the landscaping underneath.

The cornerstone on the carriage house read 1899. Harry removed his shoes and keyed in. An entirely open space, it had a soaring exposed-beam ceiling and new cherrywood floors, and it carried the odor of fresh paint. A granite-topped bar divided the small kitchen from the main living space. Along the wall were empty spaces where new appliances would fit. A small table would nestle in a nook created by a bay window overlooking a spacious deck. Beyond the window was a view of one of the vineyard blocks.

Opposite the kitchen, a rounded archway led to another room—a bedroom with a rectangular skylight nestled in the ceiling. The room was big enough for a comfortably sized bed and a chest of drawers, but not much else. Through a sliding pocket door was a small washroom. No tub, only a small pedestal sink and a glass-walled shower stall with a big rainfall-style showerhead.

Harry's phone buzzed in his pocket with a selfie from Duncan. In the bottom corner of the foreground, his brother gave a thumbs-up and grinned, his teeth flashing white against his dark beard. The background of the picture was what Harry assumed to be the floor of the pool house, absolutely covered in little islands of animal shit. A text from Duncan followed:

> Was right about the critter in the pool house. Get your ass down here.

Harry laughed and shook his head. No, it wasn't the fresh air and hard labor here that would save him.

He texted back:

> Coming. Dibs on the carriage house.

CHAPTER SIX

Rowan

Buddy Mary's—or Buddy's, for short—had been their favorite bar in the city since they were undergrads. It was packed tonight, but Rowan, T.J., and Frankie had managed to arrive early enough to score one of the high-top tables closest to the bar. Pounding house music rumbled the seats of the barstools they sat in, but the dance floor was far enough away it didn't inhibit conversation.

A lifetime ago, Buddy's had been one of the places twenty-one-year-old Rowan found salvation. It seemed silly, really, for a college bar to have played such a formative role in her life, but it would forever be the place where sweat, Obsession perfume, and watered-down Amaretto sours baptized her into a new, post–Noah Tully life.

She'd met Noah junior year. During their year-long relationship, he'd dominated her priorities, her consciousness, her entire sense of self. Her GPA tanked—she almost failed biostatistics, and consequently still struggled with stats to this day—and she lost the few casual friendships she'd had then. Noah demanded everything of her, and in her stunted notion of love, she went all in, overcompensating and overcorrecting for the lonely years of her adolescence. She'd recklessly embraced youthful romantic optimism instead of trusting the instincts that had been etched onto her bones as a child. Wanting so desperately for instinct to be wrong.

When their engagement imploded, it left her in unrecognizable pieces. She'd been in survival mode when she moved in with Temperance and Frankie, sleeping or studying whenever she wasn't in classes, scarcely emerging from the second bedroom Temperance had vacated so Rowan could have some meager privacy. Originally, her stay with them was intended to be temporary until she could find a place of her own. Instead, the two women infused themselves into her life, relentlessly and unapologetically.

Now here they still were, eight years later.

An array of perfectly fried bar foods covered the table, leaving barely enough room for their drinks. A gin and tonic for Temperance, a red wine for Frankie, and a hoppy craft beer for Rowan.

Rowan moaned around a mouthful of sloppy cheeseburger. "God, it's as good as I remember."

"I can't believe we managed to get you off my couch *twice* in the same weekend." Temperance bit into a fried mozzarella stick and closed her eyes in bliss as the hot, melty cheese stretched between fingers and teeth. Frankie watched with bare lust in her eyes.

"I'm not here for you two," Rowan muttered. "I'm here for the food."

"I'm not mad about it. A bar has no business having food this delicious," Temperance said.

Rowan waved her fingers in front of Frankie's face. Her eyes were wide and glassy. "Frances. You're not a model anymore. Eat a cheese stick."

"Screw modeling." Frankie blinked fast, like she'd

just emerged from a trance. She pressed a hand to her belly. "It's not that. Fried food makes me so gassy."

"Liar," Temperance said. "You've never farted in your life."

Rowan laughed. "Cheesesteak Friday wrecks me, and you don't see me giving that up. Eat the cheese."

Genuine anguish drew down Frankie's mouth. "But if I eat one—I'll eat ten."

"There are only five more on the plate, Frank."

"And there are five *hundred* more back in the kitchen's freezer. I can't be trusted around that much cheese." Frankie's voice rose. "Why are we having this conversation? How long have you known me?"

"Long enough to know you dumped that hot vegan guy simply because he'd never take you out for fondue." Temperance licked her fingertips with dainty precision and picked up a deep-fried pickle.

"Dante Deacon. Honestly, I should have married him. He could have been my lifelong totem against cheese overindulgence. I'd never have to be tempted." Frankie rubbed her forehead.

"Disagree. You'd want it more, because you couldn't have it," Temperance said.

Frankie's grin was sly. "Now *you're* talking about your freshman-year guy. The one you refuse to talk about."

Temperance silently lifted a dainty middle finger at Frankie.

Rowan stuck her finger through an onion ring and wiggled it around. "If you'd have married Dante, who would've been my co-chair of the Marriage Repudiation Club?"

"I'll never give up my membership card, Rosebud. Don't you worry about that."

"You also broke up with that one guy for pronouncing 'pictures' like 'pitchers,'" Temperance said.

"Ugh, that guy. Harley Patterson," Frankie said. "I am a *photographer*. I couldn't hear that for the rest of my life."

"Petty," Temperance said, smiling, and Frankie kicked her under the table with a pointed boot.

Rowan tilted the neck of her beer bottle to point at Temperance. "Let's not throw stones from our shoddily built glass houses, T.J. You're the absolute queen of dumping guys for shitty reasons."

"I resent that." Temperance sipped her gin and tonic.

Frankie snapped her fingers. "The guy who reused coffee grounds."

"Inexcusable. I should have had him arrested," Temperance sniffed and sipped her drink.

"How about Musical Myles?" said Rowan.

Temperance choked on the gin and tonic. Rowan patted her gently between her shoulders.

Frankie leaned forward across the table. "Ooh. I don't remember that one."

"Myles happened after you'd moved back home for a while. Always had a booger that whistled in his sleep," Temperance said. "No matter how much he blew his nose."

"Nope. Wouldn't have lasted a single night through that," Frankie said. "I'd have put a pillow over his face."

Temperance poked Rowan. "Please date someone so we can drag you for poor choices too."

"Oh, see, I've cracked the code." Rowan tapped a finger to her temple. "If you never date, you never have to break up."

"You're the only one at this table with any sense of self-preservation. Dating is like using the bathroom here at Buddy's," Frankie said. "Every one of the stalls has some kind of biological disaster inside. All the options suck, so you pick the option that's least disgusting."

Rowan clinked her beer against Frankie's wineglass. "It's like getting your back scratched by someone who is just, you know, a centimeter away from hitting the spot where it would really feel amazing if they could just *get there*. But they don't, no matter how much direction you give them. Reality is never as good as the expectation."

"Now you're describing your sex life," Temperance said with a smirk.

Rowan made a face and picked at the label of her beer bottle.

"Oh! Look!" Frankie said. "Picking the label means she's sexually frustrated."

Rowan rolled her eyes. "Really, Frank? Are we nineteen again?"

Frankie laid a hand theatrically across her collarbone. "I, for one, *never* drank alcoholic beverages when I was nineteen years old." Then she snatched the last cheese stick from the tray between them. "Fuck it," she moaned as she chewed.

"'Atta girl," Rowan said.

A man approached their table with slicked-back hair, reeking of drugstore cologne. He clasped his hands on the back of their empty fourth chair. His smile flashed too many teeth, and he had a pair of sunglasses holding back his hair, like a headband.

"Hey, ladies," he said.

"No," Rowan and Temperance said in unison without diverting their attention from their drinks. Frankie shrugged and shot the man an apologetic look.

"That was mean," Frankie said as the guy hustled away.

"He should've read the room. My Resting Bitch Face is pretty unmistakable," Temperance said.

"Mine is *Intentional* Bitch Face," Rowan said.

Around a mouthful of crushed ice, Temperance said, "You were nice to him, Frankie. Those big brown eyes and apologetic little shrug. He's totally going to ask you for your number the next time you go to the bathroom."

Frankie groaned. "Ugh. The ones who snipe you outside bar bathrooms are the worst." She cut her eyes conspiratorially at Rowan. "So—what's Harrison Brady's story?" Her eyebrows and the tone of her voice had both lifted, the universal expression of innocence.

"Interesting pivot," Temperance said, slowly.

Frankie tapped a finger on her lips. "I was aiming for the complete opposite of bathroom-lurker douchebag."

"In that case, solid choice. Harry is the sweetest."

"Ever date him?" Frankie asked, casually tilting a paper-lined basket to roll a few remnants of fried breading around.

"God, no."

Frankie shot a triumphant grin at Rowan while Temperance looked down at her glass.

"Why's he so broody?" Frankie propped her elbow on the table and nestled her chin in her hand.

Temperance was inscrutable. She sipped her drink and frowned.

"He has the saddest eyes I've ever seen," Rowan added.

Frankie nodded. "I noticed, too. Even before I noticed that ridiculously adorable divot in his chin."

"Alexander Skarsgård, right?" Rowan said.

"Yes! Oh, god, I've been trying to figure out who he reminded me of. Not *True Blood* Alexander, though.

Tarzan Alexander, but without the bulk. Dr. Brady needs someone to feed him some cheese."

"Terrible movie, though," Rowan said.

"Agreed, but did we watch it for the plot? I'd watch a movie with him clipping his toenails for two hours, as long as he was shirtless." Frankie sipped her wine.

Rowan nibbled her thumbnail. "He always looks so forlorn. Is that why I think he's hot? Am I only attracted to the sad ones?"

"Who, Harrison Brady or Alexander Skarsgård?"

Rowan pushed out her bottom lip, considering. She shrugged. "Both?"

They both dissolved into laughter.

Temperance scowled. "Are you two finished?" With her straw, she stabbed at the lime in her drink. The ice rattled in the glass. "Harry lost a patient."

The three of them sat silent for a while, staring at the table. Rowan felt like an asshole.

She twisted her beer bottle and thought about sharing wine with Harrison. She trusted men about as far as she could toss them into moonlit ponds. So, she'd been prepared to dislike him after the entitled way he'd yanked her around during that ridiculous game. But later, on the dock, when she'd quipped about metaphorical baggage fitting into metaphorical overhead bins, she'd seen the raw chaos of grief flash across his face before he'd restored his tranquil mask. That hint of vulnerability had both fascinated and terrified her.

Rowan wasn't built for forging new relationships. Chronic loneliness in childhood had embedded self-consciousness into her entire self-concept—she not only lacked the social skills for reaching out to new people, she lacked the initiative to bother improving them. Really, it was only plain luck she even had Temperance and Frankie in her life—it certainly wasn't because of anything she'd done right. Their love for her was more about their innate goodness than any redemptive qualities of her own.

Last night, the shirt she'd worn at the Brady party had smelled of campfire and Harrison—traces of whatever cologne or soap or aftershave gave him that vaguely sweet juniper scent. She'd first caught the hint of it when she'd undressed once she got back to T.J.'s place.

It made her feel homesick for a home she never actually had.

Then, this morning, she'd sniffed the shirt until she felt dizzy, before rolling her eyes at herself and throwing it into the laundry bin.

Temperance knocked a piece of ice into her mouth. She crunched and talked at the same time. "Speaking of the Bradys, I sent them your résumé." The words were delivered with such practiced nonchalance, Rowan almost missed what she'd said.

"You—what?"

"Your résumé. I sent it to the Bradys."

"Still not following," Rowan said, frowning.

"Your computer is always on and always open, and there's a folder there called 'résumés'—"

"I understand the fundamentals of how it happened, Temperance. You know that's not what I mean."

"They need help getting a bunch of vineyards back into shape. You're a plant person."

Sensing tension, Frankie scooted her stool backward, whispered, "More cheese sticks," and disappeared in the direction of the bar.

Rowan proceeded with caution. "That's a horticultural dream project, but I'm not the right person for the job."

"I agree. You're not the right person. You're the *perfect* person." Temperance tipped another ice cube into her mouth.

Rowan made an impatient sound in the back of her throat. "No, T.J., I'm really not. I'm a botanist, for one."

"Botanist, horticulturalist, it's all the same, isn't it?"

"Oh, sure. Cesarean section, craniotomy, it's all the same, isn't it?"

Temperance laughed. "Fine, fine. Point taken."

Rowan shredded the beer bottle's label. "There are universal plant ecology basics, but the differences become pretty big when you consider an ecosystem as complex as a vineyard."

"I attended your dissertation defense, honey. You're incredible at distilling complex ideas into understandable stuff. That's what they need right now." Temperance paused. "*Dr.* McKinnon."

Goose bumps rose along Rowan's arms. It was the first time anyone outside of her Ph.D. committee had referred to her with the new honorific.

"Three things," Rowan said, raising her fingers. "One, that's fucking manipulative. Two, how dare you. And three, say it again."

Temperance leaned forward and laid a hand over Rowan's. Gently, she said, "I need you off my couch."

"Oh, you mean I can't live there forever? You're shattering my dreams, T.J."

"Every day this past week, I've seen you staring at your computer screen, but never typing," Temperance said. "There's a laundry basket full of academic papers on my coffee table, and you haven't touched them once."

Rowan had a formidable amount of work to get done on her manuscript, but no motivation to do it. *Publish or perish* said the old research university proverb.

Academia was tainted by an underbelly of prestige-mongering, and first-author publications carried status and weight. She wasn't going any further in her career—at least, not anywhere worthwhile—without one.

Her undergrad research assistant—a pinch-faced weasel named Martin Clutterbuck—had gotten busted by the university's Ethics and Misconduct Committee for fabricating the majority of the data he'd contributed to her project. Rowan had been able to prove her own innocence, but the damage was done: after four years of work, she had a half-assed manuscript she'd previously thought was nearly ready for publication.

Martin Clutterbuck was the human equivalent of stepping in something wet with socks on.

Frankie came back with a fresh haul of mozzarella cheese sticks—two orders—and drink refills for everyone. "If I had a scientific journal, I'd publish your paper, Rosebud." She slid the tray of goodies onto the table and wiggled up on her stool.

"That's super appreciated, Frank. But publishing in your imaginary journal isn't going to land me a postdoc." Rowan stuffed an entire cheese stick sideways in her mouth and rage-chewed.

Temperance primly squeezed lime into her new gin and tonic, then pushed glasses up her nose with her pinkie. "I love you, and you know I'll let you stay as long as you need, no matter how much I joke about it. I just think you should go see what the Bradys are looking for. Part-time. Something else to occupy your mind for a little bit, so you can get your momentum back."

"Added bonus: flirting with Harrison Brady," Frankie said around a mouthful of fried cheese.

"Hm, about that." Temperance narrowed her eyes. "Rowan likes casual and uncomplicated. I promise,

Harry is neither of those things. I didn't send her résumé over there so she could hook up with him."

"Calm down, *Mom*," Rowan said. "You know the only strings I like attached are the ones on my IUD."

Frankie snorted.

Temperance let out a long breath. Nudged her glasses up again. "There's nothing for you to lose by doing this."

"I'll think about it. If they call me." Rowan arranged and rearranged the salt and pepper shakers in the center of the table. *"If."*

CHAPTER SEVEN

Rowan

Two days later, they called.

Rowan parked her ancient Honda in a round gravel parking area beside the huge Georgian-style house at the center of the Brady property. As always, she was early. Anxiety made her vigilantly punctual—being early *was* being on time. It was a way she could assert control over her environment. It provided a buffer, a pause between arrival and inevitable human interaction, a chance to wrangle her pulse and stop sweating a bit before having to exchange pleasantries.

She resisted thinking of today's visit as an interview, even though that's what Nathan Brady had called it during their brief phone call. Considering it an interview suggested it was something she'd sought out. If she called it something different, she could pretend this was all Temperance's doing, and it wasn't what she really wanted, anyway.

She'd only come because she didn't want to embarrass Temperance.

A *visit*. That's all it was. She was dying to see that greenhouse in daylight.

The property was deep in Vesper Valley, just under an hour west of the city center of Philadelphia. Rowan leaned forward to get the whole view of the house through her windshield. There were jutting dormers along the top, five windows on the second floor, and four for the ground floor. All that glass reflected a sky so blue it looked like it belonged over the Caribbean.

The home sprawled into east and west additions. The brick and stone of each wing were unique enough it was clear they'd been added during different periods in its history.

At two minutes until the top of the hour, she forced herself out of the car. The heady scent of a burning fireplace spiced the late September air. Nathan had said to knock on the front door, but if nobody answered, try the vineyard.

Of course, nobody answered.

Rowan roamed to the back of the house, and around a massive deck as large as her childhood home. Beyond, she could see in all directions. The land was all gentle slopes and sweeping green lawns reminiscent of the English countryside. In the flat areas, outbuildings nestled into the landscape like Hobbit homes. The wild vineyards curved around the outer edge of the property, the lack of regular pruning leaving them to ramble untamed along the trellises. Lively red climbing roses twisted up the end posts of the rows facing the main house, unruly as the grapes.

It was wild beauty with a cultured backbone beneath.

So different from where she'd grown up, that cramped two-bedroom house on the coast, with its peeling yellow paint and eternally muddy yard. The occasional whiff of rotting fish on the breeze, and the sticky, ever-present crust of salt on everything.

Grandma Edie would have called this place paradise.

For a few minutes, she stood there and breathed. Her

heart was far more pragmatic than poetic, but this land evoked a tenderness in her she struggled to ignore. She felt the visceral pull of the earth under her feet, and a familiar tug of yearning in her belly.

Rowan tamped those feelings down. This place wasn't hers for the wanting.

The two men at the edge of the vineyard didn't notice her as she approached. One had sleek black hair, and the other was fairer, but they were conspicuously kin. They were framed the same, though the darker one packed at least thirty more pounds of bulk and muscle on his taller body. Once they heard the crunch of her footfalls, they turned in unison and settled into the same hipshot posture, brows raised in matching inquisitive expressions.

"Hey," Harrison said.

Harrison Brady in the bright of day wasn't a thing she'd prepared for. His hair had the shine and color of browned butter, and his eyes were the rich blue-gray of woodsmoke. But his irises were clouded, like they were shielded behind a frost-hazed pane of glass.

"Morning," she said. "Don't let me interrupt."

The black-haired brother reached out to shake her hand. The movement pulled the rolled sleeve of his shirt up his forearm. His skin was solidly decorated with vibrant tattoos, each one merging into another, and his callused hands were built and weathered in a way that made it obvious he used them hard, every day.

"Duncan Brady." He removed mirrored sunglasses. Keen onyx eyes passed over her, and his smile was wide and wolfish. Gleaming white teeth, canines vaguely pointed. A tiny chip was missing from the corner of one of his incisors. She felt thoroughly sized up and analyzed, even though the exchange was brief.

Duncan Brady was the kind of attractive that made a

religious person want to sin, and a faithless one want to thank Jesus. His skin was bronzed by hard outdoor work, and the laugh lines around his eyes were the only relief to an otherwise intimidating face. He had a full black beard, impeccably trimmed to hug the lines of his jaw. His hair swept straight back from his face in a longish, thick wave, framed by closely trimmed sides.

He was the most beautiful human being she'd ever seen in person. Rowan found herself inexplicably amused by how overtly, aggressively sexy he was, standing out here in the weedy old vineyard.

"I'm Rowan." She smiled and slid her hand from his.

"You and that tall brunette crashed our party last weekend," he said, grinning. "What's her name? Frankie?"

"We weren't crashers," she laughed. "We were Temperance's plus ones."

He slid his sunglasses back on. "I think that's plus two."

"I was never great at math," she said, and Duncan chuckled. Harrison gave her a brief smile when she shifted her attention to him.

"Didn't get to meet you that night." Duncan twisted a bit of his beard in his fingertips.

Rowan shrugged. "Take that up with Temperance."

"I might do that," he said quietly, and looked away.

"I'm here to see Nathan," Rowan said. "Is he here?"

Duncan moved into the vineyard, silently encouraging her and Harrison to follow. "He went to Linden with our folks this morning. You're stuck with us for now."

The brothers fell into step with each other as they entered the vineyard, and Rowan followed a few paces behind, watching as they chatted. Harrison's directional nods and spare gestures were a stark contrast to his brother's bolder, more effusive movements. She couldn't take her eyes off the way his shoulder blades moved under the fabric of his shirt.

Stopping at the end of a row, Duncan asked, "What do you think, Rowan?"

She hadn't been listening. At all. "Sorry, what?"

Duncan's mouth curved sideways. "I was asking if you think the trellising system used here is a solid choice."

Rowan reached out to test the tension on one of the catch wires running between posts. "Well, this is vertical positioning. I assume it's well suited for these grapes, considering how long the vines have been here. I'm not sure what variety these grapes are, though."

"Apparently, they sold their crop to the winery down the road. Three Birds Winery, I think it's called," Harrison said. "We could find out."

"Wonder how they're going to feel about us getting into the wine-making game," said Duncan.

"There's plenty of room in this world for good wine," Rowan said. "It's not something you buy once, then never again. It might be mutually beneficial for you both, actually. Smaller vineyards tend to have staffing problems, since it's hard to offer enough work for folks to make a full-time living. You'd both benefit from sharing a field crew."

The men exchanged a look. "Hadn't considered that. Thanks." Duncan kicked the base of a post. "A lot of the posts are in bad shape, and I'm trying to decide if we take them all down and use a different system, or repair what's here."

Rowan crumbled a dry leaf in her hand. "Assuming you're going to keep these vines, I don't see any reason to change what's been working for decades."

Duncan laughed. "I don't know shit about grapes yet. I know a structural mess when I see one, though."

Harrison moved closer. "I think what he means is, what if there's a way that's better?"

"I'm not a gambler." Rowan looked up at him, shielding her eyes from the sun with a flat hand. Eye contact with Harrison made her feel strangely buoyant and heavy-limbed all at once. "After you get all this excess weight off the trellises, tighten everything up, and replace the weak pieces, there's no need to do something entirely new."

"So, all these dying vines need to be cut away before I can do any of my work, is that what you're saying?" Duncan asked.

"Well, they're not *dying*. They're very much alive, just ignored for too long."

"Still need to be cut away though, no?" Duncan pressed.

"Think of it as more of a haircut. They just need some love."

"I don't like being held up." Duncan's tone was playful, but in that moment, Rowan somehow felt personally responsible for every pending task in the vineyard.

"You worried about job security?" she teased.

That rakish grin again. "Not a concern when it's your family's business."

"Oh, who needs job security when you have nepotism, right?" Rowan smiled.

"Ma is proudly and insistently nepotistic, I'm afraid," Duncan said.

"How do you know you've got the best people for the job if you only hire from within the family?"

Duncan moved close enough to her she had to tip her

head back to look him in the eye. "I assume that's why we're trying to hire *you*. Branching out a bit."

She enjoyed this kind of game, and Duncan Brady was a comfortable sparring partner. He was a flirt, for sure, but the interaction with him felt low stakes. No subtext, just fun. "Aren't you scared someone from outside the family would find you to be woefully inadequate, despite the maternal confidence?"

Duncan barked a laugh, then dipped his head downward to peer at her over his sunglasses. "Bradys are rarely found to be lacking, Red."

"How would you know, if there are never any non-Bradys around to compare to?"

"I'm more than adequate at everything I do." His voice dropped, suddenly serious.

Rowan believed him. "I should warn you, the last person who called me 'Red' got a knee in the balls."

Harrison watched their banter with a subtle scowl on his face. "Her aim is garbage, though," he said.

Rowan flushed, thinking about their encounter during that silly game. How the curve of her ass had socketed so neatly into the bend of Harrison's waist in those few moments he'd arched his body over hers. The sweet heat of his cinnamon-scented breath in her hair. She swallowed.

Missing the subtext, Duncan clapped his big hands together in a single, resonant crack. "Are you this rude to all your future employers?"

She looked away from Harrison. "Future employer? I never said I'd take the job."

" 'Never' is for cowards." Duncan let out a robust sigh. To Harrison, he said, "I could do this all day. I like her. She gets my vote."

Harrison's smile was a slight curve at the corners of his lips, but it didn't reach his eyes. The pensive crease between his brows deepened.

"I'm still thinking about it," Rowan said. "You know it wasn't me who sent the résumé, right?"

Duncan's jovial mood frosted a bit. He looked at her with narrowed eyes and evaded the question. "I need to get up to the equipment garage. Don't think too long." He started back down the row of vines. "We want you to sign a contract before Harry scares you off with one of his shitty moods."

"I don't scare easily."

Duncan laughed over his shoulder. "Give it time."

* * *

SHE WAS ALONE with Harrison.

Rowan twisted the tip of a grapevine in her fingers. "Some of these plants are probably older than we are." Her voice sounded breathy to her own ears, and it pissed her off. She cleared her throat and let the woody coil spring free. "All of them are going to need to be pruned hard, possibly to the ground."

Harrison squinted against the sun. "That a professional opinion?"

"Not really. It doesn't take a botanist to see what a mess you have out here. I'm not sure what your family's goals are, anyway."

Rowan turned her back to him and walked briskly down the row.

He followed. "Grow grapes, make wine."

"Well. When you put it that way . . . ," she said, smiling over her shoulder.

"My mom's family has a multigenerational winery

in Spain, so she imagines it's in her DNA. It's been a dream of hers since she and Dad got married and came to the States."

"It's going to be years before these plants are producing wine-quality grapes again." Wayward vines hooked her shirt and hair as she moved through them, like they were pleading with her to linger.

"How many?"

"I don't know. Three? Maybe five?"

Harrison put a little jog into his step to catch up. He fell in beside her, close enough that their upper arms skimmed together. "Are we on the clock, here? I'm wondering if this is a billable consultation."

Rowan matched his pace, allowing her arm to graze his. It was entirely unnecessary for them to walk so close, and indulging in the incidental touching felt heady and forbidden. Her pulse skipped into high gear. "I think this is going to be way too much for me to handle with all the work I need to do on my manuscript." She reluctantly let space drift open between them.

Like he hadn't heard her, he gestured eastward in the direction of the big stone barn tucked into the hillside. Another structure that felt like it could be straight from Tolkien, it had been impossible to miss when she drove in. "I think Ma wants to extend the vineyard that way, too."

"You should get the existing vineyard blocks into shape before you try adding anything," she said. "There's a lot growing here that's not grapevine."

Harrison scratched his jaw. "Yeah. Lots of weeds."

Rowan stopped abruptly, and he skidded to a stop a step ahead. "Ralph Waldo Emerson said a weed is a plant whose virtues have not yet been discovered. A lot of what's growing here, you *do* want. It's healthier and more sustainable to use native plants as cover crops."

"That's what your research was about."

She blinked in surprise. "You were listening."

"Always." He smiled and pushed hands into pockets. "Got any recommendations?"

"I'd have to think about it," she evaded, moving past him again. Wild blackberries and morning glory twisted through the vines. Stands of non-native Canada thistle and baby-blue chicory grew tall as her waist. She batted them away with the back of her hand. "These non-natives need to go, though. Then, the key to keeping them gone is a healthy native community. The good stuff grows and crowds out the bad stuff."

"How do we even begin? It's overwhelming," Harrison said.

Rowan came to an archway made by joined vines at the end of the trellised row. Before ducking out of the vineyard, she looked back at him and said, "One row at a time."

A wild meadow stretched out before her. After the relative gloom of the overgrown vineyard, emerging into the meadow felt like entering Oz. The morning was so bright and crystalline, she could almost smell the sunshine.

Native grasses with downy seed heads swayed, birds darted and feasted. Wildflowers, everywhere; heath asters as white as snowdrifts, and native bee balm like lavender-pink islands throughout the sea of grass. Milkweed pods burst with fleecy seeds, ready to fly. Bees were thick on native sunflowers, black-eyed Susans, and feathery goldenrod, their fuzzy butts industriously puttering, greedy for nectar.

Beyond the meadow, the Victorian spires of the green-house roof were like a dragon's spine against a cloudless sky. She shielded her eyes against the sun glaring off a glass panel.

Rowan felt her body bend toward the sun like one of those wildflowers. She turned her face up to the sky and basked in the gentle heat, reveling in birdsong and the sibilant sound of the wind through the grasses.

This.

This was what she'd been missing. The past year of her dissertation work had been spent crunching numbers and writing her paper in her little cubicle lab office with the cold cinder block walls. And now, she was holing up in Temperance's tidy apartment, with its cream-colored paint and ivory furniture and sterile air-conditioned air, hunched over her laptop until her temples ached from eyestrain. Utterly unable to summon the initiative to make the blinking cursor on her manuscript move.

Nature was her religion, her church. Her therapy, and her muse. The thing that grounded her *and* set her free. The songbirds had no agenda for her, and plants made no emotional demands.

She felt like a green thing herself, long denied the nourishment of the light.

This felt like home.

A crunch of boots on stony soil interrupted her reverie. Rowan turned and pinched hard across the bridge of her nose to stem sentimental tears hanging heavy behind her eyes. Her breath tripped over the lump in her throat when she tried to speak.

"This place," she whispered.

Harrison gave her space. "I think you ecology types call it a meadow?"

She smiled and nudged a rock around with her foot.

"You wanna go to the greenhouse?" he asked.

* * *

AN OLD TRACTOR path cut through the meadow. It was badly overgrown on both sides, but still wide enough to pass through, and a much more direct route to the greenhouse than backtracking through the vineyard.

Harrison followed closely behind her, close enough that she heard how his breathing grew increasingly labored the deeper they delved. At the first bend in the path, Rowan heard his footfalls abruptly stop. She looked back to find him staring ashen-faced into the tall grasses alongside them.

"Coming?" she asked.

He shook his head once. Twice.

Rowan frowned. "Are you okay?"

Fresh sweat dotted his forehead and upper lip, and his chest rose and fell, rapid and shallow. He pressed two fingers to his neck, under his jaw. His eyes were round and bright as silver dollars, and he didn't respond.

"Are you sick?" Rowan asked.

Harrison shook his head. "Spiders. They're massive."

In the grasses around them, huge yellow and black garden spiders hung suspended in glittering silk webs spanning several feet across. Rowan had noticed them as soon as she'd stepped onto the path. Having spent much of her academic life in environments like this, she'd been unbothered, but the abject terror in Harrison's entire being gave her pause.

"Big, yes," she said. "But not aggressive. Don't grab one and squeeze, and you'll be fine. You don't plan to do that, do you?"

Harrison shook his head again. The spider closest to

him was motionless, placidly waiting for a meal. By the way he looked at it, it might have been a flying cobra.

"Then you're fine." She turned sideways and gestured for him to follow. "Let's go?"

"I—can't," he choked. "Can't move. Can't breathe."

Rowan went to him and laid her hand on the warm skin of his forearm. The honey-colored hairs were soft, and he had several thin parallel scratches healing there.

"Look at me," she said. Her hand tightened on his arm when he didn't respond. He stared into the meadow beyond her shoulder. "Hey. Let's breathe. We'll do it together, okay?"

Rowan placed Harrison's hand against the middle of her chest, pressing down to flatten his palm on her sternum. She took a deep breath, intentionally overinflating her lungs so he could easily feel the rise and fall.

"Find my breath," she said. "Use it to find yours."

His eyes were hazy, his skin pale. But he looked at her, finally. The hand against her chest trembled.

Once his breath began to slow, she said, simply, "Hi."

"Hi," he said back.

"When's your birthday?"

"February fourteenth."

"You're kidding."

"Scout's honor."

"Your birthday is Valentine's Day?"

Of course it is.

"Unfortunately, yes."

"What's your middle name?"

"Bryant. Harrison Bryant." A beat of silence. "Yours?"

"Mmm—don't have one," Rowan said.

"How's that possible?"

"Long story," she deflected. His respiration seemed mostly normal then, and his skin no longer looked ashen, but his hand still trembled. "Close your eyes a minute. Listen to my voice."

One of his eyebrows rose, comically suspicious. Rowan chuckled.

"You're going to have to trust me," she said. "We're probably as far from the path's entrance as it is to the exit on the other side. You have to do this. I can't carry you."

He dropped his hand from her chest and closed his eyes. His jaw was tight, and little muscles at his temples flickered as he bit down on his teeth. A bead of sweat coursed from hairline to cheekbone to jaw. Rowan wanted to sweep it away with her fingertip.

"Listen to what's around you." Birds and insects whirred and chattered. The tips of the grasses whispered and rattled. "Feel how alive it all is. Nature is simply doing what it does, and our presence here means nothing. We're irrelevant. Incidental."

His jaw relaxed, but his eyebrows remained bunched tight over closed eyes. "This is an uplifting chat," he murmured.

Rowan watched for tiny shifts in the muscles around his mouth, looking for an ease of tension. His eyelids fluttered occasionally, like it was a struggle for him to keep them closed.

"These spiders deserve to be here as much as we do. More, actually. We're barging through *their* home right now."

Harrison took a deep breath, sequestering his hands in his pockets. A ribbon of muscle in his forearm pulsed rhythmically as he fiddled with coins. Rowan moved close, near enough to feel the heat from his chest, his breath on her face. She intentionally invaded his personal space, forcing him to focus on her instead of his fear.

"We're simply another passing mammal for them.

All they care about is staying in their webs, catching insects, and having their babies."

The corner of his mouth hitched up in the barest smile. *Babies.*

No man should have lips like his. If he opened his eyes right now, he'd catch her staring right at them. "Did you know they rebuild these beautiful webs every night?" she said.

He freed his hands and flexed his fingers, then let his arms hang loose at his sides.

"They're experts at starting over. You have to admire that kind of tenacity."

His voice was thick. "Ah—*admire* is a pretty strong word."

Rowan chuckled. "Open your eyes."

The haze over his irises had disappeared—now, they shone like drops of mercury, busily surveying her face. A faint remnant of a bruise lingered around his right eye, and the cinnamon stubble on his jaw glimmered in the sun. His body was motionless except for the rise and fall of his chest.

His tone dropped to a lower register. "Experts at starting over, eh?"

"Mm-hmm. Better?"

He swallowed, hesitant. "I'll survive."

"Well, that's perfect. In nature, when you survive, you win."

A few tiny burrs clung to his shirt. She plucked them off, flinging the sticky little seed pods into the meadow.

"Thanks," he said.

"Where'd you get the black eye?"

Harrison reached up, fingertips questing along the upper curve of his right cheekbone. "Ah—falling."

Now *he* was looking at *her* mouth.

Heat shimmered up Rowan's neck and across her lower jaw. Soon, it would wash her freckled cheeks with red. She vigorously rubbed her nose and backed away.

Then one of the specks clinging to his shirt *moved*. She pinched a tiny tick between her fingers and flicked it into the vegetation.

"You had a passenger," she said. "Ready to get out of here?"

Harrison looked down at his shirt, his face gone gray again, but he nodded.

Rowan turned to lead them out of the meadow. Over her shoulder, she said, "When we get to the greenhouse, we're going to have to check each other for ticks."

CHAPTER EIGHT

Rowan

The lock on the greenhouse door looked new. When Harrison noticed Rowan eyeing the shiny key in his hand, he gave her a sideways smile. "We've got problems with trespassers up here."

"Ha, ha," she said.

Harrison hung back in the doorway as she entered, allowing the green glory of the place to speak for itself. Motes of dust and pollen floated in beams of filmy midmorning sun. It felt like a place built by eccentric wood elves—a cathedral for the worship of all things botanical. A large terra-cotta pot was filled to the top with dry, crumbly soil gone gray with age. A slim-handled spade was tucked in, like someone had planned to come back to it, first thing in the morning. Rowan's heart ached for that long-gone gardener.

Roses rambled happily along the loose floorboards, some with roots bursting beyond the boundaries of their plastic containers and into the ground beneath. Rowan cupped a velvety coral blossom and inhaled its vintage perfume, carefully avoiding the thorns.

Rosie, Grandma Edie had called her. She would have loved this place.

She paused a few steps in and smirked over her shoulder. "We've got to stop meeting here like this."

Harrison's crack of laughter was a resonant, belly-warming sound. Brief levity shimmered between them like a firework.

Something rustled, deeper within. "How does your family feel about cats?" she asked.

"Not sure. We had a dog when I was growing up, but no pets since then."

"You've got rats in here. A few mousers from the animal shelter would be good to have on the payroll."

"I thought critters deserved to be here?"

Rowan laughed. "Those spiders belong in that meadow, Harrison. Rats, however, don't belong in the greenhouse, or in any other buildings on this land."

"Fair." He leaned against a table. "I'll mention it, though it's a moot point if they're planning to raze it."

Rowan stiffened. The thought of this enchanted place being reduced to a pile of steel and broken glass made her feel sick. She righted a few tipped ceramic pots, pushed a bench back where it belonged, brushed a bit of potting soil from the edge of a table.

This place wasn't hers to fight for. And right now, there were more immediate concerns.

"Let's get this over with." Rowan gathered her shirt up to her rib cage, tipped her hips forward, and folded down the waistband of her jeans to check her belly below the navel.

Harrison muffled a cough into his hand.

She beckoned him over. "I wasn't kidding about checking for ticks. They're orders of magnitude more dangerous than those orb weavers in the meadow, Harrison."

Instead of moving closer, he turned his entire body away.

She laughed and let her shirt drop. "I'm not shy. You don't have to avert your eyes."

"Call me old-fashioned." His voice was quiet.

"I don't have anything you haven't seen before, *Dr. Brady*. Check your own waist, and then come here and look at my neck." She turned her back to him, lifting her hair.

Harrison was idle for another moment, but Rowan could feel his eyes on her skin. He quietly advanced. When he finally touched her, his fingers were gentle and deft in the hair at her nape, moving through the sensitive area with careful attention. The job could've been done in seconds, but he leisurely parted the curls there, taking his time. She pebbled with goose bumps from neck to knees.

It wasn't a stretch to imagine one of his elegant, long-fingered hands between her legs.

Stop it.

Done with her neck, Harrison sighed and sank to a crouch behind her. As she lifted her shirt again, he slid a finger under her denim waistband, tugging it down to reveal her lower back. His thumb moved along the base of her spine and nudged below the top edge of her underwear, then back up again. Twice.

"Did you find something?"

Breathy. She sounded *breathy* again.

From Harrison: silence, punctuated with more silence.

"Harrison?"

His forcefully expelled breath felt warm across her skin. Then his fingers were gone. When he finally answered, his tone was rough. "No. Ah—a freckle."

A cold void opened up behind her as he stood and turned away.

"Thanks. There are lots of those." She dropped the hem of her shirt. "Freckles, I mean."

"I noticed."

The air in the greenhouse felt cloying. Rowan had started to sweat, and soon, the little curls at her hairline would dampen and spring outward in wild abandon.

"Am I good?" She caught the inside of her cheek between her molars and bit down hard.

"Perfect. Good. Yeah." He passed a hand over his hair and scratched the back of his head.

She reached for him. "You need to let me do you now."

Harrison bowed backward like she'd come at him with a burning brand. "I'm good." He raised a hand to ward her off.

"I'm checking you, whether you like it or not. Lyme disease is no joke." She hesitated, then added again for emphasis, *"Doctor."*

When he didn't move away from her second advance, Rowan gingerly lifted the hem of his shirt. As she tugged the waistband of his jeans down, he grunted and wavered on his feet. The only thing there was a broad expanse of smooth, healthy skin and a band of navy-blue underwear.

She redirected to the nape of his neck, boosting on tiptoes to run fingers into the upturned curls there. Those waves were as soft as they looked—infinitely softer than the thick coils of her own hair.

Harrison shuddered.

"Ticklish?" She tried to keep her tone as clinical as possible.

"No."

"Scared?" Rowan skimmed her fingertips along the fine hair on the back of his neck, and down a bit, dipping under his collar.

He made a sound that was part growl, part humorless laugh. "Definitely not."

A bead of sweat raced down the small of her back. She hastily stepped away from him.

"You're clear," she said. "Find a seat, pull down your socks, check your calves and ankles."

Harrison nodded.

"The little bastards can easily hitch a ride on fabric, so we should get out of these clothes as soon as possible. You, I mean. You should get out of your clothes. I will, too. When we're done here. Separately. From you."

He raised an eyebrow.

"I don't get out much," she said, and squeezed the bridge of her nose. "Talking is hard."

Harrison chuckled and sat heavily on a bench to check around his ankles. Then he leaned forward with elbows on thighs, staring at the floor between his feet.

"You okay?" she asked.

"Yep, fine. Thinking about baseball." The tips of his ears were pink.

"Isn't baseball in the spring?"

He breathed out another laugh. "Never mind. Do you know why I brought you out here?"

"Hide-and-seek?"

"Ah, no," he chuckled, "I don't need another black eye or more bruises on my legs."

They shared a smile. He stood and plucked a delicate pink cosmos from a waist-high bunch of flowers sprouting from a basin of potting soil. He handed her the little blossom. "We could use your expertise in getting the vineyard and the grounds back into shape.

Between you and me? I think my parents are in way over their heads."

Rowan felt the unwelcome warmth of anxiety flood through her. She spun the cosmos in her fingertips like a pinwheel. "I have so much to get done on my manuscript."

Weak.

"We're not going to ask for all of your time," Harrison said.

"I really can't afford to lose momentum."

He levered himself up to sit on a table. When he laced his fingers together in his lap, his cool exterior was betrayed by the white of his knuckles. "If you want to finish that paper, holing up in T.J.'s little apartment in the city isn't what you need."

Rowan had been flailing and failing, and somehow, he knew. She blinked. "You've known me for a few days, and now you're an expert on what I *need*, Dr. Brady?"

"Harry. It's *Harry*."

She averted her eyes and touched the wildflower to her nose, even though she knew the petals had no fragrance.

"I know what I saw," he said. "Your face lit up like a carnival ride every time we went somewhere new today. This place speaks to you. Use your mind and your muscles here, get some fresh air, then go back to your manuscript in the afternoons. Bang it out. Everyone wins."

She nudged her chin up. "Research like mine is outdated and irrelevant so quickly. If I don't get it published soon, *I* become irrelevant. My life—well." Rowan shrugged. "It's my life."

"So—is your goal to stay in academia, never do anything practical with your degree?"

She took a step backward. "Whoa, wait. Are you suggesting research is impractical?"

"No, but I think a lot of people stay at universities because it's a safe option."

"Safe?" An edge crept into her words. "Are you taking a lot of *risks* with your livelihood, Dr. Brady? It doesn't seem like you're going to be practicing much meaningful medicine hidden away here with your family in rural Pennsylvania."

He stiffened. "My situation is completely different from yours."

"You don't know me."

"I know enough to want you." The words tripped out of his mouth fast, without tact or guile. His eyes slid away, and he rolled his shoulders. Cracked his knuckles. Cleared his throat. "Here, I mean. Want you *here,* to help."

Rowan's throat tightened and blood rushed to her head. She wasn't a stranger to the sensation, but it was something she hadn't felt in years. It was longing. Raw, terrible longing.

Walk out of here, she told herself, *right now.*

"Keeping my career on track is the only thing I care about," she said. "I'm selfish, and I'm messy. I'm not great at making friends. I don't think I'd be a good fit for what you need. What your family needs."

"The grapevines don't give a shit about your social skills."

"You know what I mean. I saw your family dynamic last weekend. I felt like I was in a sitcom. It was so perfect and fun and lovely. The only thing missing was a quirky pet dog and a laughing studio audience."

He considered her for a moment. "So, is your reluctance because you have a problem with my family, or is it your dedication to landing a prestigious postdoc? I'm trying to keep your excuses straight."

A headache lurked at her temples. She felt stuck in a state of disequilibrium, like he'd blindfolded her, spun her, then asked her to pin a paper tail on something. First, with that bizarrely arousing tick check, and now with his irrefutable, inconvenient logic.

Harrison pressed his palms into the table beside his thighs and leaned forward. "What are you afraid of?"

What wasn't she afraid of?

Rowan fidgeted, shredding the petals of the poor pink cosmos. For eight years, she'd managed to keep to her linear academic path. Minimizing the need for any decision-making minimized the chance she'd choose incorrectly.

"It's just—too perfect," she said. "Nothing comes without a price."

He jumped down. The thud of his feet on the creaky floor was jarring, and in two long strides, he stood before her. "Obviously. You'd be working, Rowan. It's hard work." He sounded frustrated now. "We pay *you*. That's how jobs work. An exchange of funds for services rendered."

"I belong in an academic environment where people pretend to like each other, then go their separate ways after work."

"We don't want to hire you to hang out with a field crew and braid each other's hair."

Silence.

He crossed his arms. "Why are you here?" He was plainly echoing her interrogation on the dock a few nights prior.

Rowan mirrored him, crossing her own arms. "Temperance sent my résumé, and I told her I would—"

"Bullshit."

"Do you actually want me to answer your questions, or are you going to keep interrupting?"

"You could've followed up with an email, explained that T.J. had incorrectly sent the résumé, and been done with it. So what kind of game are you playing? Why did you come?" The last four words were clipped, edgy.

Truthfully? Driving out here had nothing to do with a job—she hadn't been lying to herself about that. She'd come because she wanted to see the damned greenhouse in the daylight, and she was curious about *him*. Full stop.

Then this place also revealed itself in all its lush, wild glory, and she was ensnared. But his impatience made her dig in her heels. A man like Harrison Brady could never comprehend the decision paralysis that plagued her at a crossroads like this, because his map had always included a safe path back to a family who loved him.

If she chose poorly, it would plague her. She'd replay the mistake in her head for years.

"I don't expect you to understand. But I'm not playing a game." She ran her fingertip through a layer of sand and soil on the table. "What if I turned out to be a terrible fit?"

Harrison's voice was low. "I seriously doubt that."

"I'm not sure whether this persistence is creepy or charming."

His answering laugh seemed genuine, but it quickly distorted into a sound of frustration directed at the glass ceiling. For a moment, he paced in the narrow space between the potting benches. When he stopped, he shrugged and let his arms fall heavily against his sides.

"Fine. You want the truth?" he said. "You want to know why I'm trying so hard to make this happen?"

Rowan blinked.

"They don't need me here." The heat evaporated from his voice, and his posture went loose.

She held her breath, waiting for him to continue.

"I've been in a really bad place the last few months. The night we met, what you said about the baggage? You were right," he said. "My family wants me here so they can keep an eye on me, Rowan. Not because they need me for anything. I'm entirely unnecessary. I'm not handy like Duncan, and I don't know anything about business, like Nate. I'm so out of shape right now, I can't even climb the stairs in the house without losing my breath."

Rowan softened, but she didn't trust the feeling. It was difficult for her to interpret any overt display of vulnerability from a man as anything but performative. With Noah, it had been his way of keeping her unbalanced. Emotional theater. Nothing more than a tool in his power game.

Harrison continued, "But then, I realized—if I could get you on board—" He stalled out and turned away, scrubbing a hand across his jaw. "If I could get you to help set this whole thing on the right course, I'd have made a valuable contribution."

The words settled around her like volcanic ash, leaving her cold and hollow. At least he was honest.

"Oh. I'm a resource, then."

What more did you want, Rowan?

He forced a breath through his nose and rubbed the back of his neck. "No. Damn it. That's not what I mean, but I can see how it sounds that way." He stretched a hand toward her, fingers splayed. "Come to dinner tonight. We start early—five o'clock. Talk to my family about it. I'm really just the messenger here, and I fucked it up."

Rowan looked at him sideways. Her heart wanted to leap, but her mind pulled back hard on the reins. "I'll come to dinner tonight. But no promises."

He nodded once. "I'll, ah, leave you to explore, then."

As she watched him go, Rowan knew her apprehension had nothing to do with the self-imposed clock ticking on her postdoc plans. It had everything to do with the feelings she had brewing for Harrison Brady and his somber, storm cloud eyes.

CHAPTER NINE

Rowan

Maren Madigan Brady was Temperance's older sister—
taller and curvier than T.J., but with the same frosty
blond hair and Tiffany-blue eyes. Even though Rowan
had only met her a few times over the years, she was relieved to encounter a face she recognized when the door
to the Brady house opened. Maren gave her a quick hug.

Inside, it smelled like Murphy Oil Soap and new paint.
The foyer flowed into a central hall with doorless cased
openings on either side, all leading to rooms with unlit
interiors. To the left, a grand staircase twisted upward to
an open railed mezzanine. Down the hall, Rowan could
see all the way to the back of the house—windows and
a two-story fireplace took up much of the wall of a
sunken den.

Laughter and conversation came from her right,
where an orange curve of light spilled out from the archway. Several people sat at a long dining table with half
a dozen open wine bottles marching down the center.
Above the table hung a light fixture that looked like the
bare branches of a tree, spreading in every direction.
Homey sounds of clanking dishware came through another brightly lit open doorway at the opposite end of the
room, presumably leading to the kitchen. There were no

drapes on the big picture window, and lavender evening light spilled through condensation-clouded glass.

Harrison was at the table, his forehead cradled in one hand as he flipped through a book with the other. Duncan leaned over the back of another guy with similar swarthy good looks—clean-shaven and older, with a slimmer frame like Harrison's. Rowan was fairly sure he was Nathan, Maren's husband. She'd met him once, at Temperance's graduation from medical school.

Abruptly, Duncan and Nathan laughed—big, obnoxious guffaws echoing between the bare walls and floors. Harrison grumbled, "You two are absolute children," without looking up from his book.

"All right, Doctor Doom. Maybe if you watched more baby goat videos on the Internet, you'd be happier," Duncan said.

"Doctor Doom was a supergenius," Harrison said. "I'll take that as a compliment."

Hesitant to follow Maren into the room, Rowan shifted her weight, and a floorboard creaked beneath her feet. It was a protracted, tortured-goose sound, and *loud*. Conversation fizzled like a spent Fourth of July sparkler, and everyone turned attention to her. She raised a hand in a single, awkward wave.

"Nineteenth-century alarm system," Rowan mumbled, looking down at her feet. Someone in the room laughed.

"We have a guest," Maren said. She tucked her arm through Rowan's to tug her forward. Harrison's book fell closed, and he stood for a moment, nodding in greeting. It was such an old-fashioned gesture, Rowan imagined if he'd had a hat on, he'd have tipped it to her.

A woman with silver-spun black hair popped up from the table and padded over, barefoot. She was petite and gently rounded, the dark skin of her cheeks lit with rose. Reading glasses hung from a crystal-studded chain around her neck. A loose, plummy tunic flowed over snug jeans, and she moved with the spare efficiency and grace of a dancer.

"Welcome," she said, pulling Rowan forward into a tight, lingering hug. Jasmine perfume and the kitcheny smell of a hot oven puffed out of the woman's hair and clothing, as if motherhood had been manufactured into a wearable scent. Over the smaller woman's shoulder, Rowan's wide eyes locked with Harrison's. A brief smile hooked his mouth sideways, and he sat back down.

"Ma, you can't just—squish people without their consent," Duncan said.

The dark-haired woman released her, but Rowan could feel the reluctance in it. "Americans don't touch enough." Her words were faintly accented. "I've been here almost forty years and I've still never gotten used to it."

"Dinner in five!" a man's voice belted from the kitchen.

"Rowan, nice seeing you again." Duncan came around the table to shake her hand. "Gianna Brady, meet Rowan McKinnon. Rowan, this is our ma." He placed a big hand on the smaller woman's shoulder.

A big man with hair the same winter wheat of Harrison's emerged from the kitchen, wearing mismatched oven mitts. He carried a huge, shallow pan by its handles. Steam and the sublime fragrance of seafood and garlic and onions filled the room. Rowan recognized him from the party, the one who'd barked out the Team Tag rules from the top of the picnic table.

"Someone go get the children," he said.

"I got it," Duncan said. From where he stood, he bellowed, "Monsters! Come down for dinner!"

"I could've done that much," the elder Brady grumbled, positioning the pan on a trivet near the end of the table. When he saw Rowan, his eyes crinkled with his smile. He extended his arm for a handshake, the oven mitt still on. He made a short grunt of amused exasperation, pulled off the mitt, and shook her hand. "Will Brady. Welcome."

Gianna maneuvered Rowan to the far end of the table, putting her next to Harrison. Seated, she was close enough she felt the heat from his forearm next to hers. In her lap, she fidgeted with her cloth napkin, alternating between smoothing it flat and wrapping it tight enough around her hand to cut off circulation to her fingers.

Moments later, two kids exploded into the room. When Maren raised a single hand, they boomeranged quickly to a halt.

"Who's she?" The boy pointed immediately at Rowan and approached her.

Rowan couldn't remember the last time she'd interacted with a child. This one was five, maybe seven? She extended her hand to him, but the boy simply looked at it in confusion. His dark brows crammed together on his forehead like little brown caterpillars.

Rowan flushed. *Who tries greeting a kindergartener with a handshake?*

The girl threw an elbow to jostle her little brother out of the way. "Rude," she said to him, then she smiled at Rowan, revealing newly emerged adult teeth in the front that were too big for her face. They made her look like an adorable mouse.

The little boy reached around his sister, grasped the pointer finger of Rowan's still-extended hand, and pulled.

"Now *fart*," he commanded.

Maren snatched the boy by his shoulders and moved

him bodily into a chair. "This is Grey, and that's Alice," she said. "Occasionally, they have manners."

"Who taught him that?" Gianna demanded, wagging a finger at Grey. "That fart thing?"

Everyone looked to Duncan. He held his hands up and shook his head. "Not me."

"Uncle Harry did." Grey grinned.

Harrison slowly looked up from his book with dramatically widened eyes. He held a finger to his lips. "Our secret," he stage-whispered.

Grey smiled conspiratorially and sunk down in his chair.

Alice sat next to Rowan and spoke with the friendly confidence well-loved children had. "Everyone calls me Ace. You can call me Ace if you want."

"Okay, Ace. I'm Rowan. Nice to meet you."

Maren stood behind her daughter and smoothed a hand over Alice's hair. "She's pretty, Mommy," Alice said, looking up to Maren.

"Smart, too," Maren said. "Maybe she can tell you some neat science stuff later."

"Ever had paella?" Will Brady cut in.

"Oh, boy," Rowan said, tucking her hands in her lap. "I've never had it, but it smells incredible." She tried to not fidget with the napkin.

"It *is* incredible," Gianna said from the other end of the table. "William makes my paella better than I make my paella."

"If you don't like it, Dad makes a special kind of paella for the kids. I'm sure they'd share." Nathan eagerly tucked a napkin into the neckline of his shirt.

The children's "paella" was simple yellow rice with sliced hot dogs in it, but William served them first with all the gravitas of a waiter at a Michelin-starred restaurant. Then he passed around staggeringly large helpings of the real paella, narrating the recipe as he did. Rich rice made golden by saffron and paprika. Plump Spanish chorizo, shrimp, and clams, garnished with generous slices of lemon and bright green parsley. A long loaf of crusty bread was passed. Everyone broke off a chunk for themselves, crumbs raining to the tablecloth, and they nestled the pieces alongside their paella. Nobody bothered with knives or bread plates.

The rhythm and ritual of this family meal was obviously long established, and Rowan felt anxious about disrupting their beautiful flow. Conversation was free and constant, like it had been scripted in advance, with no tense silences or awkward pauses. The adults engaged the children in the discussions with curiosity and genuine interest in what they had to say.

Once, when Rowan was nine, she went an entire weekend speaking with a terrible Australian accent in an embarrassing bid for attention. Sybil—her mother—hadn't noticed.

Whether it was the outstanding wine, the incredible food, or the Bradys themselves, Rowan's initial unease faded, and she settled in as a comfortable—though silent—observer. Harrison loomed at the edge of her vision, and they bumped thighs a few times. He didn't say much, but he often laughed quietly, listening to the exchanges between others. Every time, the deep vibration of his laugh entered her—somehow soothing and stirring.

She'd just taken a big bite of shrimp when Gianna leaned in and said, "Tell us about your family, Rowan," like it was a normal and natural thing.

Pain was an emergency brake. Discussing her family

with this beautifully cohesive group seemed almost offensive.

"Oh." Rowan stalled, dabbing her mouth with her
napkin. "I grew up with my mom and my grandma Edie.
The three of us. Little house on the coast. Edie and I
were very close, but she passed away when I was twelve.
I didn't—well, my dad left before I was born. I didn't
know him." Everyone watched her, expecting more.
"Um. That—that's it. Just them."

Edie had been the only real caretaker she had ever
known. Her only true family. She'd insulated Rowan
from Sybil's maternal disinterest, and when Edie died,
stability and affection had evaporated like dew in the
summer sun. Sybil McKinnon had been physically and
emotionally absent, and Rowan, being an anxious, cerebral child, had always thought *she* was the problem.
So, she'd tried to be more outgoing. More typical, less
difficult. But nothing worked. At best, Sybil treated
her like a roommate, and on the worst days, a burden.
Twelve-year-old Rowan had to learn very quickly to fend
for herself, washing her own clothes, buying milk and
canned goods and maxi pads at the little gas station that
doubled as a bait shop down by the water. Forging Sybil's signature on permission slips from school and cutting
her own bangs when they drifted into her eyes.

Across the table, Maren gave her a sympathetic look.
Everyone seemed to sense Rowan's reluctance to share
more, and didn't prod for more details.

Harrison topped off her ice water with the carafe on
the table, before refilling his own. Rowan's heart lurched.
Earlier, she'd noticed Nathan doing the same for Maren,
and Duncan had done the same for his mother. William
had taken responsibility for the kids'.

In the Brady family, nobody had to fill their own glass.

The love and care that came so naturally to this family wasn't something Rowan received from her own mother. The Bradys had the kind of solid foundation and intuitive affection for each other she'd dreamed of her entire adolescence and young adulthood. It was what she, at twenty, had planned to someday build with Noah Tully, when he'd put an engagement ring on her finger. She'd build her own family and give them everything she'd never had.

That, too, had been a farce.

When the paella was cleared, Gianna brought a platter of cookies from the kitchen, and placed them on the table in front of Rowan and Harrison. "Do you like coconut?" she asked, perching on the edge of the table with hands folded in her lap, eyes glittering.

"I—do," Rowan said, cautiously.

"There are two kinds of people in this world. People who like coconut, and people who are wrong." Gianna said it like she'd declared a universal truth.

Rowan blinked.

"These are my toasted coconut chocolate chip cookies. Duncan says they taste like they have hair in them. Please, have one."

Rowan hesitated. All Brady eyes were on her. Breaths were held, as though they were waiting for her to declare a side in a longstanding war. She took a cookie, and bit cautiously. The crisp outer crust cracked, and the gooey warm center melted on her tongue. She rolled her eyes in bliss.

Gianna clapped once, leapt to her feet, and shot a triumphant finger-snap at Duncan. "See? Would someone make that lovely face if it tasted like hair?"

Duncan gave a theatrical shudder. "Ma, I have never said coconut tasted like hair. It *feels* like hair. In the mouth."

Nathan ate an entire cookie in one bite and made a show of brushing crumbs from his hands as he left the dining room. "Still on the losing side, Ducky."

"Still don't care, Nate," Duncan called back.

"Congratulations on choosing correctly, Rowan," Harrison said. He looked straight into Duncan's eyes across the table, slowly sinking his teeth into a cookie. His lashes fluttered closed, and he made a quiet, rumbling *mmmm* sound that did deeply dirty things to Rowan's insides.

Damn.

Duncan looked away, grumbling. "If I wanted hair in my mouth, I'd eat—"

"Oooookay." William cut Duncan off and glanced sideways at the kids. "You two are excused."

The kids thundered up the stairs in the foyer, a cookie in each hand. Nathan returned with a laptop and settled back down in his chair. "This is officially the least I've ever known about someone I'm about to offer a job." He opened the laptop and slid on reading glasses.

"Honestly, this has happened really fast," Rowan said, sitting up straighter in her chair. "I'm not actually prepared either."

"I didn't say I wasn't *prepared*," he clarified. "Three months ago, this family lived in several different cities and ran a successful, stable contracting business. Ma and Dad's house had been paid off for fifteen years. They burned most of their retirement savings on a down payment for a new mortgage here." Nathan cut his eyes over to William, who nodded. "Somehow, Maren and I agreed to uproot our family from our comfortable, boring middle-class life in Philly to run the business operations for this winery and bed-and-breakfast—neither of which, I should add, actually exist yet. Preparation is relative."

"I haven't committed to anything, I hope that was made clear." Rowan looked to Harrison. He'd pushed his chair back from the table to cross an ankle over his knee. Watching.

Nathan folded his hands at his waist. "What we *do* have, at this point, is a vineyard, and grounds that desperately need some professional attention. We need to know what grapes are out there. We need a workload forecast, expansion feasibility analysis. Staffing needs. Help us understand what these vines are capable of. What grape varieties we could plant here in the future. Dad says he wants to grow fresh produce for his kitchen." He paused, then went for the kill. "It's a worthy job—Dr. McKinnon."

Doctor McKinnon. A little thrill ran up the back of her neck. Damn it. Temperance must have prompted him to say it.

"Isn't all this something you should have considered before buying the place?" she asked.

"We did. That's why you're here."

"Don't you think you should cast a wider net?" she asked.

"We have. We already have two other applicants. But your résumé is the standout, by far."

"Temperance told you I wasn't the one who submitted that résumé, right?"

Maren chimed in. "She told me, then I told them."

Nathan removed his glasses and sat them on the table. "I think you're looking for any excuse not to do this, and I'm curious as hell why."

Ouch.

Truthfully? She wanted it. The challenge of it, the beauty of this land, the things she could learn. Rowan was *overwhelmed* with the wanting of it.

But there was also the matter of wanting Harrison Brady.

He hadn't taken his eyes off her. She wanted to remind him it wasn't polite to stare.

Academia had been her true north for nearly a decade. Steadfast, straightforward, sterile. Unlike Sybil and Noah, science and nature dealt in objective truths, and they were incapable of letting her down. At least, that's what she'd thought until Martin Clutterbuck sabotaged her progress with his asinine laziness. But she could recover, damn it. She *would* recover. She always did.

After Noah, she'd immersed herself in academics the same way others invested in relationships. Every aced exam, every accolade from a colleague, every time she mastered a new concept; they were her equivalent of comforting hugs and lingering kisses from a lover. The only other things she'd needed were Frankie and Temperance's unwavering friendship, and the occasional no-strings hookup.

Rowan McKinnon was her own fortress. But something about Harrison Brady made her want to lower the gates, and that made it difficult to tease apart the motivations of her subconscious—and her sex drive—from reality.

If she diverted from the course she'd set with her career, and her life went to hell, she'd be entirely to blame.

Nathan pressed on. "At least give us some pointers for how to judge the other applicants. We're building without a blueprint, here. You spent a few hours out there today. Anything we should know?"

Rowan was thankful for a redirection to something she could talk about objectively. "Oh. I'm almost certain a big part of that west block is diseased and needs to be ripped out."

Everyone blinked back at her.

"Well, shit," William said.

"Language," said Gianna.

"How do you know?" Nathan asked.

"She has a Ph.D. in botany, asshole," Duncan said.

Gianna growled, *"Language."*

Harrison chuckled.

Rowan chewed her thumbnail. "I took a semester of plant pathology. It's a virus. I remember this one especially, because I thought the red leaves were lovely." She looked around the table. "But red leaves are rarely something you want to see in a vineyard. Usually means nutrient deficiency or disease."

Nathan Brady typed on his laptop.

She continued. "Cluster size will be stunted, grapes won't ever get as sweet. It's just luck that it hasn't spread more than it already has."

More typing from Nathan, preparing notes for interviews with other candidates. Everyone else leaned in, listening to her.

Seeing her.

Rowan felt suddenly, viscerally jealous. She looked around the table, wanting to be a part of what the Bradys had here. Even tangentially. Even temporarily.

In that moment, she *was* a part of it, and it felt good.

While Nathan's fingers flew over the keys, she blurted, "I can't sign a contract. I need to be able to leave once I get a fellowship."

Nathan's hands lifted from the keyboard. He glanced

over the edge of the laptop screen. "We'd work around that. When could you start?"

Harrison went unnaturally still in her peripheral vision.

Rowan raised a finger. "I have some other conditions, as well. One, I need enough time off to be able to work on my manuscript. And for interviews, whenever that might be."

Nathan nodded. "Workable."

"Also, you agree, in writing, to not tear down the greenhouse, and you let me restore it."

"In writing? I thought you didn't like contracts?" Nathan said.

Touché.

"This is different." She sniffed and waved a hand. "Three, you need a small flock of sheep."

"Sheep?" Gianna echoed.

Every eye was on her, and she was sweating, but she didn't care. "Estate vineyards are working farms," she said. "Healthy grape production is hugely dependent on managing the vineyard floor. Weed control, cover crops, mowing. All that can be minimized with a flock of sheep in the fall and winter. Targeted grazing in late summer. It's better for the environment and ultimately, cheaper. They can be trained to return to a paddock even without a sheepdog. Just rattle a feed bucket."

"That tends to work on William," Gianna teased.

"Have you ever trained sheep?" Nathan asked.

"No. But I'd love to try."

William thoughtfully scratched his chin. He had a divot there, like Harrison's. "Could probably keep a small flock in the little barn up in the west pasture."

"Also, you need a donkey," Rowan interjected.

Duncan sat back and crossed his arms. "Plot twist."

"We already have an ass." Nathan glanced at Duncan, and Maren snorted.

Rowan swallowed before she made her final bid. The important one. The one she could use to convince herself that it made sense to do this.

"Last. You let me use my own research as the basis for cover cropping, rehabbing the grapes, vineyard maintenance. And you sign off on me writing about the work I do here, if I want to publish something someday."

Gianna's eyebrows climbed. She shared a brief look with William, who shrugged. Nathan clapped his hands and rubbed his palms together, and Duncan wore a sly grin. Maren seemed proud. Harrison looked down at his hands in his lap, an unmistakable smile tugging up the corners of his mouth.

"Well, then." Gianna slipped on her glasses. The crystal chain twinkled in the light of the chandelier. "What kind of sheep should we get?"

"And what's the donkey for?" Duncan asked.

CHAPTER TEN

Harry

Harry had an excellent view of the central vineyard block from the deck of the main house. The first week of Rowan's tenure with his family, he caught glimpses of her out there for hours at a time, her nose pressed into field guides to identify grapes and diagnose potential problems. She later cross-referenced her discoveries with old purchase orders she'd obtained from the Everetts at Three Birds Winery down the road. Soon, the Bradys knew their grapes: a three-acre block each, of Chardonnay, Cabernet Franc, and Chambourcin.

Ma spent several afternoons strolling the grounds with Rowan, notepad in hand. They often pointed and crouched to examine things, but by the end of the third day, Harry noticed Ma did very little jotting in her notebook, and a lot of smiling and laughing with Rowan.

Every autumn day was a crusade to exhaust himself by sunset. Dad welcomed his help with ongoing carpentry work in the house. Duncan always had some laborious task he needed a hand with—most recently, knocking out walls inside the decrepit pool house to open the place up. Swinging the long-handled sledgehammer had been hell on Harry's shoulders, but the catharsis that came with the sanctioned destruction made it all worth it. He sought anything that would induce the kind of fatigue that would zap his brain and his body into submission by nightfall. It was the only way he could sleep.

From the deck, he'd watched Rowan spend a week training their new flock of Katahdin sheep in the west pasture. Since they didn't have a herd dog, the sheep needed to be conditioned to return to their barn with the rattle of an empty coffee tin filled with treats. By week three, they were reliably responding to Rowan's cooing calls, and they nibbled "crunchies"—that's what she called the grain treats—right from her hand.

The donkey—a two-year-old jennet from a local rescue organization—would live with the flock as their protector. At first, nobody *really* believed Rowan, but the jennet soon proved her credibility as a guard animal by thwarting a pair of plump wild turkeys who'd wandered into the field where the sheep grazed. During dinner that evening, they'd heard the donkey's trombone-like alarm bray from all the way inside the house. Later, a macabre Internet search by Maren confirmed that donkeys were known to trample marauding coyotes to death.

The donkey also had an inexplicable and instantaneous hatred for Duncan, giving chase whenever he strayed too close. Harry had never seen Duncan run so fast. The comedy of that alone made the donkey's existence there worth it.

Harry was running again, too. Back in California, he ran a few miles any day he could fit it in. But the previous months of hiding from the world had left him so desperately out of shape that even a mile was agony. He'd been ready to give it up forever until the day he ran into Rowan working in the vineyard, surrounded by morning mist up to her knees. She'd looked like the manifestation of autumn itself in denim overalls over a crimson and gold flannel, and a sun-bleached khaki hat with a filthy, sagging brim.

She'd been hard at work digging soil samples. Nutrient analysis, she'd said. There had been a streak of dirt from her chin to her throat, and a handprint-shaped smear of dirt across the belly of her overalls. Smiling, she'd tipped her hat back to greet him. Her eyes glowed the same bright hue as her whisky-colored hair. He'd never been so close to her, close enough to notice a single dark fleck—a freckle?—in the iris of her left eye, and even a few on her generous bottom lip.

The next day, he came upon her sitting cross-legged alone in the grass, eating a peanut butter and jelly sandwich she'd brought in her little backpack. He invited her to have lunch with the family from then on, but she politely declined.

After that, Harry jogged every day, struggling lungs be damned. Now, three weeks later, he'd reconditioned himself enough that a few miles were easy, but his motivation wasn't about getting back in shape.

It was Rowan. Those few minutes of conversation each day. The shared space. The excuse to get a glimpse of her up close in that hideous sweat-stained hat, working like a force of nature in the vineyard.

Yesterday, he'd impulsively handed her a picked wildflower, like a kid with a crush. In retrospect, the damned thing had probably been a weed—though he was trying to get out of the habit of calling them that—but she'd taken it from him with a delicate flush in her cheeks and a subtle smile, and Harry knew.

He was more than a little gone.

* * *

THREE BIRDS WINERY down the road had been owned by the Everett family for decades. Now, the head wine-maker was the youngest son Colby, who'd been a few grades below Temperance in Linden public schools. Temperance had made introductions, connecting the dots between Colby, Rowan, and the Bradys. Harry overheard Nate telling Ma that Rowan had already worked out a shared staffing plan with Everett, and beginning in December, a crew of ten would float between Three Birds and the Brady place. The arrangement meant plenty of year-round work at a decent wage. A healthy win for everyone.

In early November, Arden came home from college for a visit. By that Saturday morning, she was so rest-less and bored that she convinced Harry and Duncan to go with her to the only social event in the valley that weekend: the Everetts' fifth annual Food Truck Festival at Three Birds.

The Everett property seemed immaculate compared to his folks' new place. Pennants with the Three Birds logo flapped in the wind along the paved drive in. Their tidily groomed vineyard had changed for the fall, a tap-estry of canary yellows and deeper golds. Food trucks were arranged in a semicircle in one of the grassy fields. Dozens of picnic tables sat under strings of outdoor bistro lights on high poles. Arden did a little skip when she got out of the car and insisted on a selfie in the gravel parking lot with Harry and Duncan. They had to jog to keep up with her on the way in.

It was a sensory extravaganza. The smell of fresh-cut grass and burning wood mingled with scents from the food trucks. Brisket and falafel, frying doughnuts, on-ion rings, al pastor. French fries, burgers, innumerable spices, and the yeasty aroma of pizza dough.

They mingled with locals from Linden and Shelby and Greenbriar, and a half a dozen other little townships in the valley. Harry was happy to let his brother and sister do most of the socializing. Duncan already knew people in the county via equipment auctions, construction permitting, and countless other incidental meetings with carpenters, electricians, masons, and handyfolk.

Arden was in extrovert heaven, undaunted by strangers. She had the same gregarious personality Duncan did, plus the enthusiasm of youth and the kind of self-confidence imbued by being a youngest daughter with five doting older brothers. They'd only been at the festival twenty minutes when a loudspeaker announced field games for singles in the northern field, and Arden begged Harry and Duncan to go with her. Duncan responded with "I'd rather die" and a loud laugh in her face, which earned him a sharp-fisted punch in the arm. Harry waved her off as well, offering instead to hold the dried-flower crown she'd purchased as soon as they'd arrived. Duncan invited Harry along to chat with a stonemason and a guy who owned a reclamation business to get the wheels turning on the bank barn restoration.

This new world was dizzyingly different from the bustling West Coast city Harry called home. In L.A., the air was heady with salt and sea, blooming jasmine, and pot smoke. With hot pavement, and the sterile, metallic odor of air-conditioning. Here, it was wet tree bark after rain, woodsmoke on the wind, and the sweet, earthy scent of cut grass and amber hay. In L.A., evening skies shouted the last of their daylight with aggressive purples and oranges. But here in Vesper Valley—the word *vesper* itself meant "evening" in Latin—sunsets were opalescent whispers. A gentle easing into dusk.

Here, the world was softer.

Harry wove his way through the festival, enjoying the anonymity of the crowd. Near one of the pop-up wine bars, he recognized Frankie Moreau standing with a small group of people. His pulse accelerated. The crowd milled around him, jostling, bumping, pressing. He froze in place.

If Frankie was here, Rowan might be, too.

A man with a back as broad as a cabinet blocked Harry's view of the others. Then he shifted sideways, and there Rowan was. She was backlit, tipping her head sideways to smile at something the big guy said. Her hair fell over her shoulder, bright as sunrise over the Pacific.

Harry's body went boneless.

The big guy said something to make the women laugh again, and Rowan's attention shifted, like she sensed she was being watched. Her gaze collided with Harry's, and her wide, beautiful smile faltered. She reached up to fiddle with the ends of her hair, and despite the distance, Harry could tell she swallowed hard.

Getting air into his lungs suddenly felt impossible, like his rib cage had ratcheted down several sizes.

Frankie followed Rowan's gaze, and her face lit with warm recognition when she saw Harry. She flicked a quick glance at Rowan again, nudged her with an elbow, then beckoned him over with a quick flap of her hand.

As he joined them, Frankie rubbed his arm in greeting like they'd been friends for ages. "Harry, good to see you again."

The big guy was as tall as Duncan and half again as broad. He had a sunburned forehead. "Colby Everett," he said, extending a hand.

Shaking Colby Everett's huge hand felt like palming a side of ham. A ham with calluses, and a grip like a bench vise. But a grin crinkled the corners of his eyes, and his Three Birds Winery polo shirt had a mustard stain smack-dab in the middle of the chest. It added a bit of goofy charm to his otherwise intimidating aspect. The guy's teeth were perfectly straight—clearly the product of diligent teenage orthodontia—and startlingly white against his tidy auburn beard. A beard that, Harry noted, didn't have a single gray hair in it. He absently swiped a hand across the silver-speckled stubble bracketing his own mouth.

"Don't think that one matches your shirt, man." Everett gestured to the dried-flower crown Harry held. His good-natured farm-boy wholesomeness and artfully messy man bun made Harry feel ancient.

"Ah, yeah. My sister's." Harry smiled and held it over his head like a halo. "I'd have gone with marigolds, personally."

Everett and Frankie chuckled. Rowan's smile was closed-lipped, but her eyes twinkled. Harry felt her regard like sun on his skin, and damn, did it feel good.

As if summoned, Arden plowed into Harry from the side and slipped her arm through his. Her hair was mussed, and her cheeks glowed with exertion. She plucked the flower crown out of his hand and seated it on her dark head.

She smiled at Frankie. "I'm Arden."

"I'd have known you even without an introduction," Frankie said. "You look so much like your mom. I'm Frankie."

Arden held a flat hand over her head. "Got about six inches on her, though." She grinned. "Rowan, hi. Without your overalls, I almost didn't recognize you."

Rowan blushed and chuckled, and Harry's heart squeezed.

Arden looked at Everett through lowered lashes when

he extended a big hand around Harry to shake her hand. "Colby Everett. You having fun?"

Arden nodded as she took his big hand, still a little breathless. "Didn't see you at the singles event just now."

Everett pointed to the Three Birds logo over his slab-like pectoral. "Workin', sweetheart."

Arden poked the mustard stain and gave him a wicked smile. "Snackin' too, sweetheart?"

Everett's mouth hooked sideways in a smitten grin. Before he could reply, a loudspeaker announced team field games beginning on the south lawn in ten minutes. Arden grabbed Harry's hand and tugged him in the direction of the crowd. "We're doing this."

Harry made a strangled sound of protest and did an imaginary hat tip to Rowan and Frankie as his sister dragged him away.

From behind, he heard Colby Everett call after them, "I *am* single, though!"

* * *

"NEITHER OF US live here, Arden." Harry ran to keep up. "What are we going to do with a wine club membership if we win?"

"It's not about winning. It's about *fun*. And anyway, if we win, we'll give the membership thingy to Ma and Dad. Professional recon."

Harry searched the crowd. "Let's find Duncan. He's better at this shit than I am."

"Nope. You're my guy this time."

Three Birds staff in their plum-colored polo shirts milled through the gathering crowd, handing out large burlap sacks and beach balls. Classic rock streamed through the loudspeakers. The day was warm for late autumn, and with all the color, bustle, and cooking scents on the breeze, the place had the excitement and atmosphere of a carnival.

A small woman with a silky black braid and coppery skin handed them a burlap sack. "Where's the rest of your team?"

Arden looked up at Harry and stuck her bottom lip out in a mock pout. He shrugged and took the beach ball. "How many do we need?"

"These are relay races, friends. You need to—you know. Relay. We've got games for teams of four and teams of six."

"Can the two of us run double?" Arden said.

The woman's eyebrows raised. "You can join with one of the teams of four and join the sixes bracket."

Frankie came pushing through the crowd. One hand waved in the air, and the other dragged Rowan behind. "We're here!" she panted.

"Yay!" Arden bounced on her toes and clapped. She gave Rowan and Frankie quick hugs. Over Arden's shoulder, Frankie grinned at Harry and bobbed her eyebrows up and down.

Rowan sighed with a sideways smile, gathering her hair into a quick bun. "You Bradys sure do love your games."

"Thank you *so* much for coming," Arden said.

"Don't thank me." Rowan pushed up the sleeves of her sweater. "Frankie insisted."

Each race was a heat. Losing teams were disqualified each round, and the final two teams would face off in a game of tug-of-war. The first round would require two people to get a beach ball down and back across the field, with no hands on the ball or on each other.

Frankie quickly declared herself Arden's partner by claiming Rowan and Harry were too tall for her, even though she was nearly the same height as Rowan.

Pairs moved to the starting line. Rowan propped the beach ball on one cocked hip, sizing him up. "What's our strategy, partner? Front-to-front, or back-to-back?" Smudges of color lit her cheeks. There were two little tooth-shaped dents in her bottom lip where she'd clamped down in eager anticipation.

Harry really hadn't wanted to get up close and personal with strangers for these games, but *this* he could do.

"Thirty seconds!" the voice on the loudspeaker called.

Harry knew from that first night of Team Tag how competitive Rowan was. He looked around to the other teams along the edge of the field. Some practiced sandwiching the ball between bellies, some were back-to-back. "Front to front, I think. Easier if we can see each other."

Rowan nodded. She moved close and compressed the ball between them. Wiggled. Rolled it up and down. Bounced against it. "This feel okay?"

Tension flooded his groin. There were other things he wanted to feel, front to front with her. "Yep."

The blaring classic rock faded. They waddled sideways to a line spray-painted in the grass. "On your marks!" cried a voice over the speakers.

She locked her gaze to his. "Ready?"

"Let's do this."

"Get set! Go!"

Jaunty circus music suddenly blasted from the speakers, tinny and overloud. A wacky trumpet melody and a plodding tuba bass line created an air of intentional absurdity, and when the duo next to them tripped and fell to the ridiculous beat, Rowan nearly lost it. A laugh burst from her that made the ball between them squeeze sideways. "Oh!" she said. When she pushed her belly against the ball to keep it from popping free, Harry stumbled backward and had to windmill his arms to keep upright. They spun in a circle, arms flailing, bending and contorting to try to get the ball securely between them again.

"Don't touch it!" Rowan laughed. Her hair sagged out of its bun and hung suspended from the side of her head like a huge, disorderly bird's nest.

She was the most beautiful person he'd ever seen.

"Keep it together, Dr. McKinnon," Harry chuckled.

From the sideline, Frankie and Arden alternated between shouts of encouragement and refrains of "What the hell are you *doing*?" It only made Rowan laugh harder.

They were securely in third place. They quickly passed the ball to Frankie and Arden for the second heat. As they sped away, Rowan raised her hand for a high five, breathing fast. "Nice job, partner."

Harry wanted to thrust his hands into her messy hair and kiss her hard. He studied her profile, memorizing. The tiniest upward tilt of her nose, and the curve of her cheekbones. The dip of her deep bottom lip, and the lazy lift of loose curls in the warm wind. Her chest, and the slim outline of her shoulders, still rising and falling rapidly under her thin sweater.

"Kind of fun when we're on the same team," he said.

"It is." Rowan fanned her face with her hand and turned her attention to the chaos on the field. Her expression settled into practiced neutrality, but her eyes remained glossy with excitement.

It was incredible, really, how easily she could flip that interior switch. Fiery intensity to remote coolness, in a single heartbeat. Every time he sensed a scrap of reciprocated attraction from her, she snuffed it out so quickly it felt like he'd manufactured it with his loneliness. His hormones and his heart had teamed up to sabotage his mind.

The next game was a three-legged race. Arden helped pull a burlap sack over Harry's left leg and Rowan's right leg, bundling them together to form a single center limb. To maintain balance, he had to wrap an arm around her waist. Rowan did the same, hooking a thumb through a belt loop of his jeans. Her hair tickled his face, and the outer curve of her breast was pressed against his ribs. They gripped the bag tight in the center, keeping their eyes straight ahead.

"Ready?" Rowan said.

"So ready."

"Middle legs step out first, okay?"

"You're the boss," Harry said.

They hit a solid rhythm as soon as "go!" was called. The circus music played again, but this time, it felt like the soundtrack of a weird fever dream. Rowan stumbled and laughed, the hem of her sweater riding up as he steadied her. For the rest of the race, Harry palmed the solid upper curve of her bare hip, fingertips digging into the bunch and release of muscles beneath sweat-damp skin. He adapted his movement to the pace she set, and they swept down the field in tandem, like they'd become a single organism.

Harry's composure unraveled with every flex of Rowan's body under his hand, and with each of their mingled, laboring breaths. His imagination took control, and no longer were they racing down a field surrounded by cheering strangers on a bright autumn evening. It was dark and quiet where Harry had gone, and they were alone there. Their bodies were united in an even more perfect rhythm, striving toward a different, mutually satisfying goal.

Christ.

He positioned his forearm across the fly of his jeans as he gripped the burlap in his fist—a meager attempt to hide an unmistakable and entirely situationally inappropriate hard-on.

They won the round. Harry sat on the ground with his head hung between his knees while Frankie and Arden ran their heat. Rowan quietly handed down a small cup of water from a nearby cooler. The sweet gesture made the ache even worse.

Subsequent relays didn't require them to partner up, thank god. One round, they had to balance an egg on a teaspoon up and down the field. In another, they had to run with a balloon between their knees. Rowan came alive with laughter and self-deprecating groans when she fumbled her turns. But whenever Harry made eye contact, she'd slip her gaze away and button up tight.

He tried to not watch her ass each time she hustled down the field.

He absolutely *could not* take his eyes off her ass as she hustled down the field.

Their little team made it to the final round. Frankie and Arden—now fast friends—stood with arms linked, while a short guy sporting a fauxhawk and a grapevine tattoo up the bronzed skin of his forearm declared the rules for the championship tug-of-war game.

The opposing team looked to be a family—two college kids, their parents. The mom was petite, but the dad was tall, with a thick neck and barrel belly. Harry flexed his hands and hoped he didn't make an ass of himself. He imagined being wrenched forward and flying through the air, cartoon-style.

Harry was the team's anchor, standing at the back with the rope slung around his waist, feet planted wide. Rowan was directly in front of him. When the whistle blew, the crowd around them erupted in cheers. The big guy at the other end of the rope did most of the work for his team, getting a solid lead with a vigorous tug at the outset. Harry dug in his heels, but didn't pull. Let the other guy wear himself out.

In front of Harry, Rowan was feral, yanking on the rope. Her gasping grunts and exhalations sounded so overtly sexual, he had to clear his lungs with a hard breath. He leaned away from her, focusing on the cottony clouds overhead.

"Dig in," he said after a minute, quiet enough for only his team to hear. "Wait them out."

On the other end of the rope, the teenagers got the giggles and started slipping. The mom lost her footing, and the dad was red-faced.

"Pull!" Harry called out. After a tense thirty seconds, the middle of the rope passed over their side's goal line. They won.

When the judge blew the final whistle, the big guy on the other end abruptly let go. The rope went slack, and Harry's team tumbled like a row of dominos. Rowan fell solidly backward between Harry's knees, knocking the back of her head against his sternum. Frankie and Arden rolled away, overtaken by obnoxious, snorting giggles.

Frankie shouted, "For the win!" as she helped Arden scramble to her feet. Rowan collapsed sideways with laughter. Harry laughed too as he stood and extended a hand down to her. She tucked her palm in his and let him haul her upright.

And she kissed him.

CHAPTER ELEVEN

Rowan

It was messy and quick, all surging momentum, without artifice. Rowan's lips crashed into Harrison's cheek, catching the very corner of his open, smiling mouth. Their laughter stopped abruptly, as if a needle had been lifted from a record. He jerked backward and swiped fingertips where the kiss landed, as though he could grab it in his hand to examine it.

Her body had pulled her into the kiss as surely as he had pulled her to her feet. All afternoon she'd tried to suppress the full magnitude of simple joy she felt in playing with Harrison. She'd finally been carried away by the silly thrill of the win and the delicious spontaneity of his laugh and the heat of him, and just—god, a *lightness* she hadn't felt in so long.

She was *ridiculous*.

"I'm sorry. That was—" she stammered, and pressed fingers to her forehead, her lips, her throat.

His expression softened. "What—" he began.

Rowan put up a hand in a wordless plea for silence. His tongue darted out and nudged the corner of his mouth where her lips had just been. She backed away, bumping a man pushing a stroller, and nearly knocking cotton candy from a child's hands.

Someone grabbed her from behind and gently squeezed her upper arms. Arden. She shifted around and smiled, seemingly oblivious to the tension. Then she snagged Harrison by the hand and pulled him in the opposite direction.

"Time for dancing!" Arden said. "Rowan, come on!"

Harrison looked back, his mouth opening and closing like a landed fish. The crowd swarmed around them, and once they were out of sight, Rowan took a breath so big it made her lungs burn.

It wasn't like she'd stuck her hand down his pants and propositioned him for a quick screw behind the funnel cake truck. Honestly, though—that would've been easier to recover from. She could have played that off with relative ease. The simple sweetness of the kiss made it seem somehow more audacious. More important.

Rowan wanted to sink to her knees and disappear into the earth.

* * *

PASTEL SUNSET TURNED the world watercolor. A local band warmed up, and the plaintive vibrato of a single violin wove through the noise of the crowd. A dance floor of snap-together wood panels had been constructed in the north field, illuminated by string after string of vintage-style bulbs attached to four tall poles at the corners. Farther out in the field, a bonfire was lit, and the trace of smoke in the air cushioned everything in dreamy softness.

Near the dancing, Rowan found a quiet place in the grass under a big oak. Now that the sun had nearly gone, the autumn evening felt chilly. She wrapped her arms around her legs and notched her chin between her knees. Fallen leaves around her smelled musty-sweet and familiar, and the rippled bark of the tree felt oddly comforting against her back. The band kicked off in earnest with a lively line dance, and Rowan watched the revelry from the periphery, thinking about Harrison.

The rasp of his stubbled cheek against her lips. The scent of his soap or aftershave, or whatever that sweet, lovely juniper came from. The essence of his skin, and the way his clothes always smelled sun-warmed. The intimate rumble of his laugh, and the way he made silence feel comfortable. How his breath had somehow become familiar.

The way he'd scrubbed away the trace of her kiss, then tasted the very same spot with a quick, questing tongue. How his blue-gray eyes went black when he looked at her, and how his attention always tracked to her mouth.

Damn it.

All efforts to logic herself out of her attraction to Harrison Brady were crumbling. She needed to get laid, that's all it was. Managing her own release with her utilitarian vibrator was no replacement for skin against skin, and solid male hips between her legs.

Sweet kisses in sunlit fields were not it. Rowan had given up on *sweet* a long time ago.

Temperance's words scrolled through her memory like a news ticker. *"Rowan likes casual and uncomplicated,"* she'd said to Frankie that night at Buddy's. *"I promise you, Harry is neither of those things."*

The parts of Harrison Brady that were sensitive and exposed were the same ones within Rowan that were callused over and impenetrable. There was more than simple lust in his eyes when he looked at her. Not that anyone had ever looked at her like that—but instinct told her it was not the gaze of a man who would be satisfied with casual sex.

Anyway, she worked for his family now. God, Gianna had spent *hours* with her last week, talking about perennials and her favorite eye creams and design plans for the bed-and-breakfast, and dozens of other mundane things. That uncomplicated, effortless camaraderie with the other woman had just felt so, *so* good.

Rowan pressed her forehead into her knees, hard enough to make it hurt.

A few songs later, she was shivering in earnest and checking a text from Frankie when a big silhouette blocked out the light from the dance floor.

Colby squatted down to her level. "Hey. Doing okay?"

"Yeah. Waiting Frankie out. She's got the car keys."

"She's dancing. You should come."

"I can't line dance. Big brain-body disconnect." Rowan swirled a hand above her head. "I think it's all this hair."

As if on cue, the band eased into a slow song. Colby cocked his head to the side, hiking a thumb over his shoulder. "I *know* you can dance to this."

Rowan narrowed her eyes. "You knew that was coming, didn't you?"

He shrugged and grinned, then stood. "One of the perks of running the place. It's warmer out there, you know. I saw you shivering."

Rowan caved, brushing leaves from her jeans as Colby led her to the dancing. The band was good. Close bodies and lights strung above the dance floor generated a comfortable bubble of warmth. Colby was funny and plainspoken. Undeniably cute and a bit nerdy—more Bruce Banner than The Hulk. He chatted about vineyard business while they danced. Rowan couldn't help but like him.

As the slow song flowed into a new one, he said, "I hope you'll forgive me for this."

"Oh no. What's happening?"

He cleared his throat. "I had an ulterior motive, bringing you out here. I need you to dance with Harry Brady so I can get a minute with his sister."

"You bastard," she laughed.

"I'm sorry."

"So, you're going to offer me up as some kind of trade?"

Colby grimaced. "When you say it out loud, it sounds really bad."

"I'm your sacrificial lamb."

"I'm a vegetarian, actually," he said.

Rowan shook her head and swallowed a swirl of anxiety. "You're lucky I like you."

She hadn't been able to see Harrison and Arden from where she'd sat under the oak, but Colby maneuvered to them within a matter of seconds. By the way he'd looked at Arden earlier, he'd probably had a bead on her all night.

Faint surprise registered on Harrison's face when Colby approached and tapped him on the shoulder. He gave Rowan a long, unreadable look.

"Mind if I cut in?" Colby said.

Harrison shifted his attention to Arden. Her answering blush was a gentle tint of rose on her golden skin, a pretty contrast to the blotchy red Rowan knew was beginning to stain her own.

"He doesn't mind." Arden gave Harrison a luminous smile and patted him on the chest.

Colby released Rowan and took Arden's hand, and he spun her into a theatrical twirl. Harrison's hair was glossy caramel under the gleam of lights, and wind-blown. He watched them dance away. "Did Colby Everett just use you as a distraction so he could dance with my sister?"

Rowan shrugged. "I guess you intimidate him."

"He's got fifty pounds on me. At least."

"He's squishy on the inside though," Rowan said.

Harrison laughed. "So am I. He's also not very smart if he thinks I'd try to influence anything Arden does. Or that she'd allow me to."

A new song began. Harrison slid a finger into the collar of his shirt, scratched his neck, scanned the crowd boxing them in. Then he held out his hand. When Rowan took it, his shoulders relaxed. As he pulled her toward him, he rubbed his thumb lazily, intimately into her palm. By the way her body responded, it might as well have been his tongue across her nipple.

"Everett was right about one thing," he said.

"What's that?"

"You *are* a distraction."

Rowan met his gaze. Familiar heat simmered in her belly and dropped low, lower, settling between her thighs. She shivered.

"You cold?" he asked.

She nodded, though now the shudder was less about the chill and more about being inconveniently horny. Harrison pulled her closer, bringing them belly to belly. The heat of his hand against her back branded her skin through the fine knit of her sweater. His fingers slid along her vertebrae, like she was an instrument he was preparing to play. His thumb made a long sweep southward, from the dip of her waist to the flare of her hip bone.

It felt like foreplay.

By the damp heat between her legs, her body recognized it as such. Was he trying to get a rise out of her? Tormenting himself?

Both?

She set her teeth and thought about agricultural pests, fertilizer ratios, and the care and training of Katahdin sheep.

Casual.

Uncomplicated.

"You going to be here much longer tonight?" he said.

"I'm at Frankie's mercy. She drove."

"How long's that drive? I haven't been to Temperance's place in the city yet."

"About forty minutes, when I drive. When Frankie drives? Thirty. Twenty if she has to pee."

"Ever think about staying with us once the weather turns? I assume roads are bad in the winter. Duncan says the cottage next to the greenhouse will be ready soon."

"Hmm."

Hell no.

His breath stirred the curls around her face. "Not much to say tonight?"

She shook her head. "You know I don't do small talk."

The people around them were engaged in conversation, smiling and laughing. One couple was caught up in a kiss so hot it made Rowan's mouth go dry.

"Let's talk about something meaningful, then," he said.

Rowan didn't answer.

"Tell me your favorite ice cream."

She narrowed her eyes.

"Seriously. That's not small talk, Rowan. I can't think of anything much more important than ice cream."

"What if I'm lactose intolerant?"

"God, I'm sorry."

The unvarnished intensity in his voice made her laugh and shake her head. "I'm not actually lactose intolerant, Harrison."

"Then why not tell me?"

"What is this, the half-Spanish inquisition?" She raised an eyebrow.

"Cute." His hand pressed lightly against her spine. "Tell me."

A tiny shrug. "Ice cream is overrated."

He shrank away in mock horror. "Monster."

She laughed again. "Why do we need to talk about ice cream?"

A shadow passed over his expression, then a fleeting muscle pulsed in his jaw. "I need the—ah, distraction."

Rowan felt a conspicuous ridge of heat beneath the fly of his jeans that hadn't been there when she'd first moved into his arms.

Oh, boy.

Rowan cleared her throat, brightened her tone. "I don't like ice cream. Don't have much of a sweet tooth at all, really. My real weakness is breakfast food."

"Really?"

She chattered on, fast. "My kingdom for a steaming stack of pancakes. Soaked in butter, tiny swirl of syrup. Slightly burned bacon on the side. If it's an act of true love, there's fresh-squeezed orange juice." Edie had always made homemade OJ. She'd called them her "I love you" breakfasts.

The song finished, and they swayed together a few times after the final note. Rowan leaned out of his arms, but he kept hold. When the band began the opening notes of a new song, Harrison drew her back against him.

"One more," he said.

It wasn't a question.

CHAPTER TWELVE

Rowan

"This next one is for Eve and Zoey," the band's vocalist announced, "celebrating six years of love tonight. Here's to sixty more."

The song was a steamy cover of a song she'd loved in college. "Make You Feel My Love," by Bob Dylan. Rowan sighed.

Harrison ducked his head to catch her eye. "What part do you disapprove of? The song choice, or the love stuff?"

"I doubt you actually want to know my answer."

"I never ask a question I don't want an answer for," Harrison said.

She met his eyes. "I've always liked the song."

He smashed his lips into a thin line and nodded. "Ah. So, it's the love bit that has you scoffing."

"I didn't scoff."

"Oh, I definitely heard a scoff."

Rowan shrugged.

"Love is what makes us human," he said. "I'd even argue it's a huge part of our success as a species."

"Wow. You're trying to make it about science?"

It was Harrison's turn to shrug. "We protect what we love."

Rowan leveled a cool look at him. "Animals protect what they share DNA with. It's in our genes. If your peers are safe, you're safe. Survival is a numbers game."

"Humans are different."

She smirked. "There are two things that make humans different from other mammals. Our tendency to seek self-destructive things, and our willful desire to be duped. It's why we enjoy scary movies and fiction novels, and Santa Claus and artificial sweeteners."

He breathed out a laugh. "Are all biologists as bleak as you about the human condition?"

"Why do you think I chose to dedicate my life to plants? Plants don't fuck each other over."

The smile faded from his eyes, and his arms stiffened. "Jesus, Rowan."

"People don't fall in love," she said. "They fall in *lust* and call it love, to sanitize the fact they're simply responding to the urges of their bodies."

Fingertips briefly dug into her hip. "The urges of their bodies? Really?" His voice dipped to a low enough register she felt the rumble of it in her own chest.

"How many times have you been in love, Harrison?"

He hesitated. Swallowed. "Few times."

"And how many of those people are you in love with now?" She plucked one of her hairs off his shirt and released it in the wind.

"Interesting line of questioning from someone who doesn't believe in love." Harrison's eyes lifted, tracking the long curl as it floated away.

Rowan jerked her hand back down and rested it on his shoulder. "I'm a scientist. I'm gathering data."

"Nicola and I, ah—" He spoke slowly. "We weren't what the other needed."

"Nicola," Rowan echoed the name. "But if love is real, why didn't it last?"

He hesitated. "Does a thing ending invalidate that it existed at all?"

"Don't answer my questions with a question."

"You know I'm right," he said.

She laughed. "What most people mistake for love is infatuation. Infatuation fades fast once people truly learn each other. Then they each diminish in the absence of the fantasy. See that couple there?"

Rowan nodded in the direction of an elderly couple, swaying in a tight embrace. The man was as bald as an egg and stoop-shouldered with age, and the woman had a puff of white hair so thin her scalp was visible through the teased curls. They had to be in their eighties.

"I do," he said, cautiously.

"They're fresh out of college. Married last year," Rowan said.

His crack of laughter drew the eyes of other dancers. Then he sobered. "My parents have been married forty years. Still in love. That's *my* standard. My example."

"That's precarious, don't you think? When you put a thing on a pedestal, you beg fate to tip it over."

"Oh, Christ," Harrison said, "now you sound like my brother Malcolm."

"Maybe you should introduce us," she teased.

He gave her a long look. "I don't think so."

She shrugged.

"So, love is your boogeyman," he said. "You think—if you don't believe in it, it can't hurt you."

"I'm a scientist, Harrison. Fundamentally, so are you. You know truth doesn't care about what we *believe*."

"Why did you kiss me?"

Rowan was instantly unbalanced. His tone sounded

mild, but it lied. The truth was in the rapid dilation of his pupils, and the stiff bob of his Adam's apple as he swallowed. Hard.

Earlier, she'd shivered in the cold, but now, a trickle of sweat raced between her breasts. The clasp of her bra dug into her back, and the seam of her jeans was gritty between her thighs. Her very bones wanted to leap free of her skin and dance away into the darkness.

The music and the crowd whirled around her like a carousel, but Harrison remained in sharp detail. A tiny piece of ash from the bonfire landed on his shoulder like a flake of snow. Rowan saw a tiny scar on his chin, no bigger than the edge of a fingernail. The middle button of his navy Henley was about to slip free, and the collar of the T-shirt underneath was the same tidal gray as his eyes.

Since Noah, Rowan was vigilant about maintaining the power in her relationships. No-strings sex as a matter of policy. Always and *only* with men who liked her just a bit more than she'd ever liked them. With Harrison, the power imbalance already skewed hard in his favor, and she'd only known him two months. She'd shown him her entire hand with that impulsive, half-assed kiss.

He weakened her, with his big, kind hands and solemn eyes. And his fucking ridiculous chin dimple, and those outrageous flipped-up curls at his nape, and the way he stood when she entered a room, and how he thumbed the brim of an imaginary hat every time he saw her around the vineyards, and—

Damn it.

With him, she was the one with the most to lose, and she'd never allow herself to be in that position again.

Rowan dug deep for the aloof, cerebral serenity she'd used on every other man for the past eight years. "I was excited we'd won. I'd have kissed Frankie that way too, but you were closest."

His head listed to the side. Evaluating. "Bullshit," he murmured.

"Kiss of gratitude. That's all. It was a peck on the cheek, Harrison."

"It wasn't just my cheek. You were chewing grape gum. I *tasted* it."

"I was *going* for your cheek," she snapped. The couple dancing next to them turned their heads in unison. She whispered, "You pulled sideways and made it weird."

Harrison was quiet for a while, and the band played a sweet, slow cover of "September" by Earth, Wind & Fire. Rowan stared at the half-done button on his shirt, and the throbbing pulse point in his neck. When she lifted her eyes, his face transformed. The tension in his jaw released, and he nudged his bottom lip with the tip of his tongue. His irises were bright and sharp as bottle glass, and riveted on her mouth.

"Christ. I'd been thinking it was my imagination." The rumbly tone was back. "I'm really *not* imagining this, am I?"

"I don't know what you're talking about." Her heart slammed her sternum now, rattling her ribs from the inside.

"You're as curious about this as I am. About us."

"There is no *us*."

His brows dipped into a dark ridge as he scanned her features. "Rapid respiration, flushed lips. Wide eyes, pupils dilated. I don't need to be a physician to know what physiological arousal looks like. God, Rowan, I can even smell it on your breath."

Heat climbed her collarbones, igniting her neck, her cheeks, even her goddamned ears. "Great diagnosis,

Doctor. Will you bill my insurance, or do I need to pay up front?"

He drew away like she'd slapped him.

Rowan went on the offensive. "You want to get clinical with me, Harrison? Play the doctor game?"

His answering frown was apocalyptic. "Why the hell won't you call me Harry?"

"So we're playing the *name* game, then."

"None of this is a game. I'm talking about real feelings."

"I'm talking about feeling, too." She moved closer, letting her exhale wash over his neck, weaponizing his attraction to her.

His eyes rolled and flickered closed for an instant, and his jaw locked. "No, you're only talking about *sensation*. I'm talking about emotion."

Rowan pitched her hips forward into his persistent erection. "Emotion didn't do *this* to you, Dr. Brady."

Stripes of color lit his cheeks, and a sound of frustration vibrated in his chest. "I'm talking about *both*."

"We're just two bodies, acknowledging each other as biologically favorable mates—"

"Holy shit, are you serious?"

"Try me. Let's go back to your truck."

He threw a glance at the sky, then back at her. "I'm not going to be pulled into some sexual game with you. There's something bigger here. More than infatuation, or lust, or biological urges, or whatever the fuck you said earlier."

She spoke slowly, like she was explaining a complex idea to a child. "There are two reasons humans have sex. To try to make babies, or to get off. I don't plan on having babies, so you do the math."

Genuine confusion creased his forehead. "You have

got to be the only person who uses sex as a way to *distance* yourself from someone."

"How did an obstetrician develop such puritanical opinions about sex?"

Muscles pulsed at his temples as his jaw tensed and released. "Don't mock me."

They weren't dancing anymore. Instead, they barely swayed in place, matching glares firing between them. "Do you really think all of those babies you've delivered were conceived in *love,* Dr. Brady?"

"That's reductive *and* ignorant, Dr. McKinnon," he volleyed back.

"Now you're mocking *me.* Why is this making you so angry?"

"You're punishing me," he growled. "I wounded your pride earlier today, and now you're making me pay for it."

"It was an innocent, impulsive kiss, asshole. And you jerked back like I'd spit in your face."

"Try me again," he echoed her phrase from earlier. "I won't make the same mistake twice."

The tension in him felt seismic. His restraint hovered over an active fault line. Beneath his gentle exterior lurked a well-managed intensity Rowan recklessly wanted to agitate free. Harrison Brady seemed incapable of feeling things halfway—the pain resonating out of him made everything somehow *more.* Magnified.

Fascinating.

God, he'd probably be incredible in bed.

But he wanted the kind of access she'd never grant again. He wanted to explore and expand the palpable chemistry between them, and she simply wanted to delve it for sensation and release. Harrison Brady was too wholesome for her—latent, newly discovered temper notwithstanding—and she had enough kindness in her to recognize it before she drove them both to self-destruction.

She wouldn't cast them in a story she already knew the ending to.

Rowan dropped her hands away from his shoulders and stepped back. This needed to stop here, now. "Whatever you think is going on here, you're wrong."

"Rowan." The way he said her name was both warning and supplication.

The song ended, and the band announced intermission. Everyone began to clear the floor.

She wiped her hands on her jeans and adjusted the hem of her sweater. "Probably best if you don't touch me again."

Harrison's expression darkened, a storm front passing over skin. He pushed his hands into his pockets and tilted toward her. With his mouth close enough his lips grazed her ear with every word, he said, "I won't touch you again. Until you ask."

Then he was gone, and she was alone under the glare of the lights.

CHAPTER THIRTEEN

Harry

Harry watched Rowan leave with Frankie shortly after he'd left her on the dance floor. He wasn't proud of it, walking away like he did. But he knew how his anger worked. It was a controlled demolition. First, the slow squeeze of the trigger, then a systemic breakdown that escalated into eventual ruin.

It was rare for him to lose his temper—rare enough that when his composure began to crumble, it felt like the symptoms of an illness. Metallic odor in his nose, a churn of acid in his gut. A pulse that wouldn't quite settle on a rhythm. When Rowan made the shitty quip about billing her insurance, he'd felt a familiar detonation deep within him. Practicing medicine was already a fucking sore spot for him, and her glib mockery of it set his interior simmer to a healthy boil.

Combined with the insistently hostile hard-on he'd sustained most of the day, he'd become as growly as a starving wolf. He didn't want her to see him snap. So, he'd removed himself.

Something existed between them made of highly flammable material, and Harry wasn't sure he'd survive the blaze if it ever caught fire. Rowan could be distant as the moon, depriving him of oxygen and untethering him from gravity. But she was also funny and earnest and brilliant—and before she'd put up her guard tonight, he'd heard the hungry catch in her voice when they talked about love. Something dormant and raw and aching to be explored.

For a moment, Harry clung to that.

Truth was, he hated himself a little bit less when she was around, even when she was being a pain in the ass. She quieted the commotion in his brain. Through all his years of school, he'd encountered every personality type imaginable, and it was an unavoidable truth that certain people just—clicked. On the night they'd met, he'd felt that *click* with her as certain as a deadbolt sliding home.

It wasn't that she made him forget his pain. It was that she helped him see life *beyond* it.

Arden found him at the bonfire. She looped her arm through his. "We've been here for hours, surrounded by a bonanza of delicious food, and all I've had is a lemonade. What sounds good to you?"

"Burger place. Over there." Harry pointed to a plain-looking food truck with a line a dozen people deep.

"Really? You have all these incredible options, and you choose *burgers*?"

"Arden, these aren't average burgers. Nate brought some home for everyone last week. These are the ultimate burgers. Burgers so big you have to cut them in pieces before you can eat them."

Arden arched a brow. "Did you know it's a misdemeanor in several states to cut up a burger before you eat it?"

Harry laughed.

"I'm imagining you daintily cutting a burger in half, and I'm deeply embarrassed for you."

"Come on, Arden. You have to acknowledge that

some restaurants have gotten completely out of hand with the size of their sandwiches," he said.

"Out of hand? Cute," she snorted. "Look, big brother. I've never shamed myself by cutting a burger before eating it. You smash it down, you get your mouth around it, and you chew it into submission, or you wuss out and order a meal where utensils are sanctioned. A salad, or a bowl of soup."

"I look forward to reading your anti-utensil manifesto someday."

Her side-eye was potent. "If you tell me you've used a knife and fork on pizza, I will never be able to look you in the face again."

"Fine, fine. You know what? I'm going to order the biggest, most obscenely oversized burger on the menu. Every condiment, every topping. If I have to unhinge my jaw like a snake, I'll do it. Not only will I not use utensils, I won't even use a napkin."

"'Atta boy." She squeezed his arm as they walked to the burger truck. "I'm glad your appetite is coming back."

Her enthusiasm made Harry feel a little twinge of guilt. His appetite didn't have much to do with a healthier outlook on life. It was that he flat-out needed the fuel. "Duncan has been pushing me from sunrise to sundown this whole past week. My stamina is still garbage."

"Don't let him push you too hard. I wish I was around to help."

"It's actually a good thing. I'm too tired at night to dream. I guess I should be thanking him."

"Have you thought about staying?" she asked.

"Staying where? Here? In the valley?" Harry said.

"Sure. Why do you sound so surprised?"

"Ah, I don't know. Sinclair's keeping my position open at her practice if I come back within a year."

"Stay. Be a rural doctor. I'm sure the women in this county would love not having to go into the city for their wellness and prenatal care."

"Slow down," Harry chuckled. "I still have a life in L.A., Arden."

"Do you, though?"

His smile fell and he evaded the question. Luckily, she let him off the hook, changing the subject to their parents' plans for the new property, and Arden's current class load. She fretted about how the first semester of her sophomore year was nearly over, and she still hadn't decided on a major.

It felt restorative and a little surreal for Harry, discussing college with his baby sister. He'd been eleven when she was born, the only one of the boys who'd wanted to hold her. She'd fascinated and delighted him—the swirl of dark hair on the top of her head, and her fuzzy brow wrinkled in a perpetual infant scowl. Her perfect, nearly translucent fingernails, and the little roll of chub at her wrists.

The day he met her was the day he knew he wanted to be a doctor.

Colby Everett came by again, working the crowd, chitchatting and thanking everyone for coming. He lingered with Harry and Arden a bit longer than he did with others.

"That dude has a crush." Harry nodded in Colby's direction as he moved on to other guests.

With an unreadable look, Arden watched him go. "I know."

"Does he know you're heading back to school on Sunday?"

Her answering smile was mischievous. "Nope."

"That's cruel, Arden."

"I only met him tonight, Harry," she chided. "He's practically a stranger. I don't owe him a status update."

"You give him your number?"

"Nope." She made a little *pop* sound on the last syllable. "He didn't ask."

"I guarantee, Colby Everett and his trendy man bun are going to be at our place on Monday asking around about you."

"Let him wonder." Arden's eyes twinkled, then narrowed. "Speaking of crushes—tell me about Rowan."

Harry coughed out a laugh and looked away. "Not sure what you're talking about."

"Spill it, big guy." She pinched him behind his elbow.

"Ow. Seriously, it's too soon."

"Respectfully disagree. Nicola's been out of the picture for a long time, Harry."

"You're a menace." He couldn't look at her. Arden was too much like Ma, that same soul-piercing perceptiveness in her eyes, same stubborn tilt of her chin. She'd see right through him if he met her gaze.

"I saw Rowan kiss you, bud."

"That wasn't a kiss. That was a cheek peck gone wrong. It was nothing."

"The kiss doesn't even matter. What's relevant was the aftermath. Frankie and I saw how you both reacted. Rowan turned red as one of those Spanish poppies Mama used to grow, and you looked like you could've bitten through a brick. It was gloriously awkward. If it were 'nothing,' you'd have both laughed it off."

They were next up in line. Harry took out his wallet, flipped through a few bills, snapped it shut again, and repeated the action three more times. Arden's scrutiny twisted into the side of his face like a corkscrew. He looked down at his feet.

"I like her," Arden said.

Harry caught her shrug from the corner of his eye. She pretended to study the chalkboard menu in front of the food truck, but the only thing written on it was BURGERS: YOU KNOW WHY YOU'RE HERE.

"Really?" he said.

"Why do you sound surprised?" she said. "She's awesome."

It was their turn to order, so Harry didn't have time to respond. The pasty kid working the window looked like a teenage version of Ichabod Crane. He responded with a big-eyed stare and a squeaky "You sure, mister?" when Harry ordered a burger with every condiment and topping they had available. It was an unfortunate combination of things like over-easy eggs and mango chutney, peanut butter and avocado, plus all the traditional stuff like lettuce, tomatoes, pickles—but he was determined to keep his promise to Arden. He was going to eat the damn thing without a single utensil. Grimacing, Arden gave him a thumbs-up, and ordered a burger for herself with only green toppings: lettuce, pickles, and fresh sliced jalapeño.

They found a picnic table near the bonfire, and put their order number on a clip sticking out of the top of an empty wine bottle. Arden balanced her chin in her hand and gave Harry a sideways look. "I'm not letting you off the hook about Rowan. Why would you be surprised I like her?"

Harry took a long drink of beer. "You never liked Nicola."

Arden opened her mouth and closed it quickly, then put her palms flat on the table and leaned forward. "Nicola sucked, Harry."

Harry laughed. "That's not very feminist of you."

"Being a feminist doesn't mean I have to like someone by default just because they're a woman."

"Why didn't you ever tell me?"

Arden's dark brows climbed comically high. "Really, bud? You'd have wanted your teen sister's hot takes on your love life?"

Harry's relationship with Nicola Baldwin began when they were both fresh-faced residents. The attraction had been immediate, and they worked well together, professionally. Even so, Harry had known from the jump that anything and everyone would always come second to medicine for her, and at the time, he'd expected medicine would eventually become like that for him, too—so it would be okay.

It never did, and it never felt okay.

They only visited his family once a year, and Nicola never figured out how to authentically engage with anyone. One visit, she'd called Arden "Adrienne" for an entire afternoon. Ma and Dad were gracious and kind to her, but they'd always seemed a little nervous, as though interacting with her was a perpetual audition. The only one of his brothers Nicola managed to have a lengthy conversation with was Patrick, and that had only been because Patrick was a pharmacist and could speak the same medical language she did. Duncan had only ever liked her because she'd also refused to eat Ma's chocolate coconut cookies.

Nicola wasn't a bad person. But she'd never been *Harry's* person. She was too sterile, too detached. He'd realized far too late he'd been in love with the *idea* of her.

"I ever tell you how she ended it?" Harry said.

"Let me guess. Over the phone. No, wait. She did it in a text, didn't she?"

"Worse. Email."

"No shit." Arden slapped her hands down.

Harry smirked. "I swear. One paragraph. Then she signed it, 'Regards.'"

They laughed, then Arden's expression grew sensitive and serious, and she reached across the table to touch his arm. "It's strange she's a cardiologist, as clueless as she is about the human heart."

Harry put his hand over hers. "It's okay. Really. She'd been sleeping at the hospital most nights for the last year. It's been a long time since it was real." Harry thought about his conversation with Rowan earlier. *"Infatuation fades fast once people truly learn each other."* "It might not have ever been."

Arden sat back and traced her fingers over where someone had carved their initials into the picnic table. "Honestly, I knew she wasn't right for you when she refused to play Team Tag that July Fourth at Nate and Maren's."

"Ah, to be fair, Nicola's life is medicine. Asking a cardiologist to risk a broken finger or wrist in a game with a bunch of people she barely knows is—a lot. You know how this family plays. I almost broke my nose in Team Tag the night I came home."

Arden sat back and groaned. "Hate that I missed it. Duncan told me we finally lost."

"Yep, the Bradys' brief winning streak has ended."

"I heard we have Rowan to thank?"

He nodded. "Yeah, she was—"

Sudden movement and noise erupted at the table next to them. A wineglass shattered.

"Help!" a woman yelled. She was hunched over her partner at the table, fearfully pressing a paper napkin into the palm of his hand. A crimson-black stain bloomed against the white, plainly visible in the meager glow of the string lights above them.

Blood.

Anxiety surged in his mind like a plume of oil, and he was catapulted back to a dark, rain-soaked Los Angeles highway. Inside the ambulance. Harry smelled the blood, hot and coppery, and the matching metallic odor of ozone from the storm.

The sounds. Thunder rippling against the ambulance roof. A squalling newborn. Cora Woodward's weakening cries.

Your fault.

Your failure.

Nausea crested higher in his gut, and guilt rode on his back like a four-hundred-pound gorilla. He bit his lips together and willed himself not to vomit.

His vision blackened from the outside in. His body moved in slow motion, but his heart galloped like a thoroughbred. Too fast. Too hard.

Numbness seeped into his hands, his lips. His fingers curled inward like claws, frozen against his palms.

Breathe. Fucking *breathe*.

He couldn't move.

Arden wasted no time. She punched 911 into her phone and hustled to the couple. Over her shoulder, she said, "Stay with me, Harry," but he felt himself sliding sideways.

His lungs wouldn't inflate. He was choking. Choking on nothing.

Dying. He was dying, and his little sister had to watch.

"Harry!" Arden had gone far, far away. Somewhere dark.

No. *He* was the one in the dark, far place.

He'd fallen underneath the world, where there was no air.

Everything went black.

*   *   *

HARRY SAT IN the passenger seat. Arden drove his rental truck. There were no roadside lamps outside the window, and no ambient starlight or glow from the moon penetrated the black outline of trees. They were on the rural route back home.

Home.

Was it, though?

"Hey, big brother," Arden said as he stirred.

"Shit," he whispered.

Harry had an indelible memory of overdoing it on tequila shots at a music festival as an undergrad. After barfing down his legs and filling his Birkenstocks with vomit, he'd blacked out in a stranger's bathroom at a later off-campus after-party. He'd lost the entire subsequent day, waking up after dusk, still mildly drunk. The hangover lasted another two days, and he never touched tequila again.

This? This felt worse.

"Anxiety attack." He slicked sweat-damp hair off his forehead.

"Mm-hmm," Arden murmured.

His mind had taken him somewhere his body didn't want to go. He'd been falling with his feet on the ground. Drowning in no water.

Anxiety was a canny liar. When it whispered to you

in a voice that sounded exactly like your own, it was impossible to reject the things it told you.

His jeans were damp in the front. "God. Did I piss myself?"

Arden shook her head. "That's your beer."

Harry tipped his head all the way back. "Sorry you had to see that."

Arden made a dismissive sound and reached over to squeeze his knee. "Don't ever apologize to me. I'm just sad I didn't get to see you eat that horrifying burger."

Harry's smile was weak. "How'd you get me into the truck?"

"I've been working out."

He rolled his head sideways against the headrest to pin her with a look.

"I had some help from Duncan and Colby," she said.

"Where's Duncan now?"

"I assume he went back to flirting with the girl running the barbecue truck. He said he'd get a ride home."

"How'd you explain this to Colby?"

"I told him you really hated his family's place, and you were faking it so I'd take you home," she said, dryly.

"Christ, Arden."

Gentler, she said, "I told him the truth. You have anxiety attacks, and the blood was a trigger. I hope that's okay."

"Yeah. Okay." He closed his eyes and let the motion of the truck rock him. "You give him your number yet?"

Her laugh was a whipcrack in the darkness. "Jesus, Harry. You really want me to flirt with a guy over your passed-out ass?"

"I'm willing to take one for the team. Did you?"

"No. He still didn't ask."

Harry's mouth felt like it was packed with a moldy dishrag. "Did I throw up?"

"No. You kept saying a name, though. Cora."

"Cora." He made himself say her name. "Cora Woodward. Cora Renee Woodward."

"She's the one you lost."

"Yeah."

"You know you're not to blame for that, Harry. You *know.*"

"Doesn't matter."

For a while, the only sound was the rumble of the road and the gentle, rhythmic tinkling of the keychain hanging from the ignition.

"What happened with the guy who cut himself?" he asked.

A long pause. Arden sniffed. "You won't believe me if I tell you."

"Christ, so much blood."

"Yes," she said.

"I froze."

"It's okay."

"Tell me."

Arden was quiet for a few moments before she answered. "I think he barely missed an artery in his wrist."

"Shit," Harry breathed.

A long pause. "Harry."

"There's more?"

She nodded. Her lips were pressed together, tight. "The knife slipped—as he was trying to cut his fucking burger in half."

After a beat, he said, "No shit?"

"I wouldn't joke about this."

Harry began to laugh. At first, it was a low chuckle,

but soon, he was laughing so hard he was light-headed, desperately trying to suck in enough air, trying not to hyperventilate.

He couldn't stop. He laughed and laughed.

He didn't realize he'd begun to sob until Arden touched his shoulder in the darkness. He folded forward, cradling his head in his hands.

PART TWO

CHAPTER FOURTEEN

Rowan

December in the vineyard was a stippled canvas of more browns and grays than any human artist could conceive of. Homes across the countryside burned hearty fires in their hearths, and the air smelled like warmth, though the sting of the wind told otherwise. A bank of cold mist hung over the land, pearlescent and still in the morning sun.

Earlier in the month, Rowan had moved in to the refurbished gardener's cottage on the hill next to the greenhouse. It had smooth knotty pine floors and walls painted the same gentle gray of Harrison's eyes. The tiny bedroom had a picture window overlooking one of the vineyard blocks, which let in the lemony sunshine of mid-morning. When she moved in, the first thing she did was arrange her little collection of succulents on the deep sill. She fantasized about growing herbs in the summer, and drying bundles for soapmaking on hooks from the exposed wooden beam in the living area. The place wasn't perfect—the plumbing thumped in the walls like a kicking mule, and the whole space was heated exclusively with a woodstove she hadn't quite mastered yet—but for a little while, it was hers.

She felt like an oversized child in a playhouse,

pretending her life was something it wasn't. This place wasn't anything more than a temporary stopover. She couldn't lose sight of that.

Rowan had been in the vineyard since daybreak. She pulled a knit cap down over her cold-reddened ears, and her exhale made a visible puff in the chilly air. Earlier, she'd delegated responsibilities to her small crew—six of them were to begin hand pruning the Chardonnay and Chambourcin blocks, while she and four others worked in the diseased section of Cabernet Franc. Nearly eight hundred overgrown grapevines needed to be pruned away from the trellis catch wires so they could be ripped from the earth. It would take days.

Today's work was the kind she usually loved—work that would leave her physically spent and mentally charged. But her mood was as shriveled as the landscape around her. She hadn't been eating well, and most nights she was too cold to fall into a comfortable sleep. On the table in her little kitchenette, her laptop sat untouched and unopened for weeks. She told herself it was because she'd been spending long days in the vineyard, and she was too tired to deal with the stats. But that was a lie.

Truth was, she had plenty of mental bandwidth to write in the evenings, but she was burning it all on Harrison Brady.

Her manuscript was the physical embodiment of her life's goals. And now that she'd begun falling for the charm of this place and the family who owned it, publication and a postdoc also represented a very necessary escape hatch. A built-in *out*.

Maybe she was stalling. Maybe she *wanted* to stay.

Weeks ago at the Everetts' festival, Harrison had planted a disruptive little seed deep inside her, leaving her incapable of thinking of much else for any functional length of time. *"You're talking about sensation,"* he'd said. *"I'm talking about emotion."*

He'd kept his distance since then. Orbiting her like a satellite. No longer stopping in the vineyard to chat or give her a wildflower during his morning jogs.

It sucked.

The monotony of the first hour's work put her into a trancelike state, and the morning mist made her sentimental for Grandma Edie. Rowan knew the science of this terrestrial fog's formation was different than the ocean mists Edie had called *cloud tide,* but she still found comfort in its presence. Some ephemeral familiarity.

This land was so different from where she'd grown up—a place eternally salt-sprayed and wind-whipped by the Atlantic, as harsh as an environment could be for any plant that wasn't sea oats or bayberry. Her earliest memories were of Edie in the little garden behind the ugly yellow house they'd shared with Rowan's mother. With patience, wisdom, and sheer perseverance, Edie had crafted a beautiful oasis.

Rowan could close her eyes and remember the confectionery-sweet scents of creamy cape jasmine and mock orange blossoms. Edie taught her how to prune her beloved fuchsia rugosa roses, and how to make tea with the rose hips that swelled after the blooms were spent. She nourished the garden with homemade compost tea, and Rowan learned the hard way that *that* tea wasn't the kind meant to be sipped by humans. Edie embraced the inhospitable environment and surrendered to the ecology of the land rather than trying to change it. It had been a very early and very lasting lesson for Rowan, and every day it informed the decisions she made in rehabilitating the Brady property.

Grandma Edie had been a scholar of nature. A scientist without the title, an academic sans academia.

Much of Edie's knowledge was also peppered with bits of folklore and superstition. Planting peppers should never be done while angry, otherwise they'd grow too spicy to eat. The bees were always to be greeted with a verbal *hello,* and make sure you're polite, mind. Don't forget to apologize to the herbs as you snip them so they grow back lush. And Rowan was *never* to harvest cucumbers during her monthly cycle. Back then, Rowan hadn't known what a monthly cycle *was,* but as an adult, she'd never forgotten Edie's nuggets of wisdom.

That first spring after Edie died, twelve-year-old Rowan watched helplessly as even the hardiest plants in the garden shriveled from sea spray and neglect. Her mother barely had interest in *her,* much less in helping with Edie's plants. By that autumn, much of the garden had given over to sandy, barren soil that turned to mud when it rained.

Like the garden, Rowan withered. Sybil's disinterest in her was brought into even sharper focus without Edie around to dilute and deflect it. Rather than lingering outdoors as she always had, Rowan holed up in Edie's old bedroom, reading her planting journals and mildewed gardening magazines, and watching reruns of the old *Miss Marple* mystery show she'd loved.

When Rowan finally tried tinkering in the garden the subsequent spring, Edie's rugosa roses were the only thing she managed to bring back from the brink. But it hadn't been by any skill on her part. It had been the intrinsic stubbornness of the plants themselves. A defiant, prickly insistence on *life.*

Every day, she'd worn Edie's floppy old hat. The

hat had a faint white ring around the khaki rim, as salt-stained as everything else was. That salt, though—it wasn't salt from the ocean. It was salt from the sweat of Edie's labor in the little garden. Proof she'd existed, pushed herself hard, and used her body well.

Rowan became like those rugosa roses. Resilient and determined to thrive, despite the shitty circumstances of where her roots had been put down. Plants became an obsession and an escape. By the time she turned fourteen, she'd read every botany and horticulture text in the local library. In tenth grade, she began soliciting pamphlets from biology programs at major universities in all the adjacent inland states. Green places. Places not tainted by salt and sadness.

The summer after eleventh grade, Rowan applied for scholarships at the schools with the best botany programs. She sailed over every academic goal she set for herself with grace and grit, relentless in her pursuit of knowledge, enrichment, discovery.

During Rowan's second year of college, Sybil sold the crumbling little house on the coast to a developer who'd wanted the land. She hadn't even told Rowan until months after the place had been razed. But in a rare act of thoughtfulness, Sybil had taken a picture of Edie's rugosa roses in full fuchsia bloom before the place was turned to rubble, and mailed it to her.

There hadn't been a return address on the envelope.

Rowan rubbed her nose hard and told herself the stinging weight behind her eyes was from the icy air.

"Sorry I'm late, boss," Harrison said behind her.

She'd been squatting to get at low vines, and she shot to her feet. A vine snagged her knit hat off her head as she stood. "Christ, Harrison," she snapped.

"Sorry." He snugged work gloves down between his fingers.

Like bread crumbs, the trail of cuttings must have led him right to her. His approach had been silent, a remarkable feat considering the brittle brown vegetation littering the ground.

He kept a conspicuous distance from her. *"Probably best if you don't touch me again,"* she'd said to him the night of the festival at Three Birds. Those had been the last words she'd said to him, until now.

"I'm not your boss." She extricated her hat from the brittle vine, impatiently tugging it back onto her head. "And you're not an employee here. *And* stop apologizing. I'm sure you have something better to do right now."

"Fresh air and hard work are what I need. This is the only place I want to be." His tone sounded unconvincing.

"I'm sorry for you, then. I'd much rather be somewhere warm."

That was a lie.

He looked away and squinted down the row. "Nate sent me out here, if that makes you feel any better."

"Oh." It didn't make her feel any better. "*Sent* you?"

"You may not be my boss, but technically, he is."

"That's not true either."

A stale laugh made his breath plume visibly in front of him, and he shook his head. "Fine. It's your turn to babysit me today. I'm pretty sure that's what this really is."

Rowan frowned and looked down. One of her bootlaces was loose. "Bring any tools with you?"

He lifted his coat back from his hip to reveal a leather belt holster with a pair of shiny new pruners clipped into it. "Ready to work," he said.

Rowan gave in, using an unfinished vine as a crash course for him. It looked like a giant tumbleweed suspended in midair. "These woody vines? We call them canes. The thinner canes need to be cut away from the catch wires. All we want left is the two thick, horizontal branches along the bottom wire here. They're called cordons." She reached in and pushed aside some of the twisted mess to reveal the thick T-shaped branch underneath.

"What happens after this?"

"The crew comes through with a chain and a tractor and rips them out of the ground. Then everything gets burned."

"Harsh."

"It's a necessity. This part of the vineyard needs a hard reset, if we're going to build something healthy."

"Seems to be a theme around here."

Rowan sidestepped and gestured to the vine beside them. "Daylight's burning. You take this one."

Within the hour, together they'd done thirty vines, and she was sweaty under her clothing, even though the air was chilly enough to vaporize her breath. She noticed how Harrison caught his bottom lip in his teeth when he concentrated, and how the gloves pulled tight across his knuckles as he squeezed the pruners. She noticed the little grunt he made each time he stood up from trimming low canes, and how he hummed while he worked.

She noticed how good it felt having him there, sharing labor. Sharing space.

They came together at the end of the row. From where they stood, they had a view of Lake Vesper, a long lake bordered by a forest of hemlock, white pine, and sugar maple. The shoreline was sparsely dotted with a few docks and cabins. A crescent of ice and mist covered the shallows nearest them, and a solitary blue heron glided low over the water at the deeper end.

"How many left?" Harrison meshed his fingers together and bent them backward to stretch.

Rowan chuckled and removed her hat. Damp curls clung to her forehead and cheekbones, and the air felt like heaven on her heated skin. "About seven hundred."

"Oh, fuck." He hung his head.

"I told you, you don't have to help."

"I know I don't."

"Go back. Get a hot shower and some of Duncan's shitty coffee. You can blame it on me. Tell Nate I fired you for insubordination."

"Do you not *want* me out here, Rowan?"

"I do want you. Out here." She wanted him other places, too.

He paused. Then, he gestured to her forehead. "You're steaming."

She drew off a glove and swept back clammy flyaways. "This feels like the first time I've been warm in weeks."

Harrison frowned. "What?"

Rowan waved a dismissive hand. "I haven't really gotten the hang of banking coals in the woodstove yet. Hot water in the shower doesn't last very long either."

His frown deepened and he shuffled closer to her. "Duncan should do something about that."

"It's fine. Let's take a break."

Leaves crunched under them as they sat down. Rowan hugged her knees to her chest. Harrison stretched his legs, crossed his ankles, and leaned back on his hands, long and lean as a marsh reed.

"The flannel suits you, by the way," she said after

a few minutes of quiet. "I'm trying to imagine you in scrubs. Do they make flannel scrubs?"

He gave her an odd look, his mouth twitching. "Ah, they do. They call them pajamas."

They laughed together.

"What are you really doing here, Harrison?"

"Why won't you call me Harry?"

"I'm the only one allowed to answer questions with a question. Answer me."

"I'm helping you in the vineyard."

"Why are you *here,* though?"

"You've asked me this before, remember?" he said.

"I know. I got a bullshit answer then, and you're trying to give me another one now."

He sat up straight and looked out over the lake. For a while, he fiddled with the straps on his gloves. Then, with a long exhale, he deflated.

"Bottled water," he finally said.

Rowan waited.

When he continued, his tone sounded bleak, the words practiced and measured. Like he'd recited them dozens of times. "I lost a patient in April." He wrung his hands. "Ah, she wasn't actually *my* patient. It's a long story. Changed my perspective on a lot of things. I'd only been practicing a year. I have my medical license, but I'm not board certified yet. Did you know doctors have to take a qualification exam before the *actual* certifying board exam? Failed that in June. Results didn't come until September, but I knew I was bombing, even as I was taking it."

Even with the heavy gloves on, Rowan saw a tremor in his hands.

"After that exam, I'd been holed up at home for about

three weeks, and I'd run out of food. At the grocery, I'd been standing in the bottled water aisle so long a manager came over to ask if I needed help. Like he was some kind of fucking bottled water sommelier. I think I was scaring other shoppers, the unwashed skinny guy, standing there, staring at water. Pretty sure I had flannel pajama pants on, you'd have loved it." A long pause, a sad smile. "I had three cartons of ice cream in the cart, must've had them in there sideways, because they'd started melting into a puddle on the floor."

The tremble in his hands turned into a full-body shudder. Rowan reached out to lay a hand on his knee. He glanced down at it, didn't touch her back. He dragged his bottom lip through his teeth and picked up a pebble to chuck it down the hill.

"Why do so many brands of bottled water exist? Why do we need that many options?" He threw another pebble, harder this time. "People all over the world have to drink water that might be full of disease, or full of lead. And we're regularly paying three goddamned dollars for sixteen ounces of it, just because the plastic bottle is square with pretty flowers on it."

A muscle ticked in his jaw.

"I was so fucking mad about it. The frivolity of—everything. I left. Left the full cart there with the manager, all of it. Just—walked away."

Rowan stayed silent, leaving her hand on his knee.

"As soon as Ma and Dad bought this place, they started working on me to come stay here. For months, they called me every other day. When Ma threatened to send Nate and Duncan after me, I caved. Few days after I arrived, Ma was pissed I wasn't eating her dinners. Took it as a personal attack, said I was wasting away. So, she and Dad took me to that fancy pasta place in

Linden. While we waited on a table, I sat at the bar and listened to two women talk about how they had to 'unfollow' someone's *dog* on Instagram, whatever the fuck that means. I actually looked around for a camera, to see if I was on a prank show. I couldn't believe it was something adults would waste energy getting upset about."

He took off his gloves and popped his knuckles in agitation.

"Later in the evening, the dickhead at the table beside us ripped into the waiter, really gave her absolute hell, because his steak was cooked *medium* instead of medium rare, and there wasn't enough shredded cheese on his fucking side salad."

Harrison picked up a twig and snapped it into tiny pieces. Then another, and another, throwing the fragments into the dirt before them.

"So much of what we think is important is—pointless." His voice cracked on the final word.

They were quiet for a long time while he mutilated more twigs.

"Well," Rowan began, her tone light, "some of those celebrity dogs on social media are notoriously narcissistic. I get tired of their shit too, but they're not *nearly* as insufferable as the cats are."

Harrison's fingers froze on a stick, midsnap.

She continued, "And honestly, that guy at the restaurant was an ass for thinking he could get a decent steak at a pasta place. It's his own fault."

Little pieces of wood fell from Harrison's hands like melancholy confetti. He'd gone unnaturally still, disbelief settling on his features. Rowan went cold inside and slid her hand off his leg, mentally kicking herself for being too glib, too insensitive. He slowly turned his head to look at her with pure, baffled amusement.

His laugh was abrupt. The sound of it echoed down the valley below, rich and warm and delicious as mulled wine. A startled flock of sparrows exploded from the vineyard behind them. Rowan cautiously smiled back.

Laughter faded, and his eyes tracked straight to her mouth. Lingered.

The dials on her senses cranked all the way up. Against the drab winter landscape, Harrison seemed more immediate, more alive than reality itself. He was close enough she smelled fresh coffee and caramel on his breath, and his clothes were infused with the cold, mineral bite of winter air. Beneath the edges of his wool hat, the upturned tips of his hair peeked out behind his ears.

He dampened his bottom lip with the tip of his tongue. It was impossible to mistake what she saw on his face in that moment. If she didn't move, Harrison Brady was going to kiss the hell out of her, and she'd kiss him back.

Desperate longing and desperate anxiety clashed in her mind, and she remembered Temperance's words.

"Casual and uncomplicated. I promise you, Harry is neither of those things."

Casual and uncomplicated was all Rowan was capable of.

She gave him another weak smile and hopped to her feet. He stood too, and his hands twitched toward her before he neatly tucked them with his gloves into the pockets of his coat.

"A few months ago, I thought I'd never laugh again," he said.

"Well." She fidgeted with her hat. "I'm hilarious."

"You're a lot of things," he said. The intimacy in the way he said the words made goose bumps rise under her layers of clothing.

"Right now, I'm a lot behind on this vineyard." She stepped around him to get back to work.

"Hey," he said behind her.

Rowan turned.

"Thanks for letting me help," he said. "It's hard, watching everyone play the 'what should we do with Harry today' game."

"The babysitting comment, earlier. That's what you meant."

He nodded.

"You're always welcome out here. With me." The words came too quick. Too raw. She rubbed her nose. "I mean, I can always find something for you to do. If you want."

"Let me know whenever you need me," he said. "Ah, you have some—some stuff, in your hair. Plant stuff." He gestured toward his right temple.

"It's more surprising when I *don't* have plant stuff up there." Rowan pulled off a glove and reached to her left temple, mirroring where he pointed.

He chuckled. "Other side."

She nudged around with her fingers at her right temple. Still nothing.

Harrison gestured to his own head again. "Back, a bit farther."

Rowan still didn't feel anything. "Help?" Her mouth pressed into an exasperated line.

He looked down at his feet. Then, back up. His squinted eyes were silvery in the white winter sun. "Said I wouldn't touch you, remember?"

"Oh, for goodness' sake." She snatched off her other glove and pushed them into her coat with her hat. She worked impatient fingers through her crown until she found a long tendril of woody vine, no wider than a piece of yarn. It snagged when she tugged, pulling a thick loop of hair from one of her braids. The more she fiddled with it, the more tangled it became.

Rowan dropped her arms to her sides.

Harrison moved in. Loomed. Raised both eyebrows. Waited.

"Please," she grumbled to his chin.

"Do you"—a grin tugged at his lips—"need me to touch you, Rowan?"

"You're an ass." She tried yanking her cap back on, but the knit snagged on the twig, and she couldn't pull it down without painfully pulling hair. A big, frustrated breath blew her cheeks out.

His head listed gently to the side while he watched her flail.

"Please get it for me." Pause. "You can—touch me."

He made a low sound of affirmation in his throat and reached up to extract the tendril a few hairs at a time. God, he smelled good. She tried to keep her breathing shallow, but what she really wanted to do was snort him like a drug.

"There we go." He twirled the wisp of vine. Then, he twisted it into a small circlet and slipped it onto his pinkie finger. "Think I'll keep this."

He brushed dirt and leaves from the seat of his jeans as he returned to the vineyard. Rowan's limbs felt hot and weightless as she watched him walk away.

"You're talking about sensation. I'm talking about emotion."

He'd been right. It was both.

CHAPTER FIFTEEN

Harry

Most of February had been unseasonably warm and wet, and it made Harry's life hell.

It had already rained more here in the valley than it had his entire five years in Los Angeles. He wished the temperatures would stay low enough for snow. At least then he wouldn't have to hear the incessant babble of it on his roof.

He peered out the sliding door that overlooked his small deck. The aesthetic was post-apocalyptic—gray-and-brown terrain, bruise-blue sky. The Chardonnay block closest to the carriage house had been pruned hard the month before, and now the trellises looked like rows of skeletal soldiers awaiting orders to advance.

It didn't help that most of the family had left for the weekend. Ma and Dad had gone to the mountains with Nate and Maren for last-minute wedding preparations for Patrick and Mercy's wedding next month. Duncan was out with a woman he'd met at the Everetts' party in the fall.

Urgent pounding on his front door spiked his blood pressure. When he answered, Rowan stood there, like he'd conjured her out of sheer longing. Behind her, thick clouds scudded across the leaden sky, and everything was damp with a mist too fine to be called rain. A halo of fuzzy curls shimmered around her face, thousands of tiny droplets of water caught in the fiery filaments. The chill smudged ruddy color into her cheeks and the tip of her nose.

She was breathless, pressing a hand to her side. "You know that saying about March—in like a lion and out like a lamb?"

Harry's lungs seized. He tasted the storm in the air, the enormous energy of it. The world was restless with the rising wind.

"Apparently, lambs come in February," she said.

"What the hell are you talking about?"

"One of the ewes was two for the price of one. Baby sheep. Coming now."

"How is that possible?"

Rowan straightened, cocked a hip, and withered him with an impatient look. "Well, when a mommy sheep and a daddy sheep love each other very much—"

"Damn it, you know what I mean. How did we get one that was pregnant?"

Pregnant.

Jesus, he felt light-headed just saying the word.

Rowan threw her hands up. "Love—finds a way?"

"You're an asshole."

"Harrison, she's laboring in the barn right now, and I'm freaking out. I was grafting vines in the greenhouse and I heard her bleating from all the way up there."

Laboring.

"No. Fuck, no." His jaw locked shut. He shook his head.

"Please." Rowan grabbed his wrist and tugged. He yanked out of her grasp hard enough she stumbled backward. Shame instantly seared his face.

She righted herself quickly and blasted him with a glare. "You told me to let you know when I needed you, remember?"

Another glance at the sky. "This isn't exactly what I had in mind."

Rowan blinked the wet out of her eyes. "You don't get to choose when someone needs you."

She was right. But he was fucking weak. "I'm not a veterinarian."

"If you can't help the ewe"—she visibly faltered, her body somehow stiffening even as her expression softened—"be there for *me*."

That vulnerability had cost her something, just now. It was plain on her face. And fuck it all, Harry had been aching to finally see it from her. For *months*.

But Christ, this couldn't be worse. An impending birth, a storm bearing down as sunset approached. Clouds moved faster behind Rowan, pushed across the horizon by a giant, invisible hand. His lungs began to burn, his lips began to tingle. He was going to lose his shit and have a full-on anxiety attack, right there in front of her. Harry curled his bare toes into the wood floor and willed himself to stay put until she went away on her own.

Don't throw up.

Harry tore his attention away from the sky. Forced himself to look at her. His heart and stomach did a synchronized dive to the ground. Genuine anguish overtook her features, and it felt like watching glass break in slow motion.

Harry recognized the instant she regained composure. Her face became a resolute mask. "Fine. I'll do it myself."

She turned and sprinted away.

* * *

THE ONLY THING more potent than his fear was his self-loathing.

Harry pressed his forehead and knuckles into the closed door. Slammed his palms against it. He thrust away and screamed at the wall, shaking with rage at his fucking fragility.

He closed his eyes and sucked in a few breaths through his nose, and texted Duncan:

> Get home. Rowan needs help, lamb
> being born

Duncan responded almost immediately, no words, only a photo of his dinner plate. A half-eaten baked potato. Untouched broccoli. And unmistakably, in the center of the plate, a lamb chop. A text followed:

> Well, this is awkward

Harry replied:

> I'm not fucking around

From Duncan, without hesitation:

> I'm not either. It's delicious. I'll be
> home in a few hours. Might have a
> guest

Harry grunted in disgust and lobbed the phone onto the kitchen counter. Paced. His phone chimed that a new message had arrived. Duncan again:

> Be what she needs

The words swam on the pixelated screen as Harry's eyes flooded with angry, impotent tears. Another text from Duncan arrived, rapid-fire:

> My date just ripped me for texting at dinner. Don't let my sacrifice be in vain, dick

Harry sniffed hard, blinked hard, swallowed hard. He wanted to shatter the glass of the phone against the granite countertop.

Instead, he ran to his room to get dressed before he could chickenshit out.

* * *

THE MIST MADE the grass slippery. Harry slid sideways as he ran, splaying his arms to keep from face-planting. When he reached the barn, he nearly lost an unlaced boot to the sucking mud.

Rowan didn't hear him approach.

She had her back to the open double doors, trying to separate the flock from the laboring ewe with a make-shift shepherd's crook: a long, narrow piece of ply-wood. She held it horizontally and crept toward them, clustering them in a corner. But rather than allowing themselves to be guided toward the pens she was try-ing to get them into, the sheep surged around her at the last second, scattering and bleating in irritation.

"Fuck!" Rowan yelled, kicking a puff of straw into the air.

A single sheep answered her with a defiant *meh*.

The donkey lowered her blocky head over her stall's fence to watch, puffing out her nostrils. Rowan had named her Asparagus. *"Emphasis on the 'ass,' "* she'd said on the day the rescue had delivered her, eyes twinkling. *"Get it?"*

"I'm here," Harry said.

Rowan yelped and pivoted with the plywood against her chest like a shield.

"Damn it." She sagged in on herself. "You're always sneaking up on me."

Harry braced for her to give him hell for his earlier hesitation. Instead, the plywood clattered to the ground, and she was in his arms in seconds. He buried his face in her hair as she clung to him, twisting her fists in the thick fabric of his sweater. For several minutes, they stood there, locked together in the eerie half-light of the clouded sunset through the open barn doors. As she balanced her breathing, her belly rose and fell against his.

God, she felt good.

The air was heavy with the scent of rain and the sweet, nutty fragrance of timothy hay. An undertone of animal musk and musty old timber filled Harry with some ancient, inexplicable sense of comfort.

Together, he and Rowan managed to sequester the flock into pens, while Asparagus watched, blinking big, curious with lashes like peacock feathers. Once the laboring mother wasn't crowded by the other sheep, she visibly relaxed, vocalizing less, occasionally lying down. Harry sat with Rowan on the packed dirt floor, backs against prickly hay bales.

"Thank you," Rowan said.

"Don't thank me. I'm a dick."

"You're not. It's okay. You came."

Across the barn, the ewe panted, watching them with her odd, wide-set gaze. When her barrel-like belly tightened with a contraction, she'd give a deep, gurgling bleat and raise her back leg, or scrabble to her feet for a bit before lying down again. The other sheep in the barn were restless too, intermittently peeking their weird faces out through the wooden slats of the stalls. Asparagus made occasional whistly, inquisitive donkey noises, and her ears were laid flat in apparent concern for her ovine friend.

"I bet this isn't on the list of options for the 'what should we do with Harrison today' game." Rowan's head was tipped back, her eyes closed. Her mouth curved in a little smile. Harry wanted to kiss the sleek column of her neck, bury his nose at the pulse point under her jaw.

"Nope. It's definitely on the lesser-known 'how can we fuck with Harry today' list, though."

Her low laugh was like a shot of sunshine straight into his veins.

After an hour, Rowan fell asleep and slid bonelessly into him, her full weight bearing him sideways. He had to lean into her to keep her upright. Her hair smelled floral and minty, with an undertone of cold rain. She fell so deep into sleep that her ankles collapsed inward and flopped her booted feet together. She snored softly.

The last slash of light disappeared from the barn's open doorway when the sun went fully down. A shuddering growl of thunder raised the hairs on the back of his neck like heat drawing infection from a wound. With each rumble, he heard Cora Woodward's panicked breaths in the confines of the ambulance, blood leaving her body faster than modern medicine could manage.

A peal of thunder cracked the sky above, and he startled so hard he jostled Rowan off his shoulder. She sat up abruptly and rubbed her eyes.

"I'm sorry," she said. "I haven't been sleeping well."

"Don't apologize. My shoulder is yours if you need it."

Harry wanted to give her more than just his shoulder. *Take it all,* he wanted to say. *It's yours.*

She did look tired. The usual bourbon gold of her eyes seemed as drab as the hay bales they leaned against. Her lashes cast shadows on her cheeks, emphasizing the smudgy discoloration of fatigue underneath. This Rowan was a pale version of the live-wire woman he knew.

"You okay?" he asked. "And I swear, if you make a doctor-patient wisecrack—"

"I got a 'revise and resubmit' request from the journal I most wanted—want—to publish in," she said quickly. Harry knew it was the next step toward achieving the rigorous goals she'd set for herself. But her voice sounded toneless and flat. "They liked my manuscript, but it still needs improvement."

"That's still good, though. Right?"

"It's good. None of this feels like I thought it would, that's all. I thought I'd be—more excited, finally being this close."

Before Harry had time to prompt her for more details, the ewe abruptly stood and walked stiff-legged around the edge of the pen, vocalizing loudly. Her lamb's little face was visible now, a pink nose nestled between two tiny hooves. After a few stumbly steps, the ewe lowered herself back to the hay with a grunt.

Rowan shook off her fatigue and crawled to the sheep. She made soothing sounds, settling her hands on the big contracting belly. Harry stood to switch on more of the weak barn lights, and paced.

At every birth Harry had attended, the craft and competence of the labor and delivery nurses were always inspiring. Tonight, Rowan played that role for this smelly, eerie-eyed mother-to-be. She was patience and grace in grass-stained jeans, despite being covered in muck and clinging strands of hay. Her hair had worked loose from its ponytail and slid into her face. She impatiently blew curls out of her eyes.

Harry stopped pacing and bent behind her. Quietly, gently, he took hold of Rowan's fallen ponytail, freeing it from the elastic. The curls shone like rosewood in the yellow light of the old bulbs. He withdrew several strands of straw, then gathered her hair with two slow sweeps of his hands, doing his best to re-create the kind of bun she favored. The end result wasn't as artful as her own, but it would do. He sank into a squat beside her and tucked a few wayward tendrils behind her ears, and let his fingertip linger along her jawline.

"Thank you," she murmured.

Another bolt of thunder rocked the barn, and the sky shuddered open in release. Rain pelted the ground in thick, unrelenting sheets. Harry straightened, swiped his hands over his face, and sucked in a shivering breath through his nose.

The downpour battered the metal roof of the barn the same way it had hit the roof of Cora's ambulance. The herald of all his nightmares, that white-noise scream of the rain.

Harry turned his back to Rowan. When he tried to take another breath, his lungs had locked down. He tried to swallow, a feeble attempt to make room in his airway. Couldn't do that either. He bent at the waist, hands clamped on spread knees.

Don't throw up.

A soft voice broke through the chaos. "Come back."

Harry turned. Rowan reached up a hand to him. He took it and sank down beside her. She was in complete control. Comforting the ewe, facing down her own apprehensions, soothing his fears. She was managing everything.

She *was* everything.

The ewe seemed to lose interest in the birthing process, lying on her side, chewing hay. When her water broke and the birth didn't progress further, Rowan began to fret.

With his heart in his throat, Harry let go of her hand. He set his teeth and moved behind the ewe, and gently grasped the lamb's protruding legs. To the sheep and to himself, he whispered, over and over, "We got this."

When the next contraction came, he gently pulled the lamb, and it was born in a rush. It was a tiny white thing with big triangular ears and knobby legs. Harry sat back hard on his ass, breath whooshing out of him, bewildered as the newborn. The hissing cacophony of rainfall gentled to a pattering rhythm.

Several minutes passed, and the ewe continued to chew hay, completely disregarding her baby. Rowan looked to Harry again, and frowned.

"What now?" Rowan said. The lamb quivered, covered in sticky fluids, its head weakly nudging around in the bedding hay.

"Maybe she doesn't know what to do." Harry scooted over to the baby and used his pinkie to swipe its mouth. He vigorously patted its damp little chest, then lifted it gently, moving it closer to its mother's head. When the ewe finally sniffed the baby, instinct took over, and she stood to begin nibbling the wet out of its downy coat.

Harry and Rowan collapsed back in relief, sharing a tired high five.

Together, they cleared the paddock and laid fresh bedding hay. Then they stood side by side at the old sink, washing the mess from their hands. The adrenaline-fueled high of the last hour crashed down, leaving Harry feeling weak and scattered.

"You did it, Dr. Brady," Rowan said. "You attended a patient."

He looked behind them. The lamb was already on its feet, sturdily nudging at a teat. Its tiny tail whirled like a propeller as it nursed. "It's a sheep, Rowan."

"*She* is a living creature, and she needed your help. You came through for her."

"It doesn't mean anything." Harry dried his hands on his sweater and went to the open doors of the barn to stare into the dark. The transient clouds of the storm blocked any light that would've come from the moon or stars.

Rowan moved in front of him, putting her body between his and the blackness. "It meant something to me." Belligerence sharpened her tone.

He grunted. Nothing had changed. Managing to not lose his shit while a farm animal gave birth on the floor of a barn didn't mean he was suited to practicing medicine. The only thing that had kept him grounded throughout had been Rowan's presence. She gave him space to feel his pain, while freeing him from dwelling on it.

"I'll call the vet in Linden in the morning so she can come check them both." Rowan pulled the sliding door of the barn closed behind them and stepped away.

The dim yellow lantern outside illuminated a slick

of mud. They made it three steps before Rowan's feet slipped. She twisted, trying to use Harry for balance. Instead, she knocked his legs out from under him, and they both went down hard, backs flattening in the muck.

The impact knocked all the air from his lungs. Cold suffused his ass and the backs of his thighs, and icy mud oozed into his hair and against his scalp.

Beside him, Rowan whooped with laughter.

Rolling his head to the side, he watched her attempt to stand, only to slip and fall again. This time, her legs did a cartoonish scramble before sliding sideways underneath her. Another hoot of laughter followed.

"You've lost your fucking mind," Harry said, looking back to the sky in a daze. The misty rain had transformed to wet snow. It fell toward his face in slow motion, dimly illuminated by the light on the barn.

Rowan crawled over to him and extended her hand to help him sit up.

With a playful snarl, he gathered a handful of mud and slapped it into her outstretched palm. She froze. Her eyes flashed white, going wide with surprise. A big, visible breath billowed from her open mouth. Harry squeezed her hand, making mud ooze out between their joined fingers with an audible *squish*.

Rowan's retaliation was swift. With her free hand, she flung a lump of mud straight at his chest, and it hit with a dull splat. He growled and sat up fast, bearing her backward, pinning her to the ground. Cackling with laughter, she wriggled under him and tried to stuff a handful of mud down the back of his jeans. Harry snatched her wrist before she could.

Her face was flecked and splattered with black mud. A wet streak of it crossed her chin and jaw. She was lit up like a bonfire in the darkness, breathing hard and shimmering up at him with a wide-mouthed smile.

They both panted with mirth and exertion. Their hazy exhalations dispersed together in the air between them, and time slowed.

She slowly, slowly raised a finger on her free hand and drew a smooth, deliberate swipe of mud down the bridge of his nose. Her chin quivered as she restrained a laugh. Harry's jeans had soaked through at the knees, mud oozed into his shoes, and he was fucking *cold*.

He kissed her, hard.

Rowan surged upward to meet his mouth. It was chaotic and primal, a frantic collision of lips and force and teeth and tongues. Her hand clutched at the bare skin under the hem of his sweater. Harry squeezed his eyes shut and inhaled every atom of the moment: the smell of wet earth and clean sweat, and the primitive, pristine scent of the woman kissing him back. Mud slithered down the back of his neck, sliding out of his hair.

Lust detonated through him like a bomb. He took her mouth like it was a battlefield, and Rowan answered in kind. When he pushed his thigh into the denim seam between her legs, she responded with a visceral moan. His hips thrust forward in involuntary response, seeking friction, seeking heat, seeking home.

His dick was indifferent to the cold and the filth around them, but Rowan began to shiver beneath him. Harry wrenched his mouth from hers, wincing at the bereft little sound she made. When he pulled them both to their feet, she dipped her forehead to his chest, and her strong arms twined around the back of his neck like grapevines gripping a post.

"You okay?" he said to the top of her head.

"You pulled me up so fast, I got a little dizzy."

"I'm sorry."

Rowan raised her head. This time, it was her pinning him down, though she did it with her eyes. "I'm not."

Even covered in mud and as wet as a waterbird, she was so beautiful it made his breath come short.

Water dripped from the eaves of the barn, and rivulets of runoff burbled in tiny streams through the mud all around them. Standing there with her felt like some kind of pagan baptism, and Harry never wanted to leave.

"Pulp or no pulp?" He was still breathing hard.

Rowan's teeth chattered. "What?"

"When we danced. At the Everetts' festival. You mentioned fresh-squeezed orange juice."

"Oh." She stiffened, confusion passing over her features. She nudged backward, out of his arms. "Extra pulp. I want to feel like I'm drinking an actual orange."

Harry nodded. For a few moments, they stood in silence. Snow gently eased down around them in clumps the size of postage stamps, melting as soon as they hit the ground. He didn't want her to go, but they couldn't stay here.

"Well. Thanks," she said. "For the help with the lamb. I know you were—busy."

"I'm never too busy for you." Another long stretch of silence. "We're going to have to burn these clothes."

Rowan's quick laugh turned into a grimace. "I'm not sure how I'm going to get all this mud out of my hair." She smiled a tired smile and turned to walk away. She slipped twice, catching herself with artless, balletic grace.

Back in December, she'd told him she was having trouble with her shower's hot water, and with keeping the woodstove burning for heat in the cottage. Harry shivered, imagining her crouching, filthy and cold, trying to rekindle the fire alone in the dark. Something in him broke loose.

"Hey," he said.

Rowan turned, brushing her cheek with the back of her hand. It smeared more fresh mud onto her face than it cleared away.

"My shower has plenty of hot water for both of us. I mean, ah—not at the same time."

She lifted her chin and tipped her head to the side, waiting for him to continue.

He talked fast. "I hate the thought of you being cold. Stay at my place tonight."

Rowan's exhale made a little white wisp in the air. Harry extended a muddy hand. When she hesitated to take it, he stopped breathing.

Then, she did.

"I'll take the couch," he said.

CHAPTER SIXTEEN

Rowan

It was the longest shower Rowan had taken since she'd moved there in December. At first, it hurt her icy skin, but by the time the water ran clear, she wanted to live forever in the steamy spray. The volume of mud in her hair necessitated shampooing three times, and thank god she'd taken Harry up on the offer. The hot water at the cottage wouldn't have lasted beyond the first wash. She imagined Harrison waiting out there in his kitchen— sitting on the floor to minimize tracking mud, shivering and soaked. Her heart pinged, and she didn't linger, as much as she wanted to.

After Harrison's own shower, he'd put their clothes together into a little washing machine in the nook off the kitchen. Their clothing tumbled around together, and the domestic ordinariness of it felt lovely and awkward all at once. The last person to wash her clothes for her had been Edie. She'd been twelve.

Now she was in Harrison's bedroom, wearing one of his plain white T-shirts and a pair of his boxers— loose in the waist, snug over her butt. For the first time in months, every centimeter of her body felt blissfully warm. On the other side of the closed bedroom door, Harrison prepared for sleep on the couch, which he'd surely need to bend his knees to fit onto. Before her shower, he told her he'd wait for the washer to finish so he could make sure the clothes were dry by morning. He'd also upended her boots over a heating vent on the floor, in the hopes they'd be dry enough to knock the caked mud loose when she needed to wear them at dawn.

It smelled like him there. A pure distillation of his breath and his skin, rich and earthy and male. She looped the neckline of his shirt up over her nose, inhaling until her head spun. A mystery had been solved tonight—the origin of his juniper-sweet scent revealed. It was his shampoo. Her own hair and skin smelled like it now.

Rowan sat on the edge of his bed, curling and uncurling her toes. On top of his dresser, she saw a small stack of letters addressed to him in loopy, florid handwriting. No return address. Keys to his rented truck sat in a dish with some spare change and a half-empty pack of cinnamon gum. His UCLA ball cap was next to an unopened granola bar and a half-full mug of cold coffee. A dogeared National Audubon Society wildflower field guide was bookmarked with a receipt from the used bookstore in Linden.

Rowan's heart clanged in her chest. Wildflowers.

Why couldn't it have been stuff like athlete's foot cream, or used toothpicks, or a box of tissues next to a conspicuously large bottle of cheap lotion? Was it too much to ask for a smelly pile of laundry on the floor? Something, *anything* that would make Harrison Brady less undeniably appealing?

Physiologically, she was exhausted. But her brain was lit up like a power grid, all energy and light. Sheets and blankets were a tangled hump in the center of the mattress, a manifestation of Harrison's troubled sleep. She settled her hand on them. Would he sleep better with her beside him? And was he as unsettled as she was right now?

Screw it.

Rowan levered herself off the bed and pulled the bedroom door open.

Harrison stood in the middle of the high-ceilinged living room, shirtless, holding a lightweight blanket. Billowy teal surgical scrubs were slung low on his waist. The slats of his ribs were visible, but his flat belly showed outlines of the musculature that would be defined when he weighed more. He was sharp-shouldered, his arms sparely corded with lean muscle. A flat gold-dusted vee disappeared into his thin cotton pants, bracketed by pronounced hip bones. He was far thinner than a man of his height should be, like a Renaissance sculptor had run out of materials while casting his frame.

He scratched his jaw distractedly, surprise boosting his features. His hair was clean and fluffy around his face. Rowan wanted to delve into those thick waves with her fingers, gather it in fists to steer the path of his mouth against her body.

Sleep beside me, she wanted to say. *Share my space.*

"Birds," she blurted instead.

Nice.

His eyebrows pinched. "Birds?"

Cautiously, he draped the blanket over the back of the couch, like he was afraid sudden movement would send her fleeing behind the closed door again. Rowan's hair dripped in a few places, leaving opaque dots on the thin material of the T-shirt. Harrison's eyes deviated downward, straight to her breasts. He didn't try to hide it.

"There's this, uh, phenomenon observed in migratory birds." Rowan rolled the bottom hem of the shirt into her fists. "They display this, kind of—frantic nocturnal restlessness when the daylight begins to last longer in spring."

Harrison looked from her face to her wringing hands. A single dimple in his cheek punctuated his smile like an exclamation point.

Rowan went on, talking fast. "There's a German word for it. *Zugunruhe*."

"Gesundheit."

"What? Oh." Rowan looked at her feet and laughed. "I get it."

"Rowan, are you experiencing frantic nocturnal restlessness?"

Slowly, she nodded.

Suddenly, he was in front of her, close enough she could smell the mint of his toothpaste. The damp heat of his shower-warmed skin diffused through the thin material of her clothes. Desire bloomed deep in her core—she felt the throb of her heartbeat everywhere. In her ears, in her neck. Between her breasts, between her legs.

He slipped his hands into the pockets of the scrubs. When Rowan reached up to tuck a lock of damp hair back from his forehead, he didn't budge.

Share my space.

She moved in close and tentatively settled her hands on his chest, trailing the tip of her nose up the side of his throat. His Adam's apple convulsed as he swallowed.

"Rowan. What are you doing?"

With a gentleness that contrasted to the coiled tension in his posture, Harrison slid trembling hands from his pockets and cupped her jaw. He didn't kiss her. A long, deep inhale lifted his chest under her hands. For a moment, he held the breath captive, then let it out, shuddery and hot.

"I'm asking you. To touch me."

A low, determined noise rumbled in his chest as he took her mouth. The combative force of it devastated every nerve in her body. He nipped her bottom lip, sucked it into his mouth, greedy for the taste of her. Hot hands dropped away from her face and slid under her shirt. Long fingers gripped her rib cage, and he maneuvered her backward into his room.

The pads of his thumbs grazed the underside of her breasts. Rowan arched against him, urging him to take them fully into his hands. He didn't. Goose bumps prickled the length of her body as he dragged her earlobe with the edges of his teeth.

He palmed her ass, hauling her against his hips so hard she had to go up on her toes. His fingers dug in until it hurt.

She wanted him on a molecular level. It was biological and brutal and everything.

Abruptly, he disengaged, his mouth open, gasping for breath. Her face burned from the friction of his stubble. She didn't want to stop. The frenzy in his touch revealed a wildness she wanted to explore with every fiber of her being. When she reached down to the waist of his pants, he pulled her hands up and shackled her wrists against his chest. His heartbeat was a runaway locomotive.

"Slow down," he said. His hair stood out and up in every direction. His lips were swollen, parted. His beautiful eyes were glazed, shadowed under a drawn brow. Gentle and bewildered. Tormented.

She'd done that.

"We need to slow down," he said. "You're more than a quick fuck."

"Who says it has to be quick?"

He shuddered out a tortured laugh. "I think *quick* is all I'd be capable of right now."

Hands roamed the contours of her body over the borrowed clothes, pausing to run broad thumbs along the outer curves of her breasts, deliberately avoiding the sensitive tips.

"We're two consenting adults—we can just enjoy each other's bodies. It doesn't have to be anything more than this," she said.

"Rowan." Harrison's hands paused on her upper arms. His eyes captured hers and held. "It already is."

Outside, wind wailed under the eaves. Snow became sleet, peppering the windows like handfuls of sand against the glass. Rowan blinked away the rush of aching emotion his words churned inside her. She tried to deflect and redirect by lightly scoring his chest with her fingernails.

"Stop thinking, damn it, and touch me." She set the edges of her teeth against his collarbone.

He inhaled sharply, blinking at the ceiling. "When this finally happens, it's going to last. We're going to linger afterward. For hours."

"I don't need that."

"*I* do." His voice was anguished.

Rowan's heartbeat lurched. For a moment, she sagged into him, every bit of her softening. But again, she rallied, redirecting all that creeping emotional tenderness to the furious ache between her legs. What she *needed* was the heat of a hard chest against her breasts, solid hips riding hard between her thighs, and a mind-melting orgasm.

"There's more between us than just sex, Rowan." He choked on his words as she flattened her tongue against his nipple, giving it a swirling, sucking caress. "Ah, shit."

"Touch me. Let this be enough, just tonight."

Harrison's restraint disintegrated with a resolute exhale of hot breath. He released her and grabbed his disheveled bedcovers with both hands. One swift rip sent them to the floor, leaving only the fitted sheet and pillows. The mattress was a blank canvas, ready to receive their bodies. He pulled her by the wrist, easing her down.

Flat on her back, her legs fell open at the knees. Harrison settled beside her on the bed, propped on his elbow. His free arm cradled her leg against his belly, holding her open to him. He clenched his teeth so hard she heard the strain of it. His willpower was clearly on the verge of collapse, and Rowan would've given anything to watch that dam burst.

But control rebounded in his favor. By the way his fingertips burrowed into her thigh, she knew it was hard-won.

Some of the haze of lust in his eyes was banished by new clarity of purpose. Being the subject of that resolute fixation turned her on even more than the physical things he was doing to her body.

Harrison's hand slipped into the open leg of the boxers to cup her. Rowan moaned low in her throat and angled her hips upward when he glided two fingers inside her. His neck and shoulders went momentarily boneless, and he hung his head, muffling a groan into the pillow.

He recovered fast, slicking wetness up and around, beginning with a slow, bold caress to build tension. The flat of his palm bore down on her pubic bone, and his first two fingers slipped lengthwise along the drenched heat of her. He bent his head and pressed his temple against hers, breath searing her ear and her neck.

Then, friction. Dirty, delicious friction, demanding

the attention of every nerve ending in the lower half of her body.

He knew exactly the right amount of power and rhythm to keep her right on the precipice of orgasm. She squeezed her eyes shut and tipped her hips back and forth against his hand, counterpoint to the tempo he set. Whenever she came close, he would somehow know, and he'd ease off on the pressure or slow his speed—or worse, stop touching her entirely, unapologetically keeping her at the peak without letting her crash over it.

After he eased her off the edge a fourth time, Rowan groaned and hissed through her teeth, opening her eyes. Frustration warred with the delirium of arousal—she was ready to slap his hand away and get herself off when she saw the singular intensity of his focus. She'd expected to be met with his turbulent gaze locked on her own. Instead, his attention was riveted on her mouth, fixated on each change in her breathing, every nuanced shift in the pitch and urgency of the sounds she made. *That's* how he knew when to hold off. He was playing her body like a harp.

He'd been studying her, learning her. Mastering her.

Rowan was sure she was going to die tonight.

The flex and swirl and slide of his fingers brought her once again to hitching breaths and moans, but this time, he didn't back off. This time, he was going to let her have it. Her teeth snapped together, pressure and pleasure and agony ratcheting higher and higher inside her. She dug fingers into the bedsheet, tearing it loose from the edge of the mattress.

"Go," Harrison murmured against her mouth.

The orgasm blasted through her like a grenade. Shock waves of sensation radiated upward into her belly and backward into her spine. Her knees drew up, and she struggled to keep her quaking legs spread wide as his unwavering rhythm finished her off.

As she descended from orbit, her heels slid down, and her legs fell flat. Harrison's big hand was still between her legs, trapped there by the squeeze of her closed thighs. He pressed his forehead into the pillow again, breathing as hard as she was.

Silence followed. A longer silence than she'd have ever been able to bear with anyone else.

Harrison raised his head to look down at her, enthralled. "Hi."

A simple greeting, but his eyes told a richer story. *Hello, I see you,* they seemed to say. *I enjoyed your enjoyment.*

"Hi." Rowan laughed softly.

"What's funny?" He propped his head up with a fist against his temple. He withdrew his other hand from between her legs and laid it flat against her bare thigh.

"I was going to say, I'll always have to hook up with obstetricians in the future but decided that would probably be inappropriate."

His smile was wry. "You're not the first person to have made some version of that joke."

She settled a forearm over her eyes.

"You think I'm good—at that—because I'm an O.B.?"

She rolled to face him. "It doesn't require too much of an intuitive leap."

"There isn't an Orgasms 101 course in medical school, Rowan."

"Honestly, it would make a fantastic general elective at any university." She trailed a finger down the flat of his sternum. Goose bumps rose on his skin, drawing his nipples tight. "You know that was still sex, right?"

"Right. Was it enough?"

"Are you asking me if it felt good?"

He laughed softly and glanced at his hand on her thigh. His fingers were glossy with wet. "I already know the answer to that. I'm asking if it was *enough*." The words were staccato, breaking a bit on the last.

No. It *hadn't* been enough. Rowan wanted him inside her, right now. Skin sliding, sweat slicking, hips pounding, pumping, churning.

The tip of his nose drifted along her cheekbone. "You still want more, don't you?"

"Who the hell would say no, Harrison? Really?" Rowan turned her head to kiss him, but he pulled away and sat up.

He watched her, gnawing the inside of his bottom lip. Hesitating. Evaluating. Suddenly, he surged up to his knees, tucked fingers into the waistband of the flimsy boxer shorts, and dragged them down her legs. They landed somewhere on the floor.

Pushing her legs open, Harrison hunched over her like she was a treasure to excavate. He slid his fingers between her thighs again. The friction was forceful and utilitarian, and her body was already primed from the orgasm moments before. Rowan's back bowed, and she came in his hand in under a minute. Harrison sat back on his heels with a harsh exhale, and swallowed hard, pushing hair off his forehead with the back of his wrist.

"Now?" He panted. "Still want more?" His eyes gleamed, sunlight on a glacier. An impressive erection hung heavy in the crotch of his scrubs as he kneeled there in front of her. When she reached for him, his hand snapped forward like a viper to stop her.

Rowan's eyes blazed with challenge. She flexed her fingers and yanked free of his grip, levering up on her elbows.

"Yes," she said through clenched teeth, flinging curls out of her face.

"See? Now, do you understand? It's *already* not enough, and I haven't even fucked you."

"I thought you weren't interested in *fucking*?" she taunted.

Harrison answered with a warning look. "Don't."

She loved it when his cool veneer slipped a bit, but this time, something told her not to push. "No, I don't understand, damn it, and if you're trying to teach me a lesson, you're failing. And I'm enjoying it."

"There's no lesson, Rowan. I'm trying to show you how I feel, in a language you seem to prefer."

She frowned and shook her head. "When you want more, you have more sex. More orgasms."

"I get myself off whenever I want. So do you, I'm sure." He swallowed hard, sweeping a hungry gaze down her body. He moved back up the bed to sit beside her near the headboard. "That ache you feel, still wanting more? I feel it too, but for me it's about more than physiological release. We could do every sex act known to humankind, but if that is all I ever have of you, I will spend the rest of my life wanting more." He dragged a hand over his mouth. "Christ, I think I already will."

Rowan sat up too, protectively pulling his T-shirt down between her legs. "I don't know how to respond to that."

"Let me frame it as a question, then. What if you walked out of this room, and we never saw each other again?"

His question had teeth, the sharp, needling kind that left tiny bleeding wounds before a person realized they'd even been bitten. Rowan frowned.

"It's not a trick question. You got off, right? You

wanted an orgasm, you got it. Several," he said, and Rowan didn't miss the subtle, smug satisfaction in his tone. "Would this have been enough? What we did tonight? Is this really all you want from me?"

Rowan trusted science, and the idea of sex as a biological imperative. She trusted her own raw, organic power when she got naked with someone. Sex made sense. It had no messy nuance to it, no wondering who was more invested, who was feeling more feelings. It was hormones and nerve endings and physical satisfaction. Sex was exactly what it was, and nothing more.

When feelings weren't involved, it didn't matter if the other person was fucking someone else on the side, or ten someone elses.

It was simple biology, and biology didn't have feelings.

And after the orgasm, it was over.

Rowan didn't date, she didn't do afterglow, and mornings after were absolutely out of the question, no matter how good the sex had been. She didn't hold hands in public, or share popcorn at the movies, or remember birthdays, or meet parents. She had a no-tolerance policy on expectations. Harrison was trying to establish expectations. He was asking for a pear from a lemon tree. What he wanted, *needed*—she didn't have it to give.

Noah Tully had left scorched earth in his wake. Made her shallow, and she didn't care. Far less chance of anyone drowning that way.

She could walk away from what they'd begun tonight. She *had* to walk away. Even if they did this, every night, for months.

"What if I don't have any more to give *you*?" she countered.

"You think I don't know what you're doing when you

answer questions with a question like that?" His words were sharp and fast. He sighed hard through his nose, bit his teeth together, and palmed her kneecap. "*Tell* me," he urged, "tell me you feel what is happening here."

His hand was clenched hard into her muscle, hard enough her skin dimpled inward beneath his fingertips.

She looked down at the T-shirt twisted around her fists. "I don't know."

Harrison watched her for a long time through narrowed eyes. Then, he snatched his hand back from her leg, vaulted off the bed, and gathered the bedcovers. With a rippling flip of the linens, he covered her, then tossed the discarded boxer shorts to her on his way to the door.

"Let me know when you decide on an answer."

Rowan pulled blankets to her chin as the door clicked gently closed. She'd been completely outmaneuvered, but it had very little to do with sex, and everything to do with some acutely alarming emotions. She wasn't completely ignorant. The *reason* those orgasms felt so good was because Harrison Brady had given them to her.

Hell yes, she felt it.

CHAPTER SEVENTEEN

Rowan

It was still too early in the spring for the grapevines to leaf out, but their bareness had an expectant beauty, studded as they were with swelling buds. With the help of the sheep, Rowan and her crew had cleared the non-native plants in each vineyard block, and soon, they'd plant seeds of a native cover crop. It would bloom later in May, carpeting the rows with tiny purple flowers.

Compared to the terrible condition of those same fields last September, seeing the land poised for an eruption of clean new life gave Rowan the same kind of satisfaction she got from her most difficult academic work. The work she did here was arduous—challenging for her body *and* her brain—but none of it required those Ph.D. letters beside her name.

By mid-March, she'd submitted the final revised version of her manuscript to the botany journal. Her laptop hadn't been powered on since.

Rowan worked with Gianna to begin rehabilitating the extensive landscaped beds around the property. They spent hours head-to-head on their knees in the dirt each day, pulling weeds, testing soil samples, identifying early perennials as they emerged from the still-chilly ground. Robins learned to lurk close to them, snagging worms out of the freshly disturbed earth. Gia was candid and funny, and Rowan found herself looking forward to their chats in the dirt. With Gia, it never felt like small talk. It was cozy talk.

William had given her a stack of organic seed catalogues and asked her to help him plan a kitchen garden. Every night for the following few weeks, she'd curled up in a thick sweater with a hot mug of tea, losing herself in the catalogues' colorful photos and lush descriptions, dreaming of warmer days. For Will, she ordered sunset runner beans, snap peas, and black turtle beans. Brandywine tomatoes for slicing, engine-red Romas for saucing, and a cherry tomato cultivar called Pearly Pink for eating sun-warmed straight from the vine. Sugar pie pumpkins, creamy yellow and raven squash, butternuts for roasting. Japanese eggplant. Peppers, too: bells, Cubanelles, jalapeños. For herb selections, Rowan took three whole evenings to decide. Did they really need five varieties of basil? Absolutely.

Will, Harrison, and Duncan built four enormous raised vegetable beds outside the greenhouse. Rich black soil was delivered by a small dump truck, and Rowan worked alongside the Brady men, shoveling dirt and pushing wheelbarrows for hours. Her body was more toned than it had ever been. It felt good to be so strong.

The newfound strength was only physiological, though. Inside, Harrison had weakened her. But it wasn't a diminishing weakness, like with Noah. She ached to surrender to vulnerability. It was the most frightening weakness of all, because it meant trusting *herself.*

For months, Harrison had loomed in her consciousness, crowding her out of private mental spaces that had, until him, been exclusively and uncompromisingly hers alone. He was a ceaseless ocean tide bearing down on her silent shoreline, occasionally receding, periodically returning, and inevitably transforming her.

Since the night she'd spent in his bed, she'd carefully avoided him. It was shitty of her and she knew it, but she wasn't equipped to cope with the big things he made her feel. When he'd started dropping in on her again in the vineyard during his morning runs, she changed her schedule, randomizing how and when she worked, making it impossible for him to align his jogs with when he'd bump into her. Now that she lived on-site and daylight persisted longer, it became easier and easier to do.

Several times a week, she declined the Bradys' invitations to dinner, but her excuses were beginning to sound tired, even to her own ears.

This weekend would stretch her avoidance strategies to their limits. It was Mercedes and Patrick's wedding weekend in the Poconos, and Duncan had asked her to come as his date. "Just friends," he'd emphasized, and she hadn't been able to muster the heart to decline. With her overnight bag in hand, she walked down the hill to the house, wishing she was spending the weekend alone with several bottles of wine and a few bags of cheese popcorn instead.

At least Temperance would be there too. Several days after Duncan had asked Rowan along, Temperance had called to tell her she'd be there—as Harrison's date. "Just friends," T.J. had said as Duncan had, though the qualifier had hardly been necessary.

When she arrived at the Brady house for the carpool that morning, Mercedes answered the door, greeting Rowan with a familiar hug. She was a willowy brown-skinned beauty with a luminous smile and husky laugh. Rowan dropped her bag and blinked at the ceiling with her chin squashed against the shoulder-length curls of the slightly taller woman. Rowan awkwardly patted her in the middle of her back.

Mercedes wasn't a Brady quite yet, but she hugged like one.

Harrison was already there. From the foyer, she heard the low tones of his voice from deeper inside the house.

Everyone gathered in the kitchen, chatting over coffee and mimosas. Buttery sunshine slanted through the windows, gilding the new chrome fixtures and ivory marble countertops with warmth. As he always did, Harrison stood when she entered the room. He shuffled awkwardly for a moment, sticking his hands in his pockets before removing them again. It was a little dance of apprehension only she seemed to notice. Rowan gave him a quick, tight-lipped smile.

Frankie lurked half-hidden in the doorway to the den on the opposite end of the kitchen. Her camera sported a short lens as big around as a tea saucer, and Rowan caught her snapping a photo of Harrison as he stood there. Mercedes and Patrick had hired Frankie to shoot their wedding after a glowing recommendation from Temperance. T.J. had evidently made it a personal crusade to find employment for her friends with the Brady family.

Frankie snuck out of sight as Harrison sat back down. The kitchen bustled, filled with the murmur of conversation and the burble of a new pot of coffee. Temperance stood with Mercedes's sister, Courtney, at the counter, preparing sandwiches for what looked to be an army. Arden was there too, wrapping the finished sandwiches and stuffing them into brown paper bags with chips and bananas. They greeted Rowan with genuinely cheerful "heys" and warm smiles.

Duncan perched on the countertop next to the stove like an oversized child, legs dangling down. He slapped his knee as Rowan followed Mercedes into the kitchen.

"I just realized, your name is going to be Mercedes Brady," he laughed.

Mercedes arched a brow. "Why is that funny?"

"It rhymes," Rowan said.

Duncan grinned, snapped his fingers, and pointed at Rowan in acknowledgment. "This is why she's my date. She gets me."

"Maybe Patrick is going to take *my* last name," Mercedes said.

Patrick heard his name and looked up from across the kitchen. He and Nathan were identical, except Patrick sported a short, tidy beard. He sat with Mercedes's older brother, Omar, and a scowly dark-haired guy Rowan had never met. "What'd I do?" Patrick said, blinking.

The scowly guy was rangy and lean like Harrison, but he shared Gia Brady's duskier palette with his other brothers and Arden. He had an ambiguous look about him, like a character in a fantasy movie who you couldn't quite place as friend or foe until they dramatically revealed their true motivations later in the film. Raven hair was cut fashionably shaggy around his ears and long at his neck. He had an aggressive nose and heavy brows over deep-set eyes. He scowled into a mug of coffee, looking like he'd rather be on the surface of the sun than there. When he looked up—forehead deeply creased in a James Dean frown—Rowan recognized him. He was the *famous* Brady. The author, Malcolm.

Rowan felt a pang of empathy for him, as clearly uncomfortable as he was. But when he turned his head to fire a withering look of contempt at Frankie and her camera, all her tenderness dissolved. Frankie blithely carried on with her shot of the three men at the table, pointedly allowing her lens to linger in Malcolm's direction in spite of his glower. She winked at him as she disappeared back into the den, and Rowan saw his nostrils flare at the provocation.

Good for Frankie.

The only place left to sit was on a high barstool at the center island, which was littered with magazines, cookbooks, a fruit-and-cheese platter, and a mostly empty pan of gooey homemade cinnamon rolls. On top of a stack of mail, a letter caught Rowan's eye. It was addressed to Dr. Harrison Brady, written in the same flourishing cursive handwriting she'd noticed in his bedroom a few weeks ago. Strange that someone would handwrite a letter using a person's full name and professional title. This time, she noticed a Los Angeles postmark.

When she let her attention track from the letter to Harrison himself, he was looking right at her.

Rowan quickly regretted the decision to sit on the high stool, elevated above everyone else in the center of the room. In a room so packed with people, he couldn't stare at her openly without it being obvious, but she still felt his surreptitious glances every time his eyes shifted during conversation.

She only lasted a few more minutes before escalating anxiety had her heading for seclusion. "Excuse me," she said to nobody in particular, sliding off the stool to make a break for the bathroom in the hall.

As she ducked out of the kitchen, someone grabbed her by the wrist, pulling her into the den.

Frankie.

"You owe me a month of cheesesteaks," Frankie said in a loud whisper.

"What the hell?"

"Wager. Housewarming party. September."

Rowan blinked, opened her mouth to reply, then closed it again.

"It was your idea, remember?" Frankie pressed, switching her camera off, letting it hang loose against her chest. "T.J. and Harrison Brady are definitely *nothing* more than friends. That man is desperately, catastrophically into you. And you like him, too. I have never seen you so misty-eyed and maudlin." Frankie punctuated her words with pokes to Rowan's chest. "I win, you buy lunch on Cheesesteak Fridays. We'll start in May. May has five Fridays."

"Oh Jesus, Frankie. I might be gone by next month."

"Then you can get me a gift card. I'm going to get cheesesteaks so big, they'll feed me through the week." Frankie pantomimed a cheesesteak the size of a football. "I wonder if I can make a casserole with the leftovers. I think I'll buy shoes with all the money I'll save on meals."

"Fine. I'll play along. Where's your evidence?"

"Are you serious? Rowan, I've known for *months*. I saw the way he looked at you all the way back at the festival in the fall. He has absolutely lost his mind over you."

"I'm a scientist. That's called inference. It's not empirical evidence."

"There's a photo."

"A what?"

Frankie cocked a hip to the side. "You haven't seen the picture Arden posted on Instagram?"

Rowan swallowed rising dread. "You know I don't do social media. I barely remember to check email once a week."

Frankie dug her phone out of her pocket. Her thumbs

flew over the screen. She made an absentminded ticking sound with her tongue as she scrolled through Arden's images, then sidled next to Rowan, shoulder to shoulder.

It was a gallery of sorts, a sequence indicated by little dots underneath the first photo. First, a handheld shot of Arden and Frankie, followed by one of Arden and Colby, all outrageously photogenic. Next, a macro shot of powdered sugar on funnel cake. A minimalist shot of string bulbs against the black autumn sky, and an artistically hazy photo of the bonfire. As each image scrolled past, Rowan's blood pressure climbed higher in anticipation of what was coming.

Then there it was. A photo of her and Harrison dancing, centered in a blurry sea of other bodies.

Frankie looked smug. "I'm not a scientist, Rosebud. But that's about as empirical as evidence can be."

Their posture looked intimate, at ease. Their bodies were so close no light could be seen between them. Everything about the image—down to the positions of their hands—looked *right* somehow, as if they were accustomed to holding each other, exactly so. Her fingers gripped him so tight, they pulled the fabric of his shirt taut over his bicep. She remembered how soft the flipped-up curls at his nape were as they brushed her knuckles. Harrison looked down at her with an intensity so remarkable, how had she not burst into flame then and there on the dance floor?

Rowan shook her head, darting a look at Frankie, then another back toward the kitchen. "No. Nope."

"You do realize that this is what I do for a living, yeah? It's my job to capture emotions in photographs. I am a professional feelings-capturer." Frankie tapped the screen with her fingernail. "This is a picture of two humans having some serious feelings."

"I can't believe Arden posted this online."

Frankie made a dismissive sound. "She didn't identify you by name, and anyone can take and post a photo of other people in a public space." She set a hand on Rowan's shoulder, and said more gently, "I'm sure she'd take it down if you asked."

If she asked Arden to take it down, she'd call attention to it. "Shit," Rowan said.

"Let's pretend, for a moment, that this photo is a complete fluke." Frankie lowered the bright screen, shifting tactics. "Did you see his expression when you arrived this morning? He *stood up* when you came into the room. So sweet, I almost died."

"It's what he does. He was just being polite, Frances."

"You only call me Frances when you know you're wrong. Most modern men don't stand when a woman enters the room."

Temperance peeked around the corner with her tortoiseshell glasses perched on her head.

"Oh boy," Rowan said, pinching her temples.

"Am I missing intrigue?" Temperance theatrically tiptoed into the room.

Frankie gestured her over. "Most definitely."

"Why are you two in here hissing at each other like barn cats?" Temperance asked.

Frankie handed her the phone. Temperance looked down at the photo, dipped her head closer to the screen, then held the phone at arm's length, like she didn't believe what she was seeing. She looked to Rowan, and back to the phone. "The caption says, Think I met my next sister-in-law. Is this Arden's?"

Frankie bit her lip and nodded conspiratorially.

"Oh, god." Rowan covered her face with both hands.

Temperance slid on her glasses to read some of the comments. "Christ, some of these people are thirsty. This one says, FML, I thought I was going to marry him." She looked up and took off her glasses. "What does FML mean?"

"Fuck my life," Rowan said.

"Oh, honey. I don't think this is that bad—"

"No, Temperance. That's what FML means."

Frankie snatched her phone back. "Here's another one. Do I have to stop objectifying him now? And there's a nice one about you, Ro. I would kill for her hair, it says. Wait, does this person want to murder you and make a wig of your hair?"

"There's an OB-GYN joke, isn't there? Someone definitely mentioned a pelvic exam at least once," Temperance said.

"Obviously," Frankie said, scrolling with her finger. "Here's one that says—"

"Enough. Please." Rowan turned her face to the ceiling and closed her eyes.

Frankie and Temperance were quiet for a beat. Temperance said, "What's wrong?"

Rowan looked at her friend, lovely and slight. A few silvery tendrils of hair fell artfully around her face. For all that Temperance looked delicate, she had a spine of pure titanium, and she was unyielding when it came to protecting her friends. Rowan had known for months that T.J. was in an awkward position between her and Harrison, and she was terrified to upset her, or worse, let her down.

"I don't know, T.J."

"You do know, that's why your ears have gone as red as Frankie's lipstick. You like him. You like Harry."

"I don't know."

"Bullshit," Temperance said.

"I know this is weird for you," Rowan said.

Frankie slid the phone into her pocket. "Why would it be weird for her? I think we all know Harry isn't the Brady boy for Temperance, anyway."

Temperance blanched and snapped her head sideways to glare at Frankie.

"Now *I'm* the one who's confused," Rowan said.

"It's nothing." Temperance sent a warning look to Frankie. "We're not talking about me right now, anyway. If you and Harry are kindling something, don't make me your wet blanket."

"What about what you said back in the fall? About complications."

Temperance softened and sighed. "That was Mother Hen Temperance. She's tied up and gagged right now. This is her hot, single twin sister, Wedding Weekend Temperance." She gave Rowan a breezy jazz-hands wave. "We're too old and I'm too tired to try to run interference between you two. Just please, *please* don't ask me to choose sides."

For a few moments, the three women stood in silent solidarity. Frankie flicked her camera back on. "Well. I need to get back to terrorizing Kylo Ren in there."

"Who?" Temperance and Rowan said in unison.

"You know, Mr. Tall, Dark, and Sullen. I love the ones who give me the skunk eye. They're always the most fun to finally capture a candid smile from. That broody boy doesn't realize those scowls are Frankie catnip."

Temperance grimaced. "Do you know who he is?"

"You're going to end up dead in his next novel, Frances," Rowan said.

"I know exactly who he is. I'm not scared." She winked and disappeared into the kitchen.

When Temperance gave Rowan a hug and moved to leave as well, Rowan grabbed her by the arm. "His family can't know," she said. "Arden obviously suspects something. But I work for them, Temperance. I'm technically their *employee*."

Temperance kept her expression impressively neutral and nodded once. "I get it." She squeezed her hand and said, "Love you."

"Love you, too," Rowan replied, and for a moment, she was finally alone.

She left the den, still aiming for the washroom, and was immediately intercepted by Harrison.

"Oh, for fuck's sake. It's like trying to get through a haunted house in here," Rowan growled.

He guided her into a dim room across the hall. His hand was on the small of her back, fingers subtly sweeping the flare of her waist. It was a simple touch—the involuntary kind that lovers did.

Drapes were drawn across the big window. As one of the few places in the house with carpet, it seemed supernaturally quiet. Books lined the ceiling-high shelves, looming around them like silent sentinels. At first, Harrison didn't speak. They both looked at each other, then to the open archway leading to the bright foyer beyond.

She'd been avoiding him for weeks. Standing this close to him now was like getting pure oxygen after being deprived of air. Rowan felt light-headed, a strange sense of relief tangling with an undercurrent of volatile energy.

Whoever had referred to nervous jitters in the belly as "butterflies" had never been pinned in place by Harrison Brady's solemn eyes. For her, the butterflies were the size of dragons.

"You were going to hide in the bathroom," he said.

"Not fair that you know my strategy."

"I wanted to say hi." His voice was a caress.

Rowan tried to sound casual. "You could have said hi out there."

"I know. But I wanted to say hi here, instead."

"Is that the only thing you wanted, Harrison?"

He watched her mouth and leaned in, close enough she smelled his cinnamon gum. It sent a jolt of lust from her neck to her navel. Now, she knew exactly how the swell of his bottom lip fit against hers, and how impossibly smooth his tongue was.

Harrison gently twisted the tip of one of her curls between his fingers. The back of his hand lay flat between her breasts, and her heart thumped hard on the inside, rising to meet him.

"What's Cheesesteak Friday?" His tone was light.

Oh, shit. How much of that conversation had he overheard?

"Eavesdropping?" she said.

He shrugged.

She sighed and squared her shoulders. "Since college, we've been doing these trivial little contests to determine who has to buy lunch. Cheesesteaks from Robustelli's in the city."

He chuckled. "I understand the concept. That's not what I'm asking."

A flush raced up her neck, and her mouth felt full of briars. "Girl stuff."

"Okay." His smile was dubious.

Rowan's feet began to itch, and her belly burned. At any moment, someone might appear in the open archway and catch them standing there in the shadows. "We're about to spend the weekend with your whole family."

"I know."

"They can't know about us," she said.

"I thought there wasn't an *us*."

"Damn it, Harrison." Rowan fidgeted with the hem of her sweater. "Arden already suspects."

"Does she?"

Rowan sent him a bored look. "Don't pretend you didn't see her Instagram."

Genuine confusion passed across his features. "I'm not big on pretending, Rowan."

Shit.

"Forget it," she said.

He narrowed his eyes, and for a moment, Rowan was sure he was going to press the question. Then he softened. "Are you okay?"

"No, I'm not," she muttered. "Maintaining this degree of awkwardness is hard fucking work."

"I don't think you're awkward. Not even a little bit."

"Give it time."

"Fine. I'll give you fifty years to try to convince me."

The implication in his words found an old nerve. He'd dipped down deep and yanked it, like a crochet hook pulling yarn. She swallowed hard. "Harrison—"

"Harry."

"Why?" She drifted backward a bit, opening space between them.

"Why what?"

"Why are you like this?"

A thoughtful twitch brought his eyebrows together

in a brief frown, and his eyes went earnest. "You know why. Let me in, Rowan."

"I tried to make that happen in February, Harrison."

He was so close now, she *tasted* the cinnamon on his breath. His voice dropped low, threaded with an undertone of frustration. "Do not mistake my self-control for lack of desire, because I assure you one is only barely able to overcome the other." His pupils bloomed black inside silvery irises. "Ever wondered why I'm always ramming my hands into my pockets? I'm compelled to put my hands on you. It's *constant*."

"If you want to put your hands on me, put your hands on me," she snapped back. "Consider this my ongoing declaration of enthusiastic consent."

"You said you didn't want my family to know," he said.

"They won't know what happens in your bedroom or mine."

His lip curled. He straightened. "I know what I want, and casual, meaningless sex isn't it."

"Casual doesn't have to be meaningless. It means no strings," she said. "No backstory."

Harrison put a warm hand on her bicep, then slid it down to encircle her wrist. "I want the strings. I want to tie you up in mine, and I want to get tangled in yours." His fingertips pressed lightly against the pulse point in her wrist. "Your body tells me things your words don't, Rowan. Your heart is racing."

She felt like Snow White being offered the poison apple. Everything he had was everything she once wanted. Only now, the chance to have it wasn't worth the disruption to her carefully constructed equilibrium.

You couldn't mourn the loss of something you never had.

"Anyway," he said, his tone lighter, "I just wanted to say hi."

Harrison pressed a hot, hard kiss to the tender skin of her inner wrist, then left her there with her mind as scattered as dandelion cotton.

CHAPTER EIGHTEEN

Harry

Harry and Temperance rode to the mountains in the back of Nate and Maren's big beige SUV. As soon as the cara-van of vehicles pulled from the drive, he texted Arden. He kept his phone subtly tilted away from Temperance.

Within a minute, he had a reply back from his sister confirming the existence of the photo Rowan mentioned. Within another three minutes, he'd installed Instagram, created an account of his own, and found Arden's profile.

The pictures from November were buried several pages deep. Harry had to scroll through photos of latte art, smiling selfies, people he didn't know, and a dispro-portionate number of Arden's pet tortoise, Otis. Arden loved that damned tortoise like most people loved their dogs.

Harry's phone's connection was spotty on the rural route, so when he finally found the series of images from the festival, they loaded agonizingly slowly. Each one in the sequence had a little spinning cursor in the middle of the screen before they fully displayed. He squeezed the phone so hard, the plastic case creaked in his hand.

When the mystery image finally appeared on the little screen, Harry felt gut-punched by a fist the size of a medicine ball. He remembered the way Rowan's hair had smelled in that autumn sunshine, and how the frayed rip in the thigh of her jeans revealed freckles beneath. The pale yellow sweater she'd worn had been almost as soft as the skin under it.

As they'd danced that night, he'd made a weighty gamble, challenging her to admit she felt the same things he did. Now, seeing Arden's photo, he *knew* he'd been right, even then. Rowan's expression was a mirror image of his. Wide-open longing, undisguised and undeniable.

"What are you looking at over there?" Temperance asked. Sunlight and shadow played across her face.

"Sudoku."

"Sudoku doesn't make you sigh like a lovesick teenager. You're over there pining like an evergreen." She leaned all the way over and stuck her face in his phone screen before he could switch it off, then sat up straight with a self-satisfied grumble. "Thought so."

Harry tipped his head back against the headrest. "I know you told me to be—guarded, with her."

"When did I say that?"

"Back in the fall."

A crease appeared on her forehead. "I don't think those were the words I used."

"I heard what you *meant,* T-Bird."

She sighed. "All I *meant* was that you're two very different people, and I saw the potential for some— volatility. You were in a bad place when you came here last September, honey."

"I know."

"And Rowan is—a lot."

"That's one way to put it," Harry chuckled.

"I love her, and I know her," Temperance said. "In a lot of ways, she's—stronger than you. Harder. Which is why I felt comfortable telling you to tread lightly. At first."

Harry pulled the photo up again. Stared. Sighed.

"You haven't been treading lightly, have you, Harry?"

"Back up a minute." He switched off the phone and sat up straighter. "You said 'at first.' What's that mean?"

Temperance hesitated. "She's been different. Gentler. Like some of her edges have been smoothed over."

"I like her edges."

"Well, you say that now. You might feel differently when one of those edges has you bleeding out on the floor."

Bleeding out.

Harry waited for the drumbeat of anxiety to begin in his chest, the lockdown of his windpipe, the deadened fingers. The only thing that manifested was a mild gust of nausea.

Maybe he was healing.

"Really, Temperance?" he said.

She put a hand on his knee. "God, I'm so sorry, Harry."

"You're an asshole." His tone was dry.

"It's true. I am ashamed," Temperance said theatrically. After a beat, she asked, "Does she know about Nicola?"

Harry fidgeted with a loose thread on the cuff of his sleeve. "Yes."

"Does she know *everything* about Nicola?" she pressed.

"Nicola has been out of my life for a long time, you know that. She isn't relevant."

"Rowan might not share that opinion, Harry." Temperance's expression was guarded. "You should consider giving her the full story."

"It's not—ah, we're not in a place where it would make sense for me to bring it up. But I'll figure it out."

At first, he'd kept the details of his relationship with Nicola to himself because of Rowan's dogged insistence on "casual." But now—his reticence was simple fucking cowardice. He couldn't bear for Rowan to use Nicola as ammunition in her crusade to prove that relationships—and love—never lasted.

"Be patient with her," Temperance said. "You know what a disaster Noah was."

"Wait." Harry dropped his voice when he noticed Nate flick his eyes upward at him in the rearview mirror. "Who the hell is Noah?" he whispered.

Temperance slouched low, and her ears turned pink. "She hasn't told you about Noah?"

"No, Temperance, she hasn't told me about anyone named Noah." Just saying the other man's name made his throat close.

"Shit, Harry, I'd just assumed—since she knew about Nicola . . . ," she trailed off.

Harry groaned and leaned forward to press his forehead into the back of Nate's headrest.

Temperance leaned over to put her face close to his. She whispered, "Look. I love you both, and I want the best for you. You two are the best. It's easy math. But Noah is a very sensitive subject, and I am *not* equipped to be the one to tell you about him."

He sat straight. "It's fine. Forget it."

Harry had enough pride left—and respected Rowan's privacy enough—that he didn't press for more details. Hell, he should've assumed there had been someone else. Someone who'd skewed Rowan's perception of love. But she'd exiled any backstory behind a doorless wall. Noah was as forbidden of a topic for her as Nicola was for him.

And anyway, it didn't change how he felt about her. If anything, it made him crave access to her even more.

"She's the most incredible person I've ever met, T.J."

Temperance dug a sharp knuckle into his leg. "Damn it, I thought that was me?"

"You had the title, until you made that shitty comment about bleeding out a few minutes ago," he said.

She smiled gently and patted his leg. "That's fair."

* * *

THE WEDDING WAS an evening ceremony in the lobby of the mountain lodge. Rustic wooden chairs sat in an intimate cluster around a granite fireplace, decorated with boughs of evergreen threaded with tiny lights. The huge crystalline chandeliers hanging from the slanted ceiling were an opulent contrast to the rustic exposed beams. Creamy sherbet light from the sunset lit the lobby through the wall of windows on either side of the fireplace.

Harry had spent the day with Patrick's other groomsmen, sequestered in a wing of the lodge opposite Mercedes's attendants. He hadn't seen Rowan since their hushed conversation in the library that morning. Now, as he took his place beside his brothers at the front of the crowd, he looked for her.

She wasn't difficult to find. Her bright hair shone like a lighthouse beacon on a dark sea. Harry felt his nervous system stammer, stop, then reboot back to life too keenly aware, too potent. Too everything.

He was used to seeing her in tattered old jeans, and her shabby, patched-knee overalls. In flannels, sweatshirts, or her threadbare T-shirts with the silly plant puns. Tonight, though—the champagne-gold dress she wore accentuated every curve and dip of her body, leaving her luscious arms, shoulders, and collarbones bare. Freckles adorned her skin in lieu of jewelry. Her curls were twisted in an elaborate knot at the back of her head. As she turned her head to watch the last attendant come down the aisle, he had an unrestricted view of her neck and the elegant shape of her jawline.

Harry wanted to break away from the wedding party and kiss her mindless in front of his friends and family. He didn't even try to hide that he was staring. When the audience stood for Mercedes's processional, the violin soloist began an achingly slow rendition of "Can't Help Falling in Love."

Rowan shifted her attention from the aisle. Straight to him.

Her gaze tangled with his. She looked so incandescently beautiful, Harry had to catch the inside of his cheek between his teeth and bite down hard to keep from groaning out loud.

Her cheeks pinkened. *Not polite to stare,* she mouthed, and Harry swallowed a laugh. A faint smile hovered on her lips, and her eyes were soft, like she'd yielded some of her armor. The longing he saw in her face matched the magnitude of his own, and he had to remind himself to breathe.

When the violin went silent and the officiant asked everyone to be seated, Rowan visibly startled. She cut her eyes away from Harry and swept a hand under her, smoothing the dress as she sat. A big breath raised her collarbones in sharp relief under her skin. For the rest of the short ceremony, she kept her eyes on her lap or fixed stoically on Patrick and Mercedes.

Again, that internal switch. If a glimmer of emotion slipped loose, she'd redouble her withdrawal in a way that had once made Harry think he'd imagined everything.

But now, he *knew*. This thing between them—whatever it was—was substantial. Significant. If anything, he'd underestimated the magnitude of it. Now that he knew her reluctance was rooted in damage done by another man, Harry felt confident he could change her heart, and he wouldn't risk fucking it up by allowing it to be only about messy, meaningless sex. If he did, she would put him into that box, slap a TEMPORARY label on it, and he'd never get out.

Later, at the reception, Harry and Temperance sat at a table along the edge of the dance floor with the rest of the wedding party. He pretended to be involved in the conversation, but it exhausted him. A high-key hum of tension zapped through him like an actual electric current.

After the meal, the earlier hope and optimism about a future with Rowan crumbled as he watched her dance with some asshole friend of Patrick's. Harry sat facing the dance floor with legs spread wide, leaning forward with his forearms on his thighs.

The guy was built like a rugby player, sporting a blond buzz cut and an ill-fitting dress shirt with buttons stretched to their limit across his chest. He churned his hips against Rowan's ass as her body pumped like a piston to the beat of the blaring music. She was shoeless, and her hair had slid out of its tidy twist. Every time she bent her knees and raised her arms, her dress hiked high, to where her thighs curved outward and upward. The golden material of the dress was wrinkled, the fabric darkened in all the places where Buzz Cut's sweaty hands had been.

All night, she'd catch Harry staring at her, and rather than look away or coyly pretend she hadn't noticed, she'd challenge him with a piercing stare of her own. Bold.

Unapologetic. The eye contact never lasted more than a few seconds, but each time, Harry's heart rate spiked and stumbled, like he was being defibrillated while fully conscious. His molars creaked under the strain of his clenched jaw.

He was in inescapable, voyeuristic hell.

His mouth was parched as a desert boneyard, and no amount of whisky or water or wine could satisfy the pervasive thirst. Harry flexed his shoulders and hooked a finger into his shirt collar, tugging hard. His neck was as damp as his tongue was dry.

Harry drained his nearly full cocktail in one long swallow, shredding the cherry between his teeth. Ice clattered when he pounded the empty glass down on the table. Mercedes and Temperance froze in midconversation and fixed him with matching surprised glances.

"Sorry," he growled, standing. "Excuse me."

"Harry—" he heard Temperance say, but he kept moving. He shouldered through the crowd to get outside, seeking solitude, seeking rational thought, seeking calm.

On the wraparound patio, he paced, squeezing the bridge of his nose hard enough to make his eyes water. Over the last hour, he'd thrown back Manhattan after Manhattan, and the alcohol was beginning to numb his brain all at once.

Good. Something more powerful than Rowan McKinnon was finally dominating his bloodstream.

The night wind still had winter teeth, even though it was April. Harry shuddered, the tailored tuxedo doing little to prevent the cold from slicing all the way down to his skin. Gripping the edge of the stone balcony wall, he let his head hang between his shoulders. He sucked in greedy breaths through flared nostrils and blasted hot air back out through his open mouth.

What in the hell was happening to him?

The sweet scent of expensive tobacco drifted on the breeze, preceding low, familiar voices. Harry followed the curved wall of the patio to find Malcolm and Duncan leaning against the stones.

Harry and Mal had a complicated relationship that went back to their teens. It had grown progressively worse again after they'd ended up on opposite coasts of the country, infrequently seeing each other as adults. On the rare occasions Mal did leave his posh New York City aerie to visit the family, Harry had a feeling it was only for his daughter Charlotte's benefit. Really, she was the only thing that kept Mal from being an irredeemable asshole. Regardless of how misanthropic Mal seemed on the surface, he was solo-parenting a confident, bright little girl, and that spoke volumes for who he really was.

He was still a pain in Harry's ass, though.

A wisp of smoke meandered from Mal's checkmark-shaped pipe. Duncan lit a thick cigar and used it to gesture a greeting at Harry. Then he nudged his chin toward the condensation-hazed windows of the lodge lobby. "Why aren't you in there tearing it up with your date on the dance floor?"

"T.J. doesn't dance," Harry said.

Duncan paused with the cigar midway to his mouth and raised his eyebrows. "She tell you that?"

Harry shrugged. "Go ask her yourself."

"I tend to try to avoid Temperance at weddings." Duncan clamped the cigar in his back teeth.

Before Harry could probe Duncan's comment for more information, Mal said, "What about the redhead?"

"She has a name," Harry said. "Her name is Rowan. She's Duncan's date."

Smoke poured in thick twin plumes from Duncan's nose. "What about her?"

Mal took a slow puff on his pipe and raised a single heavy eyebrow.

"Few minutes ago, she had some knuckle-dragger climbing up her back on the dance floor," Harry said.

"*That* guy. That's Pat's friend from pharmacy school. Name's Arthur. Pretty sure she can handle herself with a guy who goes by 'Art,' bud," Duncan replied. "If you're worried about her, you go dance with her."

Harry didn't respond. Duncan still had no idea of the starring role Rowan had in his thoughts and literal dreams, and he intended to keep it that way. His brother was a dog with a bone if he discovered a weakness he could exploit for the sake of humor. He'd turn Harry's feelings into a punch line, and he wasn't equipped to deal with that yet.

After a while, Mal said, "Didn't take you for quiet and broody, Harrison."

"Quiet and broody is Harry's new normal," Duncan said. "Needs to get laid."

"Fuck off," Harry said.

Mal quietly considered both brothers, and his new scrutiny made Harry nervous. Even as a child, Mal had been the family's tale spinner and pot stirrer, and the focus of his attention was never a place one wanted to find themselves. He had the uncanny ability to draw threads of information from apparent thin air, deduce a narrative from them, then show a person a reality that banged hard against the thing they most wanted to hide or ignore. It was probably what made him such a savvy author.

It was fucking diabolical, that's what it was.

Mal looked up at the starless sky and gusted out wobbly smoke rings. "I doubt Duncan's date is who he'd prefer to fuck off with."

Duncan launched an indignant glance at Mal. "I didn't ask Rowan to be my date so I could fuck her tonight. She's my friend."

Harry's brain seized on select words, and the blood drained from his head. *Rowan—my date—fuck her—tonight.* He gripped the back of a wrought-iron chair, planted his feet wide, and stared at the pavement.

"How about you, Harry?" Mal's deep voice sounded deceptively light. "You and Temperance sharing a room tonight?"

Duncan doubled over, coughed explosively, and beat his chest with a fist.

Harry leveled a careful look at Mal. "What are you doing, man?"

Mal made a thoughtful sound. "Kind of weird though, right?" His words were directed at Harry, but his full attention was on Duncan, watching for further reaction. "Did Temperance become our *relative* when Nate married her sister? Is she essentially our sister-in-law, once removed?"

Duncan was still trying to hack the cigar smoke from his lungs.

"Are you enjoying yourself?" Harry asked.

"Not particularly. But I've been observing. All day. It's what I do. I'm a watcher, a collector of information. A curator of details." Mal's tone was academic as he looked between Harry and Duncan. "Both of you are fucking clueless. You're each here with the wrong woman. Even a dismal son of a bitch like me can see it."

"Don't talk about Ma that way, dick," Duncan rasped.

Mal narrowed his eyes and didn't laugh. "Always such a clown. Everything's funny, everything's a joke. What's that humor compensating for, Duncan?"

Duncan hung his head for a moment, massaging the back of his neck with a big hand.

"Lay off, Malcolm," Harry said.

Mal turned his head and blinked at Harry like an inquisitive crow. "Ah, yes. Harrison, the protector, the hero. The most virtuous of all the Bradys. You're a self-righteous asshole, you know that?"

Harry's patience had hovered at the snapping point for hours. When the opportunity to vent some steam presented itself, he jumped on it. "The fuck is wrong with you, man? Sometimes I think Charlotte is the only thing that makes you remotely human."

That seemed to hit a mark, but it wasn't nearly as satisfying as Harry had hoped for. Mal looked briefly down at the pipe in his hand and tipped it side to side. When he looked up, his mouth was a flat line. He caught Harry's eyes, and held.

"I agree," Mal said.

For a while, the only sound was a muffled rumble of music coming through the steamy windows of the lodge behind them.

"You don't always have to be such a bastard," Harry sighed.

Mal peered at Duncan. "No wiseass comeback for that, Duncan? Isn't 'bastard' a slight to Ma *and* Dad?"

Duncan scrubbed a hand over his beard, smoothing his mustache with a thumb and forefinger. "I like you better when you don't talk."

Mal redirected his attention back to Harry. "You don't know shit about my life, Harrison."

"I know you were raised the same way we were, and

you have no reason to be such a dick to everyone. The worst thing you ever have to deal with is a bit of fucking writer's block."

Smoke had stopped curling from Mal's pipe. He methodically lit a match, paused to let the sulfur dissipate, and skimmed it over the pipe's bowl. He sipped gently at the end of the pipestem, and the air filled again with the toasty, custard-honey aroma of the tobacco. "Writer's block is a gag and a noose. Your brain takes itself hostage, puts a knife to its own neck. It's a career-killer, and I've got a kid to raise. Don't talk about what you don't understand."

Harry wanted to send his fist into Mal's nose. "Your work is about creating fictional tragedy. In my profession, *real* people *actually* die. It's not characters on a page."

Mal regarded Harry for a long moment. Then he clamped the pipe between his canines and reached inside his suit jacket to withdraw a leather-covered liquor flask. He spun off the top in a practiced motion, and the unmistakable scent of brandy heated the cool night air. "I heard about what happened," Mal said to Harry, his voice dropping low. "I'm sorry."

When Harry didn't respond, Mal took a quick drink of the brandy and passed the flask to him. Recognizing it for the peace offering it was, Harry drank, and passed the flask to Duncan.

"I'm not going to get any surprise communicables if I drink after you two, am I?" Duncan asked.

"You're the one with the questionable sexual history," Harry said, swiping his hand over his mouth.

"I resent that."

"Just drink it, dick."

The three men stood in silent truce for a while, passing the flask. Harry thought about what Mal had said about self-righteousness. With Rowan, he'd throttled any advancement of the thing between them, simply because of his own sanctimonious ideal of how it should be. He expected her to verbalize what he already saw in her eyes, when it obviously wasn't something she was ready for.

Christ, he *was* a righteous ass.

Inside, the music faded and the lights winked on as the reception ended. Through a clear spot in the condensation on the windows, Harry saw a lone shoe on the floor inside, as if it were spotlighted. Sparkly, gold.

Hers.

As Mal packed fresh tobacco into the end of his pipe, Harry excused himself and headed straight for Rowan's shoe.

Behind him, Harry heard Duncan ask Mal, "Ever put weed in that thing?"

CHAPTER NINETEEN

Rowan

It was after midnight. Rowan felt like a marionette, her joints loose and overused. She dropped her solitary shoe on the floor of the little foyer of her room, and tugged useless pins from tangled, sweaty hair. She shed the fancy gold dress and satiny underthings like a chrysalis, dropping them in a damp heap on the bathroom floor.

The past five hours of seeing Harrison Brady in that tuxedo had wrecked her. The look they'd shared during the wedding ceremony was sensual and sentimental and scary, and she'd had to avert her eyes. As Duncan's date, she'd been at the attendants' table at the reception, thankfully down the row from Harrison, instead of across from him. From the edge of her vision, she watched him pick at dinner, then ignore his ice cream. He *loved* ice cream. She watched him mostly ignore conversation with his brothers and Omar Hudson. Even Temperance. When Patrick and Mercedes were toasted by loved ones, Harry had kept his attention on his champagne, his face frozen in a melancholy half-smile.

Every moment of today's performative matrimonial charade should have left her rolling her eyes in disdain—weddings always did. But this one had the opposite effect. She'd felt infused with a new awareness tonight.

Like she'd become some kind of corporeal magnet, and Harrison was the object that drew her. Bring them close enough, they'd spontaneously snap together.

To deal with the big feelings, she'd done what any pragmatic, emotionally stunted adult would do. Duncan wouldn't dance with her, so she got shit-faced on endless cocktails, and spent most of the reception dancing with a guy whose name she didn't remember. Adrian? Austin? He'd had sour, yeasty beer breath and a short, incessant erection that poked her while they danced.

She'd used poor Alvin to punish Harrison for having the audacity to make her feel feelings. It felt like a petty reclamation of power as he watched them, his scowl deepening and darkening as the night wore on.

Yeah. Shallow *and* petty. She was a real catch.

Then Harrison disappeared. The last glimpse she'd had of him, he'd been pushing through the crowd to get outside, and the look on his face wasn't irritation. It looked like pain.

She left the dance floor that same moment, and after a futile fifteen-minute search for her second shoe, she gave up and slunk away from the celebration in shame.

Rowan let a cold shower sluice over her, washing away the traces of the night—especially the sticky fingerprints of Allen or Albert or whatever-the-hell-his-name-was. She brushed her teeth in the shower too. The chilly spray hit her in the face until it stung her skin.

She was pulling on undies when someone briskly knocked on her door. With a leg in the air, she froze like a confused, wobbly flamingo. "Nobody's here," she grumbled.

The peephole revealed a fish-eye version of Harrison. He glanced down the hallway toward the lobby, clutching her lost shoe—a sparkly gold kitten heel with an ankle strap—in both hands, like a precious artifact. His body language conveyed impatience, and his suit jacket and tie were gone.

"Are you fucking kidding me," she breathed.

Exactly twenty minutes prior, she'd have still been in her silk dress and tummy-smoothing shapewear, fortified by the cosmetic armor of perfectly winged eyeliner, mascara, and matte rose lipstick. Now, this beautiful, surly looking man was outside her door in the remnants of a designer tuxedo, and she wore a huge, hideous, lime-green sweatshirt with a SAGE AGAINST THE MACHINE appliqué and a decade-old coffee stain on the arm. Her eyes were so grainy she could *feel* the redness in them, and her hair hung lank around her face, like the mane of a russet Highland cow.

"Screw it," she mumbled, and cracked the door open. "Hi."

Her tight-lipped smile was an attempt at lukewarm and courteous, but Rowan was too exhausted to care if it came across as grumpy.

"Hi." He looked surprised she'd answered. "Busy?"

She gestured to her sweatshirt. "As you can see, I'm preparing to entertain several heads of state."

He held up her lost shoe. "This yours?"

She plucked it out of his hands and tossed it behind her. "Call me Cinderella."

Harrison smiled distractedly and glanced down the hall again. "Ah—can I come in?"

A closer look revealed genuine anguish in his eyes. She sighed and opened the door wide enough for him to step around her. When the door closed, they stood in the little foyer for several beats, motionless mirror images.

The top three buttons of his soft white shirt were open at the neck. Sleeves were tacked up to his elbows. She watched the agitated flex and release of lean muscles and tendons in his forearms as he messed with something deep in his pockets.

Rowan imagined—*remembered*—those same muscles orchestrating the movement of his fingers inside her.

Stop it.

They both spoke at the same time.

"I need you to—" she began.

"I think we—" he said.

They both cut off. Harrison winced.

"You go," Rowan said.

He freed a hand from a pocket and scratched the back of his head.

"I've—made a mistake." He straightened and squared his shoulders.

Of course. A mistake.

Something she'd done today must have finally made him see her for what she was. Amid the misty romanticism of tulle skirts and sleek black tuxedoes, silverware tinkling against champagne glasses, and all the cliché love songs at the reception, Rowan was a denier, a defier, and an outlier. The fly in the wedding cake's frosting.

This was what she'd wanted, right? It's why she'd used poor Augustus as her own personal Johnny Castle on the dance floor tonight. A human shield between Harrison and her big scary fucking feelings.

Right?

She recalled the morose way Harrison had peered into his champagne during the toasts to the bride and groom. That's probably when it had hit him. God, she was foolish. "You don't have to say—"

"Please, let me finish. Before I mess up again." He looked at the ceiling, then back to her. "Back in

September, I came home to focus. To recenter myself. To—ah, fix some things that are broken."

She tugged the sweatshirt's hem farther down her legs. It hit midthigh, longer than the dress she'd worn all night, but she suddenly felt very exposed. She braced herself for the platitudes. For the excuses, and the good-bye. "Well, tonight, you should probably go fix them somewhere else," she said.

Harrison moved in close. She averted her eyes to the carpet. The tips of his fancy shoes were stark black, aggressively shiny. They looked ominous next to her own bare, vulnerable toes.

"Where do you suggest I go, Rowan? And would it matter if I did?" He paused. She remained silent. His voice dropped to a low murmur. "Look at me."

Rowan barely breathed. Slowly, she looked up and stared at the notch between his collarbones framed by the open neck of his white shirt. She wanted to put her mouth there.

"Do you think, when you're not around, I'm not thinking about you?" he said. "You think, if I go back to my room right now, I'll take off these fancy clothes, slide calmly into that big bed, maybe read a little bit? Then fall into some kind of easy, restful sleep, where I don't dream of you?"

Oh, god.

Rowan shuffled backward and stumbled on the shoe she'd carelessly thrown behind her. As she toppled, he caught her by a handful of sweatshirt and pulled her into him. Harrison swallowed audibly. A long, controlled breath from his nose warmed her top lip, the scent and heat of him pluming around her. She smelled brandy in the exhale.

"Are you drunk?" she blurted.

"I swear, I have never been more lucid in my life."

He breathed deep and measured, but her own lungs felt ragged, ineffective. Harrison was as steadfast as she was turbulent—like an ancient reef, and she was the tide. Her pulse slammed so hard she felt it in the roots of her teeth.

"I made a mistake." He released her. "I shouldn't have made this transactional. You don't need to say words you're not ready to say." He cupped her face, fingers slipping into the curls behind each ear. "Right now, all I need is a yes, and I'm all in."

The tip of his nose grazed the side of hers. "I—still plan to leave," she managed. "Eventually. This won't change that."

His pupils eclipsed the irises of his eyes, crowding out all but a thin rim of smoke around the edge. "I'd rather have you now and miss this for the rest of my life, than never have you at all."

Rowan had never experienced the depth of feeling surging through her in that moment. It was transcendent, bigger than simply being physiologically turned on. Something in her brain had been activated—a key inserted into a lock she hadn't known existed. Her insides strained against the confines of her skin, like she'd been filled with helium. Surely, in seconds, she'd float away.

For this man, her inner fortress was really just a Jenga tower made of cheap glass, and tonight, he'd brought a wrecking ball.

"I want this," was all she managed before Harrison's mouth collided with hers. They moaned in unison, and Rowan's entire core liquefied.

He made love to her mouth with his own, deep and slow, though tension vibrated in his body like a struck clock-tower bell. He clutched her hair in his fists. Now that he'd surrendered to the desire he'd been restraining for months, it was like he was afraid *she'd* be the one to change her mind.

Rowan tilted her jaw, opening herself fully to his kiss. He tasted her, consumed her. The entirety of her consciousness became *him*. The slide of his tongue, mating with hers. The urgent ridge of his arousal against the curving bone of her hip. The clean, carnal musk of him, the impossible heat of him.

The way she trusted him.

The way she trusted *herself* with him.

He guided her the rest of the way into the room until the backs of her legs hit the mattress. In seconds, he toed off his shoes and socks, and her ugly sweatshirt hit the floor. His shirt and pants tumbled after. For a moment, they stared each other down in the dim light coming from the room's little foyer.

Rowan wanted to run her hands along every honey-dusted bit of him. There were thicker bands of muscle on his upper arms that hadn't been there in December, and his ribs were no longer visible through his skin. The generous thickness inside the front of his low-slung heathered briefs made her vision blur.

Harrison didn't give her long to look. Bare skin ignited against bare skin as he propelled them both onto the bed. The weight and heat of him was elemental. On his hands and knees above her, he buried his face under her jaw, inhaled her like she was oxygen. Rowan trailed fingertips down his belly. She palmed the insistent erection arcing sideways in his tight underwear. The fabric was damp at the head's conspicuous outline. His hips thrust hard into her hand, and he gasped like she'd scorched him.

"You good?" she asked.

"Too good." He sucked in a shaky breath and lowered his body onto hers, locking her hand between his dick and her own thigh. "Thinking about baseball."

Rowan sank teeth into the curve of his shoulder. "You've said that before."

He laughed into her hair, a short, distracted sound. "Need a minute."

She withdrew her hand, reveling for a moment in the heat of him, the feel of him pressed into her thigh. When he finally raised his head and met her eyes, the frenzy was gone, replaced by intense, hungry purpose.

A thick lock of hair fell over his forehead. She was dying to spread her legs wide and wrap around him like a vise, but he pushed back and propped up on his elbows, all focus diverted to her breasts.

"We're still wearing—" Rowan choked when the flat of his tongue swept her nipple, "too many clothes."

He reached down between their bodies, hooking a finger into the wet lower edge of her underwear. "These?" Rowan felt a slight tremor in his hand.

She dug her hands into the stretchy fabric covering his ass. *"Yes."*

A breath later, he sat up and skimmed the panties down her legs. The mattress bounced as he rolled off the bed, and he pulled his own underwear off in the same sleek movement. Rowan heard the tinkle of his belt buckle when he picked his pants up from the floor. Then, the faint rustle of a condom wrapper.

Rowan propped up on her elbows, taking him in as he stood beside her. Champagne brown hair fanned out like wings across his chest. It narrowed to a thin trail between the notches of his hips, and terminated in the hair above his prominent arousal.

His shoulders rose and fell heavily as he watched her watch him. With a negligent snap of his wrist, he flicked three wrapped condoms onto the bed beside her. It was so overtly, effortlessly sexy, Rowan's entire consciousness dropped to the desperate ache between her legs.

Three condoms. Three.

Damn, Dr. Brady.

The tremor in his hands was gone.

CHAPTER TWENTY

Rowan

Harrison's weight dipped the bed beside her, rolling her into him. He pushed her back with a hand on her breastbone, and drifted his touch down the concavity between her ribs. Over the gentle outward curve of her belly. Lower. He paused with fingers splayed wide between her hipbones, taking a moment to breathe.

"I need to hear it, Rowan." Runaway lust and a dash of fear were in his eyes. Fear she'd make them stop now. Fear she wasn't feeling the same things he felt.

"Yes," she breathed.

"Thank god."

His hand continued down her body. He found the molten core of her, sliding two fingers inside. Rowan's back arched away from the bed, and her knees fell fully open as he began his excruciatingly slow strokes.

"I know you," he murmured against her temple. "You know what comes next, don't you?"

It was thrilling, knowing he knew exactly how to get her off. She was already nearly there before he'd even touched her, and she wanted so much more than his fingers. Rowan groaned and twisted upward to sling an arm around the back of his neck, hauling him down to her. Their lips struck and blazed like a match against granite. He dominated her mouth, the heat and scent of him fanning hot against her cheek as his beautiful fingers continued their slick, rhythmic onslaught.

"Breathe," he whispered on her lips.

Rowan did, and as her lungs filled, the orgasm slammed her with primitive force. Her heels dug into the mattress, firing her hips upward. Deep in the suppressed civilized part of her brain, she realized she'd bitten his bottom lip as she came.

Harrison made a deep sound of satisfaction low in his throat, rising to his knees above her. Aftershocks of the orgasm throbbed through her, a condom wrapper tore, and seconds later, he was kneeling between her legs.

His hand flattened against the back of her thigh, just above her ass. He slid his palm up to grasp behind her knee, and pressed his lips to the inner curve of her kneecap in a brief, tender kiss. It stirred more than lust. Something bigger. And now, she had nowhere to hide from it.

"Lift your hips," Harrison said.

Rowan obeyed, and he tucked a pillow under her raised ass.

Her free leg fell open as he lowered his body against hers, snugging her inner thigh against his ribs. He let out a shaky breath as he looked down. His gaze engaged hers, and held.

An acknowledgment. An accord. Everything was about to change, no matter how much she said it wouldn't.

At first, he only nudged in, the broad tip of him teasing, stretching. She felt her own flesh convulse around him, echoes of her orgasm. Rowan bucked her hips to try to draw him deeper, and he pressed his forehead to hers with teeth clenched, resolute.

Slowly, slowly, he exhaled and sank all the way into her.

For a moment, they breathed.

Rowan felt the phantom of another orgasm lurking, like a promise. She felt the soft hairs of Harrison's chest against her nipples, and the shallow thump of his belly against hers as he breathed. The length of him pulsed inside her as he grappled for control.

He rolled his hips, only once. A pause, then again. And again, creating swirling, pressure-building magic. He guided her thigh back farther, wider, bringing the most sensitive part of her into even broader contact with his churning friction. Rowan dug fingers into the bunch and ripple of muscles in his back. Tension pooled between her legs, a powder keg of pleasure, priming for its next detonation.

Releasing her leg, he propped himself up with hands on either side of her head, pinning her down with his eyes. She slid her knees up his sides and squeezed his ribs with her thighs, tipping him even deeper inside. Other than his choppy exhalations, he was impressively controlled. Rowan wanted that self-control to snap as badly as she wanted another orgasm of her own. She locked her ankles behind his hips and twisted into him. His focus wavered for a moment, and he squeezed his eyes shut.

Then he *smiled* down at her.

The *feelings*.

With her legs around his back, he had space on the bed to spread his knees for more leverage, adding more power to the grind of his hips. When he angled higher, Rowan knew she was close again. By the way he sucked his bottom lip into his mouth as he watched her face, he knew it, too.

Laid bare underneath him, breasts bouncing, sweaty

curls clinging to her neck and face, Rowan had a rare moment of self-consciousness. "It's not"—her breath hitched in her throat—"polite to stare."

His laugh was short and explosive, ending in a low growl tempered with an edge of agony. "Ah, I'm not staring. I'm—memorizing."

Rowan's head snapped back against the pillow, her body clenching desperately against his as another orgasm shattered through her. Her legs fell bonelessly from behind his back, opening like a book with a cracked spine. The sensations were so intense, her feet scrabbled against the sheets.

Something—tears, sweat, both—ran a wet course down her cheekbones and pooled behind her earlobes.

As she returned from orbit, Harrison lowered his body fully onto hers, wrapping his arms around her back. The weight of him stole her breath. He socketed himself to her, burying his face in the crook of her neck, exhalations shallow and hot, condensing on her skin. With a convulsive, rumbling moan, he began to thrust, his hips taken by a rhythm he could no longer control. Rowan burrowed her fingers into his back and turned her head to bite his earlobe, sucking it into her mouth. She drew her legs up again and sealed him to her as he rode her hard.

Goose bumps rose down his back and across his ass. He pressed his face into the pillow beside her head. Arms tightened around her. Fingertips dug into her scalp where he cradled the back of her head. His anguished moan was muffled—he was biting the pillow. It was the sexiest sound Rowan had ever heard.

The pattern of his thrusts abruptly lost all finesse, turning erratic, and his moan escalated into a grinding, wordless exhalation. He pumped and jerked hard against her as he came, bouncing them both against the mattress with the force of it, draining himself to emptiness.

They lay there until Rowan's hip joints began to ache, and tears and sweat dried to salt.

When he finally did move, Harrison was gentle as he slid his arms from beneath her, lowering her to the mattress. The sheets were damp against her back.

He propped up on elbows and took her mouth with a gentle, melting kiss. A shocking contrast to the athletic sex of moments ago. The kisses were almost shy. Exploratory, tender. Nuzzling noses and mingled breath and gently sliding tongues.

Rowan braced for the spark of panic. The inevitable sensation of being trapped below the body above her. The need to flee.

It never came.

Harrison's biceps framed her face. As he delicately drew curls off her sweaty forehead, he remained inside her, still as hard as when they'd begun. When she realized she'd been making little dreamy swirls against his back with her fingertips, she allowed her hands to fall away limp against the mattress. A look loaded with emotion passed across his features as he gazed down at her. Then, without a word, he lifted himself away and padded to the bathroom.

Rowan removed the damp pillow from behind her hips and popped up to watch him walk away. The flex of corded muscle bracketing his lower spine and the hollows at either side of his perfect butt cheeks made her mouth go dry. She flopped back to the bed and blinked at the ceiling.

By now, she should be gathering her clothes from the floor, desperate to avoid conversation of any kind. She should want to urge him to leave, or be planning her own quick exit, even though this was *her* room.

Rowan had no idea what came after this.

As though he'd heard her thoughts from the bathroom, Harrison looked around the doorjamb and said, "Don't get up. Not yet."

"When this finally happens, it's going to last," he'd said, months ago. *"We're going to linger afterward. For hours."*

She drifted her fingertips across her bare belly, and chose lingering over leaving.

The light in the bathroom clicked off. "You didn't get up." He climbed back into the bed and palmed her hip, gathering her against his side. Her head rode the gentle rise and fall of his chest as he breathed, and his heartbeat was a slow throb against her temple. Tentatively, she traced a fingertip along the ridges of his rib cage.

Lying here with this man, Rowan understood how people fell in love. She'd thought she'd loved Noah, but that had simply been bastardized infatuation. Lust and fascination were feelings she'd experienced since then, but they were trivial compared to the intangible sense of contentment she experienced now. Somehow, lingering here with Harrison felt far more intimate than any physical sexual act. She felt bone-deep safety and *rightness*.

The dominant scientific part of her brain *knew* her body was marinated in an ocean of hormone-induced bliss. What she felt now had to be chemical—an organic cocktail of sexual satisfaction. Anything more was a social construct designed to attribute meaning to the more primal, messy instincts of human attraction.

Sex was what people truly loved. Pleasure was power. Why, then, in that moment, did she feel so weak?

Oh. There it was, the low hum of anxiety she'd been

anticipating. Rowan sat up and faced him, using a forearm to push a heap of curls from her face.

"I'm not staying in the valley."

"You've mentioned that." Harrison propped up on an elbow.

"You're not staying either."

Long silence. Then, "Probably not."

"Okay." She clutched a pillow to her chest.

"What if you *wanted* to stay longer?" He held up a hand when her mouth dropped open to protest. "Purely hypothetical."

"I've come too far with my career to not follow through now."

"That's not what I asked," he said.

"Nathan and I have already started talking about my replacement."

Impatience heated his tone. "I'm not talking about the goddamned job. I'm talking about us."

"There's no *us*. I thought you understood that when you knocked on my door tonight." Rowan pinched the pillow tighter against her breasts.

Harrison's frustration faded as quickly as it flared. He nibbled his thumbnail for a moment—an anxious behavior she'd never seen from him. "I just meant—if you—someday—changed your mind. About us."

"I'm not built for *us*, Harry. I'm messy, selfish, impatient—"

"Stop." He bolted all the way up, glorious in his nakedness. "Say that again."

"What? I'm messy, I'm selfish—"

"Not that part." His chest noticeably rose and fell as he breathed faster. "The part where you finally called me *Harry*."

"I didn't—" Rowan squeezed the pillow tighter and

frowned. "This is hard for me. I didn't expect to be so—so f-fond of you."

"Ah, Christ." He pressed the heels of his palms against his forehead. "Kill me now."

This had gone far enough. She stretched her legs to get up.

He snatched her arm, then quickly let it drop. "I'm sorry. I've never done this before." He gestured between them. "Whatever this is."

"*This* is two consenting adults, enjoying sex."

He went silent for a while, scratching the sheet with a fingernail.

"I guess you got what you wanted, then," he said.

"And you didn't?" Rowan fired back.

For a moment, he studied her. Then he grabbed the pillow out of her hands and flung it across the room, pushing her back to the mattress. With a knee, he nudged her thighs apart.

"Not yet."

CHAPTER TWENTY-ONE

Harry

May was a time of vivid transformation. The vineyard wore a mellow green haze, and the roses at the ends of the trellis posts exploded in crimson. Between the rows, the cover crop bloomed, a sea of dainty purple flowers.

Harry loved watching Rowan work. She was steadfast and strong, thinning shoots in the vineyard, tending Ma's perennials, caring for the sheep. He often saw her giving impromptu ecology lessons to Alice and Grey after school. One day, they peered into a nest of baby birds in a low shrub by the greenhouse. On another, Harry saw the three of them on the ground by the sheep barn, butts in the air, investigating a huge toad. They weeded flower beds for Ma, planted veggie seedlings for Dad, and scattered marigold seeds around the raised beds. One afternoon, the trio made mud pies in the greenhouse, and Harry later learned they'd been quietly celebrating Rowan's birthday with her. She hadn't told anyone else.

The visceral joy she took in engagement with nature was contagious, and the kids thought she hung the moon. Harry agreed.

Whenever he could get free of the rigorous schedule Duncan and Dad kept him on, Harry was by her side. In the greenhouse, they restored cabinets with new hardware, and refinished tables and benches until every bit of wood in the place gleamed smooth. Duncan installed new floorboards to replace the warped ones, then buffed and sealed the hardwood to a fresh shine. They'd spent four whole days up and down ladders, with brushes and long-handled squeegees and buckets of soapy water and vinegar, cleaning the calcium deposits and years of grime from each individual panel of glass. It was smelly work, and the vinegar burned the blisters and scrapes on his hands. But Harry had loved every wet, messy moment of it, because he'd spent it with her.

While tilling the flower bed around the front porch of the main house, they'd found a vintage Olde Philadelphia coffee tin full of antique marbles, and a few ancient matchbox cars. Rowan had done a pirouette of delight when they uncovered a big bed of purple-tipped asparagus poking out from an overgrown area near the bank barn. Harry learned the difference between pill bugs and sow bugs, about spur pruning versus cane pruning, and that hummingbirds use spider silk to bind their tiny nests. She taught him the scientific names of at least a dozen wild birds on the land, and the same for twice as many plants. He loved listening to the Latin roll from her tongue. Rowan was ceaseless in her desire to share knowledge, to cultivate in others that same affection and appreciation for the world around them. She was a born nurturer, whether she admitted it or not.

It was bittersweet for him, really. Sinclair was growing more and more insistent in her emails, asking him when he might come back to work, pressing for a return date. There had been a time when practicing medicine had infused him with the same enthusiasm Rowan had for the natural world. Harry wasn't sure if he'd ever find it again, and he'd give anything to have even a glimmer of the passion she had.

Every night, when the sky dimmed and spring peepers began to sing, Harry and Rowan belonged to each other. Often, they'd shower off the sweat and grime of the day together, lingering there under the rainfall showerhead until the water ran cold. He'd untangle ride-along twigs and leaves from her hair, and she'd gently extract splinters from his hands. Some nights, they would stay up past midnight, breaking each other's backs against the mattress of his big bed. Other nights, they'd quietly curl up on opposite ends of his couch, Rowan with her laptop, and he with a book. They'd make impromptu late-night meals together, and he'd been amused to discover she was a terrible cook. She'd been delighted to find he was an excellent one. Their conversations were effortless, and the silences were, too. Rowan hadn't made a small-talk joke in weeks.

Without fail, before dawn each day, Rowan would sneak back up to the cottage on the hill, unwilling to let his family discover her there with him. Easier when it came time for her to leave, she'd said. Avoid misunderstandings and hurt feelings.

Harry was pretty sure it wasn't only his family she referred to.

Tonight, on the lawn between the main house and the still-empty pool, the Bradys had a cookout. The air smelled of citronella candles and burnt sugar from marshmallows left too long over the campfire. S'mores weren't supposed to be until later, but Dad claimed a need for product testing and quality control on the roasting sticks he'd whittled out of grapevine canes.

It was a surprise for Harry when Rowan had joined them tonight. She was down near the pond with Alice and Grey. From where he stood, she looked small, but he could feel the gravity of her presence from any distance. Sunset was a carnival of colors across the lower part of the sky, and her hair had the shine of fresh chestnuts in the waning light. She and the kids were huddled in the grass, faces illuminated by the bright white of her phone screen. Harry watched them look up and around, delightedly look back at each other, then back at the phone. They repeated it several times.

Harry approached and squatted in the grass, thumbing the brim of his ball cap as a greeting to Rowan. "Is this a secret meeting, or can I join?"

"We're calling frogs," Ace whispered.

Harry scratched his chin. "How'd you get their number?"

Rowan's shoulders shook with a silent laugh, and she showed him the screen of her phone. She'd pulled up a university audio database of frog calls, and they were using it to communicate with the real frogs in the pond and trees around them.

"Rosie, show Uncle Harry," Grey said.

Rowan played the call of a gray treefrog. The four of them held their breath in silence, and a few seconds later, the rippling trill of several real frogs answered from the forest surrounding the water. The kids beamed, Rowan smiled, and Harry's heart grew legs and kicked him in the lungs.

Rosie.

"Hey kids," he said, without taking his eyes off Rowan, "Grandpa opened that bag of marshmallows."

Alice and Grey shared an urgent look and scrambled to their feet to race up the hill.

"Don't tell Grandma I told you!" Harry called after them.

"We won't!" they answered in unison.

Smiling, Rowan watched them go. She then turned to him, a beautiful Botticelli in weathered khaki shorts and a white eyelet tank top. Damp curlicues of hair hugged tight to her temples, and the rest tumbled like a briar patch around her freshly washed face. Her skin was the sun-kissed gold of turbinado sugar, and Harry knew it tasted even sweeter. She was so exquisitely, effortlessly beautiful, it made his whole body hurt.

He handed her a wild violet. "I heard you yelling in the Chardonnay this afternoon. What was that about?"

She sighed. "One of the sheep got in, went rogue on a whole row. You know the one with the heart-shaped patch on her head, the one you think is so sweet? Stubborn as hell."

"I like the cute, stubborn ones," he said.

"Yeah, well. She might become dinner if she doesn't cut the crap." Her tone was dry, but her eyes twinkled.

Harry chuckled. "I think we're playing Team Tag later. Tonight it's boomers and Gen X versus millennials and younger. We'll be on the same team."

"I do have an undefeated streak to maintain."

"Wait. You've never lost?"

She gave him an odd look. "Harry, I've only played the one time."

"Not even as a kid? Hide-and-seek?"

Her eyes shifted downward. A piece of grass squeaked in her fingers as she tugged it from the earth. "I had a very different childhood from yours."

Harry crossed his legs and put his elbows on his knees. "Tell me something about it. Anything."

She began peeling thin strips from the blade of grass and didn't answer.

"Rowan, I could draw a map of the freckles on your

inner thighs. Blindfolded. But I don't know anything about your family. We've spent almost every night together for the last month. Give me *something*."

She bit her lips between her teeth and looked out over the pond for a while. Just when Harry thought she wasn't going to respond, she ran her fingers over a dandelion blossom tucked deep in the grass and said, "See how this dandelion hugs the ground? The flower and the leaves are almost flush with the earth. Now look at the ones over there by the pond, where the slope is too steep to reach with the lawn mower. See?"

Harry looked where she pointed. Cheerful golden blossoms were held high on tall stems, quivering gently in the evening breeze. He looked back to Rowan.

"It's an adaptation," she said. "Here, where the mower cuts them, short ones survive and go to seed. Those seeds grow into short plants, too. Genetics. The ones over there by the pond don't have that same environmental pressure, so they get to grow tall."

She twisted three strands of grass together, making a tiny braid. Harry waited for her to continue.

"I guess—that was me. As a kid. I was a dandelion. For a while after Edie died, I got cut down by my mother so many times I just"—she nudged up her chin—"stayed small."

Harry locked his fingers together to keep from reaching out to touch her. His family was too far up the hill to be able to hear their conversation, but they all casually watched, pretending not to. But he wanted more.

Please, please give me more.

"You told me once you didn't have a middle name," he said.

"Sybil barely decided on a *first* name for me." She shook her head and laughed ruefully. "The doctor who delivered me—his surname was Rowan, so she went with that. I didn't even realize it until I was applying for my driver's license and happened to look closely at my birth certificate, and his name was there." She shredded narrow petals from a white clover, and they floated to the ground like snowflakes. "I think, for Sybil, I was just another thing that *happened* to her. She never physically hurt me. It was just—benign neglect. She was incapable of bonding with me, so she left it to Edie. Then, when Edie was gone . . ."

"Benign neglect is still neglect, Rowan." Christ, he wanted to touch her. "I'm sorry."

"Don't be." The deconstructed flower littered the grass in front of her. "Having what's traditionally a man's first name is an advantage in science." Her smile was sensible and sad.

"That's not what I mean."

"I know, but I can't deal with you feeling sorry for me for any other reason." The corners of her mouth lifted. "Did you hear Grey call me Rosie?"

"I did."

"Grandma Edie called me that. Been a long time since I'd heard it. Grey just—started doing it on his own, and now that's the kids' name for me." Her expression softened. "That ugly old hat you tease me about? It was Edie's."

Harry *loved* that hideous old hat.

He glanced up the hill. Dad and Nate quickly turned away. "They're looking at us."

"I noticed."

Alice and Grey squealed and giggled in the distance as Duncan roared and gave chase. Crickets whirred, tree frogs warbled, and Ma sang a loud, off-key rendition of "You're My Best Friend" by Queen.

Harry sighed, hard. "I really, really want to kiss you right now."

Another pause, and more evening sounds. The syncopated *ch-ch-ch* scrape of katydids. Warm wind in the grass, and the pond lapping the underside of the dock where they'd had their first conversation. Rowan's gentle exhale.

"Harry, you know why I can't—"

"It's okay. I know. Let's go before they get too many ideas up there."

On the walk back up the hill, they kept at arm's length. Harry imagined what it would be like if he could tuck his arm around her, trail his fingers down her back and across her shoulder. Or simply hold her hand as they walked, publicly declaring her his partner to the people he loved most. It was a strange kind of torture, having her *right there,* but so, so far.

During the picnic dinner, she shone like an ember beside him. Their arms brushed often. Under the table, she pressed the bare skin of her knee against his. Across from them, Temperance and Maren blinked in identical surprise as Rowan casually wiped a bit of ketchup from Harry's chin, then licked her finger clean. When she'd realized what she'd done, her ears and throat flushed red as the ketchup itself. Her skin always betrayed her, regardless of what she wanted anyone to believe.

"I hate knowing you're up on that hill alone," Ma said, watching Rowan spoon pasta salad onto her paper plate. "It's not right. You should come to eat with us more often."

"Don't pretend you make us a Spanish feast every night, Ma," Duncan laughed. "Rowan doesn't want to come all the way down here for leftovers, or Burger King, or one of Nate's weird casseroles."

"Or that nasty gas station pizza you like so much, Duncan," Maren said, pointing with her plastic fork.

Duncan mimicked her tone, pointing his own fork back at her. "You went pretty hard on that pizza the other night, Maren."

Maren smoothed a hand over a burgeoning baby bump. "That wasn't me. That was the baby."

"There is nothing weird about my casseroles," Nate said.

"Dude." Duncan slapped a hand on the table. "There were *lima beans* in the last one."

Ma puffed up like a sparrow. "Eating together is better than eating alone, even if it's just bread and milk."

Rowan put down her plastic fork to raise her glass. "Regardless of what's for dinner, I know the wine and company are always perfect."

Everyone dropped plastic utensils to grab their own glasses, and Dad relinquished his sandwich to do the same. Alice and Grey lifted juice pouches, giggling. The family toasted to good wine. It seemed rather self-referential to Harry, toasting to wine with wine—but he joined in anyway, glad for the excuse to focus his full attention on Rowan. Even for a moment.

Dad swiped his mouth with a napkin and stood, raising his glass again. "Tonight is about harmony," he said. "Wine is the harmony of humans and nature, and family is the harmony of love and friendship." His eyes connected individually, intentionally, with everyone around the table, including Rowan and Temperance. "We are so fortunate to have this family together in this new place. To beginnings."

Harry noticed Temperance awkwardly divert from clinking her glass against Duncan's. Instead, she set her wine down, rubbed her nose, and kept her eyes on her plate. Harry filed it away to dissect later.

"Most importantly, though—let's talk about s'mores," Dad continued, with pageantry. "S'mores are the harmony between marshmallows and chocolate. Let's get wasted on sugar!" He shouted the last, and the kids cheered.

A s'mores assembly line was set up on a separate picnic table closer to the fire. The traditional ingredients were there, along with candied bacon as requested by Duncan, peanut butter at Maren's request, and white chocolate for Ace, who didn't like the standard kind. Dad stood at the end of the table and handed roasting sticks to everyone. He had a big marshmallow stuck to his nose, like a clown.

Rowan was at the end of the line. Harry circled behind her and trailed a finger up her spine. He watched goose bumps lift the tiny hairs on the back of her neck and down her arms, a shimmer across her skin in the firelight.

She subtly shifted backward and dipped her free arm behind her, reaching between his legs to palm his crotch, gently clutching and lifting the weight of him. *Christ* it felt good. Harry disguised his choked sound of surprise with a cough. In seconds, he was hard in her hand, and she stroked him through his shorts. Then she blithely stepped out of his reach to browse the s'mores ingredients, her expression the very picture of serenity.

Obscuring his obvious erection with the paper plate, Harry sidled up next to her and deliberately stepped on the ends of her bare toes with the tip of his sandaled foot. Rowan turned her head to smile innocently, and her eyes widened with surprise as they tracked to the brim of his ball cap. Her smile faded.

He smirked and murmured, "I'm not falling for that shit." Then he saw movement from the edge of his vision. Something was crawling on his hat. He froze.

"Duck your head and stand still." She put her plate down. From the brim of his cap, she scooped a fat-bodied brown spider into her hand. Harry dropped his own plate, flung off the hat, and stumbled backward to put more distance between him and the arachnid.

The flying hat hit Duncan in the back of the head. "The fuck, man?" he said.

"Language," said Ma.

Temperance turned and wrinkled her nose at the spider, unimpressed. "You're so gross, Rowan."

Rowan looked unfazed. "Harsh words from a woman whose profession involves large amounts of child barf. And baby shit."

"Language," Ma emphasized again.

Duncan pointed at Rowan. "Hey, look! Rowan got *language'd* by Ma. She's officially part of the family. What'cha got there, Red?"

The spider tottered on spindly legs over her palm, then onto her opposite hand. When Duncan saw the spider, he snagged Temperance by her upper arms and plowed backward, dragging her with him like a human shield.

"Jesus citrus-scented Christ. What the fuck, Rowan?" Duncan said. Temperance wrenched away from him with an irritated growl and a punch in his tattooed bicep.

"Duncan Callum—" Ma said.

"Neoscona crucifera," Rowan said. "This little lady wanted to join the fun, you big babies. She's harmless. Harry probably walked through her web under the tree."

"Coooool." Grey pushed past Alice and Temperance to get a closer look. The spider was slow and unsteady out of her web.

"Have you read *Charlotte's Web*?" Rowan crouched to bring the spider to the kids' level.

"Grey can't read yet, but I have. The ending made me cry."

With her spider-free hand, Rowan reached up and tucked a lock of dark hair behind Alice's ear. "Me too. This spider is an orb weaver, like Charlotte was. Neat, huh?"

"Our cousin's name is Charlotte," Grey said.

Rowan's eyes crinkled as she smiled. "I know."

Duncan slowly approached. This time, he gave Temperance the same wide berth he gave the spider. He edged around to stand next to Harry, slapping him on the back a few times, hard enough to make his body jerk like a rag doll.

"Harry peed his pants once when a daddy longlegs crawled over his arm," Duncan said. "Remember that, Nate?" The children giggled.

"You're an asshole, Duncan," Temperance said.

Harry shoved Duncan away from him. "I was a *kid,* dickhead."

"Language," Ma snapped.

"Language!" Alice gleefully echoed.

"Not that it matters, but biologically speaking, daddy longlegs aren't spiders," Rowan interjected, standing.

"You say potato, I say daddy longlegs are spiders," Duncan said.

"I don't think that's how the saying goes," Rowan replied.

Harry was simultaneously hypnotized and disgusted by the spider wobbling across Rowan's knuckles. Back in the fall, she'd guided him through the gauntlet of spiders in the meadow. She'd been impatient at first, but she'd quickly softened to bring him out of a spiraling anxiety attack. He'd only known her for a few days, but even then, he'd trusted her.

He might've fallen in love with her a little bit that day.

Rowan allowed the children to study the spider for a few more moments, then she took it away from the crowd to deposit it into the trees farther away from the gathering. She returned directly to Harry and showed him her empty hands, then placed them both against his chest. His breath caught. That simple touch packed the same punch to his nervous system as when she'd grabbed his balls minutes ago. Everyone watched, but she didn't seem to care.

It felt huge.

"You okay?" she whispered.

"I am now," he whispered back.

"To them, we're simply another surface. Moving terrain. She didn't want to hurt you."

His family was quiet around them, watching. The night was alive with the chorus of insects and frogs, and he smelled the sunscreen on Rowan's skin. What would happen if he kissed her, right then and there?

Too late. She let her hands slide away, and picked up her plate and roasting stick to join everyone at the fire.

"She's the spider whisperer," Harry heard Duncan say as she walked away.

"More like—the Uncle Harry whisperer," Alice said.

CHAPTER TWENTY-TWO

Harry

After dinner and s'mores, everyone sat around the fire on the hand-scraped wooden benches Harry and Duncan had salvaged from the bank barn. Harry sat next to Temperance, with Rowan directly across the fire from them.

Grey climbed into Rowan's lap. Her arms went around him, easy and loose, and she popped a quick kiss on his hair as he settled in. His tiny fingers twined with hers, and without breaking conversation with Ma and Maren, she absentmindedly bobbled him up and down on her knees. Harry's eyes caught hers over the little boy's head. Sequins of firelight shone in her inscrutable copper eyes.

Temperance nudged a shoulder into his arm. "Anything you want to discuss, Dr. Brady?"

Harry leaned forward and looked down at his hands. "About?" He glanced across at Rowan through a lowered brow, fully aware he was as transparent as gin to Temperance.

"Really, you're going to play coy?" She leaned back a bit to fix him with narrowed eyes.

"Nah."

"Okay. Doesn't matter, anyway. I just got more information than I could have ever hoped for by the look on your face right now."

Harry cracked his knuckles and studied the dark grass between his feet. "I'm in way deeper than she is, and it's a problem."

"You're in love with her," Temperance whispered, knocking into him with her shoulder.

"I don't know," Harry mumbled back.

Bullshit. He knew.

He was irreversibly, profoundly in love with Rowan McKinnon.

But being in love was supposed to feel good. It was supposed to strengthen and uplift. As much as he tried to mask it, he'd been completely dismantled and put back together in an unstable configuration, thoroughly out of his mind. This thing they had seemed the opposite of easy, the opposite of logical. For months, she'd been actively working toward an *out*. But for Harry, this place, this life—it had begun to coalesce into permanence. It was no longer simply a temporary stopover or an intermission from reality.

He'd known it would come to this. He'd known Rowan's presence here had always been ephemeral. Losing sight of that truth was on him, and he needed to deal with the fallout.

Hell, he still had a life and a job on the other side of the country waiting, if he wanted it. Sinclair couldn't keep a position open for him forever, though. And it was starting to feel like everything he wanted was right here within the radius of this little campfire. Maybe he could do what Arden said months ago. Be a country doctor.

That didn't change the fact Rowan was leaving.

She watched him from across the flames, growing

visibly more agitated as he and Temperance chatted in hushed tones. Grey had abandoned her lap, and she was trying to maintain conversation with Ma and Maren. But Harry saw how she wrung her hands together and nibbled her fingers. She slipped her toes in and out of her sandals, and twisted the ends of her hair. To him, her crumbling composure was plain.

"She doesn't make anything easy," he said.

"Things haven't been easy for *her,* Harry."

The heat of the campfire was hot on his forehead, but the blaze in his gut was hotter. "I know her grandmother loved her very much. Her mom was absent, at best. Then, some asshole named Noah broke her. That's the sum total of what I know." Christ, he was in love with a woman who doled out bits of herself so parsimoniously, it seemed each day he discovered more about her that he *didn't* know than what he did.

Temperance squeezed his arm. "Listen. I told you I wasn't getting involved. But I know this: if you've seen over those mile-high walls she puts up, I can't imagine you're not in love with her. And I think the only way you've seen over them is if she's allowed it. That means she's in love with you too, whether she knows it or not."

He stared at the ground. "How does someone not *know*?"

Temperance folded her hands in her lap and gave him a clinical once-over. "Harry Brady, have you ever wanted a thing, and didn't get it? And I don't mean luxuries. I mean basic human needs. Companionship. Emotional stability. True intimacy."

Shame and frustration made a nauseating cocktail in Harry's stomach. Rowan had lived a very different life than his. He simply couldn't get his mind around *why,* after not having those things, she wouldn't leap at the chance to finally have them. With him.

"Paging Dr. Brady. Where'd you go?" Temperance said.

"Sorry, I think I'm tired," he said, and shook his head. "Duncan rides me from dawn to dusk right now. We're painting the pool deck tomorrow, apparently. Forecast is over ninety. Shit."

"You need to tell Duncan to take it easier on you, or I'm going to chat with him."

"You really want me to tell him that?"

It was Temperance's turn to go quiet. "No. Better not."

"Might get him off my back. I think he's afraid of you."

"Good." She turned her focus to the fire. "He should be."

"You ever want to talk to me about Duncan, T-Bird?"

She looked up. Her eyes had gone frosty. "Why would I?"

Harry laughed softly. "Oh, I don't know. But I just got more information than I could have ever hoped for by the look on your face right now."

* * *

ROWAN DISAPPEARED.

Harry hadn't seen her sneak away from the fire. While he tried to casually look around for her, he made inadvertent eye contact with Nate, who subtly pointed up the hill without missing a beat in his conversation with Dad. Harry groaned inwardly at how transparent he must be, and acknowledged with a single, silent nod. Nate lifted a curious eyebrow and nodded back.

Eventually, he was going to need to have *that* conversation.

But now, he needed to find Rowan.

The gardener's cottage was dark. Next door, a faint glimmer of lamplight shone through the foggy windows of the greenhouse. She'd set a beacon for him, intentional or not.

She leaned over the front table, watering some vegetable seedlings. When the door creaked as he entered, she straightened, but didn't turn around.

Harry locked the door behind him. The snap of the dead bolt engaged and echoed off the glass walls.

"Usually, when someone quietly leaves, it's a signal they want to be alone." She turned.

"Usually, when someone is part of a polite social gathering, they say goodbye," Harry shot back.

She dragged her bottom lip through her teeth a few times and hugged the small watering can to her chest. "Your mom sent the kids up the hill to get me earlier. That's the only reason I was there tonight."

"Okay."

"I didn't want you to think I was there because of— any other reason."

That stung, but Harry crossed his arms and maintained his distance. "Okay."

"I shouldn't have been there."

"You were invited."

"That's not what I mean. Everyone is—so nice." Her voice wavered on *nice,* and water sloshed over the side of the can when she put it down.

"You're upset you had a good time," Harry said.

Rowan looked down at her feet and continued gnawing her lip.

He frowned. "You're—upset everyone in my family adores you."

"Including you." Her expression was wary.

"What?"

"You said everyone adores me." She went pale under her freckles. "Including you."

"Is that a question?"

"You lied to me, Harrison."

"Ah, shit. We're back to 'Harrison' again?"

She crossed and uncrossed her arms, grappling for equilibrium. "You told me we could keep this casual."

Anger sparked. "I'm trying, damn it. Every time I touch you, I remind myself you're leaving. Every time you look at me, I tell myself you're not actually in as deep as I am." Heat climbed the sides of his neck. "I fight a constant, conscious battle, trying to convince myself I'm satisfied with what you decide to give me."

"See? Those aren't casual words."

No shit.

The fuse on his temper sizzled determinedly toward detonation. "If I'm a liar, you're a liar, too. You've been lying about how you feel—to me, to yourself. For *months*. You're a coward. Sneaking out of my place every night, hiding this from my family, denying it to yourself."

"*I'm* hiding? You're the one hiding. You're hiding away from your entire *life*. Hiding behind me, behind your family. All that talent, all that brainpower, just— pissed away, so you don't have to face a mountain of guilt you didn't fucking earn."

Harry rocked back on his heels. "Someone *died,* Rowan."

"Yes, someone died, and it is tragic and unfair. But how long are you going to evade *your* life because of it?"

"You know the reason I'm still here has nothing to do with that anymore," he snapped.

Rowan flinched as his words landed. "You're really putting that on me? You're staying here, digging holes, laying bricks, mowing lawns, because you—you have a—a *crush*?"

That did it. A muscle spasmed under his eye. He exploded into motion, crowding her against the table behind her. He still didn't touch her. "A *crush*. Are you fucking serious?"

They puffed at each other like two angry bulls.

"I always suspected something was wrong with me," she said, implausibly calm. "Then, once I met you and your family, I was sure of it. I'm not for you, Harrison. I'm not—this is just—you're just—too nice."

"Too *nice*?" Harry's self-control snapped like a bone in a vise. "I'm not as nice as you think I am." He reached around her to swipe an arm across the table. "Sex is all you want?" Stacks of plastic nursery pots clattered to the ground. "Fine. Fuck it."

His hands dug into her hips. In one fluid motion, she leapt, he lifted, and she was up on the high table, bare thighs clamping his chest as she sank her mouth down to his.

He rammed his fingertips under the front waistband of her shorts and nearly tore off the button.

"Not here," she muttered against his mouth.

"Yes, here. Why do you think I locked the door?"

Nice?

Fuck *nice*.

The things he wanted to do to her weren't *nice*.

"Take off your top," Harry commanded. He stepped back, out of her reach.

She hesitated. Glanced at the condensation-fogged glass walls. A box fan in one of the windows creaked in an aberrant rhythm, and the old sink in the back of the greenhouse dripped. For a moment, it seemed like she might say no, go to hell. And he would've.

Eyes blazing, Rowan smiled, drew the white tank over her head, and dropped it to the soil-dusted floor.

"I need to hear it." Harry barely recognized the low tones of his own voice.

"Yes."

Her nipples were a dark outline against the thin microfiber of her bra. Harry had the front clasp open in seconds, drawing the material away from her breasts, unwrapping her like a luscious treat. She arched her back and slipped her arms out of the bra, sending it to join the tank top on the ground.

Her breasts were the most beautiful he'd ever seen, lushly curved beneath, nipples the color of cinnamon. The same color as her eyes. Her body was all cream and spice.

"Lay back," he said.

Her knees naturally drew up as she lowered her back to the table. Harry reached under her and snagged the waistband of her shorts and panties, and tugged them over her ass, down her legs.

When he touched her and found how wet she was for him, he nearly lost it in his shorts. He was intoxicated by the scents around him: the mineral zip of clean dirt, a musky undertone of fertilizers. The lush scent of arousal from the woman before him.

Harry spread her knees and ran his hands up the outside of her thighs, bending low. He palmed her ass, lifting her, inhaling her. Then he flattened his tongue and made a few slow, broad swirls along her center. The salt and tang of her was like a drug.

Rowan's back arched off the high table, and her foot slipped, kicking him in the shoulder. He wrapped his fingers around that ankle to anchor her in place. With the other hand, he slipped two fingers inside her, then lowered his mouth to continue what he'd begun.

Harry looked up to watch her face as he swept her toward her peak. Her belly hollowed and clenched, and her breath hitched in her throat, reaching, reaching. When her legs began to shudder and she held her breath, he knew she was close.

"Stop holding your breath." He stood, using his fingers for the kind of force and friction his tongue wouldn't provide. His free hand dug into the healthy curve of muscle above her kneecap, the force of it pulling skin shiny and taut across the contoured bone.

"Look at me," he demanded. He knew the exact driving rhythm she needed. He stared her down until her eyes flashed to wildfire, flame and gold, and she clenched hard on her teeth. In seconds, she burst against his hand, hot as summer sunshine, crying out his name.

Harry. He was Harry again.

The aftershocks of her orgasm still pulsed around his fingers as he hauled her upright with his free hand. He slid her down from the table and growled into her hair, "Was that *nice*?" Pinning her against the wood, he unzipped his fly far enough to free his aching dick, and ripped open the condom he'd stashed in his back pocket. Lately, he never went anywhere without one.

"Yes, damn it." She took him in her hand, using her thumb to spread a pearl of moisture around his tip.

Sucking a swift breath through his teeth, Harry grabbed her wrist and snapped her hand away. He flipped her around and bent her over the table so her ass was high in the air. She exhaled hard as her breasts hit the wood, but no protestations followed. "You still want this?" he choked, rolling the condom on with two slick strokes.

Her voice was muffled against the table, and her hips canted backward into him. "Yes. *Now*." Before the final syllable was past her lips, Harry knocked her thighs wider with his knee and drove into her. A frenzied rhythm immediately consumed him. His fingers dug into her hips, pressing flesh hard enough to meet bone. Rowan's fingernails skidded against the surface of the table as he railed into her from behind. Hair falling in his eyes, shorts sliding down his ass with every unrestrained thrust, Harry was a mess, ablaze inside her volcanic heat. When she slammed a hand against the table for leverage to grind back into him, he thought the wood beneath them would surely burn to ash.

Her free hand was buried between her legs, working hard, greedy for another orgasm. She chased that second release, commanding him to give her more. Faster, she wanted, and faster is what he gave her. She crashed against him, rising to the tips of her toes as she came. His own roaring detonation answered hers, blasting through him hard enough to buckle his knees. He had to grip the edge of the table to remain inside her, hunching over her back to ride the sensation to the end.

She'd emptied him all the way down to the marrow of his bones.

Rational thought returned moments later. Harry straightened to look down at her back. At the body he'd used like a vessel. Her ribs were faintly visible with every ragged inhale and exhale. He traced the twin dimples above the split of her ass, and the columns of muscle bracketing her spine. The beloved freckles adorning her skin. His mouth knew every single one.

Harry slid a hand along her shoulder blades. Reverent. Soothing.

What the fuck had he done?

Shame prickled, raising every hair on his arms in gooseflesh. He took a deep breath through his nose. The air smelled like sex and soil, and the perfume of roses.

Staggering backward, he withdrew from her and deftly removed the condom, tossing it into a nearby trash bin. Rowan straightened and turned as he pulled up his shorts with shaking hands. Harry saw her wince and cup a hand around her hip.

She met his eyes. One of her cheeks was red from the friction against the table. With both hands, she pushed her hair away from her face, watching him with unnerving clarity. When she raised her arms to slip on her tank top, he saw a faint bruise springing to the surface on her hip bone. Because of him.

She padded away on bare feet and came back a moment later, wearing her khaki shorts. Pink color was high in her cheeks, and her eyes glowed like rubies.

Harry was still speechless. Self-disgust choked him. *Fuck,* he was a dick.

Drowning in the existential misery of self-doubt, he'd come here to heal, and instead exchanged that pain for the fathomless torment of wanting her. Knowing she'd never give him more than her body. Hell, he'd wanted to rediscover himself, and he'd succeeded. Only now, he had no idea who he was without her.

Somewhere in central California, Cora Woodward's husband, Wesley, cared for a son who had to grow up without his mother. Harry could close his eyes and see the man's kind, round face. He could imagine Wesley sitting up on sleepless nights with the baby, staring at the ceiling, realizing he'd started to forget the sound of Cora's laugh, or the smell of her hair.

Perhaps Harry falling in love with a woman he'd never get to keep was the cosmically cruel penance he'd earned and deserved.

God, I'm an asshole.

What a false fucking equivalence. A wife—a mother—was dead. Rowan was emotionally distant, but he could still touch her, see her, hear her voice.

He might never heal from the loss of Cora Woodward, and he hated himself even more for making her death about *him*. Disgusted, Harry wrenched up the zipper of his shorts, then pressed the heels of his palms into his eyelids until pinpoints of light flashed in the blackness.

Shame was a haze of red filling his brain. Harry slid to his knees and wrapped his hands around Rowan's waist, pressing his face into her belly.

"I hurt you."

"You didn't." She twined her fingers through the hair at his nape. "I wanted all of it. Every moment."

He clung to her there for a long time, feeling her belly rising and falling against his face, his hands clamped against the hip bones he'd bruised with his unrestrained thrusts. Several times, Rowan tried to tug him up to stand, but when he refused to budge, she dropped to her knees to join him on the floor. She took his face in her hands, forcing him to meet her eyes.

"I'm not hurt." Sweat made auburn curls spring out like fiddleheads at her temples. "It was—nice."

The words were probably meant as an olive branch. He knew her humor well enough by now. But Harry had to swallow the sourness rising in his throat. That she'd liked it made him feel exponentially worse. Of *course* she'd liked it. This was all she wanted—messy, detached sex. And he'd taken as eagerly as she'd given, like a stray begging for scraps.

She would own him until his last breath. Even if she walked out of here tonight—or a month from now, or a year from now, and left him permanently behind, this feeling would never lose potency. Harry wanted every single atom of Rowan McKinnon.

He was defenseless against her, and against his own pathetic, pathetic need.

CHAPTER TWENTY-THREE

Rowan

Harry hadn't been around to help in a week. His truck in the carriage house driveway was the only sign he still lived there at all.

Last weekend, the Bradys' campfire had been too much. Will had looked right at her during his toasts about family. When Grey had called her Rosie, she'd relived Edie's loss with a simultaneous surge of affection for the little boy. It felt so *heavy*. Then when Gia and Maren had looped her in on their conversation about baby names, they might as well have asked her to strip naked and dance around the lawn. Rowan's tool kit was utterly empty in situations like that. She'd felt like an impostor, the same hollow sense of *otherness* she'd felt the first night she'd met them. The Brady roots went as deep as their decades-old grapevines, and she was a perpetually spinning maple seed sailing through air, never landing in suitable enough soil to put down roots of her own.

After Edie died, the notion of family had become a fantasy. Something unattainable, as unlikely as becoming an astronaut, or starring on Broadway. Family was a thing so alien to her, Rowan didn't even fully understand what it meant to be part of one. Being dropped into the full Brady family experience felt like she was an actor on a movie set, where nobody had given her lines, or told her what to wear, or where to stand.

The breaking point had been watching Harry and Temperance's hushed chat from across the fire. By the way they'd both cut their eyes at her, Rowan had obviously been the topic. Harry had appeared so desolate, and T.J. seemed tense. It was too much.

Yesterday, she'd pounded on the door of the carriage house just after dusk. She'd relented after three attempts, too nervous someone would see her. Months ago, she'd told herself—and Harry—that she didn't want the professional complications of his family knowing about them. But now, the stakes were even infinitely higher. More personal. She couldn't bear Gia and Will's inevitable disappointment in her for luring Harry into this—whatever *this* was—with no promise of a future. Harry deserved so much more than she was capable of giving him, and Rowan was sure the Bradys would agree.

Her own mother hadn't been capable of loving her. How could they?

Still, she was here now, and she was worried about him. Again, she stood on the little porch of the carriage house, concern tinged with irritation. She'd knocked four times. Clearly, he was avoiding her.

After the fifth knock, Harry swung the door open forcefully enough to blow his hair back. When the waves fell into his eyes, he flicked them back with a bored upward thrust of his chin. His smoky blue eyes looked like they'd been sketched in dull pencil, rather than their usual rich watercolor.

A shadow of whiskers prickled along his jaws and his neck, and he was shirtless, wearing a pair of wrinkled blue scrubs. Long toes peeped out under the baggy hem.

His lips looked pale and dry. He ran his tongue over his teeth before he spoke.

"Hey," he said.

Frankie always teased her about her inability to read people, but Rowan *was* an expert at detecting withdrawal and annoyance. But she wasn't going to let him scare her away.

"Hey," she echoed. She had to clench the muscles in her thighs to keep from stepping forward to put her arms around him. "Can I come in?"

He grunted. "I'm busy right now."

She leaned forward to look into the house. "Busy with what?"

"Does it matter?"

"You told me once that you were never too busy for me."

"Well. Things change."

Rowan straightened and crossed her arms. "You're blowing me off."

"I needed some space. Some time."

"What are you, Doctor Who?"

He blinked. "If that's a joke, I don't get it."

She tightened her arms. "Are you trying to teach me a lesson? Make me understand what it feels like to be you?"

"I've been trying to do that for months, Rowan." His tone was dry, but his eyes were turbulent, all thunderhead darkness and energy.

"If you're going to be a dick—"

"Your double standard is bullshit, you know." He leaned out the doorway. "How many times have you run off without a word? It's okay when you do it, but not when I do?"

Rowan's first impulse was to lash out, to *win*. But

he was right. She'd done it to him all the time, and the torment in his face told her that he'd finally done the same because it was his last viable option. Her arms went slack and dropped to her sides. She kept her voice gentle.

"The times I've run away, it's been to regroup. To find the courage to come back." Rowan hesitated. "To stay."

His expression was flat as he peered at her.

"Why did you run, Harry? From California? From me? When you run, do you mean to stay gone?"

When he still didn't answer, she turned to leave.

He snagged her wrist. His eyes skimmed her body, then her face. "Wait."

Rowan fixed him with a wary look.

"Come in." He dropped her arm and walked away, leaving her to follow.

The air inside the house had a lingering odor of burned toast, and all blinds were drawn. The usual bright and glossy interior of the place now seemed dull and lifeless, like a prison cell.

By the time she shut the front door behind her, Harry had disappeared into the bedroom. She followed.

A dark bath towel was pinned against the ceiling to cover the skylight. Only a single pillow and a fitted sheet were on the bed. The rest of the linens and pillows were heaped in the corner of the room. Five empty bottles of wine sat on his nightstand, next to a stack of bent photographs. Rowan couldn't tell who was in the photos, but it was obvious they were frequently handled by rough hands.

Harry fished around in his top drawer, tugging the string at the waist of his scrubs. "Ready whenever you are." He held up a condom, expressionless. Based on how the thin fabric of his pants tented and curved out in the front, his body was not as apathetic as his mind.

Rowan snatched the condom out of his hands and flung it away. "Did you not hear what I said? I came here because I missed you, not because I wanted a quick lay."

Harry's eyes were shuttered. "Same thing for you, isn't it?"

"Not with you." That swift admission was easier than she'd ever imagined. Now that the words were hanging in the air between them, she felt relieved.

"Don't." He thrust away from her to sit on the edge of the bed, hunched over.

"So, this is where you've been hiding for the past week?" Rowan gestured to the wine bottles. "People have probably been worried about you."

"My family knew I needed some time."

My family.

Not *her.*

When she was met with more silence, Rowan kicked off her sandals and climbed up to stand on the mattress behind him. She ripped the towel down and gathered the pushpins he'd used to attach it. One of the pins sank into the center of her palm, but she bit back the pain. Late afternoon sunshine blared in like a theater spotlight.

Harry leapt to his feet and growled up at her. "The fuck are you doing?" Finally, some spark in him. It was dim, like a flashlight with a dying battery, but it was there.

Twisting the towel around her hand, she balled it up and lobbed it at him. He flinched, caught it, and threw it aside.

Rowan jumped down from the bed and dumped the pins into an empty coffee mug on the dresser. "What have you been doing, Harry? Sitting in the dark, staring at walls, drinking yourself into oblivion?"

"It's none of your business."

Maintaining her grip on calm felt like trying to grasp seaweed during high tide.

"You've spent the last eight months making yourself my business, and now that I want to have a serious conversation about"—Rowan faltered—"*us,* you're blowing me off."

"Us." He breathed out a bitter little laugh. Wouldn't look her in the eye.

"I think you're punishing yourself, punishing me, because *you* blew past the boundaries I set. You went too deep, you went too hard, and now, I'm supposed to make you feel better about it? Is that how this works?"

He flattened a hand over his eyes and paced. "I thought I could play by your rules. I can't. I fucking hate your rules." His voice broke. "And I hate the way I treated you the other night in the greenhouse."

"*And* you're mad I liked it. Aren't you?"

His head snapped up, eyes blazing pewter fire. "I hate that *I* liked it."

"Why? I loved it. I will always tell you if I don't. Have you *met* me?"

"This isn't about you. The things I feel for you are— more than that. If that's all you want, I can't—" He sat down again on the edge of the bed. "I can't."

Rowan felt the ratcheting tension in the room—she had the sixth sense of emotional self-preservation all people with shitty childhoods had. It was telling her to leave, to cut this off, right now. His withdrawal, this potent anger—it was an *out.* Her paper was publishing this month, and she had postdoc interviews in two of her top programs in a matter of weeks. Some cosmic patron saint of commitment avoidance was offering her the perfect escape hatch, all but tied up with a pretty bow. She could walk out of there right now, and it wouldn't have to be her making the call to end it.

Take the out, Rowan.

Too late. Harry hooked a finger under the hem of her shirt and drew her close, locking his knees around her thighs.

"Are you bleeding?" His voice was a sullen rumble, but his touch was gentle. He splayed her fingers open. Darkened calluses embellished his palm, and a thin curve of dirt lingered under his thumbnails—hints of wildness on typically immaculate hands.

On Rowan's own hand, the puncture wound from the pushpin was tiny, and the bleeding had already stopped. A dry, rusty smear crossed her palm where she'd wiped it on her shorts. Harry curled her fingers inward to make a fist, then wrapped his big hand around it.

They were quiet for a long time. Rowan looked at the top of his head, and at the tangle of linens in the corner of the room. At the work gloves on his dresser, laid perfectly stacked next to his shabby ball cap. The little ring he'd made of grapevine tendrils back in December sat there, too.

She looked to the nightstand. If she squinted, Rowan could make out a woman with glossy mahogany hair in the photos, and the kind of soul-stirring smile that gave you no choice but to smile back.

Harry noticed where her attention had gone. "That's Cora." His voice cracked on her name.

Rowan guided his arms around her waist. At first, he was rigid, difficult to move. When she drew his head against her belly, he unwound, and his arms tightened around her.

"Tell me," she said.

The clock in the bathroom ticked, and the refrigerator hummed in the kitchen. Outside, an eastern towhee trilled its merry *"drink your tea!"* song, and a car rumbled by on the gravel drive. Harry's bracing exhale felt hot against her middle.

"For some reason, when it rains in L.A., people forget how to fucking drive," he began.

Rowan chuckled. "That's not unique to Los Angeles."

Harry pressed his forehead into her belly, looking at the floor. "I was stuck in traffic on the 405. The sky was throwing down rain. Lightning, booming thunder. Suddenly, these people come running through the standstill traffic, waving arms, stopping at every few cars, asking for—" He swallowed hard. "A doctor.

"About thirty cars back, a woman was in labor. Paramedics hadn't arrived yet. God, I was so pumped. Pulled into the median, left my car. Cora was a first-time mom. Her husband's name was Wesley. He was freaking out, but she"—Harry laughed softly—"*she* was an absolute boss, comforting *him* during her contractions. The baby came about ten minutes after I got there. She wouldn't have needed me at all. They joked about naming the baby Storm."

"Did they?"

"Yeah. They did." His voice was barely audible. "Harrison Storm Woodward."

Rowan's heart twisted. "It's a strong name." She threaded her fingers through his hair.

"When the ambulance arrived, I tried to get them to bend the rules and let Wesley ride with Cora and the baby. Company policy said no. Insurance reasons, or some garbage like that. Wesley asked if I could stay with them, and since they'd be taken to the hospital where I had admitting privileges, I was allowed to go."

A shudder went through him.

"I promised Wesley I'd take care of her. I told them both—everything was going to be okay. That Cora had done the hard part. He gave me a big hug, both of us getting soaked in the pissing rain while they loaded Cora and the baby into the ambulance. She blew Wesley a kiss. 'See you soon, Daddy' is what she said. I can still hear the way they laughed at that."

Harry balked at continuing, his fingers curling against her back. His low groan of grief vibrated against her belly. Rowan made soft soothing sounds into his hair, and he began again.

"Everything seemed fine. Cora got tired, completely typical. Dozed with the baby in her arms, smile on her face. We'd just pulled off the exit when her vitals tanked. Hidden hemorrhage. The *blood*. The storm literally shook the rig as she started to bleed out. Those EMTs busted their asses, and I was compressing her belly with my entire body weight. But by the time we reached the hospital, she couldn't be saved."

Rowan sank to her knees in front of him and gripped his thighs. She pressed her forehead to his.

"I insisted on being the one to tell Wesley when he arrived. Took him two hours to get out of that traffic. Cora was gone before he'd even gotten off the 405."

Harry stood abruptly, stepping around her. Rowan stayed on the floor, sitting back on her heels. "Her sister blames me. Name's Lena, I've never met her." He held up the stack of photos. "A few weeks after Cora died, I started getting these at the hospital, then at home. At first, they had short, awful letters with them. Now, it's only pictures. Of Cora." He flicked them onto the bed like playing cards, one at a time. Each one was a different image of Cora Woodward's smiling face, vibrant and full of life.

"Jesus, Harry. How did she find you here?"

He shrugged. "I'm not sure. Wesley, probably. We've stayed in touch. I don't think he'd have realized this was her intent, though. He's a good guy."

Rowan stood and gathered the photos and envelopes. The looped handwriting looked familiar. "Cora Woodward deserves to be mourned, Harry. But her sister is trying to collect a debt you don't owe. You *have* to stop opening these."

"I can't help myself."

"Fine. When they arrive, give them to me. I'll take care of them."

I'll take care of you.

A quaking breath deflated him. Rowan tucked the photos into the bottom drawer of his dresser.

"You couldn't have done anything differently, Harry."

His lip curled. "I gave them false hope, and I fucking hate myself for that hubris." His gaze hardened. "How can I ever look a patient in the eyes again and tell them everything is okay?"

"It's not hubris, it's conviction." Rowan cradled his face in her hands. "Everything good doctors do is an act of willful defiance against how fragile we are as a species."

The dam burst. Rowan wrapped Harry tight while he cried in her arms. She held him until the golden sunshine coming through the skylight dimmed to a cool opal glow.

When the rise and fall of his belly against hers gentled and slowed, she led him by the hand to the kitchen and made him one of the few hot meals she was capable of: oatmeal with fresh strawberries and cream. After his belly was full of something other than wine, she pushed him into a hot, soapy shower, and snoozed on his bed.

When he emerged from the bathroom, steam swelled

out behind him, filling the space with the sweet scent of his soap. He rubbed a towel vigorously over his wet hair, making it stand out wildly around his head.

"Thank you," he said.

When he turned the bathroom light off, the room went dark, illuminated only by the weak lamp on the bedside table.

"I do make a superior bowl of oatmeal," Rowan said, stretching.

"That's not what I mean, and you know it." He dropped the towel from his waist and crawled up the bed to her, fixing his mouth to the pulse point below her ear. "Let me make you breakfast."

She tipped her chin up to give him full access to her neck, and his mouth worked its way across her skin, molten hot and slow.

"We just had oatmeal. It's nighttime."

The edges of his teeth grazed her earlobe. "Not *now*."

Realization sparked in her brain, sending a sizzle of arousal through every nerve ending in her skin. The tiny hairs on her neck rose in response.

"Oh. In the morning."

He nodded, eyes solemn. "Stay with me tonight. All night."

"Harry—"

"Only this once. I promise I'll never ask again."

"I told you earlier, I didn't come here today for sex. I don't want you to think that."

"I know you didn't. And I'm not talking about sex, either." He reached between them to open the button of her cutoffs, and slid his hand into her panties.

"Getting some mixed signals from you here, Doc," she breathed.

The dim glow of the bedside lamp skimmed his jaw

and his beloved dimple. A sheaf of hair fell over his forehead, and she tucked it back, threading her fingers through the damp strands.

"Has anyone ever made love to you, Rowan?"

The world was hushed as they took each other's mouths in a lazy, delving kiss. The only sounds were bodies crumpling sheets, skin sliding on skin, and heavy breaths, steady and deep with the sensual tempo Harry set for them. He linked their fingers and pressed joined fists into the mattress, connecting as much of himself to her as possible. His kisses were deep strokes of his tongue, a carnal echo of the slow, powerful rhythm of his hips between her legs. He kissed her as though she were the source of everything good and right, and she answered in kind.

"You are so beautiful," he whispered, his nose pressed to her temple, hot breath fanning into her hair.

Rowan responded with a watery laugh. "It's dark in here."

Harry raised above her, steady and strong. "I don't need light to see you."

Much later, he gathered her against his chest, and she tucked her head into the crook of his arm. Rowan stared into the darkness. The oblivion of sleep overtook him fast. His body collapsed a bit beneath her; his breathing turned heavy and deliberate. She eased away and propped up on her elbow beside him. Slumber softened his features, the tension that often kept his brows drawn together finally relenting. Rowan smoothed a fingertip along his hairline, and he sighed. His full bottom lip cast a crescent-shaped shadow over the subtle divot in his chin.

God, *he* was the beautiful one.

His hand rested on his chest. Rowan touched a

fingertip to the soft swirl of hair on the outer bone of his wrist, then traced the network of vessels and tendons on the back of his hand. They were a stark reminder of his humanity. Of vulnerability. That vulnerability was like a siren song to her own, calling for union.

She stayed.

CHAPTER TWENTY-FOUR

Rowan

Harry kept his word. He never asked her to stay overnight again. Rowan did anyway, throughout the rest of May, June, and into July.

It was before dawn. She awakened beside him, lingering in the murky state of consciousness where dreams were indistinguishable from reality. She'd been floating in Lake Vesper, and the water had been the color of Harry's eyes.

Sliding away from him as she did every morning, she was careful to not tug the blankets or dip the mattress too hard, or knock the headboard into the wall as she rose. She tiptoed to the tiny bathroom, where there were two toothbrushes on the sink now.

A few early birds called beyond the window, the herald of every summer sunrise. A red-winged blackbird's gurgle-trill, the slurred whistle of a lone cardinal, and the earnest *chicka-dee-dee-dee* of a chickadee. Soon, an avian choir would explode in tandem with the brightening sky, a surge of sound that was somehow both discordant and harmonious.

Those birds set a timer for Rowan each day—she had just shy of an hour before the entire world was lit. For the last few weeks, she'd been keeping work clothes

there, dressing and slipping into the vineyard before anyone else stirred or arrived for work.

Movement caught her eye from the relative gloom
of the bedroom. The bathroom light spilled forth to il-
luminate half of Harry's bare chest as he sat up to watch
her. He seemed so strong now, with bulk back on his
bones. The strappy muscles of his biceps and forearms
were more defined, and most of the hollows and angles of
him had filled in or smoothed over. So different from the
withered man she'd met last fall.

He absently scratched his chest, blinking slowly. He
tucked pillow-rumpled hair behind his ears. In another
month, the waves would brush the tops of his shoulders.
Rowan wondered if he would trim it once he went back
to practicing medicine. She imagined him in full scrubs,
white lab coat, and an irreverent nub of ponytail.

Delicious.

Those dark predawn hours had a primal quality about
them. It felt like they were the only humans in existence,
bodies tethered throughout the hours of suspended
consciousness. They might have existed at any point in
human history—ten thousand years ago, bundled in furs
under an ancient cliffside shelter, or tangled in the sheets
of a sumptuous Victorian four-poster. On the surface it
seemed a mundane thing, sleeping with someone. But
truly, it was an absolute abandonment of control. It was
trust, distilled down to the ultimate vulnerability.

It was the most intimate thing she'd ever done.

The first glimpse of Harry each day triggered a nervous, delicious agitation inside her. A heaviness behind
her sternum, a shimmer along her bones. She could smell
him on her skin as she raised her arms to put up her hair.
The insides of her thighs were tender, her muscles won-
derfully overused.

"Been watching me?" she murmured around a mouthful of toothpaste. Sexy.

"I'll never pass up the opportunity to look at you." His voice was gravelly with sleep.

She tipped her head sideways. "Hm, a little creepy."

"I was aiming for charming."

"Yeah, that's a swing and a miss, Doc."

His laugh was gentle, comfortable. "Ah, how about— charmingly creepy?"

"There's no such thing, unless you're Jack Skellington."

"Who?"

"Never mind." She chuckled and rinsed her mouth. When she shifted her eyes back to Harry, his scrutiny was intense. He always looked at her like someone she knew she was not.

"Not polite to stare," she said, lightly.

He didn't look away. "I'm memorizing. This is the last morning I get to do this for a while."

Later today, Gia would drive her to the airport. This afternoon she'd land in Austin, and her first postdoc interview would be tomorrow. Then in two days, she'd head to Montreal.

Rowan stripped off her sleep shirt, baring her breasts in the unflattering fluorescent bulbs. Harry's eyes remained fixed on her face. Funny, that eye contact made her feel more fully *seen* than if he'd swept her entire mostly naked body with his gaze.

She tugged on a bra, then slipped into an old V-neck T-shirt. "I'll only be gone a week."

"This time," he said.

"What?"

"*This* time," he emphasized. "The whole reason for this trip is to find a reason to leave. Permanently."

An indigo glow bled through the gap in the curtains, reminding her of the ticking clock of sunrise. The lingering toothpaste flavor was suddenly chalk on her tongue. He wasn't wrong.

This step should have been thrilling for her, finally moving forward after nearly a year of professional stasis. But it felt nothing like she'd anticipated it would. It felt like she was doing it for someone else—for another Rowan she barely recognized. Now, it felt like a fathomless void existed on the other side of her trusty escape hatch, and if she used it, she might tumble away into nothingness.

At the very least, she had to attend the interviews. Had to prove to herself that what she felt here with Harry was real, and not simply some whimsical artifact of being in the valley for so long. She was still a scientist, and scientists made decisions only after they had comprehensive data sets.

The last time she'd tried to listen only to her heart, it lied.

"I don't know how to respond to that," she said, pulling on her favorite cutoffs. They smelled like Harry's laundry detergent—she hadn't washed her own clothes in over a month.

"You don't have to. I shouldn't have said anything." Harry palmed the back of his neck, working the muscle there. The tension in his body language was evident, but his tone was gentle. "I don't want you to think I'm trying to influence your decision."

Rowan hesitated. "Okay."

"Okay," Harry echoed. He unfurled his long limbs over the edge of the bed and padded over to her. "Stay for breakfast. I'll be quick. I won't let you turn into a pumpkin." He kissed her forehead and slid around her, nudging her out of the bathroom. Without waiting for an answer, he pushed the pocket door closed behind him.

She gnawed her lip and glanced at the window. Indigo had phased into deep blue, and the birds were singing in earnest now.

"Rowan." Harry's voice sounded muffled through the door, but firm. "Don't go. Please."

She exhaled hard and leaned into the wall beside the bathroom.

"Only once," he said. A pause. "I promise I won't ever ask again."

She cracked an irrepressible grin at the ceiling and shook her head. The last time he'd said that—when he'd asked her to spend the night late in the spring—they hadn't spent a single night apart since.

"I know that trick," she said.

And again, she stayed.

* * *

GENTLE SOUNDS OF domesticity filled the kitchen— clinks and clanks of dishes and silverware, Harry's tuneless humming as he tended a sizzling pan of bacon on the stove top.

In the center of the table in the tiny breakfast nook, he'd filled an empty applesauce jar with wildflowers.

"You braved the meadow to pick flowers?"

"Don't get too excited. I picked from the very, very edge."

"When?"

"Around midnight. Couldn't sleep. You were snoring," Harry said.

"You went to the meadow in the *dark*?"

"I had a flashlight." Harry shrugged. "I've learned to never go out on this property at night without one." He glanced over his shoulder to make sure the joke landed before returning his attention to the stove.

"Cute," she drawled. "I don't snore."

"You do snore. It's adorable."

She rolled her eyes and propped her chin in her hands. "The orb weavers in the meadow are still tiny this time of year, you know. Wee babies."

"I didn't know that, but it doesn't matter. Even if they're tiny, they're still spiders."

"What's the story? Why are you so afraid of them?"

A deep breath drew the soft fabric of his T-shirt taut between his shoulder blades. "It's a boring story, really. A daddy longlegs walked up my arm while I was sitting in the grass during a family picnic. As Duncan took great pleasure in mentioning, scared me so bad I peed my pants."

"So, last year, then?" she teased.

"Hilarious. No, I was seven. That terror is branded on my soul."

Rowan softened. "Yet you still let me guide you through the meadow back in the fall."

He faced her. "I trusted you."

Rowan went to the table to sip the orange juice. A froth of juicy pulp skimmed her lip. Harry watched her as she drank, his task on the stove temporarily abandoned. The way he watched her seemed oddly earnest, like he was waiting for something. A reaction.

Then she noticed the contents of the small clear bin on the counter by the fridge—she'd given it to him so he could add kitchen scraps to her compost pile. It was filled with the remains of at least a dozen oranges, halved open and squeezed completely dry of juice. Rowan looked down at the glass in her hand.

The mundanity of the morning evaporated in an

instant. Their conversation from months ago came at her with the intensity of a pop-up thunderstorm.

"If it's an act of true love, there's fresh-squeezed orange juice."

"Pulp or no pulp?" Harry had later asked.

"Extra pulp," she'd said. *"I want to feel like I'm drinking an actual orange."*

Rowan's heartbeat tripped over itself, pounding hard and fast. She licked the pulp from her lip. "You knew I would stay this morning," she said. The way her heart sprinted, it was a wonder the words didn't rush out like a fast-forwarded cassette tape.

Harry gave her a small smile, then turned off the stove's burners.

"The flowers, the food." She swallowed hard. "The orange juice. This is a premeditated breakfast."

His brows twitched. "Did you just say 'premeditated breakfast'?"

"Don't tease me."

A beat of silence. Then, "Yes."

That single syllable held an entire universe of subtext.

Rowan maintained eye contact, and it felt like the hardest thing she'd ever done. "It's perfect."

Say more.

Maybe, *"Message received."*

Try humor? *"I see what you did there."*

Or maybe just, *"I love you, too."*

Instead, she took another sip of the juice, sat the glass down, and awkwardly smoothed a paper napkin over a decade-old grass stain on the thigh of her cutoffs.

Coward.

He approached with the coffee carafe, looking like a very sexy diner waiter. "I heard through the grapevine how you like it," he said.

Rowan's laugh was immediate, and the tension of the moment vented like a popped champagne cork. By choosing to respond with levity, he was letting her off the hook.

"Wow," she said.

"I know, horrible. Want coffee?"

"Mm-hmm."

He filled their mugs with fragrant fresh brew, knowing she preferred it black. For his, he spooned in two tablespoons of sugar, then changed it to pale khaki with a liberal splash of cream.

God, the metaphors were writing themselves.

Harry served her two of the most perfect pancakes she'd ever seen. Round, fluffy, and topped with pooling pats of butter. Her plate had barely burnt bacon on it, too.

It wasn't just the orange juice. It was the *entire breakfast* from that long-ago conversation. He may as well have written it in the sky.

Just say it. *"I love you too, Harry."*

"No bacon for you?" she asked instead as he settled into the seat across from her.

"Don't like it."

Rowan sucked in a melodramatic breath. "Monster."

"The piggies would disagree."

"How did I not know this about you?"

He raised a wry brow. "You never stuck around for breakfast until now."

"Fair." She took a big bite of pancake and briefly closed her eyes in bliss. "*God*. They're as delicious as they are pretty."

Harry answered with a smirk and a lingering glance at her breasts. "You just made a sex noise." He forked a big hunk into his mouth.

"Did not."

"You did. I'm an authority on the subject. An enthusiast. I'm a Rowan's sex-noises aficionado."

She chewed for a moment, swallowed, and primly dabbed her mouth with a napkin. "Maybe I'm making *pancake* noises during sex, not the other way around?"

"I need to make you pancakes more often."

They laughed. The rest of breakfast and kitchen cleanup proceeded the same—innuendo and affection, gentle laughter, and kisses in between.

Through the window, the sky burned a band of orange along the horizon. Rowan wasn't ready for the morning to be over. She had no work in the vineyard today since Gia would be taking her to the airport in the early afternoon. Tomorrow, she'd wake up in a Texas hotel room, half a country away, preparing to convince strangers to offer her a reason to leave this place.

She wanted to linger with Harry, just this once.

Struck with impulse and urgency, she said, "I want to show you something. But we have to hurry."

* * *

OUTSIDE, THE AIR smelled of mineral coolness and the lingering citrus cream scent of evening primrose. Barn swallows dove and zigzagged in the half-light, and a pair of blue herons flew over them toward the lake in the valley below. Mist, everywhere. It felt like the closest a human being could ever come to breathing underwater.

"Follow," Rowan said, leading Harry on a sprint down one of the Chardonnay rows. He followed without question or hesitation.

They ran until they reached the lower perimeter of the vineyard. Rowan climbed the short fence at the bottom of the Brady property—the latch on the gate there had rusted closed long ago.

"Trespassing? I haven't even had my second cup of coffee," he said.

"Get over here and stop talking," Rowan laughed.

Harry sighed and hopped the fence. His side-eye was almost comical.

Rowan led him by the hand to a field of short grass. Beyond the field, the southern part of Lake Vesper lapped at a shoreline of sedge and cattail. They stopped in the middle of the field, where they had a better view of the gentle upward slope of the Brady vineyard.

For the past month, Rowan had reveled in this brief predawn enchantment each time she left Harry's place, but she'd never had time to come down to see the lake up close. The mist drifted slowly down the rows of grapes, gathering and settling in the valley, mostly obscuring the surface of the water behind them.

She could feel Harry's expectant attention on her. She kept her eyes straight ahead.

"Cloud tide," she whispered.

"Hmm?" Harry murmured.

The words she really wanted to say to him were elusive—it would have been easier to grasp a handful of the vapor swirling around their legs. She squinted into the fog, tamping down a flicker of frustration. "I don't really have the vocabulary for the kinds of things you need to hear me say."

He reached down and hooked a single finger around her palm. Their hands slid together like two halves of a puzzle box. "I told you months ago, I don't need you to *say* anything—"

Gently, Rowan said, "Stop talking, Harry. This is me trying."

"Okay."

A pearl of shame existed deep inside her, buried and

smoothed by years of avoidance. Now it ached to be expelled, but she hesitated, balking at the impulse to give him the kind of access to her she'd never be able to take back. Once you cracked open an oyster, it didn't shut again.

She began slowly. "I grew up on the coast with my grandma Edie and my mother, Sybil, you know that much. Cloud tide is what Edie always called the banks of fog coming off the Atlantic."

Harry's hand tightened around hers. *Tell me more.*

"When I was little, Edie told me my dad was a deep-sea fisherman. She always said the cloud tide made it unsafe for him to navigate into shore, and as a child, that seemed a perfectly logical reason why he was never around. She made up all these fantastical stories of his adventures and heroism, but she told me to never talk to Sybil about him. Edie didn't want her to worry, she'd say. I believed every one of those stories. I'd sneak down to the water sometimes, looking for the ship lights offshore. Wishing he would sail through the fog and take me with him."

Rowan turned to face the lake. Harry gently dug his thumb into the fleshy part of her palm, massaging away the ache from yesterday's vineyard work. She closed her eyes and made a small sound of pleasure.

"After Edie died, I asked Sybil about him. I was twelve. Thought I could handle whatever she'd tell me." Rowan was silent for a moment before she could continue. "Sybil *laughed.* Told me she wasn't sure *who* my father was. Could've been any of several men, she said. It wasn't something she was upset or embarrassed about. It just—*was.*"

Harry's touch eased to a caress.

"I was used to Sybil's insensitivity. It didn't really

matter by then who my father was. What hurt the most was—Edie's stories had all been lies. I was so mad at her, Harry. It took me a year to realize she'd simply been trying to protect my little heart. Eventually, I had the thought—if Sybil didn't know who my father was, maybe there was a chance he *could* be all those things Edie told me he was. From then on, every time I saw the cloud tide, I felt her. It became like—like a symbol of the way she shielded me in my loneliness. It felt like hope."

When she faltered, Harry's hand tightened on hers, an accord between nerve endings. *I'm here. You're not alone.*

"Until I came here, I hadn't seen fog like this since I was a kid. I hadn't felt—" Her voice wavered, and her belly roiled like she was on one of Edie's imaginary ships. "Your family—" she floundered, "Harry, I—"

She couldn't say the words.

"Hey." Harry released her hand so he could cup her face. His expression was serene. Buoyant. "It's okay. You don't have to say the words for me to hear them."

He kissed her hard and fast, then abruptly released her, bending down to slip off his shoes. Then he shucked his shirt over his head and tossed it to the ground.

"Let's go," he said, dropping his shorts and his boxers to the grass.

"What?" Rowan sputtered.

"I said, let's *go*." Harry raced toward the lake.

The sun over the tree line had burned away some of the mist on the vineyard slope above. Rowan felt her confidence dissolving along with it. Fog still swirled on the surface of Lake Vesper.

"Someone will see us," she yelled after him.

"Let them," he shouted back. His bare ass disappeared into the mist.

Rowan crouched to gather his things, still warm from his body. Once again, Harry had rescued her from her inability to articulate her emotions, and that made her want to say the words even more.

"I love you, Harry."

She didn't believe in fate. But the foundation of a life did move into place, piece by piece, without a person realizing it until they were much later standing on the solid form of it. Her foundation would change again later today when she boarded a plane for Texas. Only now, that foundation felt shifty and unstable, the way sand rushes out from underfoot when you stand in the ocean surf.

Her life was on an unanticipated trajectory now, and her true north was no longer where—or what—it used to be.

In the distance, a splash, as Harry cannonballed into the lake.

"Rowaaaaan!" he shouted, dramatically drawing out the last syllable.

She took a big breath and sprinted to the lake.

Harry treaded water a meter or so out. A cabin was faintly visible behind her, but there were no vehicles there, and no lights on. She dropped Harry's stuff to the warm wood surface of the dock and slipped off her shoes.

Let them see.

Her clothes joined Harry's in the haphazard pile, and Rowan dove fearlessly into the cloud tide.

CHAPTER TWENTY-FIVE

Harry

"Let's go back and make some pancake noises," Rowan had murmured against Harry's mouth on the dock after their impromptu swim, both of them still bare naked and stippled with goose bumps.

They'd hastily tugged their clothes over lake-water-wet skin, and walked most of the way back up the valley slope with fingers linked tight. Harry tried to ignore the ache in his throat when she eased her hand out of his just before they emerged from the cover of the Chardonnay rows.

She was leaving today.

After a frenzied and inelegant quickie against the slick shower wall, Rowan didn't linger with him in the bathroom. Harry could see her mounting anxiety about being discovered there, plain as the sun now blazing in the summer sky. People were starting to arrive for work in the vineyard, and each rumble of tires along the gravel lane in front of the carriage house represented another pair of eyes who could discover their secret. She'd promised to stay until he finished so they could say a proper goodbye.

For a moment, Harry turned the water as hot as he could stand, letting it blast his neck and shoulders. The steam churned thick around him, just as the fog had shrouded them this morning at the lake.

Cloud tide.

It was almost cruel, this plot twist. Rowan had finally given him full access to an intimate part of her past, right before she was going to leave. So many things were in scalpel-sharp focus now—her issues with trust went far deeper than the mystery guy named Noah. Maybe it was *because* she was leaving that she felt empowered to share with him. Maybe she felt safe to show her hand now that she knew she'd soon be walking away from the table.

But Harry felt a spark of hope, too. She'd wanted to tell him she loved him as they stood there in the fog. He was sure of it.

She was leaving today.

Just tell her you love her, asshole.

He punched the shower faucet off with the side of his fist and forced out a wet breath.

She was leaving today, and she would leave again.

What if you went with her?

Harry dried off and pulled on a pair of shorts. He was still toweling his hair when he emerged from the bedroom. No trace of Rowan—only the hum of the fridge and the creak of his weight against the floorboards.

"Hey, you still here?" Harry said, expecting her to emerge from the little laundry room, or come in from the back deck.

She didn't.

It wasn't like her to not say goodbye, especially since she'd promised to stay until he finished his shower. Harry scratched his jaw, looped the wet towel over the back of a chair, and poured fresh coffee, puzzled. In the middle of the narrow kitchen bar sat Rowan's mug.

He'd bought it for her just after she began spending the night—it had a wide handle and said in big block letters, OOPS, I WET MY PLANTS. The coffee inside was still hot enough that a slow-motion curl of steam rose from it.

Harry froze midsip with the rim of his mug against his bottom lip. Lying next to Rowan's mug was a small array of envelopes.

The *mail*.

He hadn't left it on the bar. It had been in a clip on the fridge, blank sides out. Rowan would have seen it there when she refilled her mug. Maybe she'd taken the clip down out of idle curiosity.

Fuck.

It didn't matter *why* she'd looked. In the stack were two unopened envelopes from Lena, a piece of junk mail from the dealership where he'd rented his truck, and a letter from Nicola with a check for his share of the sale of their old Subaru. Harry looked down at her familiar slashing handwriting, and his guts bottomed out.

The return address sticker plainly read, DR. NICOLA BALDWIN BRADY. Below it, their Los Angeles address.

Harry's head snapped up. Through the sliding glass door to the deck, he saw Rowan slip into the vineyard. She was taking the incognito route back to her place on the hill.

Coffee sloshed over the rim of Harry's mug, burning his hand as he banged it down onto the polished granite. He was out the door and sprinting across the lawn before he remembered he was still barefoot and shirtless.

She moved fast. Fast enough that by the time he was in the vines, she was already out of sight.

"Rowan!" Harry shouted.

No reply. A stone jabbed into his heel as he ran. A red haze of pain burst behind his eyes.

Harry half skipped, limping as he ran. He surged out of the far side of the vineyard, squinting against the overbright sun. A twiggy grapevine cane had lodged between his toes. He impatiently bent down to yank it free and fling it away.

Rowan vanished into the meadow.

It *had* to be the fucking meadow.

"Rowan! Stop. Please," Harry called, skidding to a halt a few yards short of the weedy path into the tall vegetation. He could *see* spiderwebs from where he stood—there weren't many in the shoulder-high grasses yet, but there were plenty along the ground, dew-bright and sparking silver in the vivid morning light.

Harry bit down hard on his molars, swallowing an impotent roar of frustration. The sound emerged instead as an agonized whimper-moan behind clenched teeth. He fucking hated himself for being so pathetic.

Angry tears sprung to his eyes.

"Rowan." It came out as a croak.

The breeze in the grasses suddenly became the monotone crackle of rain on an ambulance roof. Harry's knees nearly buckled. Fingertips curled involuntarily into palms, short nails digging, clawing, until the strain of it made his knuckles creak inside his skin. The air in his lungs *burned*. He was desperate to exhale, inhale, swallow, scream—anything—but his throat locked tight, tight enough that the muscles in his neck and chest had gone rigid.

Breathe.

"Let's breathe. We'll do it together, okay?"

Harry would remember that moment in the meadow last autumn—the way his hand felt against her warm chest—until the day he died.

Breathe.

Harry gulped air. Breathed a choking breath. Lurched forward one step. Two.

"Well, that's perfect. In nature, when you survive, you win."

"Rowan!" he shouted, racing forward on the path.

Harry caught up to her fast. "Please stop," he gasped, and she froze with her back to him. The shoulders of her filmy T-shirt were darkened from the shower-damp fall of her hair.

He closed the distance between them, wincing at the debris littering the meadow path underfoot. His attention shifted to the tall vegetation on either side of them.

He would *not* lose his shit right now.

Rowan turned. Harry smelled the sunscreen on her skin, and the familiar herbal scent of her shampoo. The evening she'd showed up at his place with that shampoo and pink toothbrush in her little overnight bag was seared into his memory. It had been her wordless way of saying, *Hi, I'm here, and I plan to stay awhile.* They'd recklessly, joyfully taken each other against the kitchen countertop, and knocked an entire bowl of brownie batter to the floor. More than a month later, Harry was still finding places where the chocolate had splattered and dried.

"Someone will hear you," she hissed. Her eyes dipped to his bare chest before diverting away to the meadow.

"Let them."

Silence.

"Please," he repeated.

"Harrison—"

Oh, shit.

"No, no, no." Harry reached out a pleading hand. "Please don't do that. Don't 'Harrison' me right now."

She pulled her bottom lip between her teeth. The

latent wildness in her eyes and her spring-tight posture gave Harry pause. He let his hand fall.

Her words came fast. Defensive. "I told you I'd take Lena's letters for you, remember? I wanted to protect you."

"I know. You didn't do anything wrong."

She looked at his bare feet, then back up to meet his eyes. "I don't suppose Nicola Brady is another sister you haven't told me about." The muscles in her neck quivered.

"No."

"Cousin?"

"No."

"Who is she, Harry?"

Pressure built inside his skull. He'd dreaded this moment for months, trying and failing to decide on a way to tell her. Fighting with himself over whether he *should* tell her. Rationalizing that it didn't matter, she was leaving anyway. *No strings,* she'd said. No backstory. And then, by the time he felt like he *needed* to tell her, he was in too deep to risk losing her over it.

He'd hated himself for his cowardice. Another drop of self-loathing in an already overflowing bucket.

"My wife," Harry said. "My *ex*-wife."

Rowan's nostrils flared as she sucked in a breath. "You were married."

"I was."

"Why didn't you tell me?"

Christ, his feet hurt. Deep down, self-righteous frustration swirled with desperation. "Why didn't *you* tell me about Noah?"

"How do you know—" She stiffened, then thrust up her chin. "Don't answer my questions with a question."

"It's completely irrelevant that I was married before."

Her hands fisted at her sides. "You don't get to decide what's relevant to me."

You should have fucking listened to Temperance.

Harry's gut tightened. Frustration became annoyance, igniting the fuse on his temper. "*You* insisted this was casual. Casual doesn't require backstory, remember? What do you want, Rowan? You can't have it both ways. Do you want everything, or do you want no strings?"

She ignored that. "When did it end?"

"It doesn't matter."

"Goddamn it, Harrison. Tell me."

Harry blew a bullish breath from his nose and tamed his tone. "The beginning of the end was more than two years ago. We barely saw each other the last year of our residencies. She slept at the hospital most nights. Separation began last May. A few weeks after—Cora. Divorce was final in November."

Rowan looked beyond him as she did the math.

"November—" She dashed a hand over her face. "How long had you been together?"

"Jesus, Rowan."

"How long?" she growled.

Harry sighed at the sky, then pinned her eyes with his. "Four years."

A breath whooshed past her lips. "Four *years*?"

"Med school and residency are really fucking lonely, Rowan—"

She cut him off again. "Who wanted the divorce?"

"What?"

"Which one of you ended it, damn it?"

"Her. It was her," he bit out. "Why does it matter?"

"Are you serious?" Wetness clumped her lashes. "You spent four *years* committed to a person, in a *marriage,* that *you* weren't the one to end?"

Harry's throat tensed. "I would've ended it. She did it first, because I'm a fucking coward."

"Don't you see what this is? I've been your *rebound,* Harry. From Nicola, from Cora. All this time, you've been too emotionally compromised to understand anything you feel."

His brief laugh was dark. "You and I—it's the only thing I'm sure I *do* understand."

All color drained from her complexion, even more alarming than her dramatic red flushes. "I've been, like—some glorified therapy animal for you."

Harry's vision blanked, like a camera flash had gone off inches from his eyes. He shoved a hand through his hair. "What in the hell is *wrong* with you? Who says things like that?"

"You've been lying to me, for *months.*"

He surged forward. "I have *never* lied to you."

"Lying by omission is still a lie," she said.

"Nicola doesn't have anything to do with us. From the moment I first saw you last September, you've been the axis that *everything* else in my consciousness revolves around."

Those words landed hard. Rowan's mouth pinched into a pale line. "You think telling me that makes this *better*? I was the other"—she faltered—"other woman."

"The fuck does that mean?"

"You were still married when we met. For m-months."

"Separated. The papers were signed, Rowan. California has a six-month waiting period for finalizing a divorce—"

She wasn't hearing him. "The heated looks, the flirtation. If I'd known—"

"Damn it, when I met you, it had been more than a year since my life with Nicola remotely resembled a marriage. The divorce was final *weeks* before you and I even *kissed*—"

"Between the two of us, we have a failed engagement and a failed marriage." Rowan looked down at the splayed fingers of her left hand. Angry tears quivered in her eyes.

"Noah was your *fiancé*?" Harry blurted.

Impressively, her tears failed to fall when she thrust her chin up. "How do you even know that name?"

"Answer the question."

She didn't. "Clearly, you and I both have a serious problem with judgment when it comes to relationships. That's enough reason to not take this any further."

"See what you did right there? I'm asking you direct questions, and you give me *nothing*."

"Yes, Noah was my fiancé," she snapped. "But it was a fucking farce. It ended. Badly."

The person before him was a shadow of the warm, sensual woman he'd made love to in the shower less than an hour earlier. Her chest rose and fell in an uneven rhythm, and she sniffed, hard.

At least she hadn't run yet.

I love you, Harry thought. He ached to say the words.

Crickets resumed their whirring song all around them. A bumblebee zinged by his nose, its back legs chunky with pollen. Harry picked a dainty white wildflower and stepped closer to her.

Her mouth dropped open like she was going to speak, but no words came.

Harry trailed the petals of the flower across the back of her hand. When she took it from him, relief made his heart pummel his lungs. "Every minute I'm not with you—it's wasted."

"Oh god." Rowan's head tipped back. "How long do

you think that lasts? That intensity? It doesn't. It's not sustainable."

"How do you know? How many lifetimes have you spent with a person?"

She made a dismissive *pff* sound.

"You want to science it? Give us fifty years to test your hypothesis," Harry said. "I want to marry you someday, Rowan."

Her mouth closed with an audible clack of teeth, and she looked at him like he held a hand grenade with the pin pulled.

"I don't want kids," she blurted.

"I just want you."

"That's a lie, Harry. I've seen how you are with Ace and Grey."

"Fine. I've seen how *you* are with them too," he fired back.

Splotches of red flickered along her collarbone and climbed her neck. Harry knew she hated that about herself, but it was one of the things he loved. Her body was a canvas for all the emotion she tried to hide.

"I could turn out to be"—she fidgeted with the flower—"like my mother."

Realization dawned. Harry jammed the heels of his palms into his temples. "Oh my god, I get it now. You don't trust *yourself*. How can you ever trust me if you can't trust yourself?"

Her fire flared back to life. "I *did* trust you. I trusted you to respect that we had an expiration date. But now I'm finally leaving for interviews, and somehow we're talking about *marriage*? What happened to promising this would be enough?"

Harry's shoulders rose and fell in a shrug. "There's no such thing as 'enough' when it comes to you."

"Don't," she snapped, throwing up a warning hand.

"I made that promise to you a long time ago, Rowan. Things changed. *We* changed. I am mentally, emotionally, and physically incapable of having anything less than everything from you." His voice broke on the words.

The look she gave him was agony and anger and exhaustion. "We've never been our real selves here, Harry. It's been a fantasy. You *have* to see that. You're not a sunburned, callused handyman, and I didn't get a Ph.D. in botany to prune grapevines and tend your dad's tomatoes."

Harry squeezed the back of his sweaty neck. So much about her was rapidly coming into sharp focus, he had a hard time keeping up. "I can't believe I didn't realize this before. All this time, you expected me to make it *easy* for you to eventually walk away. You put it all on me. Well, fuck that."

"What happened to not trying to influence my decision?" she said.

"I changed my mind. If you walk away from this, I want it to hurt."

Muttering to herself, she whirled around to move farther into the meadow, to the point where the path took a sharp turn. She flung up a hand as she turned, and said, "None of this would be the same outside of the insulated little bubble this place has created for us."

If he followed, he'd lose sight of the path's entrance. Sweat slicked the crooks of his elbows and behind his knees. Something with tiny legs crawled over his bare foot, and his insides unraveled.

"You have to do this. I can't carry you."

He hustled after her.

"Rowan, *we* created this. It goes wherever we go.

You've told me you can't stay here. Won't stay. Fine. What about me going with *you*?"

They stopped again, where she'd helped him breathe last autumn. She swung around with a thumbnail notched between her teeth, posture softening. A war waged inside her—her mind and heart were the battlefields. But who was she fighting? Him? Or herself?

"I know I don't have any claim to you," Harry said. "But I deserve to know where I stand. Tell me what happens after your interviews. Do I just wake up one day, and you'll be gone?"

"I can't believe you're springing this on me hours before I have to leave."

Every moment was a tick on a clock he'd never get back, and damn it, he was tired. Tired of drifting in existential limbo. Tired of not knowing what his life would look like a month from now, a year from now. Ten years. Fifty.

"I'm retaking the board qualifying exam in Philly in a few days, and Sinclair needs me to commit to a return date by the end of the month. Tell me what to do," he said.

"It's your decision, Harry. Not mine."

"It's *our* decision. I'm talking about what's going to happen to *us*, Rowan."

"Us," she said. "There's no us."

The wildflower hung loose from her fingers. *Don't drop it. Please don't.*

"I love you," Harry said, plain and steady, like it was a universal truth.

When she sucked in a sharp breath, Harry knew he'd made a mistake. A dark thing he'd never seen before crystallized in her eyes, and she shrank away.

His left foot was bleeding. "Rowan. Do you love me?"

"I don't know." Her voice was flat.

"Answer the question."

"I don't know, Harry. I—"

"Say it," he demanded.

"I thought you didn't need me to say—"

He cut her off. "I changed my mind."

"This is some kind of emotional ultimatum—"

"It's not complicated, damn it—"

"You're always interrupting me," she yelled. "I don't *know*!"

A blackbird shot noisily out of the grass near them, sending Harry's heart further up his throat.

His patience fractured. "How can you not fucking know?" he shouted back. Disgusted with himself, he kicked at a rock, missed, kicked again, connected. Bare toes met stone. Pain twisted up the nerves in his leg like barbed wire. Harry poured his anger into that ache, redirecting it away from Rowan. Quietly, he said, "I don't understand."

"I know you don't. That's the problem."

"Help me, then. *Help me* understand."

"I can't. I don't know how." She rubbed both hands over her face. "I'm not like you. And I don't have a family to run and hide with when things inevitably fall apart."

He recoiled like her words had shoved him solidly in the chest. "That's not fair. They love you, too."

A wretched, laughing sob ripped from her throat before she pressed her lips tight and shook her head. In that moment, Harry felt the reality of her withdrawal even more acutely than when she'd been physically running away. He felt it so distinctly, he shivered in the summer morning heat.

"I need to get my head right for this trip, Harry." Her

voice was toneless. The flower dropped from her hand. "Please, if you care for me, let me go. Make this easy. For both of us," she whispered. *"Please."*

Then she ran from him, just as she did the first night they met.

PART THREE

CHAPTER TWENTY-SIX

Rowan

Gia showed up at the cottage an hour before they were due to leave for the airport. She hovered in the doorway of the little bedroom as Rowan finished packing her small suitcase. Rowan still shook from her encounter with Harry in the meadow.

"Extra socks," Gia said.

Rowan paused at the dresser. "Hmm. I won't need socks with these shoes. It's summer."

"Hotel rooms get cold. Cold feet, no sleep."

Rowan threw a single pair of socks into her bag, and Gia looked back with a self-satisfied smile.

"Have a sweater in there?"

"Gia, it's almost a hundred degrees in Austin right now."

Gia crossed her arms over her chest. "Take a cardigan. Air-conditioning."

For the past month, Gia had been bringing Rowan dinner leftovers in little glass bowls with plastic lids. Whenever she'd see Rowan around the property during the day, Gia would ask if she was hydrated. At first, she'd balked at Gia's brand of proactive caretaking. Rowan was thirty years old and fully capable of looking after herself. But now, the attention from the other woman felt natural and right.

God, she wanted to melt to the floor and cry in Gia's arms about Harry.

How different would her life have been if she'd grown up with a mother like Gia Brady? A father like Will? Was she broken because she hadn't had this, or did she not have this because she'd always been broken?

Rowan folded a gray cardigan on top of the rest of her clothes, and paused, palms pressed down into the soft knit. Feelings didn't manifest reality. No matter how she felt about any of the Bradys, they were *not* her family, and her time there had reached the closing end of temporary. She tried to disguise a renegade sob with a cough, blinking Harry's agonized face out of her mind. When she zipped the bag closed, she snagged the fabric of the sweater.

Rowan could feel Gia's narrowed eyes on her. "Could you make some of your rose-hip-and-mint tea?" Her voice sounded subtly different, too practiced in its nonchalance to be authentic. "It's still a bit too early to leave."

Alarms clamored in Rowan's head, but she made the tea anyway. They sat at the little kitchenette table by the window, quiet for a while.

When Gia spoke again, it was in the same judiciously innocent, conversational tone. "William and I were only eighteen when we married, did you know that? We met in Galicia—I still lived with my family. Will's parents were both journalists. They'd come to cover Spain's first democratic elections in forty years. He'd dropped out of college and come along with them.

"Back then, my family had the vineyards, and a tiny floristería in Cambados. I'd work in the afternoons. Will was at the café across the street, at a table on the patio. We always left the door to the shop propped open, and I saw him watching me. For *days,* he did this, looking ridiculous with those little espresso cups in his huge hands, trying to pretend he wasn't staring. I waited and waited for him to come and say hello.

"When he finally came into the shop, he introduced himself as my mierdo futuro." Gia laughed so hard, she had to put her tea down on the table. Dabbing tears from her eyes with the side of her pinkie finger, she said, "Do you know what it means in Spanish?"

Rowan knew enough Spanish to infer. "Your 'future shit'?" She couldn't help laughing along with her.

"Yes! He meant to say marido futuro. Future husband." Gia sniffed, sighed happily. "For the next two weeks, he brought me a little bouquet of wildflowers every day. The confidence of that man, bringing wildflowers to a woman working in a floristería, surrounded by some of the world's loveliest blooms! But those flowers he brought were more beautiful than anything we sold, darling. To me, they were priceless."

Gia continued, "William still brings me wildflowers, you know. I told the kids this story once, and Harry was the only one who really paid attention. He was around Grey's age, maybe seven? After that, Harry started bringing me flowers—dandelions and violets from the yard. Clover, sometimes. I asked him once, why did he do it?" She paused for a moment to smile fondly, awash in memory. "He told me—he wanted to show he loved me as much as Daddy did."

Rowan pictured round-cheeked Harry clutching a

bouquet of carefully picked flowers in a tiny fist, proudly gifting them to his ma. She sipped her tea, and it scalded her tongue, making her eyes water.

Gia shook her head, chuckling. "One year, he pulled up an entire bed of Spanish poppies I'd grown from seed."

If she tried, Rowan could probably recall every single wildflower he'd given her.

He wanted to show he loved me.

She felt her throat closing, choked by emotion. She tried listing grape varietals in her mind, desperate to redirect from where her heart was trying to take her. She managed to think of three—Chardonnay, Merlot, Traminette—before her thoughts snapped back to Harry. She repeated the chemical formula of chlorophyll in her head, and recited the seven assumptions of the Hardy-Weinberg equilibrium. The steps of the Krebs cycle. Names of women scientists. Her brain stumbled over every attempt.

Instead, a little boy toddled in her imagination with a chubby fist full of dandelions. He looked like Harry. But he wasn't Harry—he was their *son*. The image was sweet and searing, like cinnamon candy on her tongue.

Her imagination had gone all in on a family fantasy starring Harry Brady.

Gia was still talking, but her voice sounded like it was coming from the bottom of a well. "For years, when people would ask Harry what he wanted to be when he grew up, he'd reply, 'a husband.' He was the only one of us to cry at Nathan and Maren's wedding, you know." She raised a finger and wagged it. "Do not tell him I told you that."

Rowan swallowed hard and sank down a bit in her chair, weakly pantomiming a zipper across her lips.

Now her memories took her to the night of Patrick and Mercedes's wedding. How Harry had looked in his tuxedo. The tuxedo that had ended up, in part, in a pile on the floor of her room at the lodge. The first night they'd made love.

"We can just enjoy each other's bodies."

No. It had always been more.

Gia was relentless. "Harry took the red-eye twice from Los Angeles to meet Alice and Grey right after they were born. He was still in medical school then, so he had to fly back to California later in the same day. Hours and hours in airplanes and airports so he could hold those new babies. Just for an hour or so."

"If you walk away from this, I want it to hurt."

"Did you know he sings 'Happy Birthday' to each of the babies he delivers?" Gia asked.

Rowan's knuckles were as white as the ceramic mug they gripped. "I think we should get ready to go," she croaked.

"Rowan." Gia's tone grew firmer, almost strident. "Harry looks at you the same way my William looked at me through that floristería window."

She opened her mouth to respond, but Gia held up a hand, setting her mug down on the table with a purposeful *thunk*. "Don't say anything yet."

Oh, god. None of this was the casual, fond chatter of a mother about her son.

Gia Brady had come to teatime with an agenda.

"I've seen you two sneaking back and forth between each other's places for the last few months. Do not think for a moment a mother misses that kind of thing."

Oh, shit. Rowan's ears began to burn and she shrank inward, bracing for the scold. The *"how dare you."* The withdrawal of affection.

The shame.

It never came. Instead, Gia pulled three photos from the back pocket of her jeans. "I brought something to show you. Then we'll leave for the airport. Okay?"

She slid a photo across the table. The others remained facedown in front of her. Now it felt like they were playing a high-stakes card game, and Rowan was fresh out of aces.

The photo's corners were rounded, and it was orangey with age. Gia looked to be no older than twenty, laughing at the camera with an incandescent grin that looked remarkably like Arden's. She was radiant; her billowy-sleeved off-shoulder crop top revealed gleaming golden skin. Her hair was parted down the middle, sleek black silk falling to her bare navel.

Beside her, Will was virtually Harry's identical twin, born thirty years apart. One of Will's hands tucked into the pocket of his snug-hipped, quintessentially seventies jeans, and the other was wrapped around the waist of the tiny woman beside him. He looked down at Gia as she laughed into the camera.

The *feelings* in the photo were palpable. Joy, lust, love—Rowan recognized it all, as surely as if she were the one standing there experiencing it.

"Tell me my son doesn't look at you the same way William is looking at me here, and I'll never bring this up again." Gia sat back in her chair like she knew she'd laid a winning hand.

Rowan felt like she'd been flung down a dark flight of stairs.

"I can't," she said, unable to look away from the photo.

"You can't what?" Gia prompted.

I can't do this.

Gia reached over and squeezed her hand.

"What if I denied it?" Rowan said. "Would you really never bring it up again?"

Gia narrowed her eyes. "Darling, I know you. Well enough to know you're too proud to deny anything. But—a mother is always prepared." She turned over another photo and slid it across the table with one finger.

It was the photo she'd watched Frankie take back in March, as she'd arrived for Patrick and Mercy's wedding carpool. She'd captured the moment Rowan had entered the kitchen that morning. Harry stood, hands confined away in his pockets, a silent acknowledgment of her presence.

His face.

How had she not noticed then the way he'd looked at her? How emotionally stunted was she to have missed the devastating ache in his expression?

Gia pushed across the final photo.

This one was a grainy, poor-quality print of Arden's photo of Rowan and Harry dancing at the Three Birds festival last November. Rowan choked back a laugh—it seemed such a mom thing to do, to print a photo from one of her adult child's social media profiles. In the image, Harry looked down at her with the same urgent, intense gaze Will favored Gia with in the decades-old photo. Even the tilt of his head was the same.

Their conversation was as fresh in Rowan's mind as the one they'd had that morning. They'd talked about the nature of lust. And of love. That longing adoration wasn't only apparent in Harry's expression. It was also clear in her own.

God, they'd barely known each other two months.

Gia began gently, "I also know you well enough to know that until now, you've been using your career as a substitute for everything else in your life. You're a hummingbird, sipping sugar water from a feeder. The bird can survive that way, but how much flavor and color and beauty is she missing by not being nourished by flowers, as she was meant to be? You can have more. You can have both."

Rowan pushed the photos back. "I don't know how to be the person he thinks he sees, Gia. I'm not who he needs."

Gia made a small, thoughtful sound. "That's not for you to decide. What you need to decide is if he is the one *you* need. If that matches what he needs, the rest falls into place."

Rowan looked down into her pinkish tea. It reflected a wobbly likeness of her face, a monochromatic pastel Picasso.

She didn't recognize the person she saw. For most of her life, she'd seen herself through the lens of academia. Science endured. It wasn't subject to the whims of human emotion. Now, it felt like her future was as blurry as her reflection in the tea. Every day, Harry and his family's roots grew tighter around her, making it harder and harder to run. Once she was outside of the soft-focused sphere of life in Vesper Valley, her conviction would return.

It had to.

Gia stood, pushing her chair in. "I know you have choices to make about what comes next for you, and you have important work to do. You helped my son find himself again, and regardless of what happens in the future,

I will always be grateful to you for that. But make sure you're not confusing cowardice for caution, darling. It's safe to make the leap when you know who's waiting to catch you."

CHAPTER TWENTY-SEVEN

Harry

A shitty mood hung over Harry like a cartoon rain cloud.

Rowan had only been gone two days. Her presence had become the nucleus of his new normal, and without her there, he'd begun sliding back into the despair that had wracked him when he was still in Los Angeles. The last thing she'd said to him had been a request to let her go.

"Make this easy. For both of us."

Maybe he needed to be gone by the time she returned. Sinclair wasn't being gentle anymore about needing him back at the practice. Maybe he just needed to rip off the fucking bandage while Rowan was away pursuing her own out.

"Why do you run, Harry? When you run, do you mean to stay gone?"

Today he was helping Duncan with repairs after a tractor took out half a dozen posts in the Chambourcin block. He was sweating off most of the weight he'd gained back in the last few months, slamming a post hole digger into the ground with more force than necessary. The impact vibrated up his arms and along his jaw.

The first night Rowan was gone, Harry had called her. No answer. He tried not to give it too much credence, telling himself she was probably prepping for her interview the following day. Earlier today, he'd texted her to ask how it went. He'd also typed and deleted "I miss you" four times before ultimately deciding to leave it off.

Today, the glass of his phone was a smear of sweaty mud from all the times he'd checked for a reply from her. Nothing.

Again and again, he rammed the digger into the dry ground.

The greenhouse loomed like a cathedral over the part of the vineyard he was in. Rowan had breathed new life into that old building, made it her personal monument to Mother Nature. But without her vibrant light inside it, the big glass building was a lantern without a candle. Cold glass and metal.

Over the last nine months, wielding a hammer and crowbar had become as natural to him as using a stethoscope and fetal doppler. He barely recognized his own body in the mirror, or the landscape of his own mind. Much of the interior transformation had been because of Rowan, though it wasn't that she'd changed him. She'd simply revealed to him who he still was.

"I trusted you to respect this had an expiration date."

Shoulders bunching and burning, Harry raged against soil and stone. The force of it rattled his teeth. Dust flurried. Grit settled into every pore. Sweat stung his eyes as it shook down from his hair.

"Whoa, whoa, whoa, take it easy, John Wick." Duncan clapped a big hand on Harry's shoulder.

Harry stumbled backward, lifting the hem of his filthy T-shirt to wipe his face. "How is it this hot? This is Pennsylvania, for Christ's sake."

"It's not that hot. You're overdoing it. I haven't seen

your face this red since I found you sucking face with Alison Holbrook when you were seventeen."

"I was sixteen, and you ruined my first kiss, dick."

Duncan narrowed his eyes. "According to Alison, you ruined it all on your own, big brother."

Harry laughed for the first time since Rowan left. "Fuck off."

Duncan gave him a congenial punch in the shoulder and resumed on the hole Harry had started. "Take ten and get some water."

Harry only took five, reluctant to give his body too much of a break. The physical exertion took the edge off his anxiety. When he returned, Duncan was on his knees, hunched over the hole in the ground. His brother never passed up an opportunity for a prank, but Harry wasn't in the mood.

"Find buried treasure?" Harry called out as he approached.

"Jesus value-sized Christ," Duncan ground out. He gripped his wrist against his chest. The post hole digger lay beside him on the ground, and his posture was odd, strained.

"Cut the shit, Ducky," Harry said. But as he came closer, he saw unmistakable streams of blood trickling down Duncan's tattooed skin, dripping off his elbow.

Adrenaline blasted through him.

"Hit a rock, reached in to pull it out." Duncan's face had gone as gray as a fish belly. "It's like a fucking blade down there."

Blood. His *brother's* blood.

Harry's brain went blank, like sand had been dumped into his skull. He stumbled backward, sagged against a trellis post, and slid to the ground. Duncan was still talking, but his voice sounded muffled. He was usually as loud and rowdy as he was big and broad, but now his voice was quiet.

Duncan scooted toward Harry on his knees. "Hey, man. I need a hand." A nervous laugh. "Mine's fucked." A drop of blood hit the ground. It sent up a tiny puff of dry dirt, apocalyptic as a mushroom cloud.

The low tones of his brother's voice snapped Harry out of it. A deep slash crossed the pad of Duncan's middle finger, red running freely from it. Harry smelled the blood. Wet pennies. Musky and metallic. Dark spots spread through his vision, like ink dripped onto canvas. He crushed his teeth together and fought the blackout.

God*damn* it.

"Harry." Duncan remained clear and calm. "It's me. Can you help?"

Breathe, Harry.

It was basic first aid. A seven-year-old could do it.

Blink.

Think.

Move.

Harry thrust his hair out of his eyes and snatched the sweaty bandana from Duncan's back jeans pocket. He twisted it, ropelike, and gestured for Duncan to present his hand to him. After wrapping the bandana like a tourniquet around the base of Duncan's finger, Harry sat back and panted like he'd sprinted around the entire vineyard.

"Hold it up." Harry pantomimed raising his hand. "Higher."

Duncan held his hand up at eye level between them, with only his wounded middle finger extended. The wiseass grin on his face broke the tension, and Harry blew out an awkward exhale-laugh.

"Fuck you, too," Harry said.

"Hospital?"

Harry nodded and stood, holding the trellis post for support. "Gonna need stitches. When was your last tetanus shot?"

"No idea." Duncan got to his feet as well.

"Definitely the responsible adult answer I was hoping for," Harry said. He planted his hand between his significantly bigger little brother's shoulder blades to usher him out of the vineyard.

They were quiet in the truck for most of the drive, until Duncan said, "Harry. I know you've had a hard time. I can't pretend to know what you've gone through. But there comes a point where you gotta shit or get out of the kitchen, you know?"

"You just managed to mess up two idioms." Harry glanced over at him.

"You know I don't give a fuck, right?"

They laughed.

Harry helped Duncan check into the emergency department at the little hospital in Linden. The scent and sound and bustle of the place hit him like a baseball bat in the mouth. This time, though, a part of him reveled in the pain. He stood up to it, bared his teeth at it, and fed on it.

When Duncan proudly told the silver-haired triage nurse that Harry was a doctor, she smiled and commented on how well her job had already been done. "Almost as good a job as I'd have done," she'd said with an indulgent wink. "We'll get you in with a doctor as soon as we can."

In the waiting room, Harry looked down at his callused hands. Some of Duncan's dried blood was smeared across the underside of his wrist. For the first time in over a year, the notion of being a practicing physician again didn't fill him with existential dread. His heartbeat had already returned to normal, but his blood sugar had plummeted in the wake of the adrenaline rush. Soon, his hands would start to shake. But rather than feeling like he needed to throw up, he felt like he really needed a sandwich and a beer.

Progress.

Harry's phone buzzed in his back pocket. Heat rushed to his head as he pulled it out, anticipating a reply—*finally*—from Rowan.

Instead, Sinclair's cheerful face smiled back at him from their text conversation, her brown cheeks rosy and deeply dimpled. In her profile photo, she wore a hospital scrub cap covered in colorful cartoon doughnuts.

> Annie Moorhouse is expecting triplets.
> Remember her?

Harry smiled despite his disappointment that the text wasn't from Rowan. Annie Moorhouse had been one of his first patients. He'd delivered her first son just shy of sixteen months ago. He kept his reply noncommittal:

> That's going to mean a lot of diapers.

Sinclair replied:

> Great patient to add to your case list, HB.

Harry texted back:

> No point in building a case list if I can't pass the qualifying exam

Sinclair replied with a single thumbs-down emoji.

Harry swiped over to the open text message with Rowan. In the photo he'd saved with her number, her freckles had deepened with summer sunshine, and she wore a white V-neck T-shirt with a prickly little cartoon cactus on it. The cactus said FREE HUGS. What a perfect metaphor for *her*.

There were three animated dots next to Rowan's name in the text conversation, indicating she was typing something. They'd been there for two days. Harry sighed and returned the phone to his back pocket.

"What happened to not trying to influence my decision?"

"You did this on purpose to get out of work, didn't you?" Harry said to Duncan.

Duncan looked at him sideways. "Fuck, man. I'd never intentionally compromise the integrity of my wank hand."

Harry shook his head and laughed. Something shifted in him then, a solid shove against a rusted-shut hinge.

It felt good.

He knew what he had to do, though. That part hurt like hell.

CHAPTER TWENTY-EIGHT

Rowan

It was late afternoon when Rowan got back to the valley. She'd taken a cab from the airport, so nobody knew yet she'd returned. Anxiety crackled in her brain like a poorly tuned radio, and the center of her chest felt heavy, inflexible. She sat on the edge of the bed in her bright little bedroom with her overstuffed laptop bag still strapped to her back, staring at the wall. For most of her week away, she'd barely slept—the hotel rooms were too quiet, too sterile. Lying in those huge, faintly bleach-scented beds without Harry's body to anchor her felt like being adrift in a cold ocean, or free-falling through space.

She needed sleep. But first, she had to face Harry.

On the return flight from Montreal, Rowan realized—at thirty years old—she had never learned how to argue with a person she loved. At the faintest glimmer of conflict, Sybil and Noah had each had their own brand of gaslighting, pushing her into backing down, or believing she'd misconstrued or overreacted. So instead, Rowan learned to retreat. She had no idea how to stand up for herself while also giving Harry an equitable chance to share his side.

I love you, she'd typed in their text message on the first day she'd been gone, but she never sent it. It remained in pixelated limbo, even now. Perhaps she'd secretly hoped she'd nudge it in her pocket or her bag, sending it without having to obsess about the implications.

Coward.

Really, though—anything she wanted to say to him felt too big and too important to exchange via text message or even a phone call. So, she avoided it entirely.

She'd gotten so good at retreat, she could even hide from herself.

The first day in Austin, the thrill of being back in an academic environment had been enough to keep her focused. The familiar scents of formalin and institutional floor polish and textbook ink, and the enthusiastic handshakes and smiles of the faculty. But by that first evening, she missed pillows that smelled faintly of woodsmoke, and the comforting hum of Harry's refrigerator. Simply sharing space with someone who truly *knew* her. That night, she declined an invitation for drinks with a few of the younger faculty, and instead spent five straight hours in her big hotel bed watching shows on *Food Network* before falling into a restless sleep.

She couldn't stop thinking about Nicola. A woman she'd never seen. A wife-shaped phantom. Rowan imagined Harry coming home to her in the evenings. His hand, palming the back of her head as he kissed her. What did she look like? Nicola would have known the songs he sang in the shower, and his preferred cereal-to-milk ratio for his late-night bowl of Lucky Charms. Celebrated birthdays with him. Nursed him through colds, missed him when they were apart. Nicola knew exactly how Harry's eyes darkened when he—

Stop it.

She couldn't stop.

God, he'd still been *married* when she'd started falling for him.

What was it that hurt, though? The fact he'd loved someone before, or that he'd never told her?

Did either of those things even matter now? Harry was *not* Noah Tully.

Rowan shrugged the bag off her back and rolled stiffly sideways on the bed. The air still smelled faintly of rosemary and mint from her ventures into soapmaking. The bird's nest fern on her nightstand needed watering. Outside, she could hear the sheep *meh*-ing to each other in the field between the greenhouse and the equipment garage, and the insistent whirr of a leaf blower in the distance.

She was *home.*

For so long, she'd been so focused on what came next, she missed that she'd already been living it. Her carefully built fortress had enough imperfections in the walls that Harry Brady had found footholds to climb inside.

Rowan leapt from the bed.

Down the hill, Harry's truck sat parked at the carriage house. It was time to confess. To clarify. To claim all he offered, and be claimed by him. She would bang on his door in the bright afternoon sun, secrecy be damned.

Let them see.

* * *

THE DOOR OPENED quickly, but it wasn't Harry who answered.

It was Temperance.

"Hey, come in." She pulled Rowan inside. Their steps echoed in the empty space.

Empty.

The couch was gone, as was the television they'd never much watched. Two decorative throw pillows sat in the center of the floor.

Rowan listened for the familiar whistling noise of the shower through the open door of the bedroom. Nothing. The sliding glass door to the deck showed only limp and withered flowers in the pots she'd planted for Harry. They probably hadn't been watered since she'd left for her interviews. A lone coffee mug sat on the wooden table beside Harry's deck chair. He'd have ground the beans the night before and set the percolator to begin brewing just before dawn, so fresh coffee would be waiting when he woke. From the deck, he'd watch the world wake up around him, the eastern kingbirds and barn swallows darting and diving for their morning meals, and the cloud tide lingering along the vineyards and lawns. Then he would come back to bed after brushing his teeth, his mouth tasting faintly of mint, and rouse her better than any cup of coffee ever would.

"Harry's truck is out front," Rowan said, weakly.

Temperance puttered around the kitchen like a worker bee. "Yeah, I need to get it back to the rental place in Philly sometime tomorrow."

"Rental place," Rowan echoed, sliding bonelessly onto one of the stools at the bar.

Dry goods were stacked along the bar's granite top: cereals, beans, pasta, chicken stock, canned tomatoes. A gallon of milk was upended in the sink.

"He's gone," Rowan said.

Temperance nodded sympathetically. "I'm sorry, honey." She dumped a Mason jar of liquid into the sink.

The bright citrus scent hit Rowan's nose like a haymaker punch.

Fresh-squeezed orange juice. Extra pulp.

Rowan couldn't swallow. Couldn't breathe.

"He didn't say goodbye." Rowan didn't recognize her own voice.

Temperance paused with a loaf of Gia's homemade bread in her hand. Last month, Harry had wrapped it in parchment paper and plastic wrap and stored it in the freezer. They'd wanted to make bruschetta with home-made mozzarella and some of the sweet basil she'd grown from seed. Tomatoes were finally ripening. They could have done it this weekend.

"He what, now?" Temperance pushed glasses up her nose, waiting. Rowan's throat had closed tight.

It felt like only moments ago she'd been where Temperance stood now, arms around Harry's waist, cheek against his bare back as he sliced the reddest watermelon she'd ever seen. When she'd kissed him, he tasted like sticky summer sweetness.

Rowan slid from the stool and ran to the bedroom. It still smelled like Harry there. Beyond the bathroom's pocket doorway, she saw her toothbrush in the little glass atop the sink.

Only hers.

Temperance called after her. "You didn't *know* he was leaving?"

Sheets and blankets were a twisted mess in the center of the mattress. A single pillow sat centered against the headboard, folded over on itself, the way Harry liked. The other pillows were in a haphazard pile on the floor across the room.

The little grapevine ring he'd made a lifetime ago sat on the dresser. Next to it was the dried Lenten rose boutonniere he'd worn at Patrick and Mercy's wedding. A memento of the night they'd first made love.

Photos of Cora were there too, corners tidily lined up, like they'd been stacked with intention and care. Rowan was proud of him for leaving them behind, but the knife in her sternum twisted hard.

He'd left the things that hurt him.

The wildflower field guide had a folded letter on top. In Harry's handwriting, it read, T.J.

The air moved behind her, and a moment later, Temperance's hand was on her back.

Rowan sank to the floor by the pillows, squeezing one to her chest. It smelled unmistakably like her. Sunlight glinted on a few long filaments of copper hair against the white cotton. He'd banished them from the bed because there were reminders of her everywhere. Rowan imagined the anguish on his face as he threw them off.

Temperance lowered beside her, little flags of pink streaking her cheeks. "Rowan, you didn't *know*?"

A sound like a hissing teakettle filled Rowan's ears. Silently, she shook her head.

Temperance made a growly sound in her throat. "That *dick*. He asked me to take him to the airport, asked me to be here when you got back today. Said you'd need me. I thought that meant you two had decided on this together. That you knew."

"If I'd known—I—I would have—" Rowan stammered. "I might have said—"

Temperance tucked Rowan's hair back over her shoulder. *"Shh,"* she murmured. "What happened?"

"He told me he loved me." Rowan slumped forward. "Wanted to marry me."

Temperance gasped. "He *proposed*?"

"No, not exactly. He said—someday."

"I need a minute to process," Temperance said.

Rowan's laugh was brittle. "*You* need a minute?"

A grim smile twisted her friend's mouth. "Look. You and Harry are two of my best friends. I get at least twenty seconds here, damn it."

"It all happened an hour before I had to leave. I reacted—ah, poorly. I told him to let me go." Rowan clutched the pillow to her belly. "I would have told him how I felt if I'd known he was leaving. How I *really* felt."

Temperance laid her head against Rowan's shoulder. "You know as well as I do—Harry would want to hear those things because you mean them. Not to make him stay."

Rowan felt fragile and faded, like a scrap of paper with the writing erased away too many times. "He didn't let me say goodbye."

"Honey, it sounds like you did."

The sympathy in her eyes made Rowan want to scream and claw the pillow to shreds. From her vantage on the floor, she saw a lone bunched-up sock under the bed. A choked sob wracked her throat.

Beside her, she felt Temperance's shoulders shake.

She was *laughing*.

"Is something funny?" Rowan said through her tears.

A snort, then a giggle. "You're both assholes. Oblivious assholes," Temperance said.

Rowan was speechless for the second time that day.

Temperance took off her glasses and dabbed her eyes. "I *knew* you were going to do this. Both of you."

"I really don't think this is the time for 'I told you so's,'" Rowan sniffed.

"Oh, it's definitely the time. I only wish Frankie were here, too."

Rowan tossed away the pillow and stared down at her hands. "Damn it, Temperance."

"I'm sorry. I knew this would happen. Ask Frankie. We made a Cheesesteak Friday bet."

"You *what*?"

"Been a while since I've won, though. She rarely makes bets she thinks she might lose."

"Frankie has a betting problem." Rowan dropped her head into her hands. "She had one going with me, too. Said I'd fall in love with him."

"Well." Temperance slid her glasses back on. "Did she win?"

Rowan didn't answer. "Tell me about your bet with her."

"God, I just don't understand how someone could want to eat cheesesteak for an entire month—*two* months—"

"Temperance."

"Sorry." A long beat of silence passed before Temperance replied, "Frankie said you'd be engaged by summer. I said you two would get all tangled with each other, then mutually screw it up. Honestly, I hate that I was right."

"Nice, Temperance. Real nice."

"Listen." She held up her hands, innocent. "It was a jerk thing for me to say. But I know you both. Harry is a walking bundle of raw nerves, and he was halfway in love with you within hours of arriving here. But you're still letting that shitbird Noah Tully and your terrible mother dictate what you do with your heart. I didn't make any wildly unrealistic assumptions."

"This is making me feel so much better, T.J."

Temperance rested a hand on Rowan's knee. "I know you don't want to hear logic right now. But it's a language you and I mutually understand, so I'm saying it anyway. People in professions like Harry's and mine—people who see the kinds of things we do, the frailty and fragility of it all—we realize how transitory life is. We're so—impermanent. Time becomes something we don't really feel like we can afford to waste. Something made him realize that, and he took his shot with you. Someone like Harry wants forever."

"He could've given me some warning," Rowan grumbled.

Temperance turned serious. "Surely you've known for longer than a week that he's in love with you." There was plain admonishment in her voice. "I think you had plenty of warning."

Rowan stared at her hands. "I'm as shallow as a teaspoon."

"You're not." Temperance stroked a hand up and down her back. "But I'm not going to pretend my loyalty isn't divided here. Now that this is all out in the open, if you two decide to draw battle lines, I'm going to stand right in the center of them and be a massive, unrelenting monster until you both stop being so clueless."

"There's no battle to be had. It's done."

"When did you start sleeping together?"

Rowan blinked. "Jesus, Temperance."

"Oh, please." She rolled her eyes. "It's too late for pearl clutching, Lady Grantham. Tell me."

"April."

Temperance made a thoughtful *huh* sound. "The wedding?"

Rowan nodded.

Temperance pulled back in mock outrage and breathed, "You slept with my date?"

Rowan tried to give her a bored look, but couldn't help a teary smile. "Looks like he left you something," she said after a while, pointing to the dresser.

Temperance retrieved the note and settled back on the floor beside her. Fresh tears burned her eyes as her friend unfolded it, revealing Harry's compact, expressive script. Temperance read it out loud.

T-Bird,

I was ready to go. I need you to believe that.

Had a nice send-off party with the family. Duncan joked about taking the carriage house furniture, and Ma made me promise to FaceTime more. I hate that shit, but for her, I'll do it. Dad got a little teary-eyed at the end of the night, which made me teary-eyed. Asshole.

I'm glad you'll be there for Rowan. I messed it up, T.J. Mal always said I was self-righteous, but I never believed it until I saw myself through her lens. I was sure I could love her enough to change her mind. About us. But I realized— loving her means not trying to change her at all. I don't want to be just another person in her life who held her back.

You and Frankie are the two people in this world she's truly let in, and I know you know how lucky you are. Take care of her. She deserves to know how it feels when people stay.

Love you.
Harry

They sat there in silence for a while until Temperance said, "Screw this," and bounded to her feet to stalk from the bedroom.

"What are you doing?" Rowan stood to follow, stumbling over a pillow.

"You're going to tell him to get his ass back here so you can fight about this face-to-face like people in love are supposed to do. Where's your phone?"

"I left it at the cottage."

"You can use mine." Temperance was in full-on tactical advance mode, digging around in her massive purse.

"Stop." Rowan seized her wrist. "You're not getting involved, remember?"

Mouth pressed into a tight line, Temperance narrowed her eyes.

"T.J. He left. He *left* me. That's it. Let it be done."

Temperance lowered the phone and looked down at Rowan's clasping hand on her wrist. "Damn it."

"You have to *promise* me you won't call. I'm not equipped for this emotional stuff, and I can't lose him *and* be mad at you, too."

Temperance dipped her eyes to the phone in her hands and paced the kitchen like a tiny soldier. "Fine. I won't call him. I promise."

For a while, Rowan sightlessly stared at the beige rug in front of the sink. Temperance stopped pacing and leaned back against the counter with stooped shoulders, and sighed. Suddenly, her thumbs quickly flew against the little glass screen of her phone, and the silence was split by the unmistakable *zhwoop* sound of a text message being sent.

Temperance dropped the phone to the countertop and

it spun a few times, like a high-tech Ouija planchette. "I didn't *call* him," she said with a shrug.

The text said:

Come back to Rowan. Now.

"Oh, T.J. Why?" Rowan moaned.

"Be mad at me," Temperance said. "But you're not losing him."

CHAPTER TWENTY-NINE

Rowan

It took a week for Harry to reply to Temperance's text. His response had simply been:

> I can't.

He'd run, and he meant to stay gone.

Rowan didn't choose Austin. She didn't choose Montreal, either. She stayed in the valley throughout the rest of July, hoping Harry would return. Once, she thought she'd seen him from the corner of her eye, and her pulse did double-time. When she turned, it was just Will taking lemonade to Gia as she pulled thistles from her lavender bed.

In mid-August, Rowan started teaching biology as an adjunct professor at one of the universities in the city. Temperance welcomed her back on her couch for a while, but she planned to find a place of her own soon. Maybe she'd commute from Linden. She needed to be somewhere green.

She said goodbye to the Brady family on a rainy day that Harry would have hated. It was as difficult as she'd feared it would be. Ace and Grey both cried, though they perked up when she left her small collection of succulents to their stewardship. Gia made her a batch of chocolate coconut cookies, double wrapped in portions of six and sealed in a large plasticware container, so she could freeze some and make them last longer. Duncan didn't show up at her send-off. Instead, he stood at the top of the hill in front of the equipment garage and waved until she was out of sight. Rowan didn't blame him for avoiding the goodbye. It sucked.

It didn't take her long to reintegrate into the safe realm of academia. The facilities were fantastic, and her new coworkers were interesting in the earnest, earthy way natural sciences faculty always were—but her mind felt underutilized. Teaching was fun, but for her it was a stale comparison to dirt-dusted skin and muscles hot with delicious fatigue, with butterflies and birds and earthworms for colleagues.

Temperance's hours were long, so Rowan rarely saw her in the evenings. The solitude she'd prized for the past decade now felt ominous and oppressive.

Like any metamorphosis, life in Vesper Valley had often been uncomfortable. But she'd emerged transformed, and there was no going back.

Eventually, she tried to contact Harry. For weeks, she sent texts and called. He never answered. Everything she knew about his new life, she knew secondhand via Temperance, but those details were brief and obviously carefully curated. He was back at the practice his friend Sinclair had founded. In the meager spare time he had, he was training for a half-marathon. The most heartening tidbit Temperance had relayed was that he was living with a friend rather than getting a place of his own. That, to Rowan, signaled he hadn't fully recommitted to a life in Los Angeles, and she clung to the possibility like a honeybee on the summer's last sunflower.

Anytime Temperance tried to bring Rowan up in conversation, he abruptly disengaged. He never asked for news about her. Not even a generic inquiry into how she was doing, and it stung.

Soon, Rowan stopped trying to contact Harry herself. Grief sat like a stone on her chest, keeping her lungs from fully inflating. Some days, the ache made it hard to stand up straight.

The meager well of information she had via Temperance also dried up by the first of September. T.J. was quietly sympathetic and strangely apologetic, as though it was somehow her fault Harry didn't want to give her anything to pass along. It made Rowan feel even more sad. More ashamed.

She really was never going to see Harry Brady again.

Then, on September sixth, she got a text from Arden:

> Someone we both love will be home
> for Dad's birthday. See you soon?

* * *

TWO EVENINGS LATER, Rowan showed up at the Brady house. Arden answered the door and pulled her into a tight, quick hug. "I knew you'd come. This is going to be fun."

"Is he here?" Rowan asked. A forceful little jet of panic leaked through her, like air rushing from a pinpricked balloon.

"No, he can't get here until tomorrow. You can breathe."

It was cool and rainy. The den blazed with lovely warmth from the fireplace. Gia was curled up on a plush rocker with a book, and Maren scowled at a knitting project in her lap. Duncan sat with Mercy, Patrick, and

Nate at a table topped by an elaborate board game. Will paced the room with the newest Brady, baby Leo.

Rowan leaned into the molding around the entryway, silent. Someday, Harry would be the head of his own family, bouncing his grandchild around a cozy room like this, with his lifetime partner by his side. She wanted it to be her. Tears burned like acid in the corners of her eyes.

"You going to come in, Rosie?" Mercy asked without looking up from the game. After Grey began calling her Rosie earlier in the summer, everyone started to, and it made her heart feel ten sizes too big for her chest. "We have room for one more over here."

Rowan wrung her hands. "No thanks. I'm really tired. Long day."

Gia peered at her over reading glasses. "Welcome home, love."

Home.

Everyone else murmured their welcome—uncomplicated, and without fanfare. It had been nearly a month since she'd been there, but everyone behaved like she'd never left. As though they—and this place—were plainly hers to belong to. You didn't invite a person to have a seat or offer to get them a drink when they returned to their own home. You simply expected they'd do it themselves.

A mist of perspiration dotted Rowan's temples. "I need your help," she said, to nobody in particular.

Gia sat forward in her chair and took off her glasses. Will stopped pacing. A tendril of drool leaked from the baby's lip onto his hand. The four at the game table all scooted sideways in their chairs to look at her.

A year ago, this kind of focused scrutiny would have

driven Rowan directly from the room, every intent dissolving into anxious avoidance. She swallowed hard, tamped it down. This was a safe space, and the time for cowardice was over. These were Harry's people.

These were *her* people.

"I'm in love with your son."

Silence. Mercy's eyes shifted comically to Patrick, while Patrick's attention snapped to Duncan. Duncan's eyebrows crowded together in a confused frown as he absently scratched his beard. Maren and Nate abruptly laughed out loud and high-fived. Will raised brows at Gia, who sat forward with elbows on knees, her fingers linked below her chin, smiling gently.

A tear slipped down Rowan's cheek. Her watery laugh broke the silence. "Not any of these sons. Harry."

A long sigh came from Duncan. He leaned forward and pulled a wallet from the back pocket of his jeans to withdraw several crisp bills. He flicked them across the table to Patrick, who rubbed his hands together before snagging them to tuck in his own pocket. Duncan silently slid more bills to Nate, who then handed the money directly to Maren.

What in the *hell*?

"Come here, Rowan." Gia patted the couch adjacent to her chair.

Duncan bumped the table as he stood, sending game pieces rolling. "I'm going to get some air."

Rowan turned to watch him go. Before she could call after him, Gia stopped her with a hand on her arm.

"Let him go." Her black eyes were inscrutable.

Mercy and Maren ushered their husbands quietly out of the room, and Will followed with the baby. Arden stayed, joining Rowan on the couch, close enough their legs touched.

Rowan took a big breath.

"Harry blocked my calls, Gia. Arden said he'd be here. Can I stay?"

Gia's thumb stroked Rowan's arm. "He is very hurt, darling. After he first left, I tried to get him to talk to me about you, but he ended the call, every time." She made a growly sound. "Imagine, a grown man, hanging up the phone on his *mother*."

Rowan pinched her temples. "I'm so sorry. For all of it."

"I don't know what happened between you two, but I'm certain I'm not the one you need to apologize to."

"I know, but he won't take my calls, my texts. He—"

"I wasn't talking about Harry either, Rowan." Gia's voice was firm, but kind.

A tear slipped down Rowan's cheek, and she scrubbed it away with the cuff of her sweater.

"Make peace with yourself. Forgive *yourself,* and forgive Harry for leaving. Forgive both of you, for whatever happened that made him go." Gia reached over and looped a fallen curl behind her ear, and Arden laid a warm hand on her knee. "You'll stay the weekend. He can't hang up on you if you're in his face."

"You can stay in the carriage house," Arden said. "We had it ready for Harry to stay there, anyway."

"What if he's moved on?" Rowan said.

"He hasn't," the two Brady women answered in unison, without hesitation.

Rowan's answering smile was flimsy. "I don't know what I'll do if he won't listen to me."

For a while, the three were quiet. Then, Arden said, "Make him listen. Tell her about grape jelly, Mama."

Gia made a thoughtful sound. She settled into her chair, angled toward Rowan. "William and I had only been married a month when I became pregnant with the twins. Then Malcolm came along when they were barely three. By the time I was twenty-two, we had three babies and very little time together. Having children is hard enough on couples who have been together for a long time, you know? It took a toll, and we argued a lot. Especially at night. Nights with babies can feel so long. Everything seems more difficult, in the darkness.

"Every morning, I made us toast for breakfast. We were so poor, we rarely had butter, but we always had grape jelly. Some days, I couldn't get the jar lid open, and I'd have to ask Will for help before he left for work. Eventually, I realized the lid was only ever too tight the mornings after we'd argued at night."

Gia smiled fondly at Arden, then gave the same warm regard to Rowan. Tears burned behind Rowan's eyes.

"Each time, we had this little routine. I'd pass the jelly to him without a word, and he'd loosen the lid. Then he'd come very close and cover my hand with his as he gave me the jar. He'd say in that rumbly bear voice of his, 'What would you do without me?' and I would answer, 'Eat dry toast.'" Gia giggled like she was twenty again. "Then he would kiss me on the forehead and go to work, and all would be well."

"That's a really cute story, Gia, but I don't understand how this will help me with Harry."

Gia held up a finger and smiled shrewdly.

"Dad was *tightening* the lid," Arden said.

Gia nodded. "He knew it would bring me back to him in the morning, no matter how much we fought the night before." She took Rowan's hand. "Find a way to *make* Harry engage with you, Rowan. Find your grape jelly."

* * *

DUNCAN SAT ON one of the cushioned chairs of the wrap-around porch, shrouded in darkness. Rowan tapped lightly on one of the pillars, like a knock.

"What's up?"

"Got hot in there, that's all." He sat forward with his elbows on his thighs, hands knotted together. His boots tapped on the wood floor of the porch as he raised and lowered his heels.

"Duncan." Rowan wrapped her arms around her body. "You don't—have feelings for me, do you?"

His head snapped up. He skewered her with his black gaze, and his mouth twisted just short of a smile. "I love you, Red. Of course I do."

Rowan blinked.

Duncan laughed low and shook his head. "Not like that."

"Then why did you leave like you did?"

"I didn't realize you and Harry were a thing," he said.

"Honestly? Neither did I, until a few months ago."

"A few *months*?" Duncan's agitation mounted with every bounce of his legs.

Rowan slumped against the railing. "Is this a problem for you?"

"No, no." He dropped his forehead to his hand and rubbed. "*God,* no, it's not a problem. At least, not in the way you think."

"Then what's going on?"

"I just—can't believe I didn't notice."

"Honestly? I can't believe you didn't, either." Everyone else obviously had.

"I've got a lot going on. Distractions." He scratched the worn knee of his dark jeans with his thumbnail, his booted feet still tapping. He was all raw, flustered energy, and his eyes were haunted.

When he didn't continue, Rowan nudged for more. "What is it?"

"I always thought Harry and Temperance were going to end up together."

Whatever Rowan was expecting him to say, that wasn't it. "Wait, *what*?"

"Shit," he breathed, dropping his head again to stare at his hands. He let out a long sigh that ended on a half laugh, half groan. *"Shit."*

"Harry and Temperance . . . ," Rowan prompted him.

Duncan shook his head. Cracked his knuckles. "Far back as I can remember, she always preferred his company. We were teenagers when we met—when Nate and Maren got together. She and Harry always had so much in common, even back then. They'd talk about shit I couldn't even pretend to understand. Then they both became doctors, both so smart. Harry's always got his fucking arm around her, kissing her head. I always thought—you know. Then, he and Nicola split and he came back here. I thought he was coming for Temperance. But then when you said that—in there." He gestured toward the house, and fell silent for a beat. "A lot of shit came crashing down."

Rowan sat in the chair beside him. "If Harry and I are together, that means Temperance and Harry aren't."

More nervous leg bouncing. Then, he nodded.

They were quiet for a long time.

"Red," Duncan haltingly began, "you need to prepare yourself for what Harry might be like when he gets here tomorrow."

Rowan's belly turned over. "What does that mean?"

"I don't know what happened between you two, but I'm assuming since he went back to Cali, and you're here asking for help getting him back, it wasn't good."

"Fair assessment."

Pensive, Duncan rubbed his hands together. "Harry ever tell you about why Mal walks with a cane?"

"No," Rowan said. "But I've noticed Harry seems—different around Mal than he is with the rest of you."

"Short version. Mal was Harry's idol. Nate and Patrick were kind of their own duo, so Mal was *it* for us younger kids, you know? *The* big brother. Especially for Harry. Mal was home from college for Thanksgiving, and Ma and Dad couldn't pick Harry up from soccer, so they asked him to do it."

Duncan sat up straight. "Mal had gotten into drugs. I don't know the details—I was just a kid, and nobody ever talks about it. Had something to do with a girl he met at Columbia. He was high when he picked Harry up, crashed the car, fucked up his leg. Harry didn't have a scratch on him, but that pedestal he had Mal on crumbled and did a lot more damage, you know? Apparently Mal asked Harry to lie for him, say they saw a rabbit in the road, some shit like that. But Harry wouldn't."

Rowan's heart broke for teenage Harry *and* for young Malcolm.

"You know what Harry's like, Red. Cool as a cranberry, but that temper, Christ. Once that fuse burns down—" Duncan whistled.

"I think it's 'cool as a *cucumber,*' " she teased.

"Don't you start, too."

They laughed.

"Point is," Duncan continued, "Harry stayed pissed at Mal for a *year* after that. Things are still rocky between them, all these years later. And I promise you, the pedestal Harry had *you* on had to have been miles higher than Mal's."

"I can handle it." She chewed the cuticle on her thumbnail.

"He might not be nice."

"Nice," Rowan laughed. "I'm counting on it."

"You want me to step in tomorrow, you just say 'cucumber' or something, and I've got your back, okay?"

"Okay." She squeezed his knee. "Duncan. Did you have a bet with Nate and Patrick about me and Harry?"

The tips of his ears flushed pink. "You put me out two hundred bucks just now, Red. They said Harry had it bad for you. I thought—well, we just established what I thought."

Rowan sat back and clasped her hands primly in her lap. "When did you guys make the bet?"

"April."

"The wedding?"

"Jesus, I can't believe Harry made a move on my date."

Rowan reddened and laughed. "Temperance made her own version of that same joke, believe it or not."

He squinted into the darkness beyond their island of porch light. "Did she?" His smile looked sad.

"Harry and Temperance have never been anything more than friends," she said. "She's like a sister to him."

He grunted.

"You don't—think of her as a sister, do you, Duncan?"

He dropped his gaze to his big hands. "Fuck."

"Tell me."

"No."

"No, you won't tell me? Or no, you don't think of Temperance as a sister?"

His laugh was raw, and his words were rushed. "No, I most definitely do not think of Temperance Madigan as a sister."

"I see."

"We've got history, her and I."

"Do you want to talk about it?"

The easy mood evaporated, and his eyes turned glassy and distant. Big, bold Duncan Brady, with his ready, flirty grin, was nowhere to be found. The man beside her was a stranger, vibrating with dark, anxious energy. Something inside him clawed to be free, painfully tamped down with a hard swallow and a fist in his glossy hair.

Duncan Brady was an absolute mess over Temperance Jean Madigan.

"I don't ever want to talk about Temperance, Red."

"Okay, big guy."

Duncan stood and jogged down the porch steps, disappearing into the night.

CHAPTER THIRTY

Harry

"Hey Bradys, I'm home." Harry dropped his overnight bag by the stairs.

Nobody heard him. Voices and muted laughter came from the dining room. Debussy played on the vintage record player in the foyer. Harry breathed deep and closed his eyes. Dad's birthday meal had been the same as far back as he could remember. Burgers, saucy baked beans, garlicky street corn, and Ma's homemade buttercream-frosted cake. Harry also smelled Dad's familiar aftershave and Ma's lemony candles.

Home.

The ordinariness of it was a relief. During the flight, he'd been unable to concentrate on the book he'd brought. He'd stared out the little plane window, imagining the miles shrinking between him and the world he'd shared with Rowan. Obsessing over how it would feel to be back in the valley without her.

When he'd first headed back West, he'd allowed himself to marinate in simmering, self-righteous animosity. He'd indulged in his anger at Rowan, his anger at himself. It dampened the misery of walking away. Soon, California itself had proved to be a beautiful distraction. Where sunsets were aggressively orange and framed by palm trees instead of dusky pink over Appalachian oak, it was easy to pretend he lived in a different reality. A place where he'd never had Rowan McKinnon, then lost her.

Just this week, Harry got word he passed the board qualifying exam. He was still riding high on that confidence boost. Sinclair's practice was progressive and thriving, and she'd given him the space to ease back into taking patients. As a bonus, the practice was within walking distance to the Santa Monica Pier. Every Friday, he had ice cream for lunch.

Conversation halted when he walked under the dining room archway. Bodies sat up straighter around the table. Everyone was there—even Malcolm and Charlotte had driven down from New York.

Why the hell was Frankie Moreau there?

Then he saw *her*.

Rowan. Between Frankie and Dad, at the far end of the table.

Seeing her felt like taking a cannonball to the chest. The air evaporated from his lungs, and the hair on the back of his neck rose. His lungs locked down.

She held a tiny bundle in a footed gray sleeper with an owl face embroidered on the butt. A baby. With *Rowan*. For an agonizing moment, reality and fantasy clashed in his brain. It nearly sent him to his knees.

The baby curled like a comma against her chest. The thin cream sweater she wore was made of fuzzy material that created a halo around her in the candlelight. Curls were pinned up in a knot on the top of her head, giving him an uninterrupted view of her achingly beautiful face. Even from this far, he saw the thrumming pulse in her neck. Her cheeks were flushed.

Ma's voice was muted by the clamor in his head. "Welcome home, darling." The others greeted him, too. But sights and sounds were dampened. Blood slowed in his veins. Until ten seconds ago, he'd been on the path to normalcy. A quiet, ordinary life.

Now? He was right back in that moment she'd run away from him in the meadow.

"Please, if you care for me, make this easy. For both of us."

None of it had been *easy.* Admitting to himself that, no, the way he felt about her wouldn't ever have been enough to overcome her bone-deep distrust—it had been one of the hardest things he'd ever done. All of his sanctimonious confidence that he could eventually change her mind, *fix* her—it had all been a naive dream.

Gently, without taking her eyes off him, Rowan handed the baby to Frankie, who passed him on to Maren. Acid flooded Harry's gut, and he took an instinctive step backward. Damn it, when she'd shifted to hand the baby over, he imagined he could smell her herbal perfume all the way across the room. He should have sensed it the second he'd entered the house and turned to run like hell.

He could *still* run like hell.

Rowan's chair noisily scraped the floor when she stood. Everyone else had fallen silent and remained seated, even the kids. Like they'd been anticipating this moment.

What would she do if he left? Chase him?

Her lips were pressed between her teeth, and her eyes were as wide as he'd ever seen them. Pale hands with bone-white knuckles clenched a cloth napkin.

How *dare* she look so fucking vulnerable. "I thought

you said she wasn't here, Mother." Harry's scalp prickled. His gaze didn't divert from Rowan's.

Ma cleared her throat and raised a finger. "When we spoke, she was not." Her eyes turned hard as obsidian as she stepped confidently onto metaphorical maternal high ground. "And don't you call me 'Mother' in that tone of voice, Harrison Bryant."

Dad put his napkin down beside his plate and sat up taller, his shoulders somehow broadening. A timeless, wordless signal he would not hesitate to take an out-of-line child—grown or not—right the hell away from the dinner table if they didn't shape up.

Harry was trapped. This was a fucking ambush, and his entire family was complicit.

"Sit down," Dad said in his most compelling dad-voice. Rowan quickly plunked down in her chair, bobbling a water glass as she scooted up to the table. Dad chuckled and patted her hand. "I was talking to Harry, sweetheart."

Harry glowered at his traitorous father.

The only empty chair was the one directly across the table from *her*.

His stomach spasmed at the thought of having to look at her over the entire meal. But Harry sat as he was told and slapped his napkin onto his lap.

"Why is she here?" Harry asked Ma.

"I'm sitting right across from you. Ask me yourself," Rowan said.

Harry sat forward and rubbed his brow bones. Wouldn't look at her.

Conversation resumed, slow and stilted at first. Maren nursed the baby while she and Nate chatted with Frankie about promotional photography for the new website. Ma attempted to engage Malcolm in a conversation about his newest bestseller but was met with typical vague half answers. The kids were enthralled with Mercy and Duncan, who challenged them with rapid-fire riddles. Patrick was ineffectively attempting to convince Arden to consider going into prepharmacy. Dad oversaw the whole thing like it was his domestic kingdom—a glass of wine in one hand, a napkin in the collar of his shirt, and a self-satisfied smile on his face.

"You look good, Harrison," Rowan said.

Harrison.

She was baiting him. The back of his neck might burst into flames.

And that was it? He looked *good*? It was so deliberately neutral, so pleasant and polite, he couldn't keep his mouth shut. "I *feel* good, too. It's incredible what a difference a healthy environment makes." He crooked a finger in the neck of his shirt, opened a button, and finally met her eyes across the table.

When her expression briefly crumpled, guilt crept in, and he kicked it down. He *needed* to see the pain in her eyes to feed his resolve. When he finally tore his attention away from her, Maren was looking right at him, a subtle smile curving her mouth.

Shit.

He poured himself wine nearly to the rim of a tall water glass. If the kids hadn't been there, he'd have swigged straight from the bottle.

With the one-handed efficiency of a father of three, Nate deftly wielded his fork over his infant son's dusky head to take a bite of beans. Baby Leo was supported under his puffy diapered butt by only the palm of his father's other hand.

Still chewing, Nate stood and moved around the table. "You wanna hold him?" He handed the baby to Harry before he could answer.

"You just want to have both hands free for cake later, Nathan," Arden teased.

"Obviously," Nate replied.

Harry gently took the sleeping bundle from his brother, easing the infant down against his chest. Leo made tiny, grunty squeaks as he nestled in, and Harry pressed the tip of his nose to the perfect little curlicues of dark hair on his nephew's head. A trace of Rowan's unmistakable scent lingered there from when she'd held him. It mingled with the fresh sweetness all babies naturally had, and for a moment, Harry's scalding frustration was tempered by a painful longing so acute, he felt like his heart had crowded his lungs out of his chest. He could barely breathe.

To Nate, Harry quietly said, "You're a lucky man, big brother."

"I know it." Nate watched Maren as she dabbed chocolate milk from Grey's shirt. "To think she refused to date me for months before she finally agreed."

Maren looked up with a wry smile. "*Pff.* It took you months to work up the courage."

Nate wagged a finger. "You find a good woman, you don't let her go."

Maren rolled her eyes and laughed, and a dismissive snort came from Mal's direction. Duncan muttered something about "horseshit," and Patrick laid an arm across the back of Mercy's chair.

In his peripheral vision, Rowan went still.

Harry swallowed hard. "Sometimes, they don't give you a choice."

Rowan's fork clattered to her plate. Bull's-eye.

Harry didn't have Nate's fatherly grace with the baby. When he impatiently reached for his wine, his watch snagged the edge of his dinner plate, knocking it into his glass. It toppled and spread like arterial spray across the white tablecloth.

In seconds, Nate was up from his chair, lifting the baby away from him.

"Fuck." Harry tossed his napkin on the stain.

"Language," Rowan murmured around the rim of her wineglass.

Harry glared.

Duncan hooted a laugh. "Nice."

Harry rolled up the sleeves of his shirt. Christ, it had to be eighty degrees in there.

Ma stood and tossed her own napkin over the stain as she headed to the kitchen. "We'll clean it up later. It's time for cake."

After everyone sang "Happy Birthday," Malcolm and Harry both declined a piece. Duncan asked Rowan, "Chocolate or vanilla, Red?"

"Chocolate, please," she said.

"Cucumber?" Duncan said with a strangely expectant look on his face.

What the hell?

Rowan laughed and gave Duncan a gentle smile. "No, I'm good."

Rather than handing the cake directly to Rowan, Duncan reached around Mal and shoved it in Harry's face. "Pass this over, will you?"

Harry sighed. He could either take the cake or let Duncan dump it on the table in front of him. Mal leaned back with a bored look of annoyance at Duncan's big arm in his face. Impatiently, Harry snagged the cake from him and dropped it on the table in front of Rowan with a negligent bend of his wrist.

"That's the fastest I've ever seen you commit to something," Harry said to her.

A muscle ticked along the edge of her jaw. The glimmer of spirit in her eyes matched the sly curve of her lips. Harry shifted in his seat, immediately aware that somehow, the dynamic had changed, and not likely in his favor.

Rowan plunged her fork into the cake. "Duncan asked me a question I was prepared to answer."

"What the hell does that mean?"

She raised her brows in a convincingly guileless expression and licked a bit of gooey frosting from her thumb. "Within the context of tonight's birthday party, I knew someone would be offering me birthday cake. So, I was prepared for the question."

Her voice annoyed him.

Her voice enthralled him.

God, he was a masochist, but the thrill of having a conversation with her again overrode his sense of self-preservation. He countered, "There are some situations where surprise is inherent to the conversation at hand, and advance notice isn't a realistic expectation."

"I suppose. But when committing to something as important as which kind of *cake* to have, a bit of advance discussion might help one adjust to the idea of—you know—having the cake. Especially if you'd be eating that kind of cake for the rest of your life. And maybe, other kinds of cake had given you food poisoning in the past." She forked an obnoxiously big piece into her mouth and tilted her head, eyes innocently wide. "Don't you agree?" Her voice was muffled by cheeks full of cake.

"I'm not playing your game," he said.

She swallowed. "What game?"

"This feels a lot like the 'how can we fuck with Harry today' game."

She dabbed her mouth with a napkin, and her posture and expression were suddenly serious. "My reluctance in giving you an answer that day wasn't any less valid than your insistence on having one, Harry."

Harry.

So, he was Harry again. The sound of her saying it sliced through him like a blade.

Mal slowly leaned forward and placed his elbows on the table, steepling his fingers. "What—if I may—the fuck are you two talking about?"

"Language," Gia called out, while Charlotte simultaneously exclaimed "Language, Daddy!" to Mal, triggering an eruption of giggles from the other children, and a belly laugh from Duncan.

Harry felt like he was the starring character in some demented screwball comedy.

"The cake is phenomenal as usual, my love," Dad said to Ma. "I have a recipe for salted honey pie I'm planning to put on the B&B menu."

"I will not be partaking of your honey pie, Pops," Duncan said. "If I wanted some of that, I'd eat—"

"Duncan, for Christ's sake," Dad cut him off. "Not at the table."

"Do not blaspheme under my roof, William," Ma said.

Arden grimaced. "Can we at least come up with a different name for it?"

"Fresh honey!" Maren leaned forward to look down the table at Rowan. "Didn't we talk about keeping beehives on the property this past summer?"

"I love bees. That would be fun," Rowan said.

"I want fresh honey for my peach-and-jalapeño scones, too. Everything but the dry ingredients will come from right here on the farm."

"We're calling this a farm now?" Mercy asked.

"It needs a name," Nate said. He was on his third piece of cake. "A farmy name."

"I loved those heirloom jalapeños you grew for me, Rosie. And there's a nice area for a peach orchard in the pasture beside the round barn," Dad said.

"You're *all* calling her Rosie now?" Harry grumbled, but nobody acknowledged him.

"You can call me that too, if you like," Rowan said. He ignored it.

Frankie piped up, "Scones are made with eggs, though. Won't you need some chickens?"

"Chickens!" the kids cried.

Harry's head spun.

"Do you bake, Frankie?" Dad asked.

"Well, I stress-bake. Mostly as a front to eat the raw cookie dough," Frankie replied.

Harry didn't miss Mal's rare, subtle smile at Frankie's quip. *Good luck with that, bud.*

"Maybe we can share recipes," Dad said.

"You know we have to have an actual bed-and-breakfast for you to serve food to guests, right, Dad?" Patrick said.

"If I bake it, they will come," Dad replied.

"I like scones with grape jelly," Arden said. She and Rowan shared a strange smile from across the table.

Ma turned to Rowan. "Rowan, didn't you say you wanted to plant a few Concord vines along the southern fence? We could make our own jelly."

Harry swung his attention to Ma. "How the hell is she going to do that? She doesn't live here."

"I'm sitting right in front of you. Ask me," Rowan said.

Harry pinched the bridge of his nose. The rest of the evening was the same: rapid-fire conversational threads twisting and intersecting and diverting in ways that made it impossible to keep up. It felt like they were going to stay there for hours.

Maren was the one to bail them out of the endless loop of inane chatter. Nate was still chewing a mouthful of cake when he stood with her and Leo to leave.

"Well, Bradys. It's been fun," she said, "but it's late, and this cute little tyrant is going to have me up every few hours tonight wanting the boob."

"Just stick a pacifier in Nate's mouth and tell him to leave you alone," Arden said.

Nate swallowed his cake, smirked, and wagged a playful finger at her. "Real cute, kiddo. Speaking of babies, remind me to tell you about the time you crapped your diaper all the way up to your armpits during our Ocean City family vacation."

Arden laughed. "Fine, fine, I yield."

Duncan stood too, gathering the kids. "Let's go, turkeys."

Frankie followed suit. "It's a long drive into the city when you're tired and full of good food. Thank you for including me tonight. I've missed you all." She leaned in to whisper something to Rowan. As she listened, her downcast lashes looked impossibly soft over cheekbones more prominent than he remembered. She seemed a gentler version of the woman he left in July, and somehow, that antagonized him even more.

Arden looped an arm through Frankie's to see her out, Patrick and Mercy gave hugs and kisses, and Mal followed them all after a spare nod to Rowan.

Ma and Dad cleared the table, and just like that, Harry was alone with Rowan.

Stand up and leave, Harry.

The Debussy record had stopped, and the family's voices all faded as they went their separate directions. It was quiet enough he heard the grandfather clock ticking in the foyer. Harry glowered at Rowan across the table in a way that would have had a lesser person shrinking away. Not her, though. She met and held his gaze.

"You got what you wanted, you know," she said. "You told me you wanted it to hurt if I walked away. It hurt."

"You asked me to make it easy." Harry almost choked on the words. "I did."

"Was it?" She fidgeted with the stem of her wine-glass. "Easy?"

Get the fuck out, Harry.

The tip of her tongue darted out to dampen her bottom lip, and her eyes burned like garnets in the candlelight. Christ, she was almost too bright for his eyes. A living flame. Consumptive fire that would burn his body and soul to ash if he gave it the chance. He couldn't speak, and he couldn't look away.

"It's not polite to stare." She nudged her chin up.

Harry flinched. God*damn* her.

He swigged wine straight from the bottle, setting it back down with a loud *thunk*. "I'm trying to figure out what the hell you're doing here."

"Isn't it obvious?" she asked.

Rowan reached for the bottle and drank after him, as they'd done the first night they met. She nudged it gently back toward him. He didn't take it.

"To punish me?" he asked.

"Don't you think you've done a good enough job of that yourself?"

"You took my heart and my pride, and now you're taking my family too?"

"Harry, do you think I want to be here—part of this—without you?"

His short laugh was brittle. "Fuck your little questions game. Answering with a question of your own is one of the ways you refuse to commit to anything real."

Ma bustled back in from the kitchen. "Harrison Bryant, you're not being a gentleman."

Rowan held up a hand. "No, no, Gia—it's fine. I'd much rather have this than his indifference."

Well. There it was. Indifference was the weapon he needed to ward her off, but he was fully incapable of it. It would always be like this. She would toss his emotions like a coin, and he'd flounder between hating her and loving her.

Hell. He could never hate her.

"I think she's always found me to be *too* gentlemanly, Ma," he shot back.

Rowan leaned forward, slow and deliberate. "Actually, no. I've always loved how"—her voice dipped to an intimate register—"*nice* you are."

A memory of that May night in the greenhouse completely short-circuited him, simultaneously tightening his jaw *and* his balls. Now she was just being cruel.

Before Harry could retort, Dad came back, carrying a massive cookbook. "Research time."

"You might consider getting Harry's pancake recipe for your breakfast menu, Will. They're wonderful," Rowan said.

"Let's go back and make some pancake noises."

Harry had never been wound up this tight in his life. He tugged at his collar again. Unbuttoned another button. Considered slipping off his shoes.

"Solid idea," Dad said.

"There's nothing special about them," Harry replied.

"His fresh-squeezed OJ is the best I've ever had." Rowan took another drink of wine from the bottle. "Do you add something to it, Harry? A special ingredient? I *love* it."

That did it. Harry surged to his feet, shooting his chair backward with enough force it tipped over and crashed to the floor behind him.

"All right, damn it. I've had enough," he growled, slapping his napkin down. "Come with me." In two strides, he rounded to Rowan's side of the table and lifted her by the arm. He barely touched her, but she came up out of the chair with ease. Harry pulled her behind him into the foyer.

To his parents' credit, they didn't intervene. Harry had no doubt this was the outcome they'd been hoping for, anyway. This entire evening had been manufactured to force Rowan in front of him.

As soon as they were out of the line of sight of the dining room table, Harry dropped her arm and spun on her. "You have three minutes to explain what the hell you're doing here."

Her expression was infuriatingly serene. "You know why."

"Don't." He yanked his phone out of his pocket and jammed his fingers against the screen. "You're about two months too late."

"What are you doing?" She peered over the edge of his phone. She was so close, he could feel the ambient heat from her body.

"Getting you a ride to wherever you're staying."

"If you really want me gone, I can walk," she said. "I'm staying here. You'd know that if you'd have answered your damned phone, *ever,* but you blocked my number—"

Harry's agitation finally detonated into anger, a living bomb. "I never blocked your number." His voice boomed between the tile and high ceiling of the foyer. He jabbed a finger at her face. "I saw your name on my screen, every time you texted or called. *Every fucking time,* Rowan." When he saw how badly his hand trembled in the air between them, he curled it into a fist and shoved it in his pocket. "I thrived on the pain. I *needed* it to stay focused and remember why I left."

"Surely you knew why I kept trying to reach you."

"I stopped pretending I knew anything about you the day I said I loved you and you said 'let me go.'" It bolstered him when her face fell. Confidence surged. This was what she *wanted.* No fucking strings. "I said I wanted to *marry* you, Rowan. And you rejected me. You rejected *us.*"

She was still in his personal space. Harry knew exactly what he was denying himself by not reaching out to touch her. He shuddered with the effort of it.

"When I asked you to make things easy, I meant in that moment, asshole," she hissed. "I didn't mean for you to leave for good."

"I know the words you said, Rowan. But I also heard what you *meant.*"

She didn't respond to that. She simply stood there, her chest rising and falling. The scent of her breath and her skin and her hair made Harry want to fall to his knees and scream.

"I hope your postdoc is everything you hoped it would be." The words came out quieter than he'd intended.

"I didn't accept, Harry. I was going to tell you as soon as I got home."

Home.

He didn't know what terrified him more—the fact that she was here pulling this stunt, or that he might have made the biggest mistake of his life when he'd left.

"This isn't your home."

She laid a hand on his chest. A thin arc of unshed tears gleamed in her startling topaz eyes. "It was."

If he touched her, his resolve would vaporize, and he couldn't risk it again. His life in California was bright and healthy and uncomplicated. He'd spent too many years waiting for Nicola to magically become the partner he needed. He wasn't ever doing that again.

He needed to get the fuck out.

CHAPTER THIRTY-ONE

Rowan

Please, please hold me, Rowan thought. *Kiss me, show me we can heal.*

Harry was so different now. His pants were tailored, snug around his thighs, falling to a perfect length above glossy square-toed loafers. Judging by the buttery fabric of his button-down, his clothes were expensive. His hair had been trimmed into a more professional cut, short enough now it didn't need to be tucked behind his ears. It was still long enough to sweep up into familiar little ducktails at the nape of his neck, though. They made her chest hurt.

Gone was gentle, sensitive Harry. This Harry's eyes were cold as granite, twice as hard. His skin glowed with California sunshine, and there were no hollows under his cheekbones. His frame was built now with the lean muscle it was meant to have.

Maybe he'd only loved her while he was fragile. Maybe—this strong, vibrant man didn't need a woman like her.

Then there it was, in his eyes. The thing Rowan dreaded most.

Indifference.

Harry's anger seemed to evaporate like steam on hot pavement after a summer storm.

He was going to walk away, and she couldn't summon the courage to stop him.

With a disgusted shake of his head, Harry stepped around her, yanking the front door open. He whipped it shut behind him, rattling the windows along the front of the house.

She'd had him there, face-to-face, and it still hadn't been enough.

For a few minutes, she stood there alone in the foyer. She imagined him sweeping back through the door, pulling her into his arms, telling her everything was going to be okay.

Panic twisted through her. Days ago, when she'd confessed her feelings to the Bradys, they'd boosted her up with such care and confidence she hadn't even considered Harry may not come back to her.

Rowan's arms hung limp at her sides. She shook her wrists to jostle sensation back into her numb hands as she returned to the dining room.

Gia sat in Will's lap, his cookbook abandoned. When they looked up from their hushed conversation, their expressions fell in synchronized dismay.

Rowan shrugged, splaying empty hands. She seized the inside of her bottom lip in her teeth, unable to speak.

Gia hopped up and drew her into a tight hug. "What happened?"

Rowan silently shook her head.

"Horseshit," Will barked from the other end of the room. Gia shushed him.

"It's over. I saw it in his eyes." Rowan took a quaking breath. "Actually, it's what I *didn't* see in his eyes that makes me certain."

Gia squeezed her arms and studied her face. "No. You're not done yet. Neither is he."

A single tear fell, fat and hot. "How can you possibly know?"

Gia and Will shared a look, then she gestured to the foyer. "Because he slammed the door. It shook the whole house."

Will nodded in confirmation. "He's mad. You know his temper." He whistled.

"If he's that angry, he's lost control, and that means he *feels* something," Gia said. "If he'd closed the door quietly, we'd have a bigger problem."

Will stood to draw back the edge of the big picture window's curtain and made a soft *huh* sound before dropping it back into place to rub his hands together. "This is great. He's stomping down to the carriage house. Haven't seen a tantrum like this since he was a kid."

Rowan's eyes connected with Gia's, then Will's. "Why are you doing this for me?"

Gia didn't hesitate. "Because we love you."

"And so does he," said Will.

* * *

IN COLLEGE, TEMPERANCE had bought Rowan a sweatshirt screenprinted with, ANXIETY IS MY CARDIO. In that moment, as she charged across the darkened lawn to confront Harry, she'd never felt that more acutely. The evening was cool for September, but her pulse sprinted and sweat dampened the hair at her temples.

Anxiety escalated to annoyance as her heart pounded harder. Annoyance then became anger. It fueled her like a steam engine puffing diligently inside her chest. Harry had withdrawn to California, martyring himself in the wake of both of their mistakes. Leaving her to feel like she'd been solely responsible for the collapse of their relationship.

Well, screw that.

Instead of the swaying greeting she usually got from the willow outside the carriage house, its branches were motionless. It was dark inside, and the door remained locked. The back deck was also deserted. She broke off the dried head of a Shasta daisy in one of the neglected planters there and twirled it in her fingers. Where would he have gone?

The pond.

Under a wide-open starry sky, she found Harry on the dock. He sat on the fishing bench at the end of it, illuminated by the milky gray light of the full moon.

"Pool's closed," Rowan said.

He sighed when her weight dipped the dock in the water, but he didn't turn. "Forgot I didn't have a key to the carriage house." He sounded sullen.

Abruptly, he stood and tried to get around her. The dock pitched from side to side. They both splayed legs and spread arms to keep from careening into the water.

"No," Rowan said. The rocking eased. "You're going to listen to me, or I'm going to haunt you until we both die. And after, too."

Harry was the embodiment of sullen irritation. He snapped his head back to stare at the moon and locked his hands onto his hips.

"You made it seem like I was the reason we fell apart," Rowan said. "You were still legally married when we first met, Harry. The tender flirtation, all that sad-eyed charm. This whole thing between us started under false pretenses."

"We're *not* doing this again—"

"Then you left because I didn't say the things you wanted to hear."

After a beat of silence, he made a feral noise in his throat and lurched away from her, back toward the bench. The dock swayed.

Rowan kept her tone even, but firm. "You never gave me the chance to tell you why what you said in the meadow that day scared me. Why learning about Nicola hurt so bad."

"No backstory, remember?" he snapped. "I tried for *months* to get you to open up to me. You don't get to use that as an excuse."

"*You* didn't have to run all the way back to California. That's your pattern though, isn't it? Bounce back and forth between coastlines, whenever shit gets too hard?"

That found a target. He turned to face her. His bottom lip was tucked tight against his teeth, and his nostrils flared.

"You have the nerve to call *me* avoidant?" he said.

"If you'd stop interrupting—"

"I *still* don't know about Noah. The only reason I know that fucking name at all is because Temperance dropped it accidentally."

Rowan bit back, "You could've answered your phone once in the last two months, you absolute jackass."

A breeze came in from the north. It rippled the waves of his hair and rattled the cattails at the water's edge. Harry shifted his weight from foot to foot. The rapid rise and fall of his chest betrayed his outer coolness. "I am trying really hard to not walk away right now. I need you to understand that."

Rowan still blocked his way off the dock. "What are you going to do, push me in the water?"

"I'm considering it."

"I'd take you with me. From now on, you go where I go."

It was meant to be funny—a peace offering. Harry didn't laugh. Rowan's confidence sputtered like a candle on a mountaintop. When she spoke again, her words were quiet.

"His name was Noah Tully. He was a paramedic. We met when my junior-year roommate almost burned our apartment down making a silly grilled cheese sandwich."

Harry's eyes were hooded, and he was finally still. She had his attention.

"He was—incredible. Handsome, funny, competent. I was twenty-one, and obsessed with him. For six months, it was constant intensity. Everyone he met was awed by him, utterly charmed. Noah had his own gravity, this way of making everything revolve around him. And you *liked* it, being in his orbit, even though you knew you weren't the one steering the ship."

Humiliation was layered inside her. She imagined peeling back each stratum of shame, exposing the story of her year with Noah Tully the same way the rings of a tree would reveal the environment it grew in. It wasn't only that she'd been so utterly overcome by his slick charm. It was that she'd planned a life and shared a bed with a man who was already another woman's husband. Rowan had been the *other* woman.

This time, instead of burying the shame as she always did, she set her teeth and let it rise to the surface from the darkest places inside her. Rowan gathered it all—the self-contempt and the unworthiness and the guilt—and exhaled it into the clean valley air, like it was a toxin she could simply breathe away.

"After those first six months, I saw less of him. Work

was busy, he said. Being a paramedic meant unpredict-able hours. Anytime I'd bring it up, he'd sulk. Tell me I wasn't being supportive. But if *I* dared miss a single call from him, or had to cancel a date because of school, or work, or anything else, he'd *rage*. Question me—'Do you love me, Rowan?' Challenge my priorities. Mock my 'plant shit,' and how much I studied. We'd fight and make up, and I didn't realize until later he'd pick fights *just* so we could make up. He constantly chased those highs, engineering our entire relationship so it was nonstop ups and downs. I thought it was passion. I thought—that was how love was."

"That was abuse." Harry's top lip snagged upward in a snarl. "It wasn't love."

Rowan plucked a few petals from the dried daisy, crumbling each one to dust.

He loves me.

He loves me not.

"Tell me, Harry—how would I know? After Edie died, I didn't have anyone to model it for me. I didn't have any family when I met Noah. Nobody to meet him and say, 'Hey, honey, this guy seems pretty sketchy, better not.' That's why he picked me, I think."

Petals rained down from her fingers. Harry watched her, eyes shining in the moonlight. His chin trembled. The first crack in his armor.

He loves me.

He loves me not.

She went on, "You can't imagine what this year has been like for me. Being with you. With your family. To be thirty years old, feeling all these *real* things for the first time. It was like being screamed at in a language I'd never heard before. It was overwhelming and jarring and confusing."

Late-summer wind rustled tonelessly, endlessly, through the white pines and hemlocks to the east.

"Anyway. Noah," Rowan began again, slowly. "Little things started bothering me. We had no mutual friends. There was no pattern to his work schedule. I'd never met any of his family, but I tried convincing myself that was okay—I'd have just been anxious about it anyway. I'd go for a week at a time without seeing him. Once, I ran into him off campus, and he'd had two *kids* with him, Harry. Little ones, maybe two and four. His sister's kids, he'd said."

The memory of it ached, like a thumb pressed into a fresh bruise.

"A few weeks later, he proposed. It fit right in with his pattern, resetting with a flourish every time we started to slide. Anything for that emotional high."

"Fuck this guy," Harry growled.

"I thought it would all change, once we were married. I wanted a family. I wanted to mother children in a way I'd never been mothered. I imagined being someone's daughter-in-law. We'd buy a house, he'd be around more." Her laugh was ugly. "After about three months, the ring disappeared. Every night, I'd put it in a ceramic dish on the dresser, and one morning, it was gone. Noah tried convincing me I'd dropped it on campus, but I knew deep down I couldn't have. It always fit a bit too tight."

Wind sliced through her thin sweater, chilling the sweat that glazed the small of her back. She shivered.

"Noah was married, Harry. He had a wife and kids in the city. He had a family for stability, and sought other relationships in secret to feed his gross narcissistic need for the rush of something new. I'm sure I wasn't the only one he did this to."

Harry swore softly in the dark.

Rowan rubbed her nose hard enough to make her eyes tingle. "I actually saw him a few years ago. In Philly. Frankie and Temperance and I went to the Mummers Parade on New Year's Day and went to get doughnuts afterward. He was leaving the bakery with his family as we went in. I had a hat and scarf on, really incognito. He didn't recognize me at first. I will never forget the transformation on his face. Polite, impersonal smile. An apology for bumping into me, then a sly grin, like he was gearing up to say something flirty. Then, recognition. Shock. He looked at his family, then back to me."

Rowan sat beside Harry on the bench, careful not to touch him. He didn't move away. Progress.

"I'll never forget those kids' sweet faces, Harry. For them, I stayed silent. His wife—she looked tired. God, I just wanted to reach out and give her a hug. She was wearing my ring." Rowan grimaced, still destroying the daisy. "Well, it was never *mine*. That asshole used his *wife's* ring to propose to me. When she found it missing, he probably used his 'you must have lost it' line on her. Then he magically 'found' it and got to be the hero by giving it back to her."

Harry had his head in his hands now, still as a gargoyle beside her.

"Harry, when you told me you loved me during that argument in the meadow—that was a thing Noah did. He used 'I love you' to manage me. It was a dismissal, and sometimes a misdirection. Back then, I'd been so hungry for those words for so long, I didn't realize it until a long time after."

Harry stood and stepped around her, stalking off the dock. As soon as his feet hit solid ground, he went still, planted his feet wide, and balled his hands into fists. A frustrated rumble began in his chest, and with his back to her, he let out a full-throated scream at the sky.

He spun around, breathing hard. "Why didn't you *tell* me?" he pleaded.

She carefully moved to him. Tears stung her eyes. "Harry, I have spent the last eight years trying to not hate myself for getting involved with another woman's husband. *You* were another woman's husband. You can't imagine the burden of that kind of shame."

He swiped both hands over his face. "Ah, Christ, Rowan." His voice was husky from the scream. "It wasn't the same."

She swallowed hard and tipped her head back, willing the tears not to fall. "You've been surrounded your whole life by people you trust and love. Without hesitation or suspicion. My whole life? I can't even trust my *own* judgment when it comes to others."

"You should have *told* me." The anguish in his voice ripped her in half.

She blurted a watery laugh. "Before Cora, had you ever experienced *any* self-doubt, Harry? Can you imagine how it would feel to be so perfectly duped by someone you thought you loved? Who you thought *loved you*? I started thinking—maybe something about me drew abusers." She shrugged carelessly. "Gaslighting was essentially Sybil's entire parenting style, so it didn't seem strange to me when Noah did it."

Harry stepped toward her. The moon on the water reflected light onto his beloved face. Rowan saw tears in his eyes.

"So, when you told me I wasn't a rebound, and everything happening between us was real and true, my first instinct was that I was being gaslit. That I was the pawn in another game."

He shoved his hair back. Rubbed his nose. "Did I ever give you reason to think this was a game?" He dashed the heels of his palms across his eyes.

Frustration tinged her tone, and her volume rose. "No. But that, what you said, just now? That's a thing gaslighters do. They make you question reality."

"I'm not—" He cut off the words, shook his head. "This hasn't been—" He made a low, irritated noise. "I won't diminish your pain. And you have every right to listen to your gut. But some things are real, Rowan. We were real."

Tears finally overflowed. "Were?"

"I've spent the months trying to recover from you, and now you're ripping out the stitches." Harry's shoulders were drawn up in defense, or anger, Rowan couldn't tell. Maybe it was both.

The daisy in her hands was down to a nub with a few remaining petals, a pathetic husk of the bright white blossom it had been when she'd tended it throughout the summer.

He loves me.

He loves me not.

"Harry. Science is like—its own language," Rowan said. "Give me ten minutes, and I could teach Alice and Charlotte the basics of Mendelian genetics. I could tell you the scientific name of groundhogs or moth orchids or meadowlarks—but love? Love is complicated."

Harry's eyes softened, and Rowan was certain she saw a tiny upward twitch of his lips. She'd give anything to see his smile again.

"Until Frankie and Temperance's friendship, the only kind of love I'd ever known was from Edie. Spending time outside with her was the light of my entire existence, Harry. *That,* to me, was love. I'd never known healthy romantic love." She took a step toward him. "So, every time I told you the scientific name of a plant, or taught you how to work the vines, or introduced you to a toad, or tried to get you to soften a bit toward spiders—I was showing you how I feel. I didn't even realize I was doing it. It's the only love language I ever knew."

Harry squeezed the bridge of his nose, closed his eyes. A tear slipped free.

"*Rosie,* that's what Edie called me. Remember?"

He sniffed. "Yes."

"She used to say—nicknames are the name your heart chose for someone. And when you call a person by that name, you're telling them, 'I love you.'"

A pause, then a stark laugh. He shook his head and looked down at his feet, nudging the grass around. "You wouldn't call me Harry."

Say it, Rowan.

"*Harry.*" Rowan said his name deliberately, like a caress, an invocation. She waited until he raised his eyes to look at her. "I love you."

The words landed gently, quietly between them. Harry blew a hot breath through tight lips, hard and fast, like she'd just hit him with her car.

Finally, *finally*—he came close. The dock creaked under his feet as he stepped back onto it. A constellation of emotion shone in his eyes. His hair was wind tossed, and Rowan tenderly tucked a few fallen locks back from his forehead.

"You taught me how to fall in love," Rowan murmured. "And I showed you how to fall out of it."

"Sure about that?" Harry nodded at the dried daisy in her hand. One petal left. Calm settled on them both like morning fog in the vineyard.

"You told me once you knew plants better than you

knew people. What's this last petal telling you, Dr. McKinnon?"

She felt like a star about to go supernova, seconds from shattering into a billion points of light. "I don't remember this from any botany textbooks." Her laugh was wavery. Hopeful.

Harry smiled gently and took the pathetic flower out of her hand. He plucked off the final parchment-like petal, and the night wind lifted it right into Rowan's curls.

"He loves you."

CHAPTER THIRTY-TWO

Rowan

Rowan always loved spring, when the botanical world reawakened. This year, when April's flourish swept the landscape, she saw the world as not only a botanist, but as a woman in love.

After she and Harry reconciled in September, he returned to Los Angeles to tell Dr. Sinclair Berry once again he'd be leaving her practice. She'd taken the news with grace and humor, telling him she would absolutely *not* be holding his position at her practice open this time, and if he ever came back to California, he'd better have Rowan with him so she could meet her.

Rowan finished the fall semester at her adjunct teaching position in Philadelphia. In December, she presented Nate with a résumé for the Brady vineyard and future winery's principal viticulturist position. It was a purely symbolic gesture, but she insisted on making a formal declaration of intent to the Bradys, and an acknowledgment to herself that this was the official direction of her career. The work she did there was a beautiful fusion of her rigorous education, the precious bright points of her past with Edie, and the love she had for the land she'd come to know so well.

And Harry. *Harry.*

It was a life she'd never given herself the space to even dream of.

Beginning in January, Rowan audited an enology course at Linden Community College to learn more about the science of wine making. None of her fellow students knew she had a Ph.D. in botany. It was an energizing joy for her, a veteran academic getting to learn new things alongside fresh-faced youths who were just beginning their educational journeys.

The winery construction was in progress, starting with a complete gutting of the bank barn. It would have a fully equipped lab in the lower level where she'd get to dive into the chemistry of crafting wine. Gia even planned to take Rowan with her to Spain sometime that year—they'd spend a few weeks at the Vega winery as an intensive workshop with her sister Renata.

Care of the vineyards would remain under Rowan's direction. Next month, the empty section of the Cabernet Franc block would be replanted with healthy new vines. A new vineyard was in early planning stages for white Albariño grapes, which would be imported as cuttings from Vega Vineyards. The climate and soil in Galicia were remarkably similar to the conditions in Vesper Valley. It was an exciting opportunity for the Bradys, since Albariño wine wasn't yet a common offering in the States. It would set them apart from other boutique wineries.

Harry was doing part-time on-call work at one of the Philadelphia hospitals. Four months of long commutes each day had begun to wear on him. They were living together in the carriage house, but Rowan knew a change was coming—Harry would eventually get a full-time job. Likely in the city. Linden was a lovely community, and a reasonable midway point between the farm and Philly, but even so, the thought of not living there made her sad.

It wasn't the land itself she'd finally put her roots into, though. It was Harry she'd tethered to. *He* was her home.

After a lifetime of fearing attachment, now that Rowan had given over to real love, she reveled in it. Binged on it, devoured it. She wanted to experience every nuance, every morsel, scrap, and atom. She was all in. She wanted to marry Harry Brady.

He just had to get around to asking.

"I want to marry you someday, Rowan," he'd said, an eternity ago. Inside her head, a tiny, ugly voice told her he'd never mention it again, and it kept her from ever bringing it up.

Logically, Rowan knew she didn't have to exchange vows and rings with Harry to have his full commitment. But every time they'd gone anywhere special over the last few months, Rowan had a bout of nerves, wondering if it was finally going to be the time he proposed. In February, they'd spent the night in Philadelphia to celebrate Harry's birthday—incidentally, Valentine's Day. Before they left, Rowan got the first professional manicure of her life at a little boutique in Linden in preparation for a prospective question-popping. They'd had an intimate, romantic dinner, then ice-skated under the lights at Dilworth Park. All she'd come home with was a sprained ankle and a manicure that barely lasted an hour into her subsequent workday.

Still. She loved him. And she'd wait.

Earlier that day, he'd called to tell her to meet him just after six o'clock in the grassy clearing between the meadow and the Chardonnay. April evenings were still cool, but sunlight held out until nearly eight now. Rowan changed her clothes five times before deciding on dark jeans and a slouchy gold sweater that picked up the lighter flecks in her eyes. Her hair was twisted in a half bun at her crown, and the rest of her curls fell free down her back.

Harry wasn't there when she arrived. The air was hazy and golden with evergreen pollen. A breeze brought scents of powdery lilac and fruity hyacinth. Rising temperatures had triggered bud break in the Chardonnay, and baby leaves now emerged as fuzzy bronze-pink rosettes, washing the fields with a gentle blush. The Chambourcin and Cabernet Franc were slower to awaken, as reds often were. Rowan imagined the vines as sentient, reveling in finally, *finally* being properly tended for the first time in years, spreading their woody arms wide to gather the sun.

"Do they ever answer you?" Harry said from behind her.

Rowan hadn't even realized she'd been talking. She turned, expectant goose bumps stippling her skin, warmth blooming in her chest.

In one hand, Harry held a small bouquet of wild indigo, and in the other, he clutched a large old-fashioned picnic basket. He had a burnished glow now, and he seemed so *big*. Today he'd worn a pale periwinkle buttondown with sleeves rolled to his elbows, and flat-fronted khakis that hugged his slim hips. He set the basket in the grass and extended the flowers.

His hair had grown out again, long enough to be pulled back in a short nub at his nape. The locks at the front and sides were still a bit too short to stay in the elastic, so he'd tucked them behind his ears. One hunk of hair fell free, and Rowan reached up to tuck it back.

"How long have you been standing there?" She tipped her face up, breathing him in. His clothes were infused with the warm, masculine essence of his skin, and the day-faded scent of his juniper soap.

"Long enough to know you were talking to the grapevines."

"Talking to plants is an important part of any good botanist's daily routine."

"Naturally. You've also got plant stuff in your hair." He wiggled a dried flower petal free from her curls, likely blown from one of the blooming hawthorns by the sheep barn.

"That's a required part of a botanist's official uniform," she said primly.

He touched a fingertip to her nose, then turned it to her for investigation. "What's this for, then?" It was a smudge of yellow pollen.

"Botanist cosmetics," she said. "Obviously."

His laugh was low, resonating on the same frequency as her heartbeat. Slowly, he brushed his thumb across her cheekbone, then the other. A fingertip smoothed each of her eyebrows, and down the bridge of her nose, tender and sensual. He shuffled closer and cupped the sides of her neck with his hands, running his thumbs along her jawline. Every molecule of her body urged toward him, but she curled her toes into the grass and stayed put, letting him explore her. She fixated on his mouth.

"Not polite to stare," Harry murmured, hands drifting to her shoulders, thumbs caressing her collarbone through her sweater.

"I'm memorizing," she said.

"Ah."

"Why haven't you kissed me yet?"

"I'm memorizing, too." He plucked another petal from her hair. "I'm also making sure I'm not going to eat any foreign plant material if I put my mouth on you."

Rowan chuckled. "In grad school, I had a plant grow out of my shower drain. The seed must have fallen out of my hair."

"It killed you to have to pull it out, didn't it?" He tugged and released a damp curl coiled tight against her temple.

"Who says I pulled it out?"

Harry shook his head. Then he kissed her, long and slow. His breath fanned warm across her face, and she inhaled him like a benediction, lips melting, tongues gliding. Solid hands dipped into the back pockets of her jeans, squeezing her tight against him. She went up on her toes for more leverage, twining her arms around his neck, her fingers in his hair. The elastic sprang free, releasing the honeyed waves into her hands.

Harry pulled back, nudging her forehead with his. "Hungry?"

"Always," she said.

"Good. I brought cheese," he said.

"God, I love you."

They sat in the little strip of grass on one of Gia's old quilts, with the vineyard to their left, and the whispering meadow to their right. Harry opened the wooden lid of the big woven basket, withdrawing a loaf of crusty French bread and an assortment of cheeses already sliced into bite-sized bits.

"Gia made this for us, didn't she?" Rowan asked.

"Maren did. It's a grown-up lunchbox. Where are your shoes?" He gestured to her feet with the neck of a wine bottle, then poured her a glass of red.

"Mmm, over there, near that patch of dandelions. Did you know Duncan hit my favorite boots with the mower?"

"Had you left them in the field again?"

"Well, yes, but—"

"We need to have a conversation about cause and effect."

Rowan laughed and broke open the bread to pluck out some of the soft, yeasty center. "I'm aware of the concept." She popped it into her mouth and chewed. "Like, you feed me wine and cheese at a beautiful picnic in the vineyard. Resulting effect: you get laid very soon after."

Harry leaned across the quilt to drop her a quick, hard kiss. Against her mouth, he said, "If I'd known a little cheese and wine was all it took to catch you, I've have tried it the night we met." He gently pulled her bottom lip between his teeth as he withdrew.

"That's not romance. That's bait."

"Same thing."

"You consider Team Tag the first time we met?"

"Well, it was," Harry said.

"Huh," she said.

"Why 'huh'?"

"I'm just trying to decide if it can be considered an official meeting, without the exchange of names."

He grunted. "Not my fault. I tried."

"Oh, of course. That charming old chestnut, 'who the hell are you?' " Rowan growled, mimicking his baritone.

"I don't blame you for trying to knee me in the balls," he chuckled.

"*Trying* to?"

"Your aim is garbage."

"It still hurt, didn't it?"

A beat of silence. For a moment, his gaze was intense. "Agony. For *months*."

The subtext made her heart twinge. She rubbed a hand over his knee, and when the ache in his expression cleared, she popped a piece of creamy gouda into her mouth. "What does it matter, anyway?"

"What does what matter?"

"When we officially met."

"Don't you think our kids will want to know how our beginning began?" His expression was all innocence.

Rowan's bottom lip went slack, dipping into a little *oh* of surprise. She pressed her lips together, and her chest got hot. The gouda was suddenly difficult to swallow.

"I have a question for you," he said.

Oh.

This could be it. Rowan subtly squeezed the ring finger on her left hand.

Harry leaned in and dropped his voice to intimate tones. "When are you going to tell me the truth about Cheesesteak Friday?"

Rowan shrank a bit, shoving disappointment down. Lightly, she said, "The night we met, Frankie said you and I would fall in love. I told her no way. Loser owed the winner a month of Cheesesteak Fridays. I lost."

"I'm glad you lost." Harry's eyes twinkled at her. Then he tucked his hair behind his ears and looked down into the picnic basket. "I have something to show you before it gets completely dark."

Her bloodstream turned to quicksilver, and she held her breath. Was *this* it?

Harry shuffled around inside the basket. "I've been dying to share this with you."

He withdrew a small, narrow tube.

Nope.

After popping the flat cap off the end of the tube, he slid out a rolled piece of paper, then spread it on the blanket between them. He used the wine bottle and a round of wrapped brie to keep it flat. It was an artist's sketch of a lovely brick building on beautifully landscaped grounds.

A look of unfiltered joy overcame Harry's features as he looked down at it. He held his breath.

"Harry, this is beautiful." Rowan smoothed a hand over the paper. "What is it?"

"It's—ah—" Sitting up straight, he hesitated, and scrubbed a hand across his mouth. "It's a maternity and wellness center. My new practice. I mean, it will be."

Rowan was overwhelmed with a swirl of emotions too heavy to untangle. Pride. Excitement for Harry. Longing. A darker thread of envy that *this* thing, this place, was what owned his heart in that moment. She couldn't speak. Where would this take him?

Was it in California?

Could she go, too?

His brows crowded together, and he looked from the drawing to her. "Are you okay?"

Rowan blinked fast and nodded. Smiled weakly. Hated herself a little for her utter inability to not taint this with her selfishness. "God, yes, Harry, this is—wow. It's huge."

Excitement reignited in his face. He took her hand, speaking in a rush. "People out here in the valley need to drive to Linden for care. Some go all the way into Philly. I got the wild idea—well, Arden gave me the idea—why not bring care to them? I'll still need to refer some pregnancies to the hospital system, but this is going to be something new. Pregnancy isn't pathology, you know? All babies don't *need* to be born in hospitals. And easier access to wellness visits means more people will do it. I'm going to hire a few midwives, some nurses, and we're going to do it all there."

Rowan felt the blood drain from her head. "Where are you building this, Harry?"

He looked perplexed. "About two miles down the road from Three Birds. Daily commute will be, ah, about ten minutes each way."

Rowan's chin quivered uncontrollably. "Here?"

Harry scooted forward, brushing an escaped tear from her cheek. "Yes, here. Where else would I go?"

She pressed her lips tight and shook her head.

"I'm sorry I didn't tell you until now." His voice was low, soothing. "I wanted it to be perfect. The last thing I was waiting on was Wesley's blessing to name it after Cora. This is the Cora Woodward Maternity and Wellness Center."

Harry withdrew a photo from the basket and handed it over. Rowan expected a photo of Cora, but instead, this one featured Harry standing next to a bald, bearded man nearly as tall as him, both of them smiling. In his arms, Harry held a grinning toddler squeezing a floppy plush puppy.

"This is from when I flew to L.A. last month. That's Wesley." He took a big breath and smiled. "And that's little Harrison Storm. He looks just like Cora."

The photo blurred as Rowan's eyes overflowed with tears. God, she loved this man. She laid the photo aside and climbed awkwardly into his lap, throwing her arms around his shoulders. Harry buried his face in her hair, laughing as he struggled to keep them upright.

"What is it, sweetheart?" His voice was muffled.

She shook her head against his. No words.

Harry's hand flattened against her back, his warmth

suffusing her. Bolstering her. Then he gripped her arms, holding her away so he could see her face. "Rowan, did you think I was leaving to build this somewhere else?"

She nodded.

A long breath escaped him, and he threaded his fingers with hers. "I go where you go, remember? It's you and me now, always."

Rowan gasped out a laughing sob and pressed her tear-streaked face to his, kissing his mouth, his cheeks, his nose. He groaned playfully as she shoved him backward to the quilt and pinned him down with kisses.

"They can see us, you know," Harry laughed.

Through the narrow clearing between the meadow and the vineyard, Gia and Will sat on the deck at the main house. From this distance, the two were tiny figures, but it was clear they were watching. When Rowan looked up, they both turned their heads away, pretending not to notice.

Her hair fell down as she bent to kiss the man she loved. She murmured against his lips, "Let them see."

CHAPTER THIRTY-THREE

Rowan

"One final thing!" Will called out from his picnic table podium. "New rule. Due to previous"—he paused theatrically—"abuses of the privilege, buildings are now off-limits as hiding places." He pointed his whistle at Rowan. "That includes the greenhouse."

Everyone laughed. Harry's arm was slung low around her, his hand tucked in the back pocket of her cutoffs. He squeezed her butt and looked down, eyes sparkling and crinkled at the corners. Someone pelted her with a large marshmallow, and Rowan laughed as it bounced off her shoulder into the grass.

The last light of day was a glowing line of burnt orange in the sky. It was May fourth, and all the Bradys had gathered to celebrate her thirty-first birthday. Arden came home despite impending finals and preparation for a month-long hike of the Appalachian Trail. Even Malcolm was there, arriving from New York just yesterday with Charlotte. He'd surprised the hell out of Rowan with one of the loveliest gifts she'd ever received—a hardbound journal with a canvas cover, embroidered with leaves in every shape and shade of green imaginable. He gave her a terse smile and a quick nod of his head when she'd thanked him with a stilted hug. It was probably the closest he'd ever come to any overt sign of affection with her. Temperance and Frankie were the first unofficial bed-and-breakfast guests, spending the weekend in two of the newly renovated rooms in the east wing of the house. The Everetts even came—Colby, his sister, Bess, and his brother, Brennan.

Earlier that day, Gia surprised her with a luscious Spanish orange-and-almond cake, a recipe that had been in her family for generations. Harry'd helped her make the sugary citrus glaze from fresh-squeezed orange juice. The cake was studded with a hodgepodge of thirty-one candles of various shapes, colors, and sizes—leftovers from the kids' birthdays over the years.

It was perfect. All of it.

Will blew the whistle to kick off the game of Team Tag.

"You're mine this time, Dr. McKinnon!" Harry shouted behind Rowan as she sprinted into the darkness.

"Like to see you try, Dr. Brady," she shouted back, laughing.

Hiding inside buildings was against the rules, but hiding *behind* them wasn't. Rowan ran east to the sheep barn, and immediately regretted the choice. The ewes could hear her outside, and as she approached, they shuffled around noisily inside the barn, hoping for crunchies. Asparagus let out a loud, insistent whistle of donkey curiosity.

"Shhhhh," Rowan hissed. She leaned against the rough wood of the outer barn wall, trying in vain to slow her choppy breathing. Warm night air lay across the back of her neck like a sweaty hand.

Several minutes passed in silence. When she heard Asparagus make the same inquisitive noise from moments before, she knew someone else was approaching.

She could run like hell as soon as she saw a shadow, and hit the Chardonnay block a few hundred yards away. Nobody knew the vineyards like she did. But if it was Harry, she was toast. He was running half-marathons now, and even when he'd been out of shape, his ground-eating strides were difficult to keep ahead of.

The donkey went silent. The only sound was the monotone whirr of crickets, and the occasional pip of tree frogs. *Too* quiet.

It seemed suspicious, really, that she didn't hear anyone, anywhere. None of the Bradys were calling out to each other to coordinate plans of attack. Frankie was hilariously bad at the game—she surely should have been found by then, whooping with her loud, reckless laugh.

Cautiously, Rowan leaned out to peer around the barn.

Behind her, the air moved.

"Asparagus did you dirty, my love." Harry's voice was a low rumble. "Gave you right away."

Resigned, Rowan slowly turned to face him. "She's probably mad I didn't bring her a banana. Spoiled baby."

Checkered moonlight shifted across Harry's beloved face as he approached. "You're not allowed to run this time." He moved in quick and cupped her face in his hands.

Tiny hairs rose with goose bumps along the back of her neck. It felt deliciously wicked being discovered by him, there in the darkness. Outside this barn was the first place they'd kissed—exhausted, icy cold, and slathered in mud. Rowan reached around him, settling her hands on his ass. Longing and tenderness brewed inside her. The old jeans he wore were no longer loose and shapeless like they'd been when she first met him. He filled them out well, in the back—*and* the front.

"I can see your brain working right now." He brushed his nose alongside hers, whispering against her cheek. "No knees to the balls this time, either."

Rowan squeezed his butt, pulling him closer. She drew up a thigh between his legs, pressing gently into his most sensitive parts. "What if I'm gentle?"

His breath tickled her face when he laughed. "You owe me, Rowan."

"I *owe* you?" she said.

"You use rogue tactics to win. You know you do. This time, you need to play nice."

"I'm always nice." She nudged her thigh higher between his legs and nipped his neck. "Let's be *nice* together. Right now."

Harry dropped his hands to her shoulders and skimmed them down the outside of her arms. They finally settled like shackles around her wrists. "Distraction won't work either."

She tugged against his hold, testing. "Fine. I probably couldn't outrun you now, anyway."

"Bold of you to assume I'm ever letting you go." The intensity in his voice contradicted the playfulness of the game, but he gave her a soft smile to counter it. He transferred his grip, binding both of her wrists in a single hand. He pulled a long strip of cloth from his back pocket.

Rowan's eyes widened. "You're—tying me up?"

"No. This is for your eyes."

"You're joking."

"I've never been more serious." His mouth curved in a subtle grin, and his eyes were glossy with intent, lit up like moonlight on the ocean.

Rowan quirked a skeptical brow. "I'm going to fall on my ass."

"You won't." Harry brought her hands to his mouth and pressed a warm kiss to her knuckles. "I've got you."

"I'll come willingly."

A quick, answering laugh. "Cute. No."

"I promise."

"Nope. Not taking any chances tonight." He held up the cloth and waved it like a little flag. "Tonight, I'm catching you."

Sighing with phony resignation, Rowan turned her back to him and closed her eyes.

He tied the cloth and guided her with a loose grip at the crook of her arm, catching her once when her ankle turned on a stone. It was soon obvious they'd passed where base would have been. There were still no other sounds from anyone else. Moving across the lawn like this, she should have heard *something*.

"You sure you're taking me to base?" She stumbled again.

"That's the goal of the game, right?"

"But haven't we been walking too long?"

"Are you counting steps or something?" Harry chuckled.

"Stop answering my questions with a question," she said.

He made a thoughtful, rumbly sound. "Hmm. So, it's only okay when *you* do that?"

"Harry, we're walking uphill. I can tell. You're lying to me."

"Less talking. More walking." His thumb grazed the tender inside of her elbow, back and forth. Soothing.

They stopped. Rowan could tell where they were based on the scent alone. The musky green sweetness of her compost pile, the funky, acrid scent of tomato fertilizer, and the delicate perfume of the honeysuckle sprawling up a trellis she'd constructed herself last summer. Grass gave way to fine gravel underfoot, and Harry pulled her to a stop. Through the blindfold, she saw the yellow glow of a bug light. The unmistakable creak of the greenhouse door confirmed where they were.

"I'm going to take off the blindfold, but you can't open your eyes until I say, okay?"

Curiosity ran wild within her by then, but the hint of nerves in Harry's voice softened her. She obeyed, closing her eyes beneath the cloth. "Okay."

With hands on her shoulders, Harry shuffled her forward. He untied the blindfold, letting it trail a slithering caress along the side of her neck as he pulled it free. Behind her, he pressed close. Against her ear, he whispered, "Open your eyes."

She did.

The inside of the greenhouse shone like a galaxy of stars. Thousands of tiny fairy lights hung curtain-like down the walls and looped like swags from the ceiling. Every table was covered in nursery pots bursting with native flowers. Black-eyed Susans and coneflowers, blue flax and candytuft, columbine and catchfly. A dozen others.

The place had been transformed into an indoor meadow. It was the world's biggest bouquet of wildflowers.

Garlands made from pine boughs and thin grape canes wound around the pots, accented with fragrant sprigs of rosemary and sage. Wide pillar candles in lanterns with brushed brass frames were interspersed with the greenery.

She entered in a daze, tears welling in her eyes. Harry kept his distance, allowing her the physical and mental space to take it all in. It was the most magnificent thing Rowan had ever seen.

"I hope you don't mind the temporary remodeling," he said behind her.

She couldn't turn around. Not yet. "How did you do this?"

"I had a few accomplices," he said. "Colby has a ton of connections at local garden centers. And I held my breath all day, hoping you wouldn't wonder why Nate needed you to spend the afternoon with him, rehashing budget stuff."

"Harry, I swear I almost fell asleep from the boredom a dozen times."

He laughed softly.

Rowan walked between the rows of flowers, trailing a finger along the satiny wood of the tables. They were both silent for a long time.

Soon, they reached the back wall of the greenhouse, near the same window she'd climbed through to escape him the night they'd met. Only now, the hinges would move easily if opened, and the glass was crystalline clean. In the reflection, she watched Harry materialize behind her, solid and clear.

She turned. A hint of apprehension showed in his solemn eyes.

"Nobody's out there playing Team Tag tonight, are they?" Rowan said.

Harry shook his head. "Everyone's eyes were on you, so I'd know where to find you. Even the kids were in on it."

"I wondered why Duncan gave them walkie-talkies."

Harry nodded. "They were so pumped."

"Sneaky."

"Come over here. I have something to show you." He guided her to the front of the greenhouse. A wooden crate sat on a table there, roughly twice the size of a shoebox. Harry lifted the lid and moved out of the way, gesturing for her to look inside.

Flickering flames in the big lanterns made everything move in slow motion. Everything except her pulse—it sprinted like a horse with a slipped bridle. Rowan needed to lean against the table for balance when she saw the thing nestled in the shredded packing material.

It was a large brick of polished gray granite. Rowan ran a fingertip over the engraving. CLOUD TIDE, it said, with the year stamped below it.

"It's a cornerstone for the winery." Harry settled his hands on her upper arms, dropping a tender kiss on the nape of her neck. "When I told Ma and Dad your story about Edie and the cloud tide, they were all in on the name. This place is officially the Cloud Tide Vineyard and Winery, Rowan. We'll have this installed when the bank barn renovation begins."

Rowan crumpled against the table and covered her face. Harry gently turned her to him, then cuffed her wrists, drawing her hands away. "This place belongs to you now, too. And you belong to it." He nudged her chin up with a knuckle. "Think Edie would approve?"

She twisted her hands in the front of his shirt and searched his eyes. "When did you do this?"

"Oh, no. Are you going to answer my questions with a question?"

Tears spilled over. "Aren't you used to it by now?"

"Rowan." Mirth faded, and his expression transformed into raw, urgent emotion. "I have a really important question to ask you tonight. It's one you have to give me an actual answer for."

She nodded, tasting her heart on the back of her tongue.

Harry dipped into his pocket and withdrew a tiny

thing, pinched between his thumb and forefinger. With a bracing breath, he held up the little ring made from the grapevine tendrils he'd pulled from her hair on a long-ago December morning.

"Marry me," he said.

A teary laugh bubbled up. "That wasn't a question."

"You're right. Say yes anyway."

The subtle torment she saw in his face nearly undid her. Silently, she held out her hand, unashamed by the stubborn traces of soil under her fingernails, or by the way her fingers shook.

She nodded, unable to speak.

"I need to hear it, Rowan." A single tear raced down Harry's cheek so fast she'd have missed it if she hadn't been watching his face.

"*Yes,* Harry. I love you," she said. "I love *us.*"

"*Us,*" he echoed.

Harry's entire body trembled as he slid the woody little ring onto Rowan's finger. He pulled her tight against him and buried his face in the notch between her neck and collarbone.

And then, both of them laughing, he reached back and locked the greenhouse door behind them.

ACKNOWLEDGMENTS

This story began small, both conceptually and literally. In a cramped airplane seat in 2014, I wrote a scene on my iPhone: two people slow-dancing and bantering about the nature of love. My ambition was also small—I just wanted to entertain myself on the flight home. I hadn't written anything creative for a decade or so, and with three very young kids and a busy job, I scarcely had time to *read* books, let alone write one.

The characters lingered with me, though. For years, I tinkered with the story in my spare time (ask me about when it was a spec-fic romance with a dual timeline), often putting it away for six months at a time. In 2019 I got serious about finishing it, and by mid-2020 I finally let my husband, Keith, see it. He read it in a few days, cried at least once (friends, I married an archetypal cinnamon roll), and astutely observed that the book needed a donkey (thank you, honey, for that high-impact developmental recommendation). I am so grateful for his eternal optimism, and for the encouragement he gave me on countless weekends and evenings to hide from our kids to go write. He is my first fan, and I'm a big fan of his.

Some other personal expressions of gratitude: to my

parents, Steve and Belinda, for their unwavering encouragement and love through everything I've ever decided to reach for, and to Judy and Jane for their immediate and joyous support.

To Mary Shoffner, my lifelong best friend, for that bag of my very first romance novels from her grandparents' basement when we were teenagers, and for continuing to be the biggest inspiration for how I write about friendships.

Big love to my friends Carolyn, Julia, Kristin, and Tracy: my caftan crew and earliest cheerleaders. I spent so many years writing this novel in solitude, it was a bit terrifying to spill the beans about it. But y'all joined in on my joy, and I wish I could bottle that feeling for the times I question whether I can do this writing thing. By the time y'all read this, I really hope we've gotten that juice box weekend away together.

Laura Lee Cogbill, my first-ever beta reader, thank goodness for your impactful, insightful, and funny feedback on an early version of the book. My tender heart and fledgling manuscript were safe in your gentle hands.

I am immensely grateful for my agent, Laura Bradford, for seeing into the big beating heart of this story despite its quiet-on-the-surface premise, for advising me with patience and grace, and for finding the book a perfect home with St. Martin's. Also, thanks to Taryn Fagerness, my foreign rights agent, and Lucy Stille, my film and television agent, for taking Rowan and Harry to exciting new places.

Thanks to my editorial team: Alexandra Sehulster, your enthusiasm and wild love for this book made *me* love it more, and Rowan and Harry both became even more charming and dear under your guidance. Thank you, Mara Delgado Sánchez and Cassidy Graham, for being my lifeline as the book went through some of the most important steps of its journey. Susannah Noel, my copy editor, thank you for your keen eye and the lovely polish you gave to the manuscript. Endless appreciation for my cover designer, Danielle Fiorella, for the buttery sunshine cover of my dreams, and to Kelly Too for so beautifully rendering the way my words look on the page. Thank you to Katy Robitzski, my audiobook producer, for bringing the book to life in a new medium. To my production team, Janna Dokos and Ginny Perrin; my marketing team, Marissa Sangiacomo, Brant Janeway, and Kejana Ayala; and my publicist, Sarah Schoof, thank you all for your work behind the scenes to debut this book to the world in the truest sense of the word.

All the love and appreciation to my authorly crowd, including the warm, wonderful Jennifer Cox, my first writing friend, and the brilliant Ingrid Pierce, who introduced me to the group of smart, hilarious, tremendously talented people I'm fortunate to now call my critique partners and friends: Sarah Burnard, Alexandra Kiley, Maggie North, Livia Barb, Sarah T. Dubb, Risa Edwards, and Jessica Joyce. To everyone from All the Kissing (thanks Julie!), Friday Kiss, the Pitch Wars community, and my earliest readers and reviewers. You're all shining stars.

And you, reader: my endless awe and appreciation that you chose to spend time at Cloud Tide with Rowan and Harry. This story started out just for me, but now it's yours, too. You and I . . . we're "us" now.